T0090500

FLANAGAN'S LEGACY

BOOK TWO

VITO BELCASTRO

authorHOUSE

AuthorHouse™
1663 Liberty Drive
Bloomington, IN 47403
www.authorhouse.com
Phone: 833-262-8899

Published by AuthorHouse 05/16/2023

ISBN: 979-8-8230-0858-7 (sc)
ISBN: 979-8-8230-0859-4 (e)

Dedicated to an
Angel in Heaven,
My Wife,
Jeanette Marie Kane Belcastro

CHAPTER 1

WHAT THE HELL

Raptly they stared at the television screen. Mike was stunned and Nick was shaking his head in an agitated manner. He was unable to believe what he was seeing.

The movement of Nick's head sent minor spasms of pain through his damaged shoulder, but so intent was he on the televisions broadcast, that he barely felt it.

Maeve had gone to get her laptop computer and returned almost immediately with it.

Her expression was also one of disbelief.

"Look at the expression on that bastard's face." Nick said. "He knows what he's doing. That Sonuva bitch is guilty. That's the kind of shit that makes our job so freakin' hard."

"Why?" was Mike's only response.

"There's gonna be a whole lot of deep shit over this." Nick replied.

"We are going to get this crap shoved down our throats Mike. You mark my words. We are in for it."

Mike glanced sideways at his friend. He nodded, but did not reply.

The News Announcer stared straight ahead, unflinchingly, at the cameras.

"Former Minneapolis police officers, Derek Chauvin, Tou Thao, Thomas Lane, and J. Alexander Kueng have been arrested and booked into Hennepin County jail, in Minnesota for the death of George Floyd." He said, keeping his voice level and somewhat stiff.

"Good thing for them that I'm not on that Jury." Mike said softly, holding his breath until he had finished his sentence, "I'm voting guilty, as charged."

Maeve nodded in agreement, but Nick had not heard him. Nick was busy calling his precinct. He knew that they were aware of the circumstances, but they had to hear the summary from him.

His warning of but moments ago lit itself up in his mind. A shit storm was coming, for all of America's cities, especially New York.

"Wow, just think about it, Nick thought aloud, "Another example of police brutality plus all those people out of work because of the damn Corona virus. It doesn't matter how many lives you might save, or how many lost kids you find, all they're gonna see is that bastard kneeling on an innocent man's neck and killing him. Why did they arrest Floyd anyway?"

"Something about a counterfeit twenty dollar bill." Mike answered, hoarsely.

"What?" Maeve said from across the room, "I had one about a year ago, in the supermarket. They picked it up on one of those scanners. We were able to trace it back to the bank and they found a lot more there, as well as any number that they had already given out.

"Poor old Mrs. Gilbride lost her job over that. She was seventy one years old and had eyesight problems anyway."

"Manhattan will bear the brunt of this, "Mike surmised astutely, "But I can't help thinking that the whole City is in for some tough times. I wonder what the Mayor's gonna do.

"I'm gonna call Beymon. I'm sure the Brass is already hunkering down, but it won't hurt to try and be proactive."

Nick didn't hear him. Nick was too busy remembering that gathering where his ribs had been cracked by that nut-job's bullet. He wondered if the National and State Governments weren't also getting ready for what was surely coming.

With all the attention already being drawn to the Covid virus, would they even realize what they might be in for?

"So now the mayor wants to defund the Police Department." Chief Walt Agrarian was trying not to shout, but his irritated state of mind was all too evident by his gruff tone and very tense jaw line.

"I think we saw that coming Chief." Ron Beymon said firmly, hoping to allay the angry Police Chief if only slightly.

"The minute that that asshole knelt on that poor man's neck, the writing was on the wall." Beymon finished.

I've tried my damndest to clean up this department's attitude," Agrarian complained, "If only I could get some cooperation, ah, present company excluded of course."

Everyone in the room nodded. Captain Gerald "Gerry" Nathan, a precinct commander from Brooklyn, wondered aloud, "Doesn't His Honor see the ramifications of such a move? Can't he see the loss of service involved?"

Garret Holmes, an African-American civilian advisor, attached to the Police Department by the Mayor, spoke up.

"He isn't seeing that at this time, ladies and gentlemen. He is only trying to placate Liberals, both Blacks and Whites. He hopes such an action will garner him votes, for either the Governorship or quite possibly, the Presidency."

"Don't you work for him?" Agrarian asked, unable to keep the slight edge of derision from his voice.

"Yea, I guess you can say I'm serving with this police department at the Mayor's discretion, so to speak, but I don't always agree with him. If I wasn't black, he might have booted me out long ago. He displays me like an example of his liberalness. But, do not misunderstand. I am anything but a liberal.

"Certain liberal policies are beneficial to the population at large. Some are not.

"There's a certain mixture of both liberal and conservative policies which would be very beneficial to this City, this State and even this Country, if enacted. Of course, none of that takes into play that politicians are running the show, and doing rather badly at that.

"Uh, you didn't hear that from me." Holmes added with a slight cough.

"I'm gonna sign off now." Agrarian sighed, "I gotta go get my ass chewed by the Commissioner. I'm guessing that the both of us may be on our way out."

The computer screen on Natalie's credenza went blank.

"We'll talk about this later." Beymon announced. "Right now I need a break."

He went into his office and closed the door.

The three precinct commanders who had witnessed the conversation left too.

Mike and Colleen went back to their shared office, with bathroom stops along the way. Jim O'Leary stayed with Natalie.

With a dusty piece of chalk, Beymon started to write upon a green board in his office.

"Results from defunding police." He wrote at the top and drew a line beneath it. After the number, one, he wrote, "Removes funding from Rape Victims."

After looking at it for several seconds he nodded and wrote the numeral two, followed immediately by, "Removes funding from victims of Domestic Violence." After three he wrote, "Takes away resources from human trafficking."

Beneath that he wrote the word, "Children!" and drew two lines beneath the word.

"Who suffers?" he asked himself sadly as he tossed the chalk up and down several times. "Victims, naturally." Having answered his own question he shook his head ruefully.

A knock at his door brought his attention to the doorway.

"Yes?" he called out.

The door opened and Garret Holmes stood there frowning.

"A minute of your time Chief?" Holmes asked, and then added, "Please."

Beymon nodded and motioned for him to enter.

With a slight smile, which quickly evaporated, Holmes said, "I heard you had the best coffee."

Beymon pointed to the coffee maker and said gruffly, "Help yourself. If you don't want to trust the efficiency of our cleanliness, there are paper cups in the credenza as well as plastic lids."

As he made his coffee, in a paper cup, Holmes gazed at the green board. He shook his head gently.

"That looks about right, he muttered disgustedly. "but I'm afraid that list will get longer as we go along."

Beymon nodded. He sat in his chair and indicated the chair on the other side of his desk.

"What's on your mind Mr. Holmes?" he asked.

"Listen Chief," Holmes began, "I work for the Mayor, but technically, so do you. If you don't mind, I'd like to drop the Mr. and stick with either Garrett or just plain Holmes, if you'd prefer."

"Just a couple of good old black buddies slingin' the hash, eh?" Beymon surmised somewhat acridly.

"No, Sir," Holmes shot back, just a bit hotly.

He indicated Beymon's list on the green board and said, "I'm talking about that Chief. As I said, that will be an even longer list over time. It will grow, and the people of this City are going to be the unhappy recipients of whatever policies develop from this current lousy defunding that's being enacted.

"I grew up in this City. I do not want to see it destroyed. I do not want it to go the way Minneapolis seems to be going."

Beymon had calmed down. He did not smile, but his frown had vanished.

"I'm listening." He said.

"You'll still be Chief Beymon. "GOD knows you earned that rank, probably the hard way.

"Like I said, if you don't want to call me Garrett, simply Holmes will be fine. I'm just not comfortable with Mister."

"I have a set of rotten figures you will probably be interested in, if you aren't probably already aware of them. Chief Agrarian thought you might like the official report.

"Murders in this city are up 30%. Shootings alone are up 130%. Kids have been caught by those bullets, some lethally. Some of those bullets have even been shot by children. Burglaries and auto thefts are up as well.

"And, this is the real piss-off clincher. The Mayor is spending some of that money he saved from defunding the police.

"Today he and a bunch of BLM people are painting BLACK LIVES MATTER in big letters on Fifth Avenue, in front of the President's building.

"I am no fan of this President, but this ridiculous expense is simply ridiculous."

Beymon was drumming his fingers on his blotter. His brow was knit and his mouth was a tense line, bordering on a grimace.

"Here's some more bad news," Holmes related, his own expression quite fixed, "We're really stretched now, both on an equipment level and sadly, manpower.

"We've lost over twenty cruisers, between physical and rather dangerously, fire damage. At least three hundred or so have been damaged, but are still drivable. That's over a million dollars in damage, just there alone."

Beymon shook his head. In all his years on the Force he had never seen such widespread destruction.

Without actually voicing his thoughts, Beymon almost wished that the rioters would go after Gracie Mansion, the Mayor's residence.

"You already know that somewhere in the neighborhood of three hundred cops have been injured, right?" Holmes brought up.

Beymon nodded, still unable to voice his thoughts.

"And," Holmes continued, a definite edge to his voice, "Our esteemed Mayor has seen fit to sign two, not one, but two proposals that strip the NYPD of over $1 billion in funding and he has disbanded a plainclothes anti-crime unit."

"You seem to be right on top of this," Beymon replied wearily, "so I'm sure you are aware that there is approximately a four hundred percent increase in retirement applications from officers in response to all the budget slashes. The job is becoming more of a risk because of those freakin' cuts.

"Almost all of these guys and women are family people."

"I know," Holmes replied, "I'm not exactly sure of the figure, but I think it was right around one hundred and eighty for this week alone. And, his Highness closed down the Academy as well."

"And," Beymon added, "the protests and riots just keep barreling through, eating up the personnel who are not allowed to respond in force, because of that stinkin' asshole in Minneapolis. And it turns out that the victim was not all that innocent after all."

Beymon thought about what Holmes had said. He rubbed his eyes with the thumb and forefinger of his right hand. He gripped the bridge of his nose with those same two fingers, squeezing it tightly, trying to allay the screaming headache in his forehead.

The Chief took two tablets from a small bottle of common pain reliever and washed them down with a swig of his coffee.

His eyes were brighter as he looked up at Holmes and said, "If my wife asks, you didn't see that."

Holmes smiled and said, "No, I did not."

"I don't know the exact number," Beymon relayed, "but, another handful of cops have flat out resigned in response to the Mayor's decisions."

"So," Holmes agreed, "no cops, no equipment, and yet the riots just seem to continue.

"And this goes right over our smart-ass Mayor's head. He thinks he's placating liberals to secure their votes. Those same liberal voters will be caught directly in the cross-hairs of these riots.

"They will remember him at election time, and not in a good way."

Beymon stood, wearily. His shoulders ached from the tension lancing through his mind. He held his hand out and pointed to the coffee maker with his mug,

"More coffee Garret?" he asked.

Beymon's use of his first name did not go unnoticed by Holmes.

"Thank you, yes please, Chief." Holmes returned.

"Try Ron," Beymon replied with a wan smile, "it has two less letters, a victim of the Mayor's defunding."

He chuckled at his little joke.

"The head of the Captain's Union had some choice words for His Honor too." Holmes related drily. "He's blaming Agrarian as well as the Mayor."

Beymon's thoughts were mixed on that particular subject. While the Mayor and the City Council were the final authorities in most of what had already transpired, he also felt that Agrarian and the Commissioner could have done a bit more.

He had had a similar conversation with Dennis Meyer, just that morning. Dennis, the Chief of Patrol, was witnessing the utter destruction of his command, the largest of the force.

With a warning to Beymon, not to repeat any of their conversation, Meyer had expressed a desire to retire himself. He added that, "If they remove either The Chief or the Commissioner, I would not accept either job. Those guys have targets on their backs Ron. Any replacement would just be accepting that same bright, red target"

Beymon placed Holmes' coffee before him.

"I saw the President of the Detectives' Endowment Association on TV today." Beymon told Holmes.

"His point was that his people are tired of being vilified, enmasse because of that jerk in Minnesota, and a few others from around the Nation which have also been exposed."

Beymon paused to collect his thoughts.

"So it's a loss of experienced and dedicated crime fighters, in view of all this continued violence, and the politicians continue to strip themselves and this City of its protection.

"I suppose there are exceptions, but it seems like those bastards are hiding too."

CHAPTER 2
WHEN LEAST EXPECTED

Twilight had come, with the overhead lights pushing long shadows of whatever stood before and beneath them.

Melanie McGinty was very tired. Several lengthy shifts in a row had rather depleted much of her strength. Dr. O'Malley had told her to go home and get some much needed rest. It was Friday and the following Monday, Melanie was supposed to start her new position with O'Malley's sister, Dr. Sylvia Feldstrup, a noted immunologist.

Melanie was looking forward to it for two reasons. Number one, she would be getting a much needed break from the Emergency Room and two; it would be a learning experience of the highest degree.

Normally she would be riding home with Nurse Jim Cantner, a male nurse also from the Emergency Room.

Cantner was a former medic with the US Army in Afghanistan. Jim lived just a few blocks past Melanie's parents' home in Queens. Jim still had at least another shift to finish, so Melanie's brother, Kenny Keith was going to pick her up. Kenny was actually Melanie's step-brother, but in the McGinty-Keith household, such lines were largely smeared.

As she strolled from the hospital doorway out to the street, her shadow stretched before her languidly keeping pace.

She was almost to the street when she noticed that Kenny had not yet arrived.

"Hm, probably traffic." She told herself.

Since she was alone, she had pulled the surgery mask from her face and let it dangle from one ear. Her plastic visor was tilted up, above her forehead.

The aromas and scents of food being prepared and neighborhood gardens of flowers and shrubs filled her nose and she smiled.

A gruff male voice suddenly pulled her from her reverie. "Hey Babe," it called out, sneeringly, "how about a little lovin' for three weary warriors?"

She turned quickly and was startled to see three seemingly young men approaching her.

They were scruffy, apparently Caucasian, with black bandanas across their faces. Two wore baseball caps, turned backwards, and the other had a black bandana covering his hair.

One of the baseball cap wearers had on a dirty white T-shirt with BLM imprinted in the middle. The other two wore orange T-Shirts with the exact same logo.

Melanie started to back up towards the doorway. With one hand she replaced her hospital mask and with the other she pulled her plastic visor back down over her face.

Her purse was heavy and hindered her movement slightly. While she was trying to balance it she had not noticed that the three thugs had started to spread out. Their purpose was obviously to encircle her.

The hoodlum in the black scarf atop his head was almost upon her. "Two things Sweetie," he said with a snarl, "some money for dinner and a little pussy. Be nice and you won't get hurt. Otherwise, your ass belongs to us."

She suddenly noticed that he had a switchblade knife in his hand. One of the others had picked up a reasonably large leafless tree branch.

"What's it gonna be Sweet Cheeks?" the apparent leader demanded. He flipped the knife back and forth from hand to hand several times as he advanced menacingly.

So intent was he upon Melanie that he did not see Jim Cantner step up beside him. In one motion Cantner grabbed his arm, spun him around and punched him sharply in the throat.

The guy went down hard, choking and dropping his knife.

The thug with the branch advanced quickly, while swinging the rudimentary club in his hand.

"You Bastard!" he snarled, as Cantner ducked under his arm and then grabbed it almost simultaneously.

From the corner of his eye Cantner saw the third punk pick up his fallen leader's knife and swing it in a wide arc towards Cantner. Jim pulled back on the guy with the branch's arm and pressed sharply against the kid's elbow. The creep's arm snapped. He screamed and dropped the branch. Releasing the now wounded kid, Cantner caught the branch in midair and used it to block the descending knife. When he saw the knife penetrate the dry and crusty bark, Jim snapped the limb sideways, tearing the knife from the boy's grasp, and brought the club sharply down upon the last kid's head.

As all three hoodlums lay upon the ground moaning in pain, Jim walked over to Melanie and placed a protective arm around her to stop her from trembling.

Someone from within the hospital had seen the violent altercation and had wisely called the Nassau County police.

A doctor and another male nurse had come out and were tending to the three assailants who had been rather effectively neutralized.

The Police arrested them and escorted them into the hospital to continue their treatment. The kid with the broken arm was making accusations of prejudice because of their T-shirts and claiming that Jim Cantner had started the whole fight himself.

Depositions were taken from Cantner, Melanie and several witnesses from the hospital's windows. Having been read their rights by the police the thugs were being questioned as well.

It was determined that the punks were, in fact, lying, and the obvious instigators of the entire affair.

Since they had been read their rights, they were placed in custody in a secluded area of the hospital with armed guards.

Finally able to leave, Melanie kissed Jim Cantner and thanked him.

Outside waiting in the parking lot, Kenny in his Austin Sprite was apologetic. As Melly had guessed, he had been caught up in traffic.

"What's new?" he asked

Although she was frowning, there was a strange twinkle in her eyes.

"If I tell you," she answered, "You can't tell Mom or Dad. They have enough crap right now to worry about."

On the ride home Melanie twisted her hair which she had just freed from all that protection upon her head. She was humming and thinking about Mister James "Jimmy" Cantner. "A girl could do a lot worse." She told herself.

CHAPTER 3

READ HIM HIS RIGHTS

A mob of people of every conceivable race had gathered unlawfully on The Grand Concourse, Just blocks south of Fordham Road. They were protesting police brutality, with specific mention of the death in Minneapolis which seemingly had started everything.

Sergeant Vito "Viduch" Marciano stood off to one side shaking his grizzled head with its worn and tired looking eyes.

A surgical mask covered the bottom half of his face. A newly arrived plastic face shield which he had tilted upward gleamed beneath the bright streetlamp overhead.

"Be careful guys." He called out in a raspy, strained voice. We are not to engage unless something really serious and dangerous occurs.

"And neither Lieutenant Gonzales nor I will be allowed to make that call. We have to call it in and get City Hall's approval." His tone was obviously sarcastic.

A harsh expression of anger crossed his hidden features as he thought about all those newly issued guidelines.

"Yea, like that's gonna happen" he told himself bitterly.

Images of badly wounded policemen flashed through his mind.

"If you can't help it, and must act to defend yourself, well then that's different. Still don't expect that there might not be ramifications no matter what you do." He paused for a moment and then added, "No matter how badly you might be hurt. That comes straight from City Hall."

Marciano pulled his visor down over his face. Those closest to him heard him mutter, "Sonuva bitch! No wonder so many good fucking men are just retiring or even simply quitting outright. Sonuva bitch!"

One quarter of a block away, David Keith and Nunzio Italo stood side by side. They were armed with stout wooden clubs and the armor on their torsos. In addition each had a Kevlar hand shield, poised before their bodies. Their hand weapons were holstered. Neither one could guess what might be coming, but hopefully, both were prepared.

Davy was still nursing a bruised ego and a bruised forehead as well. Just three days prior in a similar situation he had been hit by a piece of a brick which had been thrown from somewhere in the crowd. One had to be watching so many different areas at the same time that sooner or later, that cop was going to get nailed. Nunzio had also been hit by something hard, probably a stone from the street. It had hit his upper thigh, just above his knee and then ricocheted back into the crowd that they were trying to hold back.

It was every cop's guess that whoever was the Republican candidate for Mayor in the next election would probably become the next Mayor. Not only would all the cops and firemen vote against the current Mayor, but the hundreds, if not thousands of small business owners who were suffering terribly between the Corona virus, and the unchecked mobs that the Mayor was not effectively protecting them from because of his new policies toward policemen, would as well.

"And Stupid can't even see that." Marciano grumbled. Stupid was obviously His Honor.

Two blocks away a sudden flicker and loud bang drew attention from the line of policemen. Most of them turned toward the sound and ensuing flash of fire.

Not all turned, however. Davy and the policewoman to his left, Patrol Woman Gerrie Contadina were scanning the crowd before them. While many policemen on The Grand Concourse witnessed the complete destruction of one of their own vehicles, Patrol persons Keith and Contadina saw a terrorist about to throw another burning bottle in the direction of Sergeant Marciano.

"Stop, red Shirt, blue hat!" Davy shouted, straining to be heard above the noise of the crowd.

The Molotov cocktail wielder's attention was briefly drawn to the sound of Davy's voice. At that moment, Gerrie shot him with a rubber bullet. The bullet hit center mass and the thug dropped immediately. Fortunately for him, the contents of his bottle spread out and away from his prone body. Gerrie was thinking that the fact that he had been saved from the fire was probably advantageous for her as well. No matter what took place these days it was always painted as a police officer's fault.

Two attending firemen, with a sudden police escort quickly suffocated the fire with extinguishers.

When the man's bottle had flashed with its brilliant flame the crowd around him had quickly dissolved leaving him standing alone. That was fortunate for them for certainly some would have been burned had they remained.

The man was lifted to his feet, choking and moaning. He was checked for worse injuries, from both the bullet and the sudden fall to the ground. Finding none, the arresting police from a group of back-ups, just behind the main police security line, hand cuffed him and half dragged, half carried him from the site.

As with many of the protestors, he was young and Caucasian. The BLM emblazoned on his sweatshirt hoodie proclaimed him to be protesting police brutality, brutality from the same group of people he had just tried to incinerate. They were in fact the same group of people who had just saved him from death and or disfigurement.

While it was agreed that more than likely he was working in conjunction with the animals that had just blown up the police vehicle just down the Concourse, Obviously, at this stage, nothing could be proven.

"Good job Gerrie." Davy said loud enough for her to hear despite the layers that covered the both of them.

"Yea, you too Davy." She answered back, with a sigh.

From Nunzio who stood to Davy's right came, "That's my girl Guys. That is my girl."

As had been the norm lately, the shift did not end at eight, ten or even twelve hours.

Fortunately, just after twelve hours they were relieved of sentry duty on the concourse and returned to the precinct house. The precinct house was also an armed camp.

Half of them were permitted to rest and get coffee in the inside. The others were posted as sentries to protect their home base. Gerrie and Nunzio entered the building together. Davy was posted on the first watch.

"Finally," Ken Grable, the man he had relieved groused, "I need coffee."

It was supposed to last for two hours, but in this day and age, who really knew what was going to be. One could only wait and anticipate, as Marciano had told them often enough.

Davy chuckled wryly as he remembered those same words coming from his Grandfather in the first year of Davy's police career.

"Sergeants!" Davy thought with a hidden smile, "They really run the show. They just let the Chiefs and captains think that they're in charge."

The next day, while they were watching the street, once more on the Grand Concourse, The danger came from a different direction. Several handfuls of small rocks, with a few larger pieces, rained down upon the unsuspecting police.

Nunzio fortunately was unhurt, but his best friend and his girlfriend were hit. While he wasn't knocked unconscious, Davy bore many of the quite solid missiles from above.

Gerrie was hit with one of the larger rocks, which knocked off her visor and hit bare flesh between her brow and her helmet. She was struck unconscious. Nunzio, and Davey, despite his lightheadedness dragged her beneath a nearby overhang.

Several masked faces appeared from three stories up, laughing and calling the cops vile names. One pulled back in time, but the other two were hit solidly in the face by rubber bullets. One of them fell backwards and was not seen again.

The other fell face forward and landed two stories below on a porch overhang. Luckily for him, he was unconscious and could not tense up before impact. That may have just saved his life. He would however, have some notable damage to his head and body.

Marciano assigned two people to climb up and get him down. They were instructed to be careful as he would probably be planning to sue the city in the near future.

At a point, he did awaken, in pain because of a broken arm and a dislocated shoulder. And as anticipated, he was calling for a lawyer and threatening to bring charges for police brutality.

Marciano personally read him his rights.

When Marciano asked if he understood those rights the man snarled, "Screw you Pig!"

Marciano then turned to the patrolman next to him and said, "Duffy, please note that the perpetrator is not intelligent enough and does not understand his rights."

"Hey Fuck you cop. I understand 'em fine. Yea asshole, I understand my rights."

Marciano snapped a cuff on the man's good arm and applied the other cuff to the dolly he was lying on.

Marciano looked over at Lieutenant Gonzales. The lieutenant was standing stiffly. He gripped a clipboard tightly in one hand and the other hung loosely at his side.

Even though Marciano's face was covered, his eyes were very grim beneath his visor.

"Sir," he asked Lieutenant Gonzales, "What was his name?"

"O'Dell, Sergeant," Gonzales replied hoarsely, "Kwame O'Dell. Sergeant Kwame O'Dell."

"He was born on a Saturday." Marciano reflected. Since his Dad was an O'Dell, he must have been named by his mother. I believe her name was Adwoba. That means Monday."

"What does all this mean?" Gonzales asked. He wasn't angry but there was an impatient tone to his voice.

"Kwame is the word for Saturday in Ghana." Marciano explained, "And Adwoba is the feminine word or name, for Monday."

The name usually given in Ghana is for the day upon which that person was born. I knew his father, Thomas O'Dell. He was an African American fireman. He married an immigrant woman from Ghana. Obviously he allowed her to name Kwame.

"I had met Kwame briefly last year. I didn't know he was attached to the precinct. He must have just made Sergeant. If you don't mind sir I'd like to notify the family. I know his Dad is dead, but I'm not sure about the Mom. I guess Personnel will have all that information."

The perp handcuffed to the gurney became wary. His eyes flitted back and forth between Marciano and Gonzales.

"What inna hell are you jerk-offs talkin' about?" he snapped, straining against the cuff which held him in place.

Marciano turned to him. The sergeant's face was bright red, what little could be seen.

"Let all here who witness my statement to be advised that since the suspect refuses to give us his name, and since he does not seem to have any visible identification, he will henceforth be referred to as John Doe. Said identification will be in effect until his true identity may be established."

Looking directly at the newly named John Doe, Marciano stated, quite sternly, "John Doe, having been read your rights and it having been established that you understand them, before witnesses, you are hereby charged with the murder of Sergeant Kwame O'Dell, a police officer who was killed while engaged in his duty to protect the City of New York, and its citizens."

John Doe was shaking where he sat. Once more he attempted to rise but was restrained by the cuff attached to his wrist. The movement caused him pain in his damaged arm and he groaned.

"You can't hang that one on me!" he shouted.

Did you throw a piece of cement block from that roof in the direction of these police officers below?" Lieutenant Gonzales asked sternly.

"No!" John Doe shot back "I threw a few pebbles and a piece of brick. It was a yellow brick you fucking asshole."

A policeman next to Gonzales held up a clear evidence bag with a third of a yellow brick in it. It was stained with blood.

"Way to go John "Asshole" Doe," Marciano snarled as he tapped the BLM logo on the punk's shirt, "You just killed a Black cop.

"Fingerprints will be taken at the house."

Marciano continued to glare at the suspect.

CHAPTER 4

ONE FOR THE BOOKS

Garret Holmes sat across from Assistant Chief Ron Beymon, nursing a semi-warm cup of coffee. Beside him sat Chief of Patrol Dennis Meyer. Meyer's coffee was hot as he had just filled his cup from the coffee maker.

"What's new?" Beymon asked, "Not that I'm in the mood for more bad news."

"Well," Holmes answered with a sly grin, "this is bad news for our esteemed Mayor, but it might be considered good news for us. In fact it involves a member of your staff Ron."

Beymon's eyes lit up as he contemplated what might possibly be good news from his department. He wondered briefly, however, just how it might reflect on him and how it might affect his day to day operations.

"Well," Holmes began, "His Honor received a small package the other day, and though he tried to hide it Joe Gundermann found it and released the information to Cathy Napoli over at the New York Post."

"Gundermann," Meyer reflected softly, "Isn't he that Republican Council Member from Staten Island?

"What was the enemy doing in a Democratic Mayors office unattended?" Meyer pondered further.

"Well," Holmes answered with a wry smile, "Despite being a Republican, Gundermann has on occasion espoused a somewhat liberal point of view. His honor was trying to woo him into his own slightly more liberal camp, but it didn't work."

"What did he find?" Meyer asked, unable to contain his excitement.

"A certain woman, who is the granddaughter of a cop, the daughter of a cop, the mother of a cop and the wife of a cop, sent back the Key To The City that she had been given.

"The harsh note which accompanied it said that, "If this foolish excuse for a city leader was going to endanger all of the people she loved as well as thousands of other forthright cops who were already in the line of fire, he could shove that key where it deserved to be, in darkness."

Dennis Meyer held his head in his hand, attempting not to show his smile.

Ronald Beymon laughed openly with warm tears running down his cheeks.

He reached for the intercom on his desk. Not knowing where any of his subordinates might be, he signaled for both offices.

"Mike" he called out, "Wherever you are could you come here please?"

He heard Mike's voice both on the intercom and just outside his door say "Be right there Chief!"

Immediately there was a knock upon the door.

"Come in." Beymon called out.

"Yes Chief." Mike said as he entered the room, closing the door behind him.

When he noticed the Chief's two guests he said, "Ah, Gentlemen, "Good Morning."

Mike immediately wondered what he had done and what kind of trouble might he be in.

"Mike," Garret Holmes began, "Uh, may I call you Mike?"

"Uh, yes sir," Mike answered, "How may I be of service, Mr. Holmes?"

"Oh, how do I even begin? Let me think about this for a moment."

Mike noticed that the two Chiefs were both smiling. He wondered just what was going on. Was he the butt of some Police Brass joke?

"Ah, yes, ah Mike," Holmes began again, "Do you know where, ah, your wife's key to the city is right now?"

Mike thought for a moment. "Well, Sir, she doesn't wear it. She thinks it's a bit ostentatious. It's probably in her jewelry........."

He stopped. He looked at each of their faces. The realization of where this conversation might be going finally hit him. His expression was blatantly aghast.

"Oh n-no!" he stammered, "S-he didn't!"

"Oh yes she did." Beymon acknowledged, "Talk about a spirited woman. I wish she was my daughter.

"Michael me boy you have yourself one heck of a wife there. Cherish her buddy. I know I would."

"Me too!" Holmes and Meyer echoed together.

"She basically told the Mayor that she could not accept something like that from a man who placed her entire family as well as other cops and their families city-wide in such terrible danger."

"Wow!" Mike reflected aloud, "I guess that sounds like my Theresa. I hope she didn't tell him......"

He was interrupted by a grinning Dennis Meyer who said, "Oh, yes she did."

Meyer could not stop laughing. His laughter was more of a high pitched wheeze, but there was no mistaking it for anything else but laughter.

"If I may Mike," Holmes interjected, "I would certainly like to meet this wonderful woman you have wed."

Although it was still light out, the sun was setting and was currently hidden by what little could be seen of Manhattan's skyline above the trees and buildings of central Queens.

As Mike pulled into his driveway he noticed that Melanie's new car was parked just ahead of his, next to Kenny's.

New car of course was a misnomer. It was actually a 2005 Hyundai Sonata, a Korean car, which it turned out had actually been assembled in the United States.

Mike had bought it from Sergeant Tim Flynn, who had been Nick Evanopolis' clerk when Mike had first returned to the police force.

Tim, still a sergeant, was now assigned to the local precinct, again under Nick. That actually was a blessing for Tim as he lived less than two blocks from the Precinct house.

The car was in really fine shape. Tim had only driven it on weekends, preferring public transportation when he worked at One Police Plaza.

Melly had supplied half the money and Mike and Theresa had kicked in the rest.

Mike phoned his landline with his cell phone. Theresa picked it up on the second ring. Apparently she had read the brightly lit window on the phone and recognized his number.

"Hello Hotshot!" she chirped into the phone. "Can you wait out there for another ten minutes or so? Melly's still in the basement shower. I already gave her clean clothing, so she should be done soon."

"My, don't you sound happy." Mike remarked.

"Well," Theresa answered, "Now that you're home all of my family is safe, at least for now. Davy just called and he's at Amy's. If he can't be here that's exactly where I want him to be.

"Oh Mike, Melly just came up the stairs. Your shower awaits you sir. I'll drop off clean clothes and when you're done, dinner will be ready. How does pot roast, carrots and roasted potatoes sound?"

"Your mother's?" Mike asked as he reached the cellar doorway at the back of the house.

"He-e-ey!" Theresa whined as he unlocked the door.

"Now, now, calm yourself, My Love. Whether you cook it or not, it's still your Mom's recipe."

"Wow, you slicked your way out of that one easy enough." Theresa remarked snidely.

She heard the shower being turned on over the phone and prepared to hang up. Mike's voice stopped her and she listened intently

"Speaking of slick," Mike said coyly, "Something came up in a meeting today that I'd like to discuss later.

"Okay, shower's just right. See you in a bit."

Dinner was a hit all around. Conversation lingered somewhat on Melly's new job and Melly's new car. They touched briefly on how everybody was feeling, especially Theresa's Mom, Marie.

Theresa reported on her daily phone conversation with Maeve Evanopolis. Nick was doing fine, although he was ever anxious to return to work. He kept in touch mainly through Tim Flynn and the acting commander Lieutenant Joseph Gustafson.

"When will he be going back?" Mike asked, "Force wide, our numbers are quite a bit depleted."

He decided not to mention the fact that he might be re-assigned to street and/or precinct duty. Theresa had enough on her mind. She was constantly worrying about Davy, Melly and Kenny.

"Well," Theresa replied, "According to Maeve, they're thinking about the day after tomorrow. It will have to be strictly administrative, but apparently they do need him."

Mike nodded and sipped the last of his coffee.

As Marie, Maria and Melanie began to gather the dirty dishes; Theresa stood and reached for her husband's hand.

"Want to take a couple of beers out onto the porch?" she asked.

He nodded and took two bottles from the refrigerator. Holding them in one hand he indicated the front door with his free arm and then offered it to her as she drew alongside him. Once they were seated and he had removed both caps, he said, "Had a discussion with Chief Meyer, Chief Beymon and Garret Holmes today."

"Holmes, isn't he that civilian from City Hall?" Theresa asked.

"Well, Mike corrected her, "More specifically, he comes direct from the Mayor's office."

"Oh, yea," Theresa remembered, "but he doesn't like the Mayor, right? Why would the Mayor keep somebody around who doesn't like him?"

"Well," Mike responded, "Holmes is a respected and influential member of the Black Community, who the Mayor is trying to court, somewhat unsuccessfully. Also, His Honor doesn't really keep him around.

"Garret Holmes has become a permanent fixture at One Police Plaza."

"Oh, the Mayor's eyes and ears, eh?" Theresa observed.

"Well, I guess that was the original plan." Mike returned with a wry chuckle, "But, it's kind of backfired.

"Which brings me to my main topic of discussion, and speaking of people who the Mayor has failed to entice, it involves Joe Gundermann."

Confusion briefly flickered across Theresa's pretty face.

"Enlighten me councilor." She replied, "The name rings a bell but I just can't place it."

"Joe Gundermann," Mike repeated, "he's the Republican council member from Staten Island."

"And how, exactly, My Dear Husband, does a Republican Council member figure into all of this? Who taught you how to tell a story Mike? You sound like my father trying to tell a joke."

"We-e-ell," Mike drew the word out for both dramatic and comic effect simultaneously, "apparently, during one of his special conversations with Councilman Gundermann, the Mayor was briefly called away and left Gundermann alone in his office.

"Something had been left on the Mayor's desk which had been intended, and quite strictly, only for His Honor's eyes.

"Gundermann, being the snoop that he is, examined the item and the accompanying document.

"He released it to the New York Post and it will appear in tomorrow's paper."

Theresa shrugged. Her confusion was rather obvious in her expression.

"My guess," Mike continued, "is that said document was printed from our computer upstairs in our room."

Theresa's confusion lingered, only for moments. As she realized his meaning, her eyes grew very large and her jaw dropped. Fortunately Mike was able to grab her beer bottle before it too dropped.

She was almost dumbfounded, and entirely speechless.

"Oh, no!" she was finally able to say. "That was for the Mayor's eyes only. They can't publish that."

"They can, My Darling, and they will. If it's any consolation, I could not be more proud of you."

"You know what I wrote?" Theresa asked, incredulously. "But, how?"

"Well, apparently, Gundermann and Holmes are friends. Also, for more consolation, all three of the others, Holmes, Beymon and Chief Meyer really admire you. Each specifically wished that you were their daughter."

Theresa's head was in her hands. She reached for and grabbed the beer bottle from Mike's hand. She downed it in two gulps. As she burped loudly, Mike handed her the other beer.

It was very dark, both in the room and outside, where the moon appeared to be hidden by clouds.

Mike yawned and recoiled at the sour taste in his mouth. Glancing to his left he noted the time on the luminous dial of his clock as four-twenty three, AM.

Reaching to his right he noted that Theresa was not beside him. With sleepy eyes he glanced towards the bathroom door. It appeared to be dark with the door open.

His attention was drawn, farther, across the room to a faint glow from the computer screen. It was almost blocked by and framed by what seemed to be the form of his wife.

"You okay?" he grunted. His voice was just as sleepy as he was.

"Well, I'm better now." She admitted with a tone that sounded relieved.

"I've read all of the early editions of all the major newspapers here on the computer. Not one of them mentions my name. And, just as importantly, none of them suggests that I told the Mayor where to place that key, which is totally inaccurate since I did not do so."

"Mike I was very respectful in my note, although I'm sure he could see that I was upset."

Mike thought for several minutes while she was speaking.

"Maybe Holmes didn't get the correct story from Gundermann." Mike suggested. "Also, maybe Holmes was able to convince Gundermann not to use your name. Actually, this way it's sort of up in the air and it gives His Honor a way out, no matter how ridiculous that might sound."

"I'm just thankful that Mom, Maria and I won't have to deal with a bunch of scrambling reporters." Theresa revealed.

At precisely nine o'clock, AM that same morning, Joseph Warren Gundermann's phone rang. He was drinking a cup of tea and enjoying a sesame seed bagel with cream cheese on it

He answered, "Hello, Gundermann!"

A very feminine voice said "Good morning Mr. Councilman. I just wanted to offer my thanks for not revealing my name."

"You're welcome." Gundermann replied without revealing his knowledge of who his caller was.

I admire your gumption Ma'am. You're one of my new heroes, or heroines, if you will. There would have been too much to deal with on your end if I had told them your name.

"I've already been down that road far too many times, myself. Please give my best to your illustrious family. I wish everyone well."

His caller said "Thank you." One more time and then hung up.

Mike McGinty sat at his desk in One Police Plaza wondering if a target was being painted on his back. Sure, he had an on-going daily target simply because of the uniform he wore.

He wondered, however if a new target was being framed as a result of Theresa sending back her Key to the City.

Granted her name had not been used in any of the newspaper articles or the brief mention of it on some of the local TV news shows. They had not even mentioned her gender. She had been referred to as a concerned citizen.

When confronted of it during his daily Corona report, the Mayor feigned no knowledge of the subject. He followed it with an admonishment to the reporter to check her sources before asking silly questions.

Theresa had admitted being troubled by the same question as she rolled about the bed trying for the sleep which eluded her.

Much later as they sat together in the living room Mike assured her once more of how proud he was of her. He said if necessary he could retire and find a counseling position somewhere.

"But you're dedicated to this job, aren't you Michael?" she answered. "This isn't just a job for you, Honey, it's your vocation. You have the Eddie Flanagan curse as much as me or any of his grandchildren, Melanie included."

"Not all of it is a curse." He had replied, smiling, and took her into his arms.

She immediately folded against him and clung tightly to him.

Theresa's mother, Marie had heard their conversation from the kitchen.

"Oh, Ed, I wish you were here right now, when we need you more than ever. "She thought, silently.

Marie stepped up to the doorway separating the kitchen from the parlor. She glanced lovingly at her daughter and the man she had come to think of as her son.

Her eyes flitted over to the family portrait on the wall.

Aligned to either side of Ed in his wheelchair and Marie were Mike, Theresa, and the four grandchildren including Melanie.

Marie saw the strong determination in each pair of piercing eyes.

"Ach, Macushla, I guess you are indeed still with us. I love you Edward. I so love you."

CHAPTER 5

OH HOW THEY SUFFER

Merriam Stodorah sat quietly, surveying the people around her. Simultaneously she was thinking about the terrible events which had brought her to this place.

Also, simultaneously, she was maintaining her vigil over the small child who sat to her left. He was Charles Stodorah, who at the age of seven was her oldest child.

Merriam had been born thirty two years previous in the African nation of Ghana.

She was a pretty woman, dark skinned with gentle black curls and large, inquiring eyes. A slender figure, not too curvy, she was dressed in a solemn black dress with a lacy white collar.

Her name at birth was Afua, which was the word for Friday, the day upon which she had been born.

Having always been a big fan of Merriam Makeba, the African folk singer, Afua, took the name Merriam as her first name when she had received her United States citizenship at age twenty one. She had maintained Afua as her middle name.

While quite proud to be an American, she never wanted to lose sight of her Ghanaian roots.

Her other two children Cara, for Irene Cara and Harry, for Harry Belafonte, were at home with their grandmother, Merriam's mother. Merriam's mother's name was Kosiwa. Kosiwa meant Sunday, the day upon which she had been born.

Charles Stodorah, whom Merriam had divorced little over a year prior to this occasion had insisted that his children remember Merriam's, and their Ghanaian roots by giving them middle names that were Ghanaian translations of the days of the week upon which they had been born.

Young Charles was Kwame, for Saturday. Cara, the middle child at age five was Afua, like her mother. Finally, little Harry, age three, was born on a Tuesday, and was named Kobla.

Although it had been her idea Merriam now regretted divorcing the children's father.

Charles had been a policeman. After he had been wounded in his leg, Merriam had begged him to give up his chosen profession. Charles, a very dedicated policeman had refused.

Although Merriam had experienced violence several times in her life, especially the murder of her father Kwame, back in Ghana, she was unable to stand the steady diet of pain that Charles' job elicited.

She wondered now whether she shouldn't have just ignored the pain so that Charles would have had more time with his children.

He had been a good father, visiting them and taking them out whenever he could.

In the last seven months he had met Calliope Hender, his new girlfriend. While he did not bring Calliope to Merriam's house, Merriam knew from conversations with her kids that Calliope was a very nice person.

Her reverie was broken as the bailiff rose himself and announced, "All Rise!"

The judge, the honorable Judge Edward Phillip Lennox strode quickly into his court and ascended the two steps to sit behind his bench.

"Are there any questions before we begin?" Judge Lennox asked.

The defense attorney, Edward Winston Preston rose and said, "Your Honor I must object to that child being in this court. These proceedings are not at all fitting for a child that young."

Judge Lennox looked over at Merriam and young Charles. He knew who she was from pictures in all of the New York City newspapers.

"Mrs. Stodorah," he addressed her, formally, "How would you respond to Mr. Preston's request?"

Merriam stood stiffly, tugging young Charles onto his feet.

"I agree with Mr. Preston Your Honor. A child should not have to view the evil, disgusting person who has killed his father. With your Honor's permission, I have someone in the hallway who can take him home to his grandmother."

Lennox noticed a trace of an Eastern African accent in her tone.

Preston immediately jumped up. His face was red and his features were contorted. "Your Honor," he demanded loudly, "I object! Mrs. Stodorah's statement is prejudicial to my client's case. Please Sir, have that stricken from the record."

"So noted," Judge Lennox replied, Mr. Priestly please strike that last response by Mrs. Stodorah."

"Wonder of wonders," Lennox told himself silently, "a victim who is prejudicial to the criminal who murdered her husband." After glancing at the documents before him, Lennox corrected himself, "Ah, former husband."

After another moment of thought, the judge again corrected himself, "Uh, alleged murderer."

A small smile crept upon Meriam's face. She had accomplished just what she had intended.

Addressing Mrs. Erica Lomonico, the Assistant Bronx District Attorney, Judge Lennox asked, "Any objection Mrs. Lomonico?"

"No your Honor, Lomonico responded with a very slight chuckle in her tone, "No objection to Mrs. Stodorah sparing her child from his father's murderer."

Preston was almost apoplectic. If possible, his face was even more brightly red.

Before Preston could say anything, Judge Lennox snapped, "That'll be enough of that Counselor. You should know better. Mr. Priestly strike Mrs. Lomonico's statement from the Record as well."

As Merriam turned to remove little Charles, she could swear she saw a gleam in Judge Lennox's eyes.

At the defense table a woman with short dark hair and a lighter African-American complexion began to cry. She laid her face upon her crossed arms and began to sob violently.

Her long sleeved pale violet blouse immediately became soaked in tears.

"There. There." Preston crooned softly, slowly rubbing her back. He noted that her back was also damp, with perspiration. He wanted to remove his hand, but was afraid that if he did so she might break down completely.

"Don't worry," he consoled her, "All that was said and done will be stricken from the record. I'll still get you off."

Eleanor Revental, her hair slightly disheveled looked up at him. Her eyes were wide and a grimace had twisted her mouth. Streaks of tears had left pale lines in her ruined make-up. Her lip gloss was completely gone and now it was staining the sleeves of her blouse.

"Are you out of your fucking mind?" she gasped sharply at her lawyer, "That poor kid just lost his father and all you can think about is your gaddam case.

"What kind of an animal are you?"

Silently she thought, "What kind of an animal am I?"

Seeing no possible hope for a peaceful adjustment to the case as it now stood, Judge Lennox called for a two hour break. Hopefully Preston and his client could make some sort of determination on how they might proceed.

As he left the Bench, however, the Judge warned himself, "Don't hold your breath, Ed, my lad."

As the defense team left to plot their new strategy, Merriam Stodorah reentered the court room. She went directly over and sat beside Calliope Hender.

Gently, almost tenderly, she laid her hand upon Calliope's shoulder.

"I'm so sorry Calliope," Merriam said softly, "He told me that he did love you."

Charles had never told Merriam that, but she thought it might be something that Calliope might need to hear.

Calliope's eyes were damp with her own tears.

"Th-thank you Merriam. I'm so sorry for your loss as well. Charles told me that the insurance policy was still in your name. He increased it when all this crap in the City began. He wanted to make sure there was enough to bury him and even more for the kids."

Merriam squeezed Calliope's hand, and nodded.

"So what's up here?" she asked, sweeping the emptying room with her hand.

"After you left, the defendant broke down. She was sobbing and she called her lawyer an idiot. The Judge called for a two hour recess."

"Want to get a cup of coffee?" Merriam asked.

Unsure of how to react, Calliope just stared at her with widely open eyes.

Merriam placed her hand on Calliope's arm. "Listen, she began, "I still loved him, but it had been my decision to end the marriage.

"Admittedly, when the two of you started dating I was a bit jealous. But, and this is a very big but, he left me protesting the divorce, and I kept pushing him away. He found love again with you Calliope, and for that I will be eternally grateful.

"Yea, we both lost him, and yes, we both loved him. Let us rejoice in the fact that before he died, he knew that he too was loved.

"Now, how about that coffee? Although," she added, "I'm really a tea drinker."

There was a small café just a block away from the Courthouse. As they sat waiting, for the waitress to return with their beverages, Calliope asked, "Do you have any of the details? They said because I wasn't really related to him, they could not tell me."

"Well," Merriam began, "I got to know his sergeant, Marciano fairly well."

"You mean like the boxer?" Calliope asked, somewhat surprised.

"Yes, same spelling but no relation." Merriam replied, I asked him the same thing.

"Anyway, Marciano said that Charles died from asphyxiation. Thank God he wasn't burned up, although not being able to breathe seems horrible enough."

"Dead is dead!" Calliope stated with a catch in her voice.

She began to cry again. Her tears elicited tears from Merriam as well.

The two women commiserated with each other silently. They reached up to hug each other after pulling their chairs closer.

When their drinks were brought they had both quieted down.

"So, how was this Revental woman involved?" Calliope asked.

"She and several others threw Molotov Cocktails at Charles' squad vehicle. Supposedly, the way the vehicle was positioned they did not see him in it, so they all say.

"It was running with the air conditioning on and the windows closed."

"Didn't they think that a running police car was suspicious?" Calliope asked.

"They claimed that there was so much noise that they didn't hear the vehicle." Merriam explained, "Apparently Charles turned the car off before it could actually explode. Marciano had a fire extinguisher, but as I said, Charles died from lack of oxygen."

"You said there were three of them, but only that woman was there today." Calliope questioned.

"Well, from what Marciano told me, that lawyer is an activist himself. He usually only takes cases where he gets the glory no matter what happens to his client.

"Apparently the other two were a white man and a Hispanic. Since a black cop died, this Preston guy apparently thinks he'd have an easier time defending a black woman, and so he petitioned, successfully, apparently, to have her trial separated from her co-defendants."

"Wow," Calliope observed, "You really have all this legal language down pat."

"I guess Charles didn't tell you. When we first married I was a legal secretary. I stopped when little Charles was born and became a stay at home Mom. I have to admit, however, I'm somewhat addicted to all the old Lawyer dramas on TV. They run them all on Cable."

Calliope looked tired. Her eyes were drooping and face seemed a little pale.

"I really don't want to go back to that courtroom," Calliope revealed, "But I'm not looking forward to that drive back to White Plains, uh, that's where I live."

"I know where you live." Merriam revealed, "I Googled you a little while back. I'm not proud of it, but I was a lot more jealous back then.

"I have an idea though. I rode in with my cousin and she took little Charles back home. I could drive you to my place in New Rochelle. You could rest for a while before going home or if you'd like you could spend the night.

"I know for a fact, that there are three very small people in that house that would love to see their Aunt Calliope."

"Y-you wouldn't mind?" Calliope asked.

"Honey," Merriam replied, earnestly, I still haven't figured out how to tell them about their father. It would be really stupid and heartless to deny them Auntie Calliope too."

Unfortunately, neither one of them had expected the children's reaction when they saw Calliope.

"Where's Daddy?" Little Charles asked with a happy, expectant smile upon his face.

"Daddy, Daddy!" Cara and Harry chimed together, dancing up and down.

The next hour was not an easy one for the two women.

Explanations of Heaven and a new guardian angel were prominent.

Harry didn't really understand, but Charles and Cara certainly did. Their crying however brought tears from their baby brother.

Finally quiet, the three children were placed in bed.

"This isn't over." Merriam told herself.

What might have been a peaceful night was not. Little Charles woke up several times crying with nightmares.

Merriam and Calliope alternated staying with Charles and sleeping in a chair in the room with Cara and Harry.

The two younger kids were fresh the next morning. Charles was worn out and fell asleep with his cereal spoon in his mouth.

CHAPTER 6

DOES THE LAWYER EVEN CARE

Edward Winston Preston arrived in a large black Cadillac SUV. He had three assistants, Monica Germaine, a legal secretary, William Romanesque, a lawyer like Preston and Carlene Whelles. Carlene was his current girlfriend and her position on his team was strictly so that he might pay her and not have to worry about the money on his taxes. On occasion, David LeCorse, his accountant would have been a part of the entourage, but David was currently recovering from the Covid Virus and not available.

Preston was a New York scion, the son and principal heir of a noted family that spent little time in Manhattan, but owned some rather expensive Manhattan real estate.

The location was the Bronx County Courthouse on 161st Street and the Grand Concourse. The Bronx County Courthouse is known as the Mario Merola Building and is located in the Concourse and Melrose neighborhoods of the Bronx. The Mario Merola Building stands two blocks east-southeast of Yankee Stadium.

Sometime in 1988, former Mayor Ed Koch had renamed the Bronx County Courthouse. It had become the Mario Merola Building to honor the Bronx County District Attorney Mario Merola who had recently died. It was also the Bronx County Government Building. They and the courthouse shared the space.

The court room was thinly populated, in keeping with the new rules brought on by the pandemic.

Preston and his Secretary sat at the defendant's table. He sat at one end and she at the other.

Directly behind him sat Attorney William Romanesque, two rows back in the general seating area.

Preston's personal assistant, Carlene Whelles, sat behind Monica Germaine, the secretary, and again, two rows back.

A television monitor, beside Monica Germaine framed the defendant, Eleanor Revental who had chosen to remain in the nearby Bronx House of Detention. Seated beside him, but at another table, was another of Preston's associates, Attorney Carlos Montoya.

Along the wall where a jury might normally sit were four uniformed police people. They each sat with an empty chair between them, more precautions because of the Corona virus.

The Judge, Edward P. Lennox sat in his place, atop the bench and the bailiff stood to one side. The recording secretary sat at his desk, with his fingers dancing, alert and ready to type. Everyone in the courtroom was masked and had hospital caps upon their heads except for the police, who wore police baseball caps and the judge who was bare headed.

Both the judge and his bailiff were African American.

When not masked against an unseen virus, Judge Lennox was a tall, bright eyed for fifty eight years of age, somewhat lean, handsome man. He had decided not to wear a protective cap on that day and his silvery white hair was bright beneath the equally bright courtroom lights.

Ten feet to the right of the defending team, at another table sat the prosecutor, Assistant District Attorney for the Bronx, Erica Lomonico. Her co-prosecutor, Maria Sanchez, sat at the other end of their table.

"Your Honor," Preston asked, rising and indicating the four officers sitting to the side, "Must we have a small army to guard the court room? I'm sure they would be just as effective in the corridor."

"Miss Lomonico," Judge Lennox said in a somber though sonorous tone, "those are your people. How would you respond to Mister Preston?"

"Your Honor, they are my witnesses. Mr. Preston has a list of their names. I'm sure if Mr. Preston is afraid of the New York Police, we can have them wait in the hallway, as he suggested."

To the side, Officer David Keith inadvertently chuckled. It was not heard, except by his fellow police officers on either side of him. Officer Contadina bit her lip to avoid laughing, but Officer Italo chuckled as well.

Addressing attorney Preston, Judge Lennox asked him, "Well Sir, is that true? Are you afraid of her witnesses, or is it just a police presence of any form?

"I should point out, Mister Preston, while a police force of any size will certainly have personnel problems; I'm inclined to think that not every cop is like that bad cop and his cohorts in Minneapolis. Might you agree, or perhaps, disagree?"

"Ah, ah, no, of course not Your Honor." Preston stammered.

The defense attorney looked down at the papers in his hands. He shuffled them slightly as he thought about his next statement.

His political aspirations at present seemed just a bit wispy in his mind.

Preston had done his homework studiously. He knew Judge Lennox to be a liberal in his politics, and that the Judge had ruled against several conservative elements in his court previously. Preston was beginning to suspect that being anti-police was not one of Lennox's convictions.

He knew he had to change his tactics slightly.

Of course, as an attorney he wanted to have his client freed. But, as a liberal activist, he wanted to make the trial a statement.

His attention was drawn back to the bench as Judge Lennox began to speak again.

"Mr. Preston, Miss Lomonico, and all here in this courtroom, I wish to make something perfectly clear. I shall make a statement now, and if either of the parties feels that I should recues myself, then I will take that possibility into consideration."

Preston noticed immediately that Lennox had not said that he would actually recues himself. All he had revealed is that the matter would be duly considered. This old guy was sly.

"Better watch myself." Preston resolved.

"When a police program is defunded, any number of people are affected." Lennox continued, "They include battered spouses, missing children and missing adults. Considering the beating that our New York police have taken recently, with a loss of personnel and equipment, this magistrate is totally against the defunding of our police department.

"I should also include mention of this virus in our midst as well.

"Sadly, the defunding decision was made by our illustrious Mayor, and I and my fellow judges are left to sift through the shambles it has created.

"Mister Preston, Miss Lomonico, do you have any questions or perhaps a statement of your own?"

Erica Lomonico wanted to correct Judge Lennox and tell him that she was married, and therefore a Missus, but felt that now was not the time.

"No, Your Honor." She said firmly and sat down.

Needing more time to assess the situation, Edward Preston said, "Not at this time Your Honor." and also sat down.

"Well," Lennox replied, "at my age, pontificating takes a lot out of me. Let's take a thirty minute break. We'll decide about Mister Preston's concern with Miss Lomonico's witnesses when we return."

"All rise." Tom Wilcox, the bailiff called out as Lennox left the bench.

Edward Preston glanced over at Monica Germaine, his legal secretary. "You know that I don't like surprises Monica. Why wasn't I informed of Lennox's stance on police defunding?"

Used to a myriad of complaints and childish outbursts, Monica shrugged and said, "I'll look into it boss. Anything else? I have to pee."

He dismissed her with a wave of his hand.

Erica Lomonico, meanwhile, stood before her witnesses. Their eyes all sparkled with what they had just seen.

"Well," she announced, "That went well."

The following day in a separate case the anteroom outside the office that Erica Lomonico shared with Maria Sanchez was full. Besides John Doe's attorney, Edward Winston Preston and his assistant, Carlene Whelles, There was a Lieutenant McGinty from One Police Plaza and a man from the Mayor's office named Garret Holmes.

Erica knew who Holmes was and McGinty's name sounded strangely familiar.

She dismissed McGinty with the thought that it was probably a fairly common name. When you prosecuted as many cases as she had in her ten year plus career, you ran across a great many names.

Only one of her witnesses was there, patrolman Keith. Perhaps McGinty was one of his supervisors.

At the last minute a woman, Sergeant Eberstein had reported to McGinty with some documents.

While she attempted to get her thoughts in order, Erica had Maria herd everyone down to one of the larger conference rooms.

Just as everyone started to leave, she called out to Garret Holmes, "Mr. Holmes, a minute of your time please?"

Holmes entered her office followed closely by McGinty and Eberstein.

"Oh, no," Lomonico told them, "I just want to see Mr. Holmes, not his entourage."

"Well, actually, Holmes informed her with a smile, "I'm a part of Lieutenant McGinty's entourage."

To Erica Lomonico's confused expression Holmes explained the entire situation to her in as few words as possible.

When he was finished, she seemed less confused, but still was unable to fully grasp the entire position.

Garret extended his hand towards Mike and said "McGinty, you have the floor."

Mike opened up one of the files that Natalie had given him.

"Uh, Mrs. Lomonico, we now know that your John Doe is really Brian O'Dell. He's a white supremacist from Springfield Massachusetts. He belongs to a group known as Caucasian Infinity."

"But he wore a BLM tee shirt!" Erica exclaimed, "He was protesting the police presence."

"That's what he and his organization wanted us to believe." Holmes interceded, "They were causing additional havoc and damage and it was being blamed on the entire BLM movement. Although, I'm relatively sure he isn't a fan of the police, either."

"One thing we have to get straight here," Mike told her, "There are elements in the BLM movement who are solely destructive and self-serving. They are criminals taking advantage of the unrest caused by the actuality of police brutality in certain circles. Yes, it exists here in this city, but Walt Agrarian is doing his damndest to root it out of his department. There are of course, peaceful protestors. They are protestors who oddly enough, realize the need for proper law enforcement.

"But, and this is a very definite but, there are some criminal elements, both black and white who are seriously taking advantage of this unrest here in our country.

"Add to that the scores of politicians who are making bad, no, make that dangerous decisions in regard to the wellbeing of all of our innocent citizens.

Mike stopped to catch his breath and to sort his thoughts.

"And now we have yet another facet to this problem." Natalie added, wanting to be heard, "These freaking white supremacists posing as BLM protestors in order to incite even more riot and hatred with their stinking actions."

Mike patted her on the shoulder and said, "Way to go Nat."

Erica Lomonico tapped steadily on her blotter with her manicured fingernails. She was obviously deep in thought.

Towards the end she was humming a simple tune under her breath.

Standing, she took a step towards the door. Urging with her moving forefinger, she said, "Gentlemen, please follow me. I have some information which the law compels me to share with my esteemed colleague, the defense attorney."

When they arrived in the conference room, Edward Preston was beaming. Erica recognized a writ in his hands, no doubt for either a change of venue or quite possibly for a total release of his client either in his or the client's own recognizance.

As she sat down, and the others all took places around the table, she pointed at Preston's document and said, "Oh that can wait for the moment Mr. Preston. I have evidence which I must share with you. We'll get to your writ in a few minutes."

Preston nodded for her to continue. There was a gleam in his eyes.

"Before I begin, I will have supporting documents to turn over to you, but would you like Miss Whelles to record this?"

"You're okay with that?" Preston asked, but a suspicious tone had crept into his voice.

"Well, of course, it's entirely up to you, but yes, I'm fine with that. Oh, and do you want your client to be a party to these proceedings?"

While he was digesting all of her statements and questions, she added, "Uh, on your laptop, naturally. There's no need for Brian to come all the way over here."

Both Preston and Carlene Whelles looked up sharply. Preston regained his composure immediately, but Whelles seemed quite nervous.

"H-how did you know that?" she stammered, her voice an octave higher.

"It's my job to know." Erica answered, somewhat sweetly, "Which brings us back to our disclosure topic.

"Here are the documents supplied by our rather efficient police department.

"His full name is Brian Eugene O'Dell. He's twenty seven years old, a high school graduate, a warehouse worker and single.

As Preston seemed to be breathing deeply, although somewhat unevenly, Erica Lomonico added, "Oh yes, and he's a member of Caucasian Infinity, a white supremacist group, who have openly stated their superiority over and hatred of Jews, Hispanics, Homosexuals and…."

Her voice trailed off as she tapped the document before her with her bright red fingernail. It picked up as she said loudly, "Oh yes, Black people, especially people in the BLM movement and Black people in positions of authority."

At the last, she glanced sideways at Garret Holmes, who simply nodded.

Preston asked for a little more time. Erica Lomonico could see the wheels turning in his head. Having a white supremacist for a client would certainly not jive with his highly liberal values.

She agreed and made a mental note to contact Judge Lennox. She informed Preston that she would square it with the court, but urged him to contact Judge Lennox as well.

CHAPTER 7

IT'S A WAR ZONE

As they were walking out to the parking area Mike offered Davy a ride to his precinct.

Natalie was in the back seat and Garret Holmes was already seated in the passenger side front seat.

"I guess he didn't hear you call shotgun." Mike whispered to Davy with a chuckle.

Davy raised his eyebrows and shook his head solemnly from side to side.

Mike asked his step-son if he was scheduled for duty.

"Not exactly scheduled," Davy told him, "but with the various personnel and vehicle shortages, everyone is expected to put in as much time as possible.

"Nunzio, Gerrie and I have all been reassigned back at the old Four-Eight. They need people a bit more than the Four-Seven or even the Four-Six does.

"I think, of all the places I've worked, namely the Four-Seven, Four-Eight and One Police plaza, I like the Four-Eight the best.

"It's where I started, met Nunzio, and eventually, his sister, Amy.

"Plus, I really like and trust Sergeant Marciano."

"Yea, I like him too." Mike admitted. "He kinda reminds me of your grandfather."

Davy smiled and nodded.

Traffic was fairly light and within minutes they were on the Cross

Bronx Expressway. Several minutes more and they were exiting the highway to reach the precinct.

Garret Holmes had been past this particular precinct, many times on his way from Manhattan to Westchester and New England, but had never really noticed the building.

He was suitably impressed. It was a reasonably new building compared to many of the other precincts in New York City.

It was a large building of a darker brick construction. It had a series of flat roofs, and the main entrance was on the second floor. A relatively steep handicap ramp led up from the street level. While not a walled building, it still looked at least moderately defensible. There were approximately five patrolmen and women strung out across the front sidewalk, at a loose parade rest. Several more could be seen up on the several roofs.

Mike pulled into an empty parking space. Within moments, a sturdy, hospital masked sergeant stepped up to the driver's side and said, "You can't park here sir."

Mike was driving his own SUV. The sergeant spied the shield first and then Mike's lieutenant bars.

"Oh," he said, "ah, Lieutenant. How may I help you sir?"

"I'm just dropping off one of your officers Sergeant. I'll be gone in several minutes."

The Sergeant noticed Holmes in the passenger seat, and mistook him for a detective. His eyes also noted the female sergeant in the backseat next to a patrolman.

Davy was just pulling his own hospital mask into place and the sergeant recognized him immediately.

"Oh, Keith," he said, "Marciano's waiting for you inside."

"Thanks Sarge." Davy said, "They'll probably send me back out to you after I've been checked for Covid."

The sergeant nodded and backed away from the car. He raised his hand in a modified salute as Mike backed up and then drove away.

Davy was almost to the top of the ramp and waved as Mike drove off.

Davy was cleared and reported to Marciano. He had not specifically been told to report to the Sergeant, but after his brief conversation with

Sergeant Ramirez outside, he felt that doing so would be the best course of action.

As he sought out Marciano he reflected on how Ramirez was pretty much the Assistant Intelligence man in the precinct. In a crisis like the one they were going through, however, every man was a front line soldier.

While Davy had not known at the time, he now knew that Ramirez had been Jimmy Martinez's handler when Martinez was posing undercover as "Bobby J" Jimenez, the leader of the gang, the Bronx Choppers.

He wondered where Martinez was in the midst of this Pandemic- riots crisis.

He met Marciano finally, coming out of Captain Rodriguez's office.

Despite the fact that they were both masked, they recognized each other immediately from their individual body types and the ever helpful nametags. Plus Marciano, of course, was wearing his sergeant's stripes.

"I'm guessing outside, eh Sarge?" Davy offered.

"Yea," Marciano answered in a somewhat beaten voice, "But up on the roof."

Davy guessed correctly that Marciano had not gotten very much sleep either.

"I have a few coffees for the guys on the roof." He stated, "Any chance you can take them with you, what with your equipment and all?"

"Sure Sarge," Davy replied, I'll manage."

"Good, and Keith when you get up there, tell Contadina to come down for a rest. I imagine she's exhausted. She's been up there the longest. And tell her, no arguments. That's a direct order from me."

"Will do Sarge!" Davy snapped back and went to get his equipment.

As he emerged out upon the roof, Davy heard a familiar voice call out, "Finally! It's about freakin' time."

Smiling beneath his face covering, Davy said, "And it's good to see you as well, Officer Italo."

"Davy," Nunzio exclaimed loudly, "When did you get back? Was that you in that SUV?"

"Yea!" Davy answered, "Mike dropped me off."

"Well, what's the story? Where do we stand on that punk's case?"

"I'll explain it in a few minutes." Davy assured him.

"There's coffee in the box. All we have is black, unless you want sweeteners; we have plenty of them, but no sugar or creamers."

"Black's just fine." Nunzio declared, reaching for the box.

He then announced, "Hey guys, coffee."

"Where's Gerrie? Davy asked, "Marciano wants me to relieve her."

"That's her over there, leaning on the wall." Nunzio answered, "I had her take the rear in case she started to doze."

He then yelled in Gerrie's direction, "Hey Contadina, your relief is here. Snap to, Officer."

Languidly, Gerrie turned in their direction. She half waved and started toward them.

Like Marciano, she recognized Davy's body type and immediately zeroed in on his nametag."

"Hi Davy," She said lazily, "Anything new on John Doe's case?"

"I'll fill you in later," Davy replied, "Right now Marciano wants you to go down and rest. He said to tell you that's a direct order, Missy!"

Without answering, and with another half wave, Gerrie left the roof.

"Wow," Davy exclaimed, "No back-talk. She must really be tired."

"Yea, she's been up her the longest." Nunzio answered, "She's really beat. And those headaches are driving her nuts."

Davy pulled out his cell phone and dialed Marciano.

When Marciano answered, he said, "Hey Sarge, this is Keith. Gerrie's still getting severe headaches. I wonder if she doesn't have a concussion."

"I'll get her checked out." Marciano assured him.

As Davy placed his phone in the holder on his belt, Nunzio lowered his coffee from his lips. "Now," he said, "About our case with John "Frickin' Doe?"

Davy explained all that had happened in the DA's office. He was especially colorful as he described Ed Preston's reaction when he found out that his client was a racist.

Tears of laughter ran down Nunzio's cheeks. He slapped Davy on the shoulder.

Minutes later Davy's eyes were scanning the street, up and down. He spotted something which seemed out of place. The traffic was relatively light, but a late model European, possibly German car was traveling somewhat slowly.

"Look at that Nunz." He said to his friend, "What's that look like to you?"

"I'm not exactly sure," Nunzio returned, "But it doesn't look Kosher to me."

"Hey guys," Davy called down to their fellow patrolmen below, "that blue car riding so slow looks outta place."

The guys on the street immediately took notice. Sergeant Ramirez had them quickly take cover behind whatever they could.

For some it was parked police vehicles. For one it was a privately owned vehicle, for Ramirez and two others it was the area just to the left of the ramp, behind an industrial sized generator left there by workmen.

Seeing the police reaction, the car speeded up and the barrel of some sort of rifle extended from the passenger window.

"GUN!" Davy and Nunzio shouted together as loud as they could and quickly peeled their weapons from their holsters.

As the street assailants were emptying some sort of automatic weapon fire at the hiding police, both Nunzio and Davy were firing from their superior position at the open passenger window as the car tried to speed away.

Several bullets must have found their mark as the automatic weapon fell from the shooter's hands to the pavement. The car, itself clipped a parked car and ricocheted into a parked pickup truck.

The driver recovered however, and sped off. "But, not before Ramirez and one of his men, Tom Remar, had started a police SUV and were quickly after him.

As it turned out the driver had also been hit from a bullet ricocheting off of the dashboard. That of course was unknown to the policemen following.

It had hit and penetrated his thigh and he was bleeding badly. He passed out, hit another parked car and spun through the intersection into the path of an oncoming dump truck. The car turned over, trapping both occupants within it. A ruptured fuel tank and dripping gasoline was ignited by the sparks of the vehicle sliding across the pavement on its roof. If either occupant had been alive upon impact, they no longer were.

From atop the precinct house, Nunzio said, "Sonuva bitch!"

While squinting, Davy merely said, "Yea!"

Sergeant Marciano, who had led several other policemen out of the building with weapons drawn said, "There'll be hell to pay for that. Mark my words."

There was indeed a price to pay however, but not the one that had leapt into the Sergeant's mind.

Marciano saw it immediately as the sound of groaning drew his attention to the man who had ducked behind the privately owned vehicle. It was a car which belonged to a Merchant from Fordham Road whose bodega had been firebombed in the middle of the night.

Lying prone upon the pavement, Patrolman Jonathan Pierce Overton was bleeding to death. A single bullet had hit his belt buckle as he had been turning sideways to check on the guys hiding behind the generator. That movement had lifted his body armor just high enough that the bullet had driven deeply into his abdomen. Several vital organs had been pierced. What blood was held in by his armor quickly flooded his abdominal cavity. He was dead before Marciano could get to him.

Jonathan Pierce Overton was an African American policeman. He had been proud of his heritage and proud of his shield. He would have become a sergeant by the end of the year, if not sooner.

As the vision of the vehicle exploding, just down the street flashed through Marciano's mind, he whispered a husky, throaty, "Good! Fuck 'em!"

From the roof, both Davy and Nunzio glanced back and forth between Marciano kneeling over Overton and the flaming crash approximately one block away.

"Damn," Davy told himself silently, "I sure picked a hell of a time to become a cop."

CHAPTER 8
WHY HER OF ALL PEOPLE

As news of the problems in the Four-Eight Precinct reached the McGinty household Theresa was beside herself. Although a phone call from her son to tell her that he was okay removed that particular worry, it was not enough.

Stories flew throughout the police dependents community. She knew of his head wounds from thrown rocks and debris. She knew of the two black cops from his precinct that had died. One had been hit by a brick and the other by a bullet.

"What the hell has happened to our City?" she lamented.

"Damn this City government and its freaking vainglorious Mayor."

It was the wrong time for an almost beaten, almost robbed and possibly even almost raped young nurse to emerge from the cellar.

"And you," Theresa screamed, throwing her hands into the air, "Why did I have to find out about your problems from someone else?"

"Because I was afraid of this." Melly told her pointing at her Mothers histrionics.

Theresa lowered her arms. She was trembling. She suddenly threw those arms around Melanie and drew her daughter tightly into her embrace. Even at that she could not stop shaking. The movement shook loose the towel wrapped around Melly's damp hair and it fell to the floor.

"What can I do?" Theresa rasped softly, "Whatever can I do?"

"What you do each and every day," Melanie answered, tearfully, "be my Mother. Be the woman who cared for me when I was young without my own Mom and with a Dad who tried to escape his sorrow with other people's problems."

Together, the two women embraced tightly, almost squeezing the air from each other.

Releasing Melanie, and stepping back from the girl that she did regard as her own true daughter, Theresa gazed upon the tearful young lady before her.

"You know," Theresa observed with a certain amount of pride, "You do look a lot like Jennifer. She was a beautiful woman, and you seem to have all of her best features.

"I'm sorry Melly. That must have been a terrible ordeal for you."

"Coffee, cake and discussing it might just be a cathartic experience." Marie, Theresa's Mom called out from the kitchen.

"I've got two cups already made and I'm working on mine and Mom's tea." Maria, Theresa's other daughter added.

Once they were all settled Melanie related all that she remembered of that night's events.

Both Theresa and her Mother, Marie shuddered as they listened. The expression on Maria's face was not much better.

Although Theresa kept her thoughts to herself, Melly's narrative brought back memories of Theresa's deadly encounter with the home invaders.

Grandma Marie also had other thoughts as she remembered just a few of Ed's cases. They too were cases where people she loved had been in danger. Ed was so very often in danger.

Even though they were not of her own blood, Mike McGinty and Nicky Evans almost seemed like her own sons when they too were in peril. Little did she know at the time that McGinty, the big lug, would someday be her son-in-law.

She chuckled inwardly, but none of the others noticed.

"Thank GOD for Jim Cantner." Theresa remarked with an exhalation of relief.

"Amen to that." Marie added.

Melanie smiled. Buck still visited her in her dreams from time to time, but she had found herself falling for Nurse Jim Cantner long before he had come to her rescue.

It was a Tuesday. The sun was high in the sky and Nunzio Italo descended the stairs from the upper level of his Mother's restaurant in The Bronx, not far from the Yonkers, NY border.

He had slept late since he had worked the night before and was scheduled to do another midnight shift.

His former partner, Davy Keith was working the current day shift. Davy was engaged to Nunzio's sister, Amy, and hopefully when all of the craziness in the City calmed down there would be a wedding.

Davy was partnered with Nunzio's girlfriend Gerrie Contadina. The two of them were getting along a lot better recently, but occasionally had their flare-ups.

When Nunzio entered the kitchen he gave his Mother a hug and a kiss. "Where's Amy?" he asked, referring to his sister.

"Uh, she went out back." Ronnie, whose name was actually Rhonda said, indicating the back door with her thumb. "She had a phone call."

After pouring himself a cup of coffee, Nunzio went to find his sister.

He found her sitting on a stack of discarded wooden pallets. Her hand clutched her phone upon her lap. She was crying.

Rushing to her side, and imagining any sort of scenario he dropped his coffee and sat beside her. Hoping desperately that it wasn't Gerrie or Davy he wrapped his arms around her and murmured softly, "Who?"

"M-Meg T-Thebes." Amy sobbed, followed immediately by another deluge of tears.

"T-traffic stop and they opened fire on her before she even got to their window. Teddy Winthrop was backing her up. He immediately opened fire, nailing two guys in the car.

"Meg's dead. She died on the way to the hospital. That was Gerrie on the phone. She's all torn up. Davy was with her trying to console her. She called me first because she thought I would be more level headed when I told you. I guess I screwed that up huh?"

Nunzio drew her even more tightly into his embrace.

"You did just fine Sis." He said, "I gotta get to the precinct to see Gerrie. Can you tell Mom? She's gonna be devastated too."

"There's more." Amy related, reluctantly in a soft voice.

Nunzio stopped at the door. Picking up his discarded coffee cup he looked back to his sister. "What?" he asked tentatively.

"A reporter from some liberal rag came upon the scene just before backup arrived. He told the Sergeant responding that maybe Teddy should be brought up on charges. He didn't even witness anything, Nunzio and he comes out with a load of crap like that"

"Piece of shit!" was all Nunzio could say as he clenched his free hand tightly.

He walked back over to Amy and put his arm around her shoulders.

"C'mon Amy, we'll go tell Mom together."

The sun did seem a bit hotter, but that might only have been the uneasy feeling which Nunzio seemed unable to shed. He knew Gerrie would be upset. He only hoped that he would be able to console her properly.

He knew that he could be childish from time to time. Too often he knew that he craved to be the center of attention. The feeling often resulted in his silly jokes or just as often grousing about things which really did not matter.

The precinct interior did seem a little cooler. He stood in a line waiting to be checked by Peggy Romaine, their sometimes resident nurse.

Peggy's expression was somewhat noncommittal above her hospital mask until she noted his nametag. Her normally bright eyes dimmed considerably when finally they met his.

"She's in the back room Nunzio." Peggy said softly and indicated the area with a rearward sweep of her hand.

"Carole Amendola and Davy Keith are with her. Meg's husband has been notified. He went to see her body at the hospital, even though Inspector Malinowski told him not to. They have a three year old little boy Nunzio."

"Stosh came back last night from Medical leave. He's heartbroken."

"Thanks Peggy." Nunzio murmured as he pushed past her brusquely.

Nunzio found them just where Peggy had said they would be. Davy was sitting beside Gerrie, holding her hand and Carole sat on the other side.

When Hc saw his friend, Davy rose and offered Nunzio his seat.

"Are you alright Honey?" Nunzio asked and then admonished himself for opening like that.

"No you idiot." He said aloud, "Of course she's not alright. I'm so sorry

Ger. I know how close you two were. We all loved her Gerrie, the entire precinct loved her."

Gerrie was sobbing softly. The blue of her police blouse was darker in the front where her tears had stained it.

She squeezed his hand tightly and he drew her into his embrace.

Her tears began to darken his shirt as well. He removed his shield with his free hand to make sure she did not scratch her face.

"Italo," Stosh barked from the doorway, "Stay with her. She needs you more than the people of the Bronx do.

"Keith," Sergeant Gronkowsky snapped, "You up for a bit more overtime?"

"Sure Sarge." Davy answered, "D'you want me to cover for Nunzio?"

"If you don't mind." Gronkowsky answered, flatly.

"Meg Thebes had been one of Gronkowsky's favorites. He was presently able to control his emotions, but he wasn't sure for how long.

Davy laid his hand on Gerrie's shoulder. He kissed the top of her head. "I'm so sorry Gerrie. He said softly, and started to leave.

"Davy." Gerrie said between sobs.

He stopped and looked back at her within Nunzio's arms.

"Be careful Davy." She said firmly, more firmly than she had meant, "I can't lose any more of my friends."

"I will." He assured her along with a nod, and was gone.

Davy was assigned to car fourteen, with a seasoned patrolman, Jimmy Castile, as his partner.

"Sorry about Thebes, Keith." Castile said as they walked towards their vehicle, "I really liked her. Why is it always the good ones?"

"Yea," Davy echoed in his mind, "and she was certainly one of the best."

While Nunzio sat holding Gerrie Contadina, Sergeant Stosh Gronkowsky went to get them both coffees. When he returned he sat both cups and a small bag of sugar, sweeteners and creamers along with the cups before them.

"Sorry," he apologized, "I wasn't sure how you took them.

Nunzio prepared Gerrie's coffee for her, just as he knew she liked it.

Foundering for conversation, he asked, "So were they black guys or white?"

She stared at him. Her expression had changed, just slightly, but certainly noticeably.

"Why?" she demanded more than asked, "What difference does that make?"

"I'm sorry Ger. I was just tryin' to ascertain what kind of motive they might have had."

"Why did you lead with black instead of white?" she once more demanded. Her jaw was set firmly and her tears seemed to have stopped.

"Gerrie," he asked, obviously confused, "Where are you goin' with this? What did I do wrong? The very last thing I would wanta do right now is to upset you more. Gerrie I love you. You know that."

She calmed slightly. Her expression changed again. He saw an unfathomable question in her eyes but could not figure it out.

Gerrie sat quietly, staring at her hands which were clasped together in her lap.

Finally she said, in a tightly controlled tone, "Do you know Bianca Brown down in the Four-Seven?"

The name elicited a specific memory in Nunzio's mind. She was a pretty African American woman in the Four-Eight when he had arrived. He had thought about asking her out when he had first joined that precinct. She had, however, let him know that no way would she ever date a rookie, especially one as dumb as he appeared to be.

With injured feelings he had avoided her as much as possible after that.

She warmed up to him slightly after he had been wounded in the altercation with the Fordham Freaks in Sánchez's bodega. Remembering her words of his first days there however, he was never more than cordial to her again.

Then had come Geraldine Contadina, also a fiery young woman. There seemed to be more to Gerrie though, and Nunzio had fallen in love with her.

"Yea, I know Bee. "He said, using Bianca's nickname. "What about it?"

"If we ever decide to marry, she will be my maid of honor."

Her voice caught in her throat as she said, "It would have been Meg."

Her voice trailed off into a quiet moan and the tears returned.

"How do you know Bianca?" he asked, thinking he might already know the answer.

Despite her previous animosity, Nunzio sat again beside his girlfriend. He wrapped his arms around her once more, feeling her stiffen within his embrace.

"Let me guess," He said, "She's either an old friend or a relative. Judging how this has unfolded, I would think a relative. So tell me. How am I going to be related to Miss Bee Brown?"

She looked up at him. There was less animosity and her expression was more curious.

"How did you come to that conclusion?" She asked in a slightly weaker voice.

"It's all just too intense." He replied. "I don't know if she ever told you, but I asked out when I was a rookie.

"Uh, I guess more of a rookie than I presently am." He corrected himself.

Her eyes opened a bit more widely. Tears still glistened on her flushed cheeks.

"She never told me that." Gerrie admitted and wondered silently where he was going with his story.

"She not only said no," Nunzio returned, "But she had some rather harsh things to say about rookies in general and me in particular. I guess I carried a grudge after that, but it had nothing to do with her skin color. It was her attitude towards me when I was only trying to be friendly."

Gerrie shook her head gently. It all made sense now. Apparently she and Bee were more alike than either of them had realized.

Gerrie's expression was softer as she gazed back at Nunzio. The pain was still etched upon her face, but any animosity had disappeared.

"Bianca's mother and my mother are sisters." She said softly.

"Well then," Nunzio announced with certain finality, "Then Miss Bee will have to get used to having a rookie for a cousin-in-law."

At that he kissed Gerrie's cheek and hugged her even more tightly.

CHAPTER 9
WHERE DID THAT COME FROM

With the hearing over for the moment, the four police officers adjourned to the courthouse cafeteria.

Surprisingly it was open, although large spaces had been created between tables and there were only two chairs at the opposite ends of each of those tables.

With each officer taking a seat at those opposing ends, and each at two adjacent tables which were seven feet apart, they sat and drank the much needed coffee.

Davy pulled a bottle of over the counter pain reliever from his pocket and washed two of them down with his caffeine loaded coffee.

"Still getting the headaches?" Gerrie asked.

"Davy nodded, feeling a slight stab of pain when he did. After a moment, he retrieved the bottle from his pocket, and called out "Heads up."

He started to toss it to Gerrie, but still feeling the pangs from his own headache, changed his mind and walked them over to her.

She thanked him, pulled down her hospital mask and smiled.

He admitted to himself, that despite her very spicy and sometimes obstinate nature, she was a very pretty woman, even without makeup and a red bump on her head.

He sighed, and thought, "My future sister-in-law."

The assistant DA, Maria Sanchez showed up to inform them that the judge had decided to postpone the trial until, as he put it, "Both warring camps can get their damn acts together."

He had added, "My courtroom is not a television comedy show. Everyone get their damn facts straight and try to remember to present their cases with some kind of decorum."

She added her own observation, "I'm sure he was talking about the defense counsel, but he has to include all of us to avoid any thoughts of impropriety."

The four of them returned to the precinct house. Marciano greeted them with new assignments. Nunzio and Jimmy Castile were sent out on patrol. Noting that the other two still had bumps upon their heads, Marciano kept them in house for sentry duty.

They were assigned to the somewhat steep ramp which led from the street sidewalk to the precinct's front entrance.

It was a fairly big building. Smaller than a few, but larger than many, as police buildings go.

Of course, it was not THE Headquarters building. That naturally was One Police Plaza in southern Manhattan.

Considering the threat, they had each been issued Heckler & Koch MP5s a 9x19mm Parabellum submachine guns. As they exited the main entrance onto the ramp, Davy held it down at his side and said, "I could get used to these."

Gerrie laughed. Hers was strapped to her shoulder, also pointing downward.

"More than a shotgun?" she asked.

"Whoa," he returned, "I'm not too sure on that thought."

They both had Tasers and flashlights. Both were clad in armor vests with Kevlar helmets.

Davy wasn't sure about Gerrie, but his helmet was pushing against the red welt and bump on his head. He lifted the helmet back slightly. The pain eased up, but obviously, quite obviously, his forehead was exposed. He had placed a thin kerchief on his head to soften the feel of the helmet, but it was not working.

He pulled the kerchief lower when he had adjusted the helmet. It was of course, no protection, whatsoever, but at least it hid the damaged area from view.

They stopped talking when they reached midpoint on the ramp.

Sergeant Carl Brimley, an African-American policeman was standing at the foot of the ramp. He was in charge.

Davy and Gerrie both waved slightly to Brimley, who waved back and then indicated that they stay just where they were.

A variety of people came and went. Gerrie suggested that one of them take the outer area of the ramp, while the other stood closer to the building.

"The better to avoid any surprises from people already on the ramp." She explained.

"Good idea." Davy remarked, "Are you sure you didn't know my grandfather?"

"No," she answered, "But I have certainly heard a lot about him."

"Yea," Davy laughed, "From me."

"Actually," Gerrie replied, "From several people, including Marciano in there." She indicated the building behind them with her thumb.

"In fact, one of my first sergeants, a Manny Romano in Brooklyn used to quote him often. It was always Ed Flanagan this and Ed Flanagan that. I didn't really connect the dots until a week or so ago. He was a well-liked guy, I have to admit."

"Oh, I don't know, Gerrie, you strike me as someone who doesn't have to admit anything if you don't want to." Gerrie chuckled. It was muffled by her hospital mask and helmet visor, but Davy heard it and smiled.

"So, how did he look?" Theresa asked. She stood, on the porch, leaning against the front door frame. Her hand was on her hip. Her hair was tousled from the late evening breeze and several curls hung down upon her forehead.

Her position made her breasts jut out prominently, but with all that was on her mind she did not notice.

Mike, sitting loosely in a deck chair before her, noticed it and could not stop staring. She wasn't wearing a bra and Mike found it slightly difficult to concentrate upon what she was saying.

She was, of course, speaking of her son Davy.

Mike and Davy had been consulting together on a court case then taking place in the Bronx. Mike had dropped Davy off at his precinct the day before and then driven himself and a civilian dignitary back to One Police Plaza.

Not long after Davy had been dropped off there had been a drive by shooting incident at that very same building. According to the news, only one African-American police officer had been hit, but quite sadly that man had died.

Davy had called soon after the incident to tell his Mother that he had been on the roof and none of the assailant's fire was directed at them. His voice had been strained, however. There were little nuances, clues that his tone had revealed. They were things that a Mother noticed.

Apparently tired of standing, Theresa pulled over another chair and sat beside her husband.

Mike was both happy and disappointed to see her blouse billow outward as she sat.

"Well, how about it?" Theresa asked again. "Mike are you even listening to me?" Her voice had risen at least another decibel.

Having banished all the prurient thoughts to another room in his mind, Mike was indeed able to recall all that she had previously said.

"I'll be honest with you Honey." He began, "At least then you'll be able to face your fears head on."

Her eyes grew large and her jaw dropped slightly. She was imagining the worst.

"He has a big lump on his forehead, surrounded by an ugly welt. He didn't complain, but he took several pain relievers while I was with him.

"What kind of pain relievers?" she demanded, a touch of panic in her tone.

"Don't worry about that Honey. I examined them visually as he poured them from the bottle. They were standard over the counter stuff, but extra strength. He didn't swallow half the bottle, but at one point he did take four instead of two."

She was unable to keep from gasping.

"I told him to get it looked at as soon as possible. I told him if I didn't get a satisfactory report by today I was going to call and speak to that Sergeant Marciano myself. You remember him Theresa; he was the guy that ushered us into the hospital when Davy gave that guy mouth to mouth."

Theresa nodded, but Mike could see deep concern etched upon her face.

"I also told him that I would be reporting to you and that I would not lie for him. GOD knows, I know as much as anybody how serious our depleted manpower is, but he would not be doing the force any good if he was at less than one hundred percent."

"As if on cue, the phone inside rang. Someone picked it up immediately. It was a standard rule in their household that the phone or cell phone must always be picked up.

Telemarketers could be dealt with, but the odds were always too high that the call might involve someone's dire peril.

Theresa's daughter, Maria stepped out onto the porch. She held the phone against her abdomen, muffling it as she spoke.

"Would you like to speak to my older brother Mom or should I tell him you've moved away.

Theresa had risen as soon as Maria had appeared. Without a word she snatched the phone away from her daughter and placed it to her ear.

"Where are you?" she snapped, "What's going on with your head? Did you get it checked out?"

"Yes Mom," Davy answered sounding like a petulant child, "Marciano had a local doctor come to the precinct. He actually brought X-Ray equipment and a tech to handle them."

"So you're alright?" She demanded.

There was a bit of silence at the end of the line. She could hear him breathing. She wanted to yell at him, to make him answer her, but wisely kept quiet. He in fact could hear her breathing as well.

"It isn't as bad as it could be," Davy answered, "But no, I'm not okay. I have a mild concussion, not unlike football players. Dr. Nelson assures me that it could be much worse, but all things considered it will heal. I've been taken off of duty for at least two days. They have a cot set up for me here in the house and Nelson will check back tomorrow and the next day.

"Please tell Mike that Captain Rodriguez has been in touch with Judge Lennox's office and so that trial adjournment will remain in place at least until next Monday. The DA's office will contact Mike and Mr. Holmes as well."

Mike noticed how much Theresa's expression had softened. She wasn't smiling, but neither was she frowning. She brushed the hair up away from her brow as she asked Davy to thank Sergeant Marciano for her.

"I will Mom." Davy answered, followed by "I love you Mom." And he hung up.

Theresa gazed back at her husband. With a sprightly gleam in her eyes she said, "He mentioned Sergeant Marciano. You know Marciano Mike. He escorted me into the hospital that day."

With a toss of her hair she added, "Oh, I really need a glass of wine."

Davy was better, although a mild headache still persisted from time to time. He, Nunzio, Gerrie and Patrolman Tom Remar all sat outside Judge Lennox's courtroom awaiting the Judge's appearance.

Erica Lomonico was in the courtroom with all the various defense team members. The defendant was still on a computer screen, allegedly for his own safety. The excuse was the Covid virus, but Davy suspected that Edward Preston was having qualms about representing the man since he had proven to be a racist, after all.

ADA Maria Sanchez was sitting with the four police officers awaiting word of when they would be needed.

The exact same thought was crossing the minds of all four officers, namely that they would be of better use on either patrol or sentry duty at the precinct house.

Davy had seen and greeted Mike when first his step-father had arrived. Mike was accompanied by Mr. Holmes from the Mayor's office. Davy knew just how much Mike disliked the present Mayor and wondered how well he was getting along with the Mayor's representative.

They heard the loud, clear baritone voice of Bailiff Thomas Wilcox, as he announced, "All rise, for Judge Lennox."

"Well," Davy thought, at least the show is opening up."

Lennox sat quietly at first, surveying his courtroom. His eyes zeroed in on the defendant's image emblazoned on Monica Germaine's laptop computer.

Certain things were meant to be kept hidden until they were deemed ready to reveal in an open court.

Lennox prided himself, however on knowing everything, whatsoever, which might actually be revealed in his court. He knew of the defendant's membership in a white supremacist organization.

It was not lost on Judge Lennox that the defendant, a racist white man had probably murdered a young black police officer, a father and a breadwinner for his family.

Principal upon Judge Lennox's mind, however was that both men shared the same last name.

"The irony of it," The Judge told himself, "The fucking Irony."

Returning his attention to the courtroom, Judge Lennox addressed his audience in general, but Mr. Preston and Mrs. Lomonico specifically.

He asked if any decisions had been made regarding any pending motions. He specifically named them as pending, since none had actually been presented at the preceding hearing.

"Specifically," Lennox asked them, "Are there any requests by either party for me to recuse myself, based on my avowed stance on Police Defunding?"

As he said that, he scanned the room for the four officers that had been present in the earlier hearing. They were not there. He did see the Police Lieutenant, McGinty, and Garret Holmes of the Mayor's office, however.

Lennox knew that despite working for the Mayor, Holmes was no fan of the Mayor. He felt that maybe Holmes and he thought along the same lines in so many ways.

Edward Preston rose. He accepted a document of some sort from his Legal Secretary, Monica Germaine. He made a show of rustling the paper importantly before clearing his throat.

"Your Honor," Preston said, seemingly scanning the paper in his hands, "The defendant, ah, Brian Eugene O'Dell, has chosen to release me as counsel for his defense. He apparently felt he could find a better lawyer, than I."

What he neglected to say was that he had informed Mr. O'Dell that Preston's plan now was to include him as a group of defendants, including both white and black men to show the solidarity of the movement. The move would have identified young Mr. O'Dell as a member in good standing of the BLM movement.

The White Supremacist movement might not have looked so kindly on such a move by Mr. O'Dell.

Fifteen minutes later the courtroom emptied out.

Mrs. Lomonico informed everyone in the hallway of the court's decision. She also told them that there might not be a new trial. With the prosecuting business booming because of the riots and all, The City was pushing for easy dispositions for as many cases as possible. There would be several reduced sentences as well as quick dismissals for minor infractions. Mike could hear the weariness in her voice and could tell that she was not in favor of City Hall's deplorable policies.

"Of course," Lomonico added, "A dead policeman does not equal a minor infraction in any way possible."

"I just called Marciano," Mike announced, to the police witnesses, "I have a police SUV and there's plenty of room for everyone so I'll drive you back to your precinct. One thing, though, I'm calling shotgun for Mr. Holmes. Unseen by the others, Gerrie and Nunzio both punched Davy lightly on either shoulder.

Davy did not respond. He was thinking of the last time Mike had driven him back to the Precinct. Jon Overton had died that day.

A bit later a hospital light overhead was rather bright. Once again darkness gave way to light as Mike McGinty was able to force open his weary eyes.

"Well, Mike surmised as pain spider webbed from his cheek, up his face into his hairline, "This seems a bit familiar."

He resisted the call for a minor groan that his body was then soliciting.

He did however; hear a somewhat louder groan come from his right.

Unlike the time he had been shot defending Assistant Police Chief Vincent Dobrinetti, Mike had a little more flexibility. Despite the ever-present pain he turned to his side to see what might be ailing his thus far unknown roommate.

Garret Holmes occupied the neighboring bed. His left arm was bandaged and a cast was wrapped around his elevated left leg.

He appeared to be sleeping as opposed to being unconscious. The telltale sign was a light snoring.

Turning, however had intensified Mike's pain, and he did groan out loud.

The noise seemed to waken Holmes; however, who stirred, as his eyes snapped open.

"Sonuva bitch!" Holmes muttered groggily, "This really sucks."

He turned his head slowly in Mike's direction. His eyes grew bigger and a faint smile creased his face as he saw that Mike was finally awake.

"I don't think that this is One Police Plaza." Mike observed astutely. He slurred the words police and plaza, which sounded more like pliss plassa.

"You are right Sir!" Holmes returned in his best Ed McMahon imitation, which actually fell somewhat short.

"I have a general idea of where we are," Mike related, "But I'm not really sure exactly where we might be." His voice seemed to be getting stronger and his words were less slurred.

"Me neither," Holmes replied, "But did you get the number of that bus that hit us?"

"We were hit by a bus?" Mike asked.

"No," Holmes answered, "I believe it was a shotgun blast. You did some fancy driving there too, Buddy. I think you saved our lives.

"The blast was fairly close. It shattered your driver side window.

I'm surprised that you weren't knocked unconscious immediately."

"Who shot us?" Mike asked, feeling just a little lightheaded.

"I'm not sure." Garret answered, "They were wearing BLM hoodies, but after that trial earlier, who knows who's a rioter and who's an agitator. I'm pretty sure however that they weren't White Supremacists."

To Mike's puzzled expression, Holmes said, "Two of them were black."

"How many were there Mr. Holmes?" Mike asked.

"I'm not sure," Holmes responded, at least five. Oh, and if we're going to get shot together, it's Garret. I'm not going to stand on formality with the guy who probably saved my life."

Mike just stared at him. "I assume the leg is busted, eh." He stated as much as asked.

"Yea," Holmes replied, "and I have a few gashes on my arm.

"Luckily there were some Manhattan cops nearby who arrested the bad guys and called for paramedics to take care of us. You were out cold by then. The one cop said that you had had the sense to turn off the key, which may have kept the car from exploding.

"Apparently we had hit a city bus to stop our forward motion."

Mike laughed out loud, followed immediately by another groan as pain again spider webbed around his head.

"What's so damn funny?" Holmes asked with an obvious strain in his voice.

"We didn't get hit by a bus," Mike observed, "We hit the bus."

He laughed and groaned again.

Not wishing to feel any more pain than was necessary, Garret Holmes only smiled.

Just then Mike's own smile vanished as he heard out in the hallway, "My name is Theresa McGinty. Where's my husband, Michael?"

"Oh my GOD!" he heard from the doorway. He was already looking at the opening but was not prepared for the apparition that was his wife.

She was wearing cut-off jeans and a threadbare blue cotton blouse. He recognized them as her gardening clothes. She would never appear publically in that outfit, so he knew she had been shocked from her daily routine by the announcement of his injuries. She had probably rushed off in a panic and she didn't have time to change.

A pink surgical mask with a small plastic breathing vent covered the bottom half of her face. Her eyes, while bright seemed just on the verge of shock.

An equally threadbare blue and gray hound's tooth scarf covered her auburn tresses, some of which were dangling to either side of her ashen face.

She pulled the mask from her face and stuffed it in the oversized gray purse dangling from her shoulder.

He had only been conscious for a short time, and that time had been occupied with his conversation with Garret Holmes.

She was at the side of his bed in five long strides.

"Oh, Michael." she called out. The use of his complete first name was rarely a good sign. Her fingers were immediately touching his lips and lower face. The upper part of his face, including his left eye was swathed in bandages. He blinked rapidly and grabbed her one hand. With a bit of effort he pulled it to his lips where he kissed it somewhat sloppily.

"Are you awake?" she ranted wildly, then realized her error.

"Of course you are." she corrected herself, "Oh Mike, what in the hell happened. Can you speak? Can you?"

"Honey, he answered wearily, "I don't really know what I look like, but I don't feel as bad as I must look. There's some pain, but at least I'm not as wiped out as I was when I helped Dobrinetti."

Looking over towards Holmes Mike said, "Ah, Dobrinetti is............"

"I know who Chief Dobrinetti is Mike," Holmes explained, "And I know how you took a bullet for him."

Even though she was presently in no mood for humor, Theresa thought wryly, "But do you know who Sergeant Marciano is?"

"Why don't you save your strength for your wife?" Mike's roommate advised.

Despite a slight spasm of pain in his arm and neck, Holmes nodded at Theresa, and said, "Hi, I'm Garret. We were riding together when this happened. Mike probably saved my life with his quick thinking. Apparently he makes a habit of that."

"And you are?" Theresa asked, unable to keep the suspicious expression from her face. Her brows were knit, and even though she wasn't scowling, her mouth was a very tight tense line.

"Wow," Holmes thought to himself, "Even frowning, that is one beautiful woman.

"Uh, I'm Garret Holmes......." he began, but was interrupted by Theresa.

"Oh, I know who you are." Theresa snapped. The straight line of Theresa's mouth did indeed become a grimace and her brows became descending lines which would have formed a Vee had they been touching.

"Hold on Honey," Mike intervened with a soft, somewhat weak voice, "He may work for His Majesty, but he neither likes nor gets along with the Mayor. That's why the Mayor hides him at One PP, to keep Garret away from City Hall."

Theresa's features relaxed. She was not smiling, but neither was she still frowning.

"W-why were you together then?" she asked both men, but her eyes were leveled at Holmes.

"We had that trial thing in the Bronx and were on our way......."

"With Davy?" Theresa exclaimed loudly, "Was he......?"

Holmes held his good hand up defensively. "No, he replied quickly, "We had left him at his precinct house......"

"Like that's a safe place!" Theresa snorted, derisively, and then was silent.

She placed her hand tenderly on Mike's shoulder, but continued to stare at Garret Holmes.

Holmes wanted to look away but he was captured by Theresa's beauty. He blinked several times until she returned her attention to Mike. Then he sighed and closed his eyes.

CHAPTER 10
THOUGHTS AND EXPLANATIONS

Mike felt terrible, even with Theresa massaging his shoulder. He perked up slightly when he heard Theresa apologize to Garret Holmes.

"I'm sorry Mr. Holmes," she began, "But this entire situation has me absolutely frazzled. I'm the daughter and mother of two cops, not to mention the two darn cops that I married.

"Is there a psychiatric ward in this hospital? I think maybe I should have my head examined."

"Now Honey,….." Mike began.

"And you, you Paddy Sonuva Gun, "She remarked snidely, poking him in his side, "You should've had that head examined before I even married you. "Why are you always putting yourself in these dangerous situations?"

"Beats me!" Mike answered, "I was only driving down Second Avenue. Who knew my judge and jury would be strolling against the traffic with a shotgun. At least, I think it was a shotgun."

"Has Chief Beymon been notified?" Theresa asked.

"He has indeed." Came Beymon's voice from the doorway, "And I agree with you Mrs. McGinty. How do these situations find Mike? How indeed?"

As he entered Beymon pulled the mask from his face. He was in full uniform including a chief's formal garrison hat.

"If I'd known that sooner, I might have taken the Subway." Garret Holmes chided.

He laughed at his own joke and then groaned for the pain that it brought.

"Garret," Beymon said, walking over to Holmes' bed, "How are you Buddy? I don't know who looks worse."

"Well, Mike took a face full of glass, maybe shotgun pellets and an airbag fully in that hard-ass head.." Holmes said, seriously, almost gravely.

"I hope he doesn't lose that eye."

"It's okay," Mike Chuckled, as much to cover his own concern as anything, "I have another one on the opposite side. Plus, if and when I may need glasses, I can get a monocle for half the price."

Theresa was frowning again. A tear had rolled down her cheek. Mike could not see it because she was standing on his currently blind side.

"Knock it off Mike." She snapped hotly, "None of this is funny, none of it. Stop it now!"

Her voice had risen and her face was a bright red.

Mike turned his head so that he could see her. It caused him physical pain, but he ignored it.

He was also wrought with emotional pain, but he embraced that pain. She was trembling, and before his eyes the red of her face turned very pale.

He reached out to clasp her hand. The movement continued to cause him pain, but he still ignored it.

"I'm so sorry Tere," he said gravely, "Please forgive me, even though I guess I really don't deserve your forgiveness."

Beymon stepped out of the room to give them privacy. Unable to do the same, Holmes just turned away.

The single tear had become a deluge. Her cheeks and chin and the top of her blouse were all very wet.

She grasped his hand back with both of hers. Placing her face against his shoulder, her own shoulders were wracked with sobs.

He stretched his good arm to form a crude embrace.

Just then Ron Beymon stepped back into the room. He had reapplied his own surgical mask.

"Theresa," he called to her, "The nurse is coming. Better cover up."

Snapping out of her sorrow, Theresa was able to retrieve her mask and reapply it just before the nurse entered the room.

Addressing the uniformed policeman first she said, "Who are you here for?"

Lowering her glasses from her forehead she glanced at Chief Beymon's nametag and the portion of her face which could be seen registered sudden surprise.

"C-Chief Beymon!" she stammered slightly, "It's you!"

"Have we met?" Beymon asked, slightly confused

"Uh, no sir." The nurse answered.

Looking down she noticed that the stethoscope hanging around her neck was blocking her name tag. Brushing the instrument aside she pointed to the tag which read Lois Conway.

"Uh," Lois Conway began, "my Bobby is supposed to come to work for you on Monday."

"Oh, of course, Sergeant Robert, uh, Bobby Conway. Oh, it's good to meet you Mrs. Conway. We're looking forward to working with the sergeant.

Beymon indicated the two men to either side of him. "These men will be working with Sergeant Conway as well, if they're out of the hospital by then."

He indicated Mike and said "This is Lieutenant Mike McGinty."

Indicating the other bed he said, "And this is Mr. Garret Holmes of the Mayor's office. He's a part of my team as well.

"Forgive me Mr. Garret," Lois Conway said, "But I'm no fan of the sitting Mayor." Her mask hid her clenched jaw.

"Neither is Garret, Mrs. Conway," Beymon interrupted, "But unlike policemen and their spouses, he isn't allowed to admit it in public."

"How nice of you to include police wives Chief." Lois Conway replied, her tone slightly less than acerbic."

"Well, Beymon replied, "I have my own personal experience with police wives, including my own, and Mrs. McGinty here.

"Theresa McGinty, please meet Lois Conway. Your husbands are about to become co-workers."

Lois Conway immediately offered her latex gloved hand. Noting the moisture on both Theresa's blouse and Mike's hospital gown, Lois Nodded, and said, I've been there Theresa, far too many times. This last time I thought I had lost him forever. Thank GOD that he'll be working at One Police Plaza for a while."

Theresa shook her hand warmly, but then pointed to the two men in the hospital beds.

"A fat lotta good it did for them Lois. Do whatever you can to keep ah, Bobby is it, keep him safe."

Theresa gave the others a somewhat defiant look before she tugged her mask down and kissed Mike on the cheek. Replacing it she announced, "I have to go to the Ladies Room, but I'll be right back."

After she left, Nurse Lois said, "Boy, she seems a little bitter and kind of tough too."

"You don't know the half of it!" Beymon exclaimed with a wry chuckle.

He quickly ran down a synopsis of Theresa's life including her two marriages, her actions on Barclay Street, on Nine-Eleven, being shot, and then sometime later, shooting two home invaders while killing one."

Lois was shaking her head. "Wow!" she exclaimed, "That is one tough cookie."

Beymon looked over at Mike, who was enjoying his Chief's praising of his wife.

"Okay if I tell her about the return?" He asked, as his eyes twinkled merrily over his own surgical mask.

"Sure," Mike replied, "Why not?"

Beymon asked Lois Conway if she had read the article a while back in the Post about a police wife returning the Key for New York back to the Mayor, stating that she could not accept such a gift from an executive that placed so many city employees at risk with his defunding program."

"That was her?" Lois said, unable to keep the admiration from her tone.

Beymon, Mike and Garret Holmes were all nodding simultaneously.

Holmes and McGinty were both feeling pain from the movement. Mike felt it slightly more so.

Minutes later when Theresa reentered the room, all eyes were on her, except of course for Mike's left eye which was bandaged.

Just before her entry she was intercepted by a tall man dressed in white with a stethoscope draped around his neck.

"Are you Mrs. McGinty?" he asked.

When she nodded, he said, "I'm Doctor Abriello, Chip Abriello. Your husband is lucky to be alive Mrs. McGinty. Another inch lower and he would have lost that eye. He has what we call Ecchymosis. It's basically a contusion........"

"I know what a black eye is Doctor." Theresa cut him off, "I trained as a nurse and I recently went back to work."

After a brief conversation she returned to her husband.

Her face had been washed and her clothes, as much as possible under the circumstances, were much neater.

"What?" she asked, warily.

"Honey," Lois Conway answered, I just got the quick version of your life. You are my newest heroine. I want you for my new best friend."

"Well, actually, that title belongs to Mike," Theresa offered, with a smile, "Despite his latest dopey exploit." At that she pointed at her husband with her thumb.

"Then comes Maeve Evanopolis, My Mom and my kids. But I think I can fit you in just ahead of the other two gentlemen in this room."

Beymon and Holmes were both chuckling. Unlike Beymon, however, Garret Holmes was still in pain.

"I've actually met the Evanopolis family." Lois confessed. For a short while I was working with Kings County Visiting Nurses. It was kind of a fill-in job when they lost a few of their regular nurses to the Covid virus.

"Also because of the virus we were covering parts of Queens.

"I attended to Captain Evanopolis after his second incident when that woman shot him. I must say, Maeve really let her have it with that frying pan, twice I'm told."

"Yea," Theresa admitted, "She's the sweetest person, but threaten her family and she is hell on wheels.

"She and I were friends all the way back in grammar school. After my Mom, she's probably my oldest friend in the world. We talk almost every day, mostly on the phone since the Covid."

The name Evanopolis stirred up new thoughts in Mike's mind.

Speaking in a whisper, he asked "How did you get here? As upset as you are, I hope you didn't drive yourself?"

Theresa glanced around nervously. Her eyes briefly settled on Beymon and then snapped back to Mike.

"Uh, I had someone uh, drop me off."

She felt an arm on her shoulder,

"Theresa," Beymon intoned softly in his quiet sonorous voice, "I'm in management because I wasn't all that good of a detective. However, despite the common feeling among the rank and file that the Brass doesn't know its butt from a hole in the ground, I can put two and two together. I almost always come up with four.

"I bet he's wearing that wrinkled Mets baseball cap. I'm also sure that he's wearing sweatpants or possibly shorts. Pulling on a tee shirt with that shoulder would probably be a little tough too, so I'm guessing a button down shirt. Have I left anything out?"

Theresa was smiling. It was a wan, wondering what might yet happen, kind of smile.

"Pull on shoes," she informed him, "He's wearing brown pull on shoes."

"The ones with the tassels?" he asked her, "The golf shoes?"

She nodded slowly, her expression becoming one of surprise.

To her side, Mike was chuckling.

With his own expression of surprise, Garret Holmes was thinking, "My tax dollars at work."

The receptionist on the desk, nine stories below was holding her phone aloft. She looked over in the direction of a middle-aged couple. The man was wearing a Mets baseball cap and brown golf loafers, just as the caller had described.

"Nicky?" she called out, "Are you Nicky? A woman named Theresa would like to talk to you."

Nick went over to the desk with Maeve in tow. Accepting the phone he said, "Yea Theresa, has the 'Old Man' left yet?"

"Not that damn old!" Beymon exclaimed, surprising Nick into silence.

"Here's how it works Evanopolis," Beymon continued, obviously enjoying his little joke, "You give me fifty million dollars and I won't tell Dennis Meyer that you're in the City."

"If I had fifty million dollars Chief, I would have retired after that woman shot me.

VITO BELCASTRO

"How about you give me fifty million Chief, and I won't tell Agrarian that you're shaking down his employees."

"Okay, I'll hand him the phone." Beymon replied, "You can tell him now."

Beymon's voice was slightly muffled as he placed his hand slightly over the phone's mouthpiece.

"Sorry Walt, it's no go. Now he's tryin' to shake us down."

Nick knew better, but for a very long minute, much longer than sixty seconds, his throat became dry and his hand shook just a bit. "Come on Nick," Beymon said more firmly, "you know he isn't here. Although, I'm not particularly sure that he doesn't' have eyes and ears all over this city.

"Come on up. Neither Holmes nor I will say anything, and I'm sure Mike would like to see you. They have that silly X amount of people in the room thing, so I'll be gone when you get here.

"When you're feeling better stop over to One Police Plaza.

"And for cryin' out loud, don't wear that damn Met's cap. I'll buy you a Yankees hat if you'd like."

As it turned out, Beymon was waiting for the elevator when Nick and Maeve stepped off. The chief tugged down his mask and kissed Maeve upon her cheek.

Holding up his hand for a fist bump, Beymon said, "No kisses for you Evanopolis. You tried to shake me down."

A smile made Nick's eyes brighter and he replied, "Hey, you started it."

"Nah," Beymon answered as he dodged quickly between the closing elevator doors, "It was all Mike's idea. I was just his helpless pawn."

Both Nick and Maeve were thoroughly shocked when they saw Mike's appearance.

"From Garret Holmes' bed came, "So this is the famous Nick Evanopolis. I'm not sure if we ever met, but I remember you from that Hospital stand-off in Queens.

"Boy, people just like to shoot you, don't they."

"Tell me about it.," Maeve chimed in, "And I'm left to pick up the pieces."

"Not according to what I've been told," Garret replied, "I understand that you wield a rather mean frying pan."

Maeve giggled.

She pulled down her mask and gave Mike a kiss, on his cheek just below the bandage.

"Looking' good, Mikey Boy." She said, and then turned to Theresa.

"Sweetie," she said, what are we gonna do with these two old reprobates?"

Theresa just shook her head.

An hour later, Lois Conway herded all the visitors out into the hall, citing the need for her patients to get some much needed rest. She also mentioned the fact of doctors and pertinent examinations.

Before they walked to the elevator, Nick mentioned that he worked with a Sergeant Bobby Conway up in Astoria before getting transferred to the One-Ten Precinct.

"Yea, Lois replied excitedly, "That's my Bobby."

"Oh," Nick replied, "I'm so sorry. I heard he was hurt pretty badly."

"Yes," Lois answered, but he's recuperating now. Chief Meyer has placed him on Chief Beymon's team. He'll be working with Lieutenant McGinty and Mister Holmes."

While he did not say it out loud, Nick thought to himself, after seeing both Mike and Holmes, "Yea, like that's any safer."

Maeve and Theresa were thinking the exact same thing.

Just before the elevator arrived Theresa begged off in order to say goodbye to Mike. She said she would be down directly and they should all go home at least for a while.

She kissed Mike and apologized for her earlier theatrics. He assured her that he did not consider them drama, and apologized himself for making her fret and worry.

She surprised both of them by giving Garret Holmes a kiss on the cheek too. "Get better Garret." She said and was gone.

CHAPTER 11

EVER THE INNOCENT

Charles Stodorah's body was being released to the Cresskill Funeral Home the following day. Cresskill's was an institution in the Bronx. They were a business that had been founded decades before by the brother of a man who had risen to the rank of Deputy Inspector in the NYPD. Both brothers, Ernie and Jerry Cresskill, had passed on, but the Home was still run by family and still catered to the NYPD.

Apparently, a group of the people who were rioting in New York was aware of Cresskill's lineage too. That night, the building was firebombed.

The first and second floors as well as the basement were used by Cresskill's, who actually owned the entire three story building. The third floor however consisted of two apartments, one on either side of the building, and facing the street.

The fire escape however was on the right side of the building, the Southern side, in a wide alley. People from the Northern side had to access their neighbor's apartment in order to use the escape way.

As it turned out, there was a woman with a child trapped in that Northern side apartment.

In the distance fire engines could be heard, sounding their sirens as they fought their way through traffic.

Thinking quickly, Sergeant Vito Marciano retrieved a strong, reinforced leather blanket from the trunk of his car. With stout leather handles, it was perfect for what the sergeant intended.

Calling out to some civilian spectators, he directed them to grab an old dirty mattress leaning against the wall in another alley across and just down the street.

As they ran off to complete the task he instructed Davy Keith, Nunzio Italo and patrolman Raheem Davis to grab the blanket along with him.

The mother, immediately seeing Marciano's plan said, "Here he comes officers. Please, please, catch my boy. If I don't make it, his name is Mikey, Mikey Sanchez."

The child panicked slightly as his mother dropped him.

A minute plus seconds later he was caught quite easily by the four strong men.

Marciano lifted the frightened child from the blanket just as the civilians with the mattress arrived. He quickly handed the boy to a middle aged woman, and told her to watch him. She could see how agitated the little boy was and hugged him tightly while crooning softly.

The woman in the apartment above them called down, "I guess I'll go check the hallway."

"NO!" Marciano shouted, emphatically, "If you open that door, those flames will envelope you. I have a mattress to help cushion your fall. We've done this before. We'll catch you."

He knew he was lying, because only he and Davis had ever done this before. He had seen Keith and Italo in enough situations however, that he had complete faith in their ability.

Just then another police vehicle pulled up. Officer Gerrie Contadina jumped out and ran immediately to Marciano.

Just as she reached him, even before she could ask for instructions, he rasped loudly, "Contadina. We're going to catch that woman up there. I need you to push this mattress under the blanket wherever we have to position it."

Both reluctantly and yet still expectantly, the woman positioned herself and then stepped out of the window.

As per Marciano's instructions she let herself fall instead of leaping.

Anticipating the fact that her trajectory could go in any direction, as well as down, Marciano directed his team closer to the building, directly beneath her.

On the ground, Gerrie Contadina pushed the worn mattress as quickly as she could, beneath the widely spread blanket.

"Remember guys," Marciano called out, "She's gonna be a lot heavier. Hold tightly.'

As Marciano had predicted to himself mentally, the blanket did fold slightly upon impact.

Fortunately, Contadina was right there with that mattress.

It wasn't much of a cushion, but with the strength of the four men to hold the blanket tightly, thankfully it was enough.

Although slightly stunned, the woman immediately called out for her child.

Marciano had her placed on the seat of the police SUV Contadina had just vacated, and her son was placed in her arms. She held him tightly and he held her just as tightly.

"Mikey," she crooned softly, intermittently kissing his cheek as her tears stained his dirty shirt.

After several minutes of holding him and cuddling him, Mikey's mother, Kathy Novalski, finally had him calmed.

When she asked Mikey if he was alright, the boy pointed to the blanket and said, excitedly, "Do again, Mommy."

Sadly, the remains of several already dead customers were damaged in the fire. Since the fire was climbing upward when the Firemen were able to finally force their way through traffic, the damage to the three customers, one on the first floor and the other two in the basement was from falling debris.

Fortunately, Charles Stodorah's body was being released from the morgue the following day.

Cresskill Funeral Home was owed any number of favors by the Hastings-on-Hudson Funeral Home up in Westchester County. Cresskill was able to have them perform the needed service. This made it slightly easier for both Merriam and Calliope since they both lived in Westchester, albeit on the side of the county nearer to Connecticut.

For most police funerals, especially for an officer killed in the line of duty, an Honor Guard is in order.

However, with all that was presently affecting the City, an Honor Guard was deemed unacceptable by a representative from City Hall.

Garret Holmes assured the Police Chief that his sources in City Hall had assured him that such an edict had not come from the Mayor, himself.

Just to be safe, however, only three policemen from Charles Stodorah's home precinct were sent. They were Sergeant Vito Marciano, Patrolman Nunzio Italo and Patrolman David Keith.

The town of Hastings-on-Hudson also supplied nine of their own policemen, making it an even dozen. One of the Hastings policemen was also a bugler and played Taps at the grave side.

Sergeant Marciano had prepared two of the Blue Line American Flags, per a request from Merriam Stodorah. He gave her one and then presented the other to a very surprised Calliope Hender, sitting at Merriam's side.

After the funeral, Merriam announced that she must go pick up her kids.

"I'm sure they are driving my mother crazy by now." Merriam surmised, "Mother loves them as only a grandmother can, but she is aging quickly and I'm sure she needs a break."

"I was thinking of getting them a pizza or two. Care to join us?"

With a slightly puzzled look upon her face Calliope agreed.

"I don't have any nefarious plans for you, My Dear." Merriam assured her new companion.

"I'm only thinking of the needs of six people I care about."

"Six?" Calliope asked.

"Yes, them, me and you."

"From their point of view, you are as much a part of this family as any of us. And, I have to admit it. I am beginning to think that way too."

CHAPTER 12
DOES IT EVER EASE UP

Once back at the Precinct house, Marciano relieved Sergeant Jimmy Ramirez just outside the building. He stationed Nunzio and Davy on the ramp, relieving two other very tired men.

As he strolled down the ramp past them, Marciano said, "Be alert you guys. This shitstorm isn't over yet. You're both well aware that we do have targets painted on our backs."

As he reached the bottom of the ramp, he was thinking, "Maybe this shitstorm will never be over.

"How's it goin' Jimmy he asked Sergeant Ramirez as he approached him. "I'm your relief. Why don't you go drink some coffee or maybe catch a few Zees?"

"Nothing new Viduch," Ramirez answered, "But it's almost One PM. The crazy wild ones will probably be making their presence known soon. I know I don't have to say this, but be alert buddy. We can't afford to lose you."

Marciano nodded and immediately scanned the street, up and down. Although his eyes were slits from the bright overhead sun, he was taking in everything.

As Ramirez walked up the ramp, he greeted Nunzio and Davy. Indicating Marciano with a nod, he said "Watch him guys. We can't lose him."

Both young patrolmen said, "Yea Sarge."

Being such a large and imposing Precinct house is what probably made the Four-Eight such a prominent target.

It was also easier because of the quick entry to the Cross Bronx Expressway. Not only did the Expressway have east and west access, but it intersected with all of the North/South major roadways, avenues of escape from the area. However, being one of the top ten busiest highways in the United States, sometimes the Cross Bronx could be a virtual nightmare.

The desk sergeant, Pete Amalio, at the Four-Eight had just gotten notification of a stolen EMT van from over in the Four-Four precinct. Before he could alert his personnel, that stolen vehicle was just then cruising past the Four Eight precinct house. Davy was looking east and Nunzio spotted the van slowing up. Having not heard any mention of injuries in the precinct house, he became suspicious.

"Funny Van!" he shouted as loud as he could.

Davy's head snapped forward, as did Marciano's.

Marciano was a big, noticeable man. He drew all of the fire from the automatic weapon which suddenly appeared at the van's window.

Four bullets hit the sergeant in his torso, driving his breath from his lungs and pushing him heavily to the ground.

Nunzio opened fire on that open window, but the assailant had pulled quickly back after shooting.

Davy ran down the ramp, as quickly as possible to help his sergeant.

Tugging Marciano's hospital mask down, as well as his own, Davy also lifted both of their plastic visors. Dropping to his knees, Davy began to administer mouth to mouth resuscitation. Within a minute, Marciano was breathing on his own. He was also gasping to pull the air into his lungs.

"Sarge, Sarge," Davy asked of Marciano, "are you alright?"

"I-I think so." Marciano gasped.

Davy pulled back a foot or so to allow Marciano to draw from the air around him.

Sergeant Ramirez came running from the building. He brushed passed Nunzio as the young patrolman maintained a defensive stance.

"How is he?" Ramirez asked as he knelt beside Keith.

"He had the wind knocked out of him Davy replied, but he seems to be breathing a little better now. I haven't loosened the armor just yet, and there could be cracked or broken ribs."

Davy knew that even though he may have saved Marciano's life there would be a lecture when the sergeant could talk again.

There's an EMT van on the way." Ramirez said, "A real EMT van."

Ramirez thought for a minute and then said, "Well, actually, that was a real EMT vehicle as well. It was stolen from a facility just about a mile or so from here."

Ramirez stood up. He shouted up to the guys on the roof. "Anybody see which way they went?"

Officer Ronny Whitcombe called down from the roof, "They went down Washington Sarge."

"Probably headed for Bruckner Boulevard." Ramirez remarked thoughtfully, "That's also an east-west road.

"I'm guessing either the Tri-Borough Bridge, or northeast to Connecticut. Could be western Long Island as well."

"Or Westchester or even Jersey." Davy thought out loud, hoping that Ramirez did not think him a smart-ass.

"Yea." Ramirez said, calmly and then fed all the information into his mike.

"Hm, that's Four-Two territory." Pete Amalio inside the building remarked, "Notify all the precincts south of here with this information." He told the dispatcher, "Tell them it comes straight from me."

Sergeant Jimmy Lomax and Patrolman Jerry "Doc" Carroll were cruising undercover in a plain light tan vehicle on the Bruckner Boulevard. They were a pair of African-American policeman, who also appeared somewhat non-assuming.

Minutes after being notified of the stolen van approaching their area, they became even more alert.

Minutes after that, the EMT van, with gunshot damage to the passenger side window whisked past them at approximately ten miles over the speed limit.

"Bingo!" Lomax, in the passenger seat said, "There they are."

He immediately called it in and instructed "Doc" Carroll to just fall in behind them and to lay off of the portable dome light and siren. He naturally gave his precinct their position and all other pertinent information.

Traffic was relatively light for an early afternoon, and everyone but a few cars in the slow lane, was speeding. Carroll and Lomax fit in nicely with all the other traffic.

Three miles down the road, near the access to the Whitestone Bridge, combined elements from the Four-One and the Four-Three Precincts were in the process of setting up roadblocks.

Several Queens's precincts were guarding their side of both the Whitestone and Throgsneck bridges.

"They're coming fast." Lomax warned his fellow cops, "Very fast."

"We're ready." was the response.

Three patrol vehicles with flashing lights blocked the highway. Behind them seven officers with rifles were eyeing the oncoming traffic. All the supposedly innocent vehicles were pulling themselves to either side of the highway.

As the stolen EMT vehicle spotted the barrier up ahead, they quickly braked and spun their van about.

As they headed in the opposite direction, Lomax and Carroll drove straight at them.

"You okay with this?" Lomax asked nervously.

"Oh yea," Carroll answered with just a touch of glee in his voice, "I always wanted to do this."

"Yea," Lomax answered, "but let's just hope that they don't want to go out in a blaze of whatever they consider glory."

Fortunately, for the two undercover cops, the bad guys did not want to go out in a blaze of glory. Their vehicle screeched to a halt and immediately several weapons, both automatic rifles and pistols were thrown out of both windows. As police vehicles drove up behind the van, and Lomax and Carroll maintained their position, a machete and a hunting knife were also tossed to the pavement.

Officers approached warily as no one had as yet disembarked the EMT van.

Within seconds the pair of thugs was surrounded by a small army of policemen.

As the criminals slowly emerged from the van, hands up, Lomax and Carroll also exited their vehicle, with their pistols drawn and their shields displayed from lanyards around their necks.

The thugs lay down upon the asphalt, with their hands spread widely over their heads. "I give up." One of them said hoarsely, "We, uh, both give up."

Sergeant Lomax was greatly disappointed to see that they were both young African American men.

"You and me helped to get this collar," he told Doc Carroll, but the news will see it as white cops got the bad black men."

"Hey," Doc offered, "life sucks, and then you die." He shrugged as he said it.

Lomax only snorted.

Just as Sergeant Jimmy Lomax had predicted, that evening on almost every broadcast TV news show, the picture was of the two black men surrounded by seven white cops and three black cops, other than Lomax and Carroll. The three African-American police men were held in the background, and none of them had been interviewed.

Probably because they had been caught in another precinct, was Carroll's reasoning, as he and Lomax's names were omitted. However, Lomax had made sure that their names were on their own reports.

Two hours later, their shift having ended, Lomax and Carroll parked two blocks away from their precinct house.

They did not want anyone to tie that particular vehicle to the NYPD.

As they strolled into their base of operations, Lieutenant McCovey, the day's operations officer jerked his thumb in the direction of his own office. As they passed, he mentioned, "Good job guys. It did not go unnoticed."

When they got to McCovey's office there was a burly white police sergeant sitting in one of the visitor's chairs.

He was bulky, without really being fat. They could see the hardened muscles pushing out against his shirt, and in his arms.

"I brought you guys coffee." He said in a somewhat growly voice. "I know it's not enough, but I figure it's a start."

Carroll was shaking his head, confusion obvious on his face.

"My name is Marciano." The sergeant informed them.

"Like the fighter?" Carroll replied, with a silly grin.

"Yes, but no relation either," Marciano answered, "If I was, I'd be retired by now."

"Actually, you'd be dead. Be glad you ain't no dead boxer." Lomax observed with a chuckle.

"Well," Marciano responded with his own chuckle, "That brings me to the reason I'm here. You guys helped catch those jerk-offs that did almost kill me today. I saw a brief news snippet, with all of those white officers and those two black kids on the ground. I know better. If it wasn't for you two guys they might have gotten away.

"That was a ballsy move on your part. I'd rather have you guys on my team than all those guys who hid behind their vehicles with rifles pointed out."

"They did come after them though." Lomax pointed out.

"Yea, but would they have been quick enough if you hadn't blocked their way. I think not. Those EMT vans are just as fast as our cars, and those guys had a head start." Marciano returned.

"Nah, as far as I'm concerned, you guys are the heroes of the day."

"Now, the other reason I'm here. Chief of Patrol Dennis Meyer has instructed me to tell you that there will be awards. It will be a private ceremony since they don't want to expose your identities. "You're also being transferred to another precinct. Despite every effort being made, you guys were featured on another newscast. Somebody, somewhere here in this area is gonna put two and two together."

"I can handle that." Doc Carroll admitted, "I don't even live in the Bronx."

"There are a couple of problems though." Marciano added.

"Uh, Doc, is it, will you be able to stomach having a lieutenant for your ride-along boss?"

"What?" Carroll and Lomax said simultaneously, Lomax just a bit louder.

"Yea, but you can't tell anybody until Chief Meyer makes it official.

"Oh, and, ah, Jimmy, there is one other provision. You have to give all your sergeant stripes to Doc, since they're promoting him too.

"Still keep it under your hat until its made public.

Lomax was nodding, but Carroll was grinning from ear to ear.

CHAPTER 13
WE CAN ADJUST, I GUESS

The hall lights were dimmer than normal, a cost saving attempt, but certainly not a solution. Chief of Police Walt Agrarian and Chief of Patrol Dennis Meyer emerged together from the Police Commissioner's office. They looked as if they had been in a drawn out battle, which in some ways, they had been.

Neither wore a cap and Meyer was carrying his uniform jacket loosely, over the crook of his arm. Both of them had hospital masks, but each wore his dangling from one ear.

Together they walked, no; make that trudged, down the hall towards their respective offices.

Attempting levity, Agrarian said, "You know that which came first, chicken or egg story right?" he asked Meyer.

"I suppose so Walt." Meyer replied, "What are you getting at?"

Here's one I heard on the radio this morning. What's worse, a politician or the millionaire-billionaire that owns him?"

Meyer chuckled softly, too worn out for a loud guffaw.

Then, something clicked in his head. Pointing rearward with his free thumb, he asked, "You don't mean…..?" He let his words trail off dramatically.

"Once never really knows, now do we?" Agrarian answered.

The Chief of Police thought for several moments, mulling his thoughts.

Finally he said, "He's been a good boss as bosses go. I know he has friends in Albany."

"One very important friend." Meyer agreed."

"Yea," Agrarian echoed, "and he might just need that friend, sooner than any one of us thought.

"His honor, The Duke of Gracie Mansion is going to blame all of the fallout from defunding on someone. He certainly won't take any of the blame himself."

"Well, Chief, right along those lines, both of us have targets on our backs as well." Meyer quipped.

"Yea I know Dennis. I sometimes wonder why I don't just retire and attempt to fade into the sunset."

"Because you're just like me Walt." Meyer replied, "We both came up through the ranks like most police chiefs.

"Hell, I still remember my first patrol, in Manhattan South. I was both scared and simultaneously excited to be there.

"My Mother had taken a photo of me in my brand new uniform. Years later when miraculously I was in charge of Manhattan South, I had it blown up and hung it on my office wall."

"It's still there." Agrarian told him. "When Beymon had command there and I was Chief of Patrol, he asked me if I wanted to take it down and reframe it to give to your Mother, rest her soul. I said to have a copy of it made and so it's still there, at least the copy is."

Meyer glanced down the corridor. A Sergeant, with his cap placed between his arm and body seemed to be looking for something. He had a small piece of paper in one hand and was currently reading it. The sergeant's squinting told Meyer that either he needed glasses, or perhaps had forgotten his glasses.

The man was also limping noticeably but at present had a shining black cane hooked over his forearm.

As they reached Agrarian's office Meyer bid the Chief good day and headed for the Sergeant who he assumed must be lost.

As Meyer approached, the sergeant suddenly spotted him and snapped to attention. He did not see Meyer's nametag, but the stars on Meyer's collar were a dead giveaway.

Going out on a limb, Dennis Meyer cleared his throat and said, "I'm guessing that you're Robert Conway."

"Y-yes Sir." Conway answered, totally surprised that a Chief of Police would know who he was.

"Well, I'm Dennis Meyer. You used to work for me. And I should say, you did one hell of a job. I'm sorry for your injuries Sergeant."

"Uh, Yes Sir." Conway answered, "But how did you know it was me?" To the best of Conway's knowledge they had never met before.

"Well, with all the crap out on the street now-a-days, you're the only sergeant I know for certain who was reporting here. Your limp was a dead give-away too. Again, I'm sorry for that.

"But, I'm guessing that we have a new receptionist on the desk downstairs. She sent you to the wrong floor.

"You're to report to Chief Beymon. He's a couple of floors below us.

"C'mon, I'll walk you down. I have to talk to Ron Beymon, myself. In a way, you still work for me, but Ron is the main honcho in your life now.

"Oh, by the way, I met your wife the other day. I stopped by to see Lieutenant McGinty and she was his nurse. Lovely woman. You're a lucky man Conway."

"Uh, yes Sir, I do know that, uh, for a fact, ah Sir."

As they entered Beymon's outer office both Natalie and Mike were talking.

"McGinty," Meyer called out, "I thought you'd be home by now. What're you doing here?"

Mike pointed to the bandage on his head. Meyer noticed that his eye, itself was no longer bandaged. It was however, somewhat red, both the eyeball and the skin around it.

"Uh, I need to take my mind off of this, Sir. If I stay home, I'll just sit around thinking about my problems."

"Okay," Meyer answered, "but take it easy. A face full of glass and shotgun pellets can slow down even a big galoot like you."

Mike smiled and said, "Yes Sir, will do."

Just behind Meyer, Conway was thinking, "Glass and pellets in the face. And I thought I had problems."

Meyer brought the sergeant forward.

"This is Sergeant Robert Conway folks. He's your new man. Mike that was his wife taking care of you.

"When I was there the other day, Mrs. Conway, uh, Lois, I believe, was the one who was gushing over Theresa."

Turning back to Conway, Meyer explained that Theresa was Mike's wife.

"Oh, yea, I heard all about Theresa Sir. She's Lois' newest hero."

"Yea, well don't repeat everything she may have told you Sergeant. We try to keep some of that stuff under wraps. It's all true though."

Sweeping his hand towards Natalie, Meyer said "This is Sergeant Natalie Eberstein, Conway. You will be replacing her once she trains you. She's also one hell of a cop, uh, Bob."

Natalie blushed as Meyer praised her.

"Now, where's His Majesty. We're supposed to have a meeting."

As he said "His Majesty," Meyer winked at Natalie who blushed again.

Uh, he went up to your office Sir." Natalie informed the Chief, "You probably passed on the elevators."

"Uh yea," Meyer replied. Pointing to Conway with his thumb, he said, "I uh got side-tracked.

"Let this be a lesson to you Sergeant, Chiefs are not as infallible as we think we are. Okay, now forget that I ever said that.

"Natalie, please do me a favor. Call Nancy and tell her to inform Chief Beymon that I'm on my way."

"Yes Sir." Natalie called out to his retreating back.

Conway was wondering what part of "Wonderland" he had stumbled into. This was certainly not the One Police Plaza he had envisioned. His eyes roamed around the room and his attention finally returned to Sergeant Eberstein who was watching him intently.

"We'll do this at your pace Sergeant Conway." She said, "And for now we'll share this desk. However, eventually it will be yours.

"If you don't mind, I would prefer Bob and Natalie or Nat. But again, that'll be your choice."

CHAPTER 14

BEGIN AGAIN, SHALL WE

And at the Midtown South precinct, its newest Lieutenant, Colleen McNamara was meeting with her commander. Deputy Inspector John Robert Bowen.

"I'll ask you flat out, Inspector, do you have any problems with female cops?" Colleen demanded, as much as asked.

Bowen unsuccessfully tried to hide his smile and brief chuckle.

He pointed to his African American face and said, "Do I look like I'm prejudiced?"

"I'm sure you've faced more than your share of prejudice Inspector, but it isn't really the same thing." Colleen replied, toning back her attitude just a bit.

Bowen grew serious. He appeared to be thinking.

"No, I suppose that it isn't quite the same, unless perhaps we we're speaking of a black female cop. I apologize for the chuckle, but the smile was sincere.

"Lieutenant, have you kept up on the news other than here in New York?"

"Uh, yes sir," Colleen replied, but what does…..?"

He cut her off with, "Sergeant Ella Braithwaite in Atlanta this past weckend was shot while successfully apprehending three BLM rioters who had beaten up an old white man with his own cane. Sergeant Braithwaite, thankfully will recover.

"Despite several Atlanta politicians calling for an investigation of

Sergeant Braithwaite's tactics and the fact that the poor rioters ONLY had one gun between them, The Atlanta police hierarchy has held up her arrest as righteous, and commended her bravery and dedication to duty."

Colleen sat watching the animation in Inspector Bowen's face. She wondered where this was going, but had already decided that perhaps he felt that female cops were indeed as worthy as male cops.

"Sergeant Braithwaite's maiden name is Bowen. If our Mother were still alive, I know she would be as proud of her as I am."

Colleen smiled. "I can only hope to prove myself to be as good as your sister, Inspector." She assured him, "Thank you for sharing that story with me."

After her interview Colleen reported to Captain Jim Svenson. James Stephen Svenson was the deputy Commander of Midtown South. He, like Colleen was a recent addition, having previously been in charge of the One-Two-Oh Precinct in Staten Island.

His former precinct covered the northern part of the Island, from New Jersey to the Verrazano Bridge.

The Staten Island Ferry had been within his jurisdiction as well.

While probably the busiest precinct on Staten Island, it in no way could match the ultra-activity of Midtown South.

"We have a lot going on here." He told Colleen.

"I know Captain." She replied, "I used to work here, and I live over in Hell's Kitchen."

Svenson's eyebrows, a couple of furry white tufts lifted appreciatively. "Is that Midtown South too?" He asked.

"No Sir," she answered, but we cover each other's territory and often back each other up. Hell's Kitchen isn't the hotbed of crime it once was, but when the Westies were in control, there were problems every day, uh, all day."

"Well, then I guess you know your way around the area don't you?" Svenson acknowledged.

"Say is there anywhere around here for good coffee?" he asked. "They seem to be serving swill in the break room."

"Well Sir, I know of one. It was where we went when I was a Sergeant.

"It's only a short walk from here, but it was designated as NOAOP."

"NOAOP," Svenson echoed, "What inna hell is that?"

With a sparkling smile on her face, Colleen said, "No Officers Allowed On Premises, Sir, NOAOP!"

Scratching his head, Svenson said, "Really? How do they enforce something like that?"

"Well, Sir, it's not actually a rule. It's more like a guideline.

"I was there a few weeks ago and became friends with the owner, Mr. Aprierte. He likes me, so I'm pretty sure I can get you in there without a problem, uh other than the angry stares of patrolmen and sergeants."

With Svenson in tow, Colleen entered the establishment called Aprierte's Luncheonette.

There were no other police personnel in the café.

Obviously the double whammy of Covid and the riots were taking their toll on the place.

Mr. Aprierte's smile was engaging as he came around the counter to greet them.

"Lieutenant McNamara," he chortled, "It's so good to see you. I don't get my clientele like I used to.

"They were here on Thursday, however when some young toughs were threatening to tear my place up."

He showed them to the booth in the back. Colleen introduced Captain Svenson, informing Sal that they were both new to the precinct.

Sal gushed over the both of them and soon reappeared with coffee, a couple of buttered rolls and two cinnamon buns.

Svenson was suitably impressed.

"Well, he's certainly a fan of yours Lieutenant." Svenson acknowledged.

"Uh, yes Sir," Colleen answered, "but the reason is somewhat embarrassing."

Svenson seemed deep in thought. "I know you come from One Police Plaza," He admitted, "but I don't see the connection."

"Do you remember the Lieutenant who was almost killed in Queens by the Russian Mob Sir?"

"That was you?" Svenson stated as much as asked, as his eyes grew large and his mouth dropped open slightly.

Although he did not realize it he glanced nervously about the room.

"Yes Sir." Colleen answered, "Apparently it had been arranged by a dirty cop that I had had an affair with. I don't know which is more embarrassing, that he turned out to be a dirty cop and that I did not know......or....."

She paused to collect her thoughts, "Or that Internal Affairs was recording all of our trysts.

"I'm a good cop Captain, I really am. I just made that one mistake.

"Well, perhaps two mistakes." She declared ruefully.

"Svenson held up his hands in a defensive manner. "Lieutenant, although this in no way is an arrest situation, I really must insist that whatever you say might be used against you. I like you Lieutenant. I must say, you remind me a little of my daughter, although she's still a teenager.

"Don't say anything that might implicate you in anything."

"Oh, Sir, it's not all that bad. Chief Beymon placed me in charge of an investigation out in Queens. It involved a precinct Captain and a Lieutenant whom I was currently working with. I just may have let my emotions initially run the investigation."

"I'm thinking that it was the one that City Hall took away from you and Chief Beymon made that big stink about it being taken away because you were a woman." Svenson acknowledged.

Colleen nodded.

"I read about that Colleen. May I call you Colleen?"

She nodded again.

"Colleen, I'm no stranger to politics. You see them constantly on a Captain's level. I believe that the one lesson we should take from that incident is that an Assistant Police Chief felt so strongly for you that he extended himself in your defense. We all knew that he had, in fact, jeopardized his own career to do so. Fortunately, Chief Beymon is held in such high regard here in our community, so that it wasn't really an issue.

"You're okay in my book Lieutenant Colleen McNamara. I only wish you were Norwegian."

"I'm Irish Sir." Colleen stated with a shy smile, "Anyone who's Celtic has Nordic DNA somewhere in their background. I got that from Lieutenant Mike McGinty. I should mention that he not only saved my life, but he bore the majority of my ire during that investigation that I mentioned. I should also tell you that he and I are still good friends."

CHAPTER 15
A TIME TO REFLECT

It was a single shot. The sound of it pierced the air of the canyon created by erecting five, six and seven story apartment buildings side by side in a seven block area. The Apartment houses were lined on street level with stores, restaurants, salons and a small theater.

That single shot was much louder than the grunt of its victim or the slight thump of his body hitting the ground.

It was then that Vincent "Vinnie" Amadullo made his first mistake. He decided that he should have the dead police officer's gun and shield for souvenirs.

His second mistake was in assuming that the dead cop was alone. Aiden McDermott was the dead cop. His partner, Jeff Costolano came running out of Epstein's delicatessen, dropping the bag and two coffees in his hands and drawing his pistol at the same time.

Vinnie saw Costolano at the last minute. He quickly brought up his pistol to stop the advancing cop.

Jeff's first round shattered Vinnie's right elbow. The second shot pierced the right side of Vinnie's chest. The bullet missed Vinnie's heart but it lodged in Vinnie's right lung.

In the back of his mind for some unfathomable reason, Jeff envisioned some civilian review board member demanding to know why Jeff had fired that second shot.

The thought evaporated almost immediately as Jeff spied Aiden's inert body.

The first shot, from Vinnie had caused several merchants and apartment dwellers to immediately call the local police precinct, the One-One-Oh.

As Jeff knelt over Aiden's body, two more police vehicles pulled up.

Jeff's and Aiden's commander, Captain Nick Evanopolis, cursed softly when he saw his fallen policeman.

"Is he......" Nick began.

"Yea Cap," Jeff responded in a teary voice, "He's gone, Aiden's gone. Oh CHRIST! Who's gonna tell Candy? Who's gonna tell his Mom?"

Candace Imigliaro was Aiden's fiancée. Aiden's Mom was Moira McDermott.

Nick held his face between his fingers as he realized it would be his duty to tell the two women.

Normally he could get a police chaplain to perform that particular task.

A chaplain simply would not do for this notification.

Nick had dated Moira McDermott for at least two years before he met Maeve. Nick had known Aiden's father Aiden Senior, another policeman who had also joined the force just after the Navy. They had not known each other in the Navy, and Aiden McDermott Senior had been almost a year senior to Nick.

It became a joke among friends that Moira, a McDermott had met the one man named McDermott that she had not been previously related to. "Of course," Aiden Senior had reasoned, "somewhere, probably back in Ireland, there was a common relative."

Moira was only happy that none of her legal documents, including her driver's license had to be changed.

Aiden Senior had died of a heart attack around three years previous to this moment in time.

While Nick had known Moira since High School, he had started going out with her just before he had left the Navy.

Even though Nick and Aiden Senior were just casual friends, Nick had introduced him to Moira shortly after Nick had begun to date Maeve.

His body still ached from being shot those two times, but the cracked ribs had healed.

With some difficulty he knelt beside Aiden's body.

The boy had not died immediately, but since the bullet had pierced his carotid artery, he had died relatively quickly.

Nick pressed Aiden' eyes shut with two of his fingers. He took off his own Jacket and laid it over the young man's head and damaged neck.

Looking up at the blue sky, decorated with moving whitish grey clouds, he made the sign of the cross.

Grainne McDermott Finley opened the door to her sister's house slowly. The three sharp raps upon its surface had alerted her to yet another mourner and well-wisher.

She was surprised when two police officers of a higher rank with two women stood before her.

"Aren't you Captain Evanopolis? You were here earlier, this afternoon." Several thoughts gathered together in her mind as she also realized that he had both dated Moira and later introduced her to Aiden's Dad.

Nick had earlier come directly from the site of Aiden's murder to inform Moira of her son's death. It had not been pleasant, not for Nick and definitely not for Moira.

"This is my wife, Maeve, and our friends Mike and Theresa McGinty. Theresa's son David was a classmate of Aiden's at the Police Academy up in College Point."

Grainne noticed the large bandage covering Mike's forehead. She did not say anything though.

After hellos the two couples were shown into the parlor. The wake had not yet been set up.

Moira McDermott was seated on a sectional sofa between two women that looked very much like her.

Her eyes were red and puffy, overexposed to a deluge of tears which had not stopped since Nick had arrived earlier.

When she saw him she reached up. "Nicky" she called out, "Come sit by me."

Maeve pushed him gently towards the grieving woman.

Moira caught sight of Theresa.

"I know you." She said, her tears having briefly stopped, "You were at Aiden's graduation from the Academy. Your son graduated too, didn't he? How is he in all this shit that's threatening to break our city? What's your name, dear?"

"I'm Theresa McGinty." Theresa told her. "Davy's okay for now, but we've come close to losing him a few times now."

"I remember now," Moira thought out loud, "you killed that home invader. Didn't you?

"Good! These scumbags think they can just hurt and kill anyone they please."

She began to cry again and buried her face between her hands.

"There, there, Darlin'" the woman beside her crooned softly, "Let it out. Oh, I'm so very sorry Moira."

The woman who had met them at the door said, this is our sister Siobhan." She pronounced it Shiv-on. "My name is Grainne." which she pronounced Grawn-ye.

"And that's our sister, Deirdre on the other side."

Both Maeve and Theresa said "Hello."

Mike only nodded.

An hour or so later the McGintys and the Evanopolis left.

Nick was driving despite his sore shoulder. Mike had a headache and even though both Maeve and Theresa had both volunteered Nick had insisted.

They stopped at a small café for dinner. Tables were arranged upon the broad sidewalk before the restaurant in accordance with the current Covid-19 rules.

All four tugged their hospital masks into place before exiting the SUV. Dinner, mask-less of course, went quickly and somberly as young Aiden McDermott was on everybody's minds, especially Nick's and Theresa's.

Aiden's name was only mentioned twice, but both times, Theresa's mind automatically substituted Davy's name for Aiden's.

She resolved to call her son when she got home to tell him of poor Aiden. However, her ulterior motive was to check on Davy's safety.

To change the subject in her own mind, Theresa asked if the McDermott's had known her father. She assumed that they had. Nick's eyes flashed a very startled expression. Maeve, unaware of whatever might be bothering him just sipped her tea. Nick quickly glanced at Mike who appeared to be just as startled.

Laying his napkin on the table, Mike smiled nervously. "Well, Honey, that's kind of a touchy subject.

"I'm guessing that between your name being McGinty and Davy's name being Keith, Moira didn't realize just who you were."

Theresa's eyes had narrowed. A slight frown was dominating her expression. She wasn't sure if she really wanted to hear what Mike had to say.

Suddenly sensing the new tension at the table, Maeve paused in mid-sip to take in her dinner companions.

"What's going on here?" she asked. Defensively she placed her hand over Theresa's.

"Well," Mike answered tentatively, "Nothing bad on Ed's part. If anything, it's just another example of how Flanagan believed in things being absolutely correct.

"Aiden McDermott Senior was a bit of a racist. He wasn't too fond of Jews, blacks or Hispanics. He tried not to let it influence him, but occasionally he did go over the line. Your dad called him out on it. Aiden told Ed to mind his own effing business if he didn't want to get hurt.

"Well, you know your dad. His blood boiled over and soon enough, McDermott found himself in a pitched, knock-down battle.

"Ed gave him the choice of retirement or a hearing.

"McDermott chose retirement and died sometime there afterwards.

"At first Moira held a grudge, but she slowly came to see how wrong her husband had been. She went out of her way to make sure that young Aiden was nothing like his father in that respect.

"It's no excuse, but Aiden Senior had been raised by a father who beat him constantly and pretty much raised him to be the way he turned out. Aiden senior for the most part was a pretty decent guy, and went out of his way not to treat his son the way he had been treated. All of his anger and resentment however manifested itself in his prejudice."

Theresa was holding her head in her hand. "Ed," she asked herself, "what more can I expect?"

Mike and Theresa, having been dropped off at their home, were presently enjoying the cooler evening air. Autumn had arrived and the smell of it infiltrated the neighborhood.

They sat side by side on their front porch. Both Theresa's mother Marie and her daughter Maria had joined them. Mike was drinking coffee and the three women were sipping hot chocolate.

Maria's spring flowers, long gone now, had been replaced with several different shades of chrysanthemums and dahlias. Mixed in were small clumps of autumn cabbage with red yellow and green leaves.

Her Grandmother, Marie had been her fellow gardener.

"Mom, did you know the McDermotts over in Corona?" Theresa asked.

Mike tried to keep from choking on his coffee.

"Why?" Marie asked curtly, "What has Mike been telling you?"

Theresa explained exactly what Mike had told her, prefacing it with the death of young Aiden.

At the mention of Aiden's murder, Marie made the sign of the cross, and mentioned, "Oh the poor boy." Immediately after that she said, "Och, and poor Moira too.

"I saw Aiden's name at the graduation. I thought he might be related. I see now that he was." Marie revealed with a sigh.

"Well everything Mike has told you is absolutely true.

"Apparently we didn't recognize each other at Davy's graduation. I guess Ed and I were just too much into Davy's moment at the time, and Ed was really looking forward to looking up this one afterwards." At that she had pointed her thumb at Mike, beside Theresa.

"Plus, him bein' in that wheelchair, and his age." Her voice trailed off.

Just then, Theresa's phone rang. Retrieving it from her pocket she saw that it was Davy.

"Hi Honey" she said into the phone, "Listen, everyone in the family is okay, but I have some bad news."

"Is Nick okay?" Davy asked with a touch of panic in his voice.

"Yes, Dave, Nick's okay. I would think that by now you would realize that Nick and Maeve are family too.

She went on to tell him of Aiden McDermott's death.

"Oh no," Davy muttered, so very obviously upset. "he was one of the good guys.

"We're supposed to avoid gatherings of any size, but I'm gonna try and go to his funeral. Are there any announcements yet?"

"No, Davy, not yet." His mother answered. "Mike, Nick, Maeve and I were over to see Aiden's mother today. She's absolutely crestfallen. Her sisters are with her, so maybe we'll know tomorrow. I'll let you know when I know."

They said goodbye after Theresa assured him that all of his family said hello and wished him well.

Aiden's funeral had indeed been a small affair. Nick and Maeve attended as well as Davy. The sisters sat together with nieces and nephews in the rows behind them. A piper from the nearby firehouse played Amazing Grace. Moira insisted however that the young piper stand beside the casket and not in the hallway. But despite promising herself that she would not cry, her tears were a torrent.

CHAPTER 16

SO, THIS IS THE PLACE

Captain Jim Svenson was sorting documents at his desk in Midtown South Precinct. He looked up just as Lieutenant Coleen McNamara came out of the ladies room. She looked fresh and ready to tackle the day's events in what was often called the busiest precinct in Manhattan. There were those who called it the busiest in the World.

Despite her slight limp she was walking with her head erect and her shoulders thrown back.

Svenson knew it to be a hazy day. Even though it wasn't raining yet, the forecast had been for rain. His own joints agreed readily with the weatherman.

The upcoming rainy weather was playing havoc on all of Colleen's mending joints. She was so much better than she had been, but all that damage had truly left its mark.

She had taken a couple of over the counter pain reliever tablets in the Ladies' room. They had not yet kicked in. She had vowed, however that nothing was going to keep her from performing her job.

"Lieutenant McNamara." Svenson called out while simultaneously waving her into his office. "Have you got much on your schedule today?"

Colleen was presently the assistant intelligence officer for the precinct.

"Uh, I'm not exactly sure." She told him. "Yesterday, Chip and I tied a lot of loose ends together. I guess it pretty much depends on what's coming in today."

Indicating one of the chairs in front of his desk, he said, "Please, sit down."

Svenson dialed a number on the interdepartmental phone. When it was answered, he said, "Chip, this is Jim Svenson.

"I have some business down at One Police Plaza today. Do you think you can spare Colleen to show me around down there?"

"Sure," Captain Charles "Chip" Dellagrio answered. "It looks like it might be a light day today, although between riots and the virus, who can really tell. I have Benny Cruz if I need him. Just ask her to sign in first, so we know she was here."

"Chip said fine Colleen, just sign in. I'll get a car and meet you out on Thirty Fifth Street. I'll be the nervous looking guy. Manhattan traffic always scares me. Sometimes I long for the easy traffic back on Staten Island."

"If you like, I could drive." Colleen told him.

"When I was at One PP, my friend Natalie did almost all of the driving. She could be a real nut-job sometimes.

"One time we had Chief Beymon's car and he had warned us to have it back by five o'clock, or else.

"She had dropped me off out at Aprierte's Luncheonette. No sooner had I gotten out and she was off, siren blazing and Beymon's dome light spinning like crazy.

"Now, that's a Manhattan driver." Colleen chuckled at her last statement.

After signing in, Colleen checked with Chip, just to be sure. He waved her off and told her to have a good day.

Outside, idling was a vehicle with Captain Svenson in the back seat. She was entirely surprised to see her current boyfriend, Danny McBride in the driver's seat and grinning like a fool.

While he had lost his sergeants stripes for speaking out of turn at City Hall, apparently he had pleased the right people there on the Force and now had them back.

He was smart enough, however to greet her as Lieutenant as she entered the vehicle.

"I got us a driver." Svenson announced with a chuckle, "In fact he volunteered. You know Sergeant McBride, don't you?"

"Very well, Captain." Colleen answered, "Sergeant McBride and I are very well acquainted."

McBride sat with the vehicle while Colleen and Svenson went into 1PP.

Colleen knew the civilian receptionist Ivy LeMoyne and introduced Svenson. She and Svenson both were wearing surgical masks and protective visors.

Colleen was wearing a soft cap while Captain Svenson wore a full garrison type cap.

Svenson was informed that his appointment had been pushed back for another hour and that if he liked, he could sit in the lobby and partake of coffee, water or canned soda.

"I'm going up to see Chief Beymon Ivy." Colleen told the receptionist, "Can he come up with me? I'll get him down to Payroll in time."

"Well, ah, sure," Ivy answered, "But, rules have gotten a little tighter now. You're responsible if he runs amok."

The lower part of Ivy's face was covered, but Colleen could see the twinkle in her smiling hazel colored eyes.

Colleen gave Ivy a crisp salute and said, "Yes Ma'am. We'll be careful."

As they entered the elevator, Colleen could tell that Svenson was mildly amused.

"Not at all what I expected." He told her, with a wry chuckle.

"Oh, it's a bit more relaxed here than you'd think." Colleen informed him, "Although I imagine it has gotten a bit more dour since his Majesty's defunding program."

"His Majesty.....? Svenson questioned, and then said, "Oh, yea." when he understood the reference.

The outer door to Beymon's small suite of offices was open. Colleen noted that there were two desks, on either side of the room. The one on the extreme right was empty. She assumed that it must be Mike's.

There were two chairs at the other desk, but only a male sergeant was seated there. She remembered that his name was Robert Conway.

Beymon's door was closed.

"I'll bet Natalie and Mike are in there with him." Colleen told herself.

Stepping into the room, with Svenson right behind her, she said, "Hi, Sergeant Conway, I'm Colleen McNamara. I used to sit right there and do whatever it is you're doing."

"Oh, yes," Conway responded, "Natalie speaks of you, often. Uh, she's in with the Chief right now, uh, with Lieutenant McGinty and a couple of guests. They've been in there for almost an hour now. The meeting should be breaking up any minute now,"

As if on cue, the door to Beymon's office opened.

Out strode Chief of Police Agrarian and Chief of Patrol Dennis Meyer. Svenson gulped audibly.

Agrarian muttered something and walked out into the hallway. "Come see me later Dennis." he grunted to Meyer.

When Meyer saw Colleen his eyes brightened considerably.

"Lieutenant McNamara." He called out, "What, they aren't treating you well up at Midtown South? Did you think Ronnie might stand up for you?"

His eyes were bright and his smile was infectious. She could easily tell that he was kidding.

Svenson wasn't so sure.

"No Chief," she answered with a twinkle in her own eye, "I'm here with Captain Svenson. He's one of my bosses at South. He has business here today."

At that, she indicated Jim Svenson, off to her side.

"Oh yes, Jim Svenson, I remember now. We snagged you off of Staten Island. How do you like the middle of Manhattan?"

At that, Meyer extended his hand for a shake.

Svenson reached out tentatively, but Meyer enveloped the Captain's hand with his own.

"How long are you here for?" Meyer asked.

"Uh, I have an appointment in payroll, ah Sir, in about thirty or so minutes."

Meyer thought for a couple of seconds and then said, "After you're done here come see me. Colleen can show you where I am. I'll let Deputy Inspector Bowen know you're with me. I don't want him to think I'm sneaking around behind his back."

At that Meyer left and Mike, Natalie and Chief Beymon came out of Beymon's office. All three were very glad to see Colleen.

Natalie gave Colleen a cursory hug, which did not go unnoticed by Svenson. Then when the lieutenant and the Chief each gave her a kiss on either cheek, he told himself silently, "Damn, I'm brown-nosing the wrong people.

"Sooner or later I'll probably be working for McNamara."

After Colleen introduced Captain Svenson and pleasantries were exchanged, Beymon retired to his office. When Colleen and Natalie went to the Ladies Room together, Mike offered Captain Svenson a chair at his own desk.

"It gets a little lively around here from time to time." Mike admitted., "But definitely not as crazy as it gets up in your neck of the woods. I was a patrolman out of South, so I know."

As Mike shuffled some papers together and clipped them, Svenson studied his face. At first, thrown off by the scar tissue above Mike's one eye, Svenson suddenly placed the face with the name and realized that he was in the presence of a legend.

"Y-you're Mike McGinty!" Svenson exclaimed. You shot that guy at the hospital a while back, and, and you were at Nine-Eleven."

As he always did, Mike became rather embarrassed. His features reddened and his smile slipped from his face.

Over at his desk, Bob Conway wondered what had just happened.

"If you don't mind, ah, Sir," Mike began, "I, ah would rather not discuss any of that. It's history and I'm not at all comfortable talking about it."

Just then, the ladies returned. From Mike's demeanor they both knew exactly what was going on.

Colleen stepped up and said, "Ah, Captain, maybe we should get you down to payroll, and then that more important appointment with Chief Meyer."

Unconsciously she tugged at Svenson's sleeve.

"Uh, I'm sorry Lieutenant." Svenson apologized, "I meant no harm."

"I know Captain." Mike assured him, "You just caught me off guard. I guess cops aren't supposed to get shaken up that easily. Sorry for my reaction."

"Oh, that's okay." Svenson assured him as the Captain allowed Lieutenant McNamara to escort him from the room.

After they had left, Mike looked over at Conway and said, "Sorry Bob. That was uncalled for."

Conway only nodded.

After a moment, Conway said, "If it makes any difference Sir, I do understand."

"Police Combat Cross, with a gold leaf, as I recall." Mike said softly, smiling as he did.

"And, I also recall three civilian lives were saved, and you took a bullet in the knee and one in the thigh. Almost hit your femoral artery. Thank GOD it missed."

Conway's eyes were wide open and his mouth hung loosely as he stared back at McGinty.

"The Chief checks out everyone who comes to work for him." Mike answered Conway's unasked question.

"Get used to it. He isn't trying to invade your privacy. He just likes to know our backgrounds."

Bob Conway nodded once more.

He glanced over to Natalie, beside him. "How about you Sergeant?" he asked, "What's your story?"

"Look, uh, Bob, since we are working together, at least for now, it's either Natalie or Nat. Your choice Sweetie,

"And, no, there's nothing in my file."

"Don't listen to her Bob." Mike remarked without looking up, "She's a real hellion. If you don't believe me, ask Colleen."

Natalie made a rude gesture in Mike's direction and gave him a Bronx cheer. After pausing a moment, she added, "Sir!"

Still smiling, Mike just waved, casually.

Conway stared at the two of them and once more shook his head.

A little later, when Natalie was running errands for both herself and Beymon, Conway asked, "What exactly did she do Lieutenant?"

"You've heard of the cable ties on door handles scam, haven't you?" Mike asked.

"Uh, yes Sir." Conway answered.

"Well our Natalie was jumped in a mall in Jersey and she crippled one guy and then was forced to kill the other. The guy she wounded ended up giving the Jersey cops names and locations, both there and even here in the city. Natalie did real good on that day. Several hostages were recovered. Plus she was able to meet her current boyfriend. Jim was the lead detective on that case."

His problem in Payroll solved, Captain Svenson reentered the waiting room of that specific area.

Colleen was waiting on a stiff metal chair near the door. She tried to maintain her cool as she rose, but Svenson could see the pain in her eyes above her hospital mask.

"All set?" she asked and turned to exit the room.

"Are you alright Lieutenant?" he asked as he followed her out.

"Well, the weather outside isn't helping any, and I left my painkillers back on my desk at Midtown."

Svenson reached into his jacket pocket and retrieved a white plastic bottle. Offering the container to Colleen, he said, "They're extra strength, if that's okay."

"That's the strongest I'll allow myself." She told him, "When I worked Narcotics before going to work for Chief Beymon, I saw too many cases of Opiate Dependence. When I was in the hospital I vowed to never go that route."

They had to wait a few minutes in Chief Meyer's outer office. His aide, Nancy said he was on an important phone call but did not elaborate.

Finally, after a call from Meyer, Nancy told them to go in.

"I've had my eye on the two of you for some time now." Meyer told them. "Nothing is positive yet as all this defunding has thrown a bit of a wrench in the process, but there might be openings elsewhere in the City.

"I spoke to Deputy Inspector Bowen about it, and he claims that he can't spare either of you. Of course, that only makes you both look a lot better to me.

"For now, we're gonna hold back a bit, but I wanted you to be aware of what may, or may not be happening."

A twinkle entered his eye as he mentioned, "Uh Colleen, one of my advisor's on this matter was Ron Beymon. He seems to think you would be better off back in his department.

"I hope you don't mind, but I quashed that idea immediately." Meyer chuckled.

"Well, that's it for the time being. I promise to keep you both informed. If you don't hear from me, then no progress has been made.

"I will tell you this however, If we only get approval for only one person, it will be Captain Svenson. Nothing personal Lieutenant, but that's just the way it is."

"To be honest Chief," Colleen replied, "Just to be considered is pumping air into my ego. No matter what happens, thank you for thinking about me."

The ride back to Midtown South was quiet. Neither officer wanted to discuss the situation in front of Sergeant McBride. Colleen thought silently that perhaps she might not even tell Danny later.

After dropping Svenson and Colleen off, as instructed by radio, Danny McBride sat with his engine idling on Thirty Fifth Street waiting for a couple of rookies. His newest assignment was to drive them around the precinct to familiarize them with its layout.

Robbie Carlson and Debbie Kelso were both nervous. While awaiting the return of the Sergeant who was to escort them, they had heard any number of stories on how much of a hard-ass he was.

They had not realized that as the very lowest on the totem pole, they were being hazed by silly fellow cops who at that time had nothing better to do.

Carlson held open the front door to the vehicle so that Kelso might enter. He then got in himself, into the rear seat.

They were both startled when a female lieutenant appeared at Kelso's window. Her nametag read McNamara.

Kelso reached to open the window. She was again startled when McBride did so from the master control panel on his door.

She smiled at the two rookies and then told the sergeant that she wished to speak to him later.

He smiled at her, tipped two fingers to his cap and said, "Yes Ma'am, no problem."

The Lieutenant then smiled again and told the new people, "Welcome aboard. Listen to this guy. He knows as much as anybody in this precinct. Oh, and laugh at his jokes, even though they aren't funny."

As she turned to go back into the Precinct House McBride frowned and groaned, "He-e-eyyy!"

Although none of them could see it, the Lieutenant was grinning as she walked away.

Rob Carlson had no idea who she was, other than a superior officer. Debbie Kelso knew exactly who she was. She was that police woman who had been targeted by the Russian Mob.

She was still around though, while two dirty cops had been put away and at least three members of that Mob were dead.

They were in Hell's Kitchen. McBride had explained that while they were assigned to Midtown South, sometimes the lines between precincts became blurred.

They were presently in the One-Oh Precinct. However, should the need arise, patrol people from 'South', as he called it, were required to respond to situations in adjacent precincts whenever needed. And, along the same line, other precincts might be called upon to respond to any crisis which might occur in 'South'.

As if to illustrate his point, gunfire erupted from an alley just down the street. McBride immediately called it in to Midtown South, who patched him over to the One-Oh Precinct over on West Twentieth Street. McBride and his pupils were on West Thirty Eighth Street. Their Desk Sergeant assured McBride that help was enroute.

Telling the Rookies to stay down, McBride inched his way to the alley opening. Just then two young men came running out waving handguns. McBride could hear crying in the Alley.

"Hold it," He called out loudly, "Police!"

Both young men dropped behind a beaten and faded blue older Chevrolet that had seen better days. One fender was painted with rust colored primer and a fairly large dent marred the driver's side door. The two men slipped into the vehicle through the passenger's door. One of them tumbled over the seat into the back seat. He physically cranked open the window. He fired several times at the crouching policeman. McBride's first shot hit the Driver's side window. While the bullet did not hit the driver, dozens of shards of sharp glass did. The guy grabbed his left eye with both hands just as the car slammed into a parked SUV.

The man in the back seat slammed forward, hitting the gun's trigger simultaneously.

His bullet did pierce his partner's head and he was immediately sprayed with the driver's spouting blood.

He was attempting to wipe the blood from his eyes when he felt the barrel of McBride's pistol against his forehead. It was still warm from having been fired and the hoodlum felt a mild burn against his skin.

As Rob Carlson and Debbie Kelso cautiously advanced one of the One-Oh Precinct's squad vehicles pulled up. A sergeant and two patrolmen took the live perpetrator into custody as McBride holstered his weapon.

An ESU van with two Firemen pulled up minutes later. After being informed that the Perp Driver was already dead they ran into the alley as directed by McBride.

Charlie Rossario appeared to be dead, but actually was not. He was, however, clinging tenaciously to life. His girlfriend, Alicia Graver was kneeling over him. She had never given CPR before but was attempting to do so then. Jimmy Hansen, the lead ESU pulled her gently away so that his partner, Ronnie Dombrowsky might tend to Charlie properly. Fortunately the Firemen were just in time.

As Alicia hovered nearby, the two ESUs tended first to Charlie's shoulder wound. It was so close that at first they thought it had pierced his right lung. Of course tests would have to be administered at the hospital, but from the sound of his breathing, they both felt that the lung was undamaged.

Alicia sighed deeply when they informed her thusly. She felt an arm encircle her shoulders. A glance to her left revealed a somewhat worn and tired looking police sergeant.

When two much younger patrol people, a man and a woman, arrived the Sergeant instructed them to stay with her. He then walked over to check on Charlie too.

Coming back he told her, "He's gonna be alright Miss, although the next forty eight hours are gonna be critical. The ESU's think the bullet missed his lung, but they'll know better at the hospital. They're taking him over to Manhattan Emergency. I received permission to drive you over myself."

The young woman nodded nervously. The even younger police woman placed her arm around Alicia's shoulder and steered her toward the police vehicle.

After instructing his two subordinates to occupy the back seat, McBride held open the front door for the young woman.

"Thank you Sergeant McBride." She said after noting his name tag.

Looking first to the backseat, and then back to McBride she said, "I'm Alicia Graver. That's my boyfriend, Charlie Rossario, up in the ambulance.

CHAPTER 17

CHANGE AND THEN MORE CHANGE

Ron Beymon sat at his desk contemplating any number of all the more recent occurrences.

The events of several days previous immediately came to mind.

Beymon remembered when he had slowly entered the outer office of his little suite. He had been tired and perhaps just a bit grumpy. He had known this day was coming and was not looking forward to it. That had been the day that "Beymon's Team", as he liked to call it, would be disassembled. They had done good work together. There had been disagreements along the way, but hey! They were a team of bright, clear thinking individuals. Differences of opinion were a key to such unique character.

Still, that day had come. It was a day that each of them dreaded, yet, oddly looked forward to.

Assistant Chief Ron Beymon's office had been filled with all of his subordinates, and the Chief of Patrol Dennis Meyer, as well.

Accompanying Meyer had been his administrative assistant, Sergeant Nancy Adreano.

Sergeant Adreano had been equipped with a variety of recording devices so that everything said would be available for future reference.

They were all there at the direction of NYPD Police Chief Walter Agrarian and the Police Commissioner as well, both of whom had been far too busy to attend.

Meyer had called the meeting to order. Even though everyone there knew precisely what the meeting was for, Meyer had Nancy read the minutes of his meeting with Walt Agrarian so that there would be no misunderstandings.

In essence, they were all there to be reassigned to precinct duty in the quickly dwindling ranks of the NYPD.

"I generally like to save questions for the end of the meeting." Meyer had announced, but I think for this one, I'll field any you might have beforehand. So, are there any questions?"

"There had been none, with some of the participants shaking their heads.

"Well," Chief Meyer had continued, "Starting at the top, Ron, as you may have surmised by now, you'll be assigned to my office. You've been around though, and so you know that anything can change at any time.

"Until you've been truly established, Walt feels that you will need an assistant. Nancy has her hands full, so I really can't share her. Either Sergeant Eberstein or Sergeant Conway are your choices. While it's entirely up to you, I think we all know what Natalie thinks.

Natalie blushed. She was watching Jim O'Leary with her peripheral vision. His mouth was a tight line and his brows were drawn closely together.

"I have to admit, however, I have examined both of their records. Either one would be an excellent street cop. And it pains me to lose either of them to administrative services.

"But, we all know Bob Conway's situation. At least for now, One PP is his best option."

Conway blushed and looked down at his hands. When he looked up Beymon was watching him. The Chief nodded and his meaning was obvious. Bob exhaled his pent up breath.

"Maybe you could get someone to free me for street duty as well." Nancy Adreano had offered, with a sly grin.

"Uh, duly noted Sergeant." Meyer had answered, nervously, "Let me think about that one too.

"Okay, for certain, Mike McGinty, you'll be in Midtown South. Deputy Inspector John Bowen is in charge there. I think you two will get along fine."

"Ah, yes Sir." McGinty had answered, "I know Inspector Bowen.

We've worked together before. He was one of my sergeants at that exact same precinct when I was a rookie."

"Good, good." Meyer murmured. "As you all know, Colleen is already there. I believe she's the assistant Intelligence Officer.

"Jim O'Leary," Chief Meyer continued, "Since most of your experience is right in this area you'll be going to the Oh-Five. Your commander will be Deputy Inspector Otis Manley, another good guy. The Fifth is over on Elizabeth Street."

Chief Meyer seemed deep in thought. His eyes lit up as a revelation entered his mind.

"Forgive me folks." He asked of his audience, "I'm getting old and everything that is occurring in this city, my city, keeps me up at night.

"Let me make a phone call and I'll get right back to you."

He had stepped out into Beymon's outer office.

A few minutes later Meyer had leaned through the doorway and asked Beymon to join him in that office, which Beymon, of course, did.

After another couple of minutes both men had returned. Both were wearing grave expressions but neither was frowning.

"Sorry to have excluded you Nancy," Meyer had said to his assistant, but until my thoughts were more organized and 'til I had discussed this with Chief Beymon, I wanted this off the record.

"All that being said, I have made a decision and Chief Beymon has agreed.

Sergeant Robert Conway will be staying with Chief Beymon as his assistant. As all of you know, Sergeant Conway is from a Bronx precinct and was injured not too long ago in one of the so-called peaceful demonstrations in which several patrol vehicles were firebombed. Sergeant Conway we know that you were shot twice and are recuperating. I know that you are anxious to be of value again, but so far you are unable to return to any kind of patrol work just yet.

"Sergeant Eberstein I'll need you to stay on for a time to show him the ropes a bit more. When you and Chief Beymon think he is suitably ready you will be re-assigned to the Fifth Precinct with Sergeant O'Leary."

At that, Meyer had winked. The meaning was all too clear. Natalie's expression was not sad, but neither was it particularly happy. While she was more than happy to help Beymon she knew that she would miss O'Leary for the time being

"Well then," Meyer summarized, "You all have your assignments. Now, are there any questions?"

Just then Natalie's phone had rung in the outer office. Beymon answered it from his console.

He said hello, but immediately began to listen, attentively.

The thoughts from that call and what it had led to flooded Beymon's mind.

"Yes," he finally said, "He's right here, but if this is a private call, I'll have to relay it to his office and you'll have to wait until he gets there. No, I'm his boss. I'm Assistant Chief Ron Beymon.

"Sure, hold on."

He had handed the phone to Mike and said, "It's a Sergeant David O'Toole out in Nassau County. He says it's important."

Mike glanced over to Dennis Meyer as he tentatively accepted the phone.

"Go ahead," Meyer urged him, "Until the end of the day you're still on Chief Beymon's dime."

Mike had taken the call and Beymon herded everyone out into Natalie's office to give him a little privacy.

They were just getting settled when they all heard Mike exclaim, "Sonuva Bitch!" followed quickly by "Where, when?"

After several minutes he had appeared at the door. His face was pale and his mouth was a grim line.

"I just got some news which affects all of us, but it's especially pertinent to Chief Beymon's now former committee."

He looked over to Chief Meyer and asked, "With your permission Sir?"

Meyer had nodded.

"That was Theresa's cousin in Nassau. As you may have guessed, he's a Nassau police sergeant. They had an incident the other night involving my daughter, which I just learned of just now. But, more importantly there were further ramifications, which you really have to hear."

Mike had stood silently for several moments weighing his thoughts. Everyone else in the room waited patiently.

He wondered how Theresa would react. He wondered if she didn't already know. And if so, why had he been kept in the dark.

"As it turns out, while my daughter was waiting for her step-brother to pick her up she was attacked." Mike related grimly.

A series of sympathetic murmurs encircled the room. Mike held up his hands defensively.

"It's okay, ah, she's okay. Her friend, a fellow nurse who was a medic in Afghanistan apparently beat up all three of them and she wasn't hurt.

"The touchy part came afterwards. It seems all three of these guys, young white men, were wearing BLM tee shirts.

"During the attack, before her friend, Jim Cantner stepped in they kept mentioning the movement, and so they were booked in regards to all that is going on right now, with the additional charges of attempted assault and possibly attempted rape.

"Well, it turns out that Nassau Internal Affairs was watching a sergeant out in Williston Park where the three hoods were being held. I wasn't given his name but he was suspected by Nassau IA of brutality similar to what took place out in Minnesota.

"Unknown to him when he went in to interrogate those three BLM prisoners, he was being filmed by a hidden camera.

"He began his interrogation by slamming the one kid's head into the table. He used the N-word accompanied by the word lover. Dave said it was just like the old protests when white freedom riders were beaten and often disappeared in the South back in the fifties and Sixties."

"Sonuva......" Meyer began, but was cut off by Beymon snorting a loud "Oh yea!" while shaking his head angrily.

"Wait," Mike said breathlessly, "There's more.

"Just as the Internal Affairs guys got ready to rush in there before he hurt them any worse, The other two guys started yelling that they were white supremacists who had infiltrated the Black Lives Movement.

"What?" Beymon and Meyer said simultaneously.

Mike repeated much of what he had already said. He then added, "They mentioned a group from New England called Caucasian Infinity.

"It turns out that not only did the cop recognize the name, but he had strong sympathies to just about any white supremacy group.

"He immediately apologized and began to make the injured guy feel better with ice on his head and drinks followed by sandwiches.

"Dave says that it's an ongoing investigation, but would not reveal anything else other than the three guys are still incarcerated."

"Hold on," Meyer spoke up, "Let's hold off on the reassignments until next Monday. Ron, I'd like you and your guys to investigate this further. I'm also gonna give you back Garret Holmes. He can smooth over wrinkles between Nassau and the City.

"Let's find out how much of this interacts with all this crap we have going on here.

"If I may Chief?" Mike asked, raising his hand like a schoolboy.

"Yes Michael, you may go to the bathroom." Meyer said with a silly grin.

He then apologized, adding, I always wanted to do that. I suffer through very few meetings where I would be able to.

"Go ahead Mike. Speak your piece."

"Well Sir, my step-son, David Keith is involved with a BLM case up in the Bronx Sir. Once more it was white youths bombarding police from up in a building

"A black cop was killed. His name escapes me right now, but it should be easy enough to find out. It was an altercation on the Concourse. Davy, uh, Officer Keith was injured as well."

"John Doe, I'm aware of that." Meyer replied.

"Bronx ADA Erica Lomonico is handling that case." He added.

"We finally got an ID on the kid from his fingerprints. I don't recall his real name, but he's from Massachusetts, I believe western Massachusetts, and he's also a member of Caucasian Infinity.

"Look into that one too Ron." Meyer urged.

"Maybe Monday's not such a viable date after all." Beymon suggested.

As Chief Meyer left he could be heard muttering to himself.

One half hour later, as Beymon's group sat in his office discussing the events of the day; a knock upon the open door drew their attention to it.

Garret Holmes had stepped into the room and greeted everyone.

"Dennis Meyer asked me to report to you Chief Beymon." He said while rubbing his hands together briskly.

"He mentioned Nassau County, but he did not elaborate. Can you fill me in?"

Instead, Beymon had asked Mike to explain the circumstances with Mr. Holmes.

"That's gonna be a little touchy." Holmes informed them, "While it is a Democrat led government, His Honor has a habit of stepping on toes. I'm not sure, but he may have made a little sisters remark in regards to Nassau and Suffolk Counties. The obvious gist is that they are both subservient to the Big City. That did not go well with our Eastern neighbors.

"But, as we say here at One Police Plaza, we don't sweat the difficult and we always tackle the impossible head on. Let me see if I can find a helmet that fits."

After Holmes had left, more news arrived in the nature of a telephone call from Chief Meyer.

Beymon was instructed to keep Natalie', Bob Conway and Mike on his crew, while as formerly directed Jim would be assigned to the Fifth Precinct.

Natalie stifled a groan. Jim held her hand gently.

The loss of O'Leary had obviously upset Natalie.

They would also lose the extra office, and so must make allowances.

Beymon had thought at least one of them should move into the inner office but he still had not decided who.

Finally, he informed them that Mike would be his office mate until Conway was brought up to speed and then who knew what sort of personnel changes might be enacted.

There was always the possibility that once they cleared up the Nassau business the crew might be split up again.

Once more, in Police business, nothing is ever definite and absolutely nothing is ever permanent.

As he presently sorted through those thoughts, Ron Beymon sighed audibly.

"And life goes on, doesn't it?" He muttered softly.

CHAPTER 18
POLITICS......SONUVA.......

Morton Lieberman tapped his ballpoint pen nervously upon the pad of lined paper before him. He inhaled and exhaled several times quickly. While everything about his mien seemed a bit anxious, it was actually a carefully timed ploy. All of Morton's movements were calculated and deliberate. Intimidation was Morton's way of thinking, even as he used it to creep up upon his unsuspecting quarry.

Besides, when one's opponent was zeroing in on Morton's uncertainty, it gave him additional time to decide upon his next course of action.

With a thin webbing of wrinkles surrounding each of his facial features, and thinning silver hair, Morton appeared easy to fool. He was anything but.

Lieberman stared intently at the young man before him. Officer Nunzio Italo stood loosely in a relaxed version of a military parade rest. He clasped his left hand in his right hand before him.

"Hm," Morton thought to himself as he continued to tap his pen, "A righty. Good to know."

Lieberman tried to use both hands in his pen tapping ritual in order to throw any others off.

"Time to shake this puppy up." He told himself with a self satisfying smirk.

"Officer Italo," Lieberman announced commandingly, "Did you not have your gun drawn? Were you not able to force Mister Slovak to drop his own gun?"

A smile graced Lieberman's face as he sat back.

From off to one side of Officer Italo came the gruff, husky voice of police Sergeant Vito Marciano.

"Please let the record show," Marciano elucidated, "That Mister Lieberman has completely disregarded all of the prior testimony given by Officer Italo."

Marciano cleared his throat before continuing.

"Unless, of course, Councilman Lieberman has completely forgotten or disregarded that testimony on purpose.

"Please, Sir, ah, Mr. Councilman, refresh my own memory, would a reading of the minutes help at all?"

"That's it," Lieberman shouted, standing up suddenly, "Mister Chairman, I want this room cleared of any unwanted personnel immediately!"

"Excuse me Councilman Lieberman," Nunzio Italo interrupted, "But is it your desire to deprive me of my chosen representative and advisor?"

Nunzio glanced innocently over at Marciano who was hiding his smile with a hand over his face.

Before Morton Lieberman could respond, Nunzio said in a sugary, and just slightly louder voice, "As I said Sir, the perp, uh, perpetrator, Eddie Slovak, was standing directly behind Miss Nunez. He had his weapon to her head, just behind her ear."

At that Nunzio nodded toward Katherine Nunez, just to the right of Sergeant Marciano. She smiled faintly and nodded back.

"I could see Slovak's eye, just behind the silhouette of his weapon. That is not a good target. Had I taken that shot it would have been more likely that I would have hit Miss Nunez. I did not want to kill an unarmed, innocent civilian.

"The department and all of society frown upon just such an action. I certainly frown upon it, myself, most vehemently Sir, as I'm sure that you do as well."

Lieberman's face was a crimson scowl. His brows were drawn and his eyes were blinking rapidly.

"Did he not kill an additional two people while trying to escape?" the Councilman demanded hotly.

"No Sir, he did not." Marciano answered crisply. Abject rancor could be easily discerned in the Sergeants reply.

"He accidentally killed one of his own men, and shot Officer Italo in Italo's protective vest while still hiding behind Miss Nunez."

Katherine Nunez unconsciously touched her own ear, noting the ringing still there from the gunshot fired at the side of her head.

"Italo, though having trouble breathing returned Slovak's fire, once Slovak had thrown Miss Nunez to the ground, violently." Marciano continued.

"Well Sergeant Mariano, are you aware that Slovak's family is suing the City for wrongful death?" Lieberman had purposely mispronounced Marciano's name.

"Well Sir," Marciano returned with a slight grin, "I suppose that's why we are here today, instead of policing and defending the streets of the Bronx."

"I don't like your attitude Sergeant." Lieberman snapped angrily."

"Well then Councilman Lieberman," Marciano snapped back, "I guess I won't be backing your program to supply all the City's criminals with protective vests and helmets."

"That's it Sergeant," Councilman David Claren, the committee chairman warned hotly, "you are way out of order. We are adjourned for the present.

"Everybody out for now. We'll reassemble tomorrow at nine in the morning."

As everyone began to leave, Claren said, "Not you Mort. Stay for a minute or two."

After all the others had vacated the meeting room, Claren said, "Mort, you were egging both him and Italo on. If you continue to do so, we can expect more of what we saw today. If you want respect, you have to give it back in kind. Think about it.

"See you tomorrow."

Once Claren was alone he dialed a single digit on his cell phone. He explained all that had occurred to the person he had contacted.

After listening for several minutes he chuckled, said "Goodbye." and clicked the phone off.

His contact also chuckled. She held down the touchtone button on the phone upon the desk she was sitting at.

"Yea, what is it Nancy?" NYPD Chief of Patrol Dennis Meyer asked.

"Oh, Boss," Sergeant Nancy Adreano answered, "You're gonna love this one."

CHAPTER 19

OLD TIMES, GOOD FRIENDS AND CAKE!

Jaycee Steele sat calmly by the window, absorbing the mid-morning Sun as it warmed his face. The window was slightly open, barely an inch, letting in a cool morning breeze in as well as the Sun. He smelled flowers in the air but could not identify them. In his mind he saw fields of brightly colored flowers stretching for dozens of yards all about the building. Reality punched his dream apart as he realized there were probably less than a dozen blossoms in what was possibly no more than a two foot by five foot patch.

Jaycee was blind.

He remembered going to Longwood Gardens in Delaware on his honeymoon with Ella, his wife of over forty seven years. Those were such beautiful flowers as he remembered fondly.

Ella had been gone now, for the last five plus years. The memory triggered the sight in his memory of the many flowers, of every conceivable hue, displayed around her coffin, as she had lain there finally in peace.

She had not been his High School sweetheart, although they had known each other in High School.

He had dated her older sister, Corina, once, but apparently Corina did not really care for him.

"Ah yes," he told himself with an inward smile, "The good old days."

That had been Boonton, New Jersey, back in the early nineteen sixties.

With no prospects on the line for a young African American in Boonton, he had gotten a ride with Benny Colson's father over to Morristown and there he and Benny had joined the Army.

After Basic Training in Fort Dix, NJ they had both gone to North Carolina to become meaner, leaner and tougher.

It seemed as if the life's purpose of the drill sergeant, Staff Sergeant Bobby Culpepper, had been to crush the spirits of Privates Benjamin Colson and Jamal Charles Steele. He had come close several times, but something within the two young men valiantly seemed to resist the Sergeant's efforts.

Culpepper was so very obviously prejudiced against black soldiers in his army.

He had a southern accent, but neither Benny nor Jaycee cared enough to inquire where from. It didn't really matter. As both young men knew, that particular type of prejudice existed in the North, as well.

Deciding that perhaps they might be leaning upon each other for support, Culpepper separated them, placing Colson in one platoon and Steele in another.

He was especially hard on Steele, as the boy's name irked the hell out of Sergeant Culpepper.

"Steele," he would shout into the soldier's face from less than three inches, "You are not now, nor will you ever be a soldier. You are not steel Boy. You are only soft, easy to break, lead."

Jaycee would stand there, stiffly at attention. He would absorb the sergeant's anger, hatred and very bad breath.

Unknown to Culpepper, Jamal Steele used that bad breath as a shield against the man's even more toxic personality.

On a very rare twenty four hour pass into town he revealed his strategy to Benny, and together, although in separate situations, they weathered Sergeant Culpepper's efforts to make them quit.

Culpepper stood to one side, glowering darkly as they finally received their graduations.

Culpepper was a little more elated as he announced that the two of them were headed to Vietnam to join the Ninth Division in and about the Mekong Delta.

They had deployed out of Long An Province, and had even probed into Cambodia at one point. Somewhere along the line, Benny Colson had been hit by friendly fire as he and several others had pushed a bit farther than the rest of their company.

When Jaycee had finally caught up, the medic was kneeling over a very dead caricature of Jaycee's friend and shaking his head.

For the next month or so whenever Jaycee tried to sleep he saw Benny's strained features with wide open eyes in his mind. He hoped, oh so desperately that it hadn't been his bullet which had pierced Benny's back.

His visit to Benny's parents once he had been discharged was even harder than facing the 'Cong had been back along the Delta.

But, that too had been a very long time ago.

Jaycee was presently, and once more, the guest of the United States Government. Two years after Ella's death, he had begun to go blind. He had been living with the younger of his two sons, Roger, in Montville, New Jersey. With Roger and his wife Carla both working there was no one to care for Jamal.

At his own urging he had been placed in the Paramus Veteran's Hospital and Soldier's Home. It was at his room's window, on the second floor that he had smelled the unknown blossoms.

Jaycee was seventy three years old. He had spent a good portion of his life after Vietnam with the New York City Police Department. He still had a few friends in the NYPD. Occasionally one of them would make the trip from the City to see him.

If that friend was a retiree, he would come from wherever he had ended up.

Two such friends were also patients right there in Paramus, NJ.

Since the pandemic had begun, however, no one had visited except his son, Roger and Roger's wife, Carla.

The older of his two boys, Jamal Jr., lived out in Portland Oregon. While Jaycee was unable to watch television, he listened to whatever his roommate, Gary Pentallo was watching.

More often than not, Gary's choice of entertainment was the daily news. Like Jaycee, Gary thought the country was going mad.

A lifelong Republican, like his father had been before him, Gary understood why the sitting President had been elected. What Gary did not understand was why he still had any supporters left, at all.

"The man is single handedly ruining this country." Gary grumbled loudly, unable to disguise his anger.

"Oh no," Jaycee would counter, "He has lots of help, Gary, both Republican and Democrat. Together they are fucking this country up royally.

"Maybe it's just me Gary, but it seemed as if things were a lot different when we were younger. Sure, graft and corruption existed then as well. But, it also seemed as if those politicians tried to balance out what was best for this country with their various self-given gifts from rich benefactors."

Grudgingly, Gary agreed with him. In fact, whenever a group of the veterans gathered, anywhere in the building, almost everyone agreed with Jaycee's assessment.

Still, however, with Jamal and his wife Terra and their four kids, two boys and two girls out in that powder keg of Portland, Jaycee slept very little. Even though blind, his mind's eye saw quite clearly the areas of destruction all around the nation.

Jaycee concentrated on the aroma of the flowers and thought fondly of his darling Ella.

He had been a New York cop for almost two years at the time of their hook-up.

Standing on the corner of Fifth Avenue and Fiftieth Street during the Saint Patrick's Day parade he was mildly surprised when a pretty black woman standing less than three feet away said, "I know you. You dated my sister, Corina."

"Are you from Boonton?" he asked her. "You do look very familiar."

When she answered yes, he replied, "I took her out once, but we did not really date. I wasn't quite what she was looking for."

"Well," the young woman responded with an enchantingly bright smile, "Perhaps I shouldn't say so, but I kinda had a crush on you back then. I was sorry when you enlisted in the Army with Benny."

Her smile dissolved into a sorry frown. "I wanted to write to you, but I didn't know where you were. I guess I could have asked your Mom, but I was kinda scared of that as well.

"I was so sorry to hear about poor Benny though."

"Jaycee faced briefly back down Fifth Avenue at the mention of Benny's fate. Some things take so much longer to heal, if they ever heal at all.

"Why are you here, today?" Officer Steele asked, turning back. Obviously the parade was a factor, but Jaycee was struggling to keep her interested in their conversation.

From his tone Ella could tell that he really might be interested in her. Her own interest was greatly piqued.

"Would you believe that I came to meet you?" she asked with a shy smile.

"No," he answered with a much more engaging smile, "But if you wouldn't mind dating a cop, I would certainly like to ask you out."

"I'm interested." Ella replied and stepped right up next to him.

She felt his bicep through his shirtsleeve and smiled just a bit more broadly.

"Do you date college students?" she asked coyly.

"I haven't yet," he answered, "But if you're a student, I would certainly like to try it.

"Once the parade passes Saint Pats, I'm off duty. My car is all the way over by the Hudson River, but we could take public transportation if you like. How did you get here, and do you still live in Boonton?"

"Well, yes, I still live in Boonton, and I drove in with some friends. Those three girls behind me who I'm sure are grinning like idiots. Let me tell them where I can meet them and I'll go with you."

"If you'd like," he offered, "I could drive you home, and I would spend the night at my Mom's house."

"Well, I currently live on campus, Fairleigh Dickenson, in Madison, but I could spend the night at my Mom's house too."

Ella introduced Jamal to her friends and explained the situation to them.

Twenty minutes later the tail end of the parade had passed and was several blocks further up Fifth Avenue.

Jaycee introduced Ella to his partner for the day, Patrolman Ed Flanagan and started to look for a taxi cab.

"I don't mind walking, if you don't." Ella told him, and they set off for Twelfth Avenue, carefully avoiding all the rowdy Irish bars and pubs.

That had been a very long time ago. The bittersweet memories swirled around in the blind man's mind.

Thoughts of her always elicited so many wonderful memories.

Those thoughts of her also brought sorrow because she was no longer with him, except in those heartfelt memories.

Just then, one of the orderlies, Rob Stevens, entered the room. Jaycee knew it was Rob from the cologne he was wearing.

As was always the case, Jaycee surprised Rob by announcing his name and asking the orderly what he needed.

In a slightly exasperated voice, Rob asked Jaycee if he was up for visitors.

Jaycee figured that since the pandemic was still raging, they must be Veterans Affairs officials. He nodded and said, of course Rob. I'll clear a spot on my busy calendar."

When he heard the booming sound of a man, whose voice he recognized but couldn't quite place, he was utterly surprised.

In the recess of his mind he associated the voice with Ed Flanagan, but knew that Ed had passed away not all that long ago.

In his best, although somewhat lacking, Sammy Davis Junior voice, Mike McGinty said, "Do the name McGinty ring a bell?"

"Mike," Jaycee asked excitedly, "Is that really you Mike?"

"It is indeed," Mike replied, and I have another surprise for you. It's me darling wife, Theresa, daughter of your old partner Eddie Flanagan."

Before Jaycee could respond, Theresa was at his side, kneeling and kissing the old man's cheek.

Her warm affection surprised him and even surprised Mike.

Looking up at her husband, she said, "I'm sure you didn't know this, but I used to call his wife Mama Ella or sometimes Mama Ellie. She was one of my baby sitters whenever Mom and Dad needed some alone time.

"This fine gentleman was Papa Jay."

Jaycee chuckled fondly. He remembered those times well. He and Ella would also place their two boys in Marie Flanagan's hands whenever they needed time alone. Both of his boys still made Hot Dog stew and Irish stew, and especially Marie's strawberry short cake.

When they were young it was made with a wee dram of bourbon as Marie used to call it. He had last eaten some when he and Ella had visited Ed and Marie in Florida, some ten years ago. Marie had switched to Amaretto. The cloying almond aftertaste was a wonderful change.

"How is your Mom, anyway?" Jaycee asked. "She was a dynamo of a woman if ever there was one. She and my Ella were so very close."

"Well," Theresa began, without releasing her embrace, "she's as well as she can be. Since Daddy left us, she has her moments of sorrow, but she's a real trooper.

"Mike brought her into our house after Daddy died, so I see her every day.

"Naturally, there are moments when we get on each other's nerves, the old mother and daughter story, but we're always there for each other. She's a fantastic influence on my kids.

"As you know she and Daddy helped to raise them when we lost Dom."

As she had been talking Jaycee was nodding. His expressions were a mixture of joy and sadness as he recalled his old friends.

His reverie was interrupted when Theresa looked up at her husband and asked, "Mike?"

McGinty knew what she meant, and had, in fact, already dialed his home phone.

On the other end, Marie Flanagan had tears of joy in her eyes, having heard most of what her daughter had said.

Theresa pressed the phone into Jaycee's hand and said softly, "Here Papa Jay, someone wants to talk to you."

The conversation had been pleasant as both Jaycee and Marie remembered old times with their loved ones who had already passed.

Mike and Theresa sat off to one side. Theresa sat in the only other chair while Mike sat upon the bed. Mike noticed that Theresa was beaming.

This man was probably as close as she could get to any man who reminded her of Eddie Flanagan.

Of course, Jaycee was in no way as cantankerous as Eddie could sometimes be.

The conversation lasted for at least fifteen or more minutes. A salty tear slid down Jaycee's cheek as he handed the phone aloft to whoever might grab it.

"She sounds good." Jaycee admitted. "She brought back some happy memories. Even after your Dad and I were no longer partners, we stayed close."

Jaycee sighed audibly.

"I miss them both." He said softly, "But, what's this gift she mentioned?" They could hear excitement in his tone.

The blind man heard paper and then plastic rustling. All at once, the faint scent of amaretto filled his nostrils.

"No-o-ooo!" he sighed, unable to conceal a new found enthusiasm.

"Yes, yes indeed." Theresa answered sounding triumphant, "And it's all yours."

From across the room, Gary Pentallo asked "What's all his?" they heard a soft grunt from Rob Stevens who had reappeared at the door.

"Jaycee was grinning broadly and told her, "Nothing is all anybody's in this place Theresa.

"We all share and share alike.

"Gary," he asked his roommate with a smile, "Did your Mom or Grandmother ever make strawberry short cake?"

"Did she?" Gary said resoundingly, "You betcha."

"Mine too!" Rob echoed as he stepped into the room completely.

"About how many slices we got here Theresa?" Jaycee asked expectantly.

"Well, she answered, if you keep them slender, around twenty, I'd guess. Of course, Mike and I won't be eating any."

From the corner of her eye she saw Mike's grin dissolve into a frown.

"Yea, she's right." Mike agreed, but the frown remained in place.

"Rob," Jaycee asked, "Would you get twenty paper plates and plastic forks and slice this baby up for us, uh, naturally you and Billy included?"

Billy was Bill Harnten, the other orderly on their floor.

"When all was said and done, and everyone on the floor had been fed, Rob leaned over and whispered into Jaycee's ear, "One piece left, Buddy. It's wrapped and in the refrigerator whenever you want it. I labeled it Liver and broccoli, so no one will take it."

Jaycee gave Rob the high sign.

While Rob spoke to Jaycee, Theresa slipped her arm into her husband's.

"Don't be upset Big Guy," she whispered into his ear, "When we get home I have a special dessert only for you."

Mike's eyes brightened considerably. He did not answer, but his gleaming smile said it all.

Just over an hour later, Jaycee started to fade.

Without being rude, Rob Stevens asked Theresa and Mike if they could leave and come back on another day.

After Theresa kissed Papa Jay goodbye, they left.

Down in the lobby, as they prepared to leave, a medium tall black man was just entering. Theresa surprised both Mike and the man by kissing the new man's cheek.

The man stepped back a pace and was about to say "Excuse me." When Theresa said, "Whatsa matter RJ? Don't you recognize your little sister?"

Roger Steele blinked several times until moments later he recognized her.

"Theresa!" he exclaimed, "Boy, you really grew up!"

His attention was immediately drawn to the man standing behind her. The man's expression had just relaxed from consternation to a broad smile. His head was bandaged with a white patch from his eyebrow up into his scalp. Several small scratches ringed the bandage.

RJ reached up with an extended hand. "Hi, I'm……."

"Roger Steele." Mike interrupted, "I just figured that out. You might not remember me, but when I was a rookie cop, and you were a young man, I met you a couple of times. I'm really sorry about your Dad's condition.

"Oh, yea, I'm Mike McGinty. Your Dad and I both partnered with Ed Flanagan over the years."

"Yes," RJ answered with a smile as it all came back to him, "I remember.

"And you invited us to your wedding, but Dad's blindness was just starting to affect him and we had to decline."

He turned back to Theresa, with a smile. "Carla should be in at any minute." He said, "She's parking the car. She picked me up at work."

Just then a pretty African American woman came rushing in. She stopped short when she saw her husband talking with some people which to her were strangers.

"Carla," RJ called out, "Come meet my little sister, and I guess my brother-in-law.

"This is Theresa and Mike McGinty.

"Our moms used to exchange babysitting duties. Her mom is Marie Flanagan. You've heard me mention her."

Carla extended her hand first to Theresa and then to Mike. "Hi!" she greeted, tentatively, "Yes, RJ has spoken of Theresa and Marie often.

"I remember getting an invitation to your wedding, but we were caring for Dad at the time and couldn't make it.

"I guess congratulations are in order."

Theresa embraced the startled woman. When released, Carla was unsure as what to say.

Mike filled the void by announcing that they still had a bit of a trip back to Queens, and RJ and Carla still had Jaycee to visit with.

As they left, Carla wondered what might have caused the damage to Mike's forehead.

On the trip home, conversation skirted a variety of subjects, including the Corona virus; the Mayor's defunding program and its effect on all their lives. And, of course, they discussed their kids.

Mike and Theresa discussed Melanie's near assault in Nassau. Theresa explained that she felt that Mike already had a lot to worry about and that was why he had been kept in the dark.

Mike wondered why whenever he had used the exact same argument he was always admonished.

Eventually, the conversation swung around to the blind man they had just left.

"He once told me that your Dad might have gone at the very least, to be captain if he hadn't been so acerbic." Mike revealed.

At first, Theresa took exception to what Mike had said, and then realized the truth of it. Her Dad had really possessed quite the mouth on him.

As her mother had once pointed out, Ed saw things as they were, and quite sadly, he saw things as they really should be.

He always felt it necessary to address the inadequacy of whatever the situation.

Like any organization, large or small, politics would rear its angry head.

Sometimes, especially back then, a man or woman's ability fell behind that of another's whose talent was more in brokering slick deals.

Ed had been very vocal when his friend, Jamal Steele had been passed over for a sergeant's promotion. The powers that were back then did not take it lightly.

Eventually Jaycee had risen to sergeant, but Ed forever bore the stigma of a troublemaker.

Theresa chuckled as a thought entered her mind.

"What?" Mike asked simply.

"When I was around ten years old," she told him, "We went on a trip to the Long Island South Shore.

"We were on Route Twenty Seven, on our way to Sag Harbor, up on the north shore of the South Fork, if that makes any sense.

"I think we were approaching where Route Twenty Seven heads south east and we were going to switch over to Route Seventy Nine.

"I was in the first car with Papa Jay and Mama Elly. I was seated in the back between RJ and Jammy. They were both older than me, but not by too much.

All of a sudden I felt Papa Jay apply the brakes

"What is it? Mama Elly asked. She had a worried tone to her voice.

"I don't know." Papa Jay answered, "I wasn't speeding. Maybe my brake lights are out."

"Well, we sat there for several minutes, and all of a sudden a policeman appeared at Mama Elly's window. I got scared because he had a gun in his hand.

"Then another policeman appeared at Papa Jay's window. He wasn't holding his gun, but he was resting his hand on it."

Theresa paused. She was trying to remember the incident exactly as it had occurred. Her expression changed slightly.

Gazing back and forth from the road to his wife, Mike noticed it immediately.

Although he had not heard this story before, he could see exactly where it was headed.

"The cop looked into the back seat. When he saw me with my very bright red hair and my freckles, his expression became angry, mean.

"Whatta you doin' out here boy?" he demanded of Papa Jay. He kept staring at me the entire time. I glanced out Mama Elly's window and his partner had brought his gun up higher and was holding it with two hands.

"Quite suddenly he turned his attention back to Papa Jay and screamed at him, "I asked you a fucking question boy."

"Even if I hadn't been there, Papa Jay's two young boys were in the back seat. His wife was in the front seat. There was no need for that kind of language. I grew very scared.

"Just then I heard my Dad's voice come from behind us."

"What're a couple of Asshole Jerk-off deputies doing, stopping a decorated NYC policeman for?" he snarled. "Does Chester Knowles know you're wasting the tax payer's money like this?"

"I didn't see it, but RJ later told me that as soon as my dad mentioned the name Knowles, the cop on the passenger side holstered his weapon.

"Who are you?" the driver side guy asked. His voice was still angry, but decidedly less so.

"I'm the guy who's renting half of Chet Knowles' house up in Sag Harbor." Dad told him, "Jamal here is renting the other half.

"Maybe Chet and I need to have a discussion about how New York cops are treated in his jurisdiction. Maybe we ought to include The New York Daily News in that particular conversation.

"Hey, I have an idea. We could include Larry Kelso as well.

"Having just looked at the driver side cop's ID tag, Dad added, "How does that strike you patrolman Haggerty?"

"I later learned that Larry Kelso, uh, Lawrence T. Kelso was a big deal out there on the South Shore. Before retiring however, he too had been an NYC cop.

"The cop on the passenger's side got very nervous and told Haggerty that he'd wait for him in the car.

"I guess Haggerty thought that maybe he could still bully his way through the situation. He pointed at me and said, well, he's got a white girl in the car."

"My daughter!" Dad exclaimed angrily "Why Patrolman, what's your problem?"

"Well….." Haggerty muttered, and then he just waved, disgustedly and stalked past Dad, back to his car.

"Dad made sure that Papa Jay was okay and we went on to Sag Harbor.

"I found out that later that day, my father did call Chet Knowles and they had a very explicit conversation. We never did go back to that area of Long Island again. Daddy said that things had changed out there, somewhat, but the incident had left a bad taste in his mouth."

CHAPTER 20

WHERE DO THEY COME FROM

The McCobbs had been in Manhattan since early in the Nineteenth Century. No one really knew the reasoning behind the family's immigration to America, and for the most part, nobody really cared.

James "Jimmy" McCobb lived on 49th Street between Tenth and Ninth Avenues in the area of Manhattan known as Hell's Kitchen. The "Kitchen" was an extremely tough area.

His wife Ciara had given him five sons and three daughters. When his oldest son was twenty nine, Donnie was born. The strain of it was too much for Ciara and she died giving birth.

While still carrying Jimmy's newest addition, Ciara had been an ardent fan of the singer, Donovan. She had instructed that the boy's name should be Donovan in his honor. Of course, everyone shortened it to Donnie. It was left to Donnie's three sisters, Meg, Sylvia and Connie to care for and raise the young child.

While Connie, the youngest, was thrilled to be placed in the role of mother, both Meg and Sylvia resented it. Too often they left their younger sister with the complete burden of it.

Connie, or Constance, was fifteen years old at the time. Since she had school to deal with, during the day, Sylvia, who worked a night shift in a factory in Queens, was left to watch young Donnie. Donnie's closest sibling was his brother Stephen, age nine. When Sylvia had to leave for work, since Connie would not be home for another twenty minutes or so,

Stephen was left in charge of his baby brother. Stephen was not the most accomplished of babysitters.

Donnie was often neglected.

Jimmy McCobb earned his living by working for the local gang, a group called The Cork Boys, named for the large county and second largest city in Ireland. None of the Cork Boys had ever been to Ireland, but loved the name anyway. Of course, not all of the members could trace their heritage back to Cork either. They just liked the name.

They were also not the final authority in Hell's Kitchen, the area where the McCobb family resided.

The Cork Boys reported to and were totally subservient to the Westies, a local gang which rivaled and occasionally challenged even the much vaunted Italian Mafia.

Jimmy ran numbers for the Cork Boys and often took advantage of the highly rumored "Fell off of a truck" merchandise.

It was on Donnie McCobb's first birthday that a soft Brown and tan teddy bear fell off of one of those trucks.

Since Stephen was nine, he wanted no part of a sissy teddy bear, but still thought it his duty to constantly make fun of Donnie's love for his new toy.

Being the youngest of nine siblings can be a somewhat toughening process, especially if that child does not have a mother to defend him.

While Connie was his surrogate mother, Connie was also discovering boys. As Donnie grew older, more often than not he was left alone.

Being the youngest of nine can also make a child who is left alone so often somewhat aggressive and feisty.

Add to that fact, the additional fact that Donnie's brothers and sisters had taken to calling him Teddy, because of the bear. It was not a term of endearment except when used by Connie.

It was in fact, somewhat derisive.

Teddy/Donnie learned how to fight. His rules for fighting were not the Marquis of Queensbury's, either. Teddy's rules involved biting, gouging, kicking and handfuls of dangling testicles.

Understanding that he would be inflicting pain, Teddy assumed that at some point he would be experiencing pain as well. Even at that young age he steeled himself for what he knew that he would have to endure.

Almost all of his siblings suffered the little fellow's anger at one time or another.

At one point even Big Jim felt his son's unnatural rage. Teddy of course was rewarded with a closed fist to the mouth which removed three of his teeth.

After shaking off the pain, Teddy noted, even though still a child, "Lesson learned."

As he grew, young Teddy understood more and more of the art of aggression. At first, playmates mocked what they deemed his sissy nickname. It became a hard lesson which they noted sorely as their bruises and cuts had begun to heal.

As a middle teen, Teddy McCobb had become the toughest young man in the neighborhood. The Cork Boys took note of this, but were told to back off by the superior Westies. They too had taken note of young McCobb's abilities and decided to recruit him as one of their own.

However strong and cunning Teddy was, he was also a very intelligent young man. He saw things in a certain way and reacted in a decisive manner.

The leadership of The Westies took note of this and allowed him to act in whatever way Teddy thought might be best. It had proven so far to be a wise course of action.

One of Teddy's major quirks was that even though the police were in place to prevent crime from being committed, they, he reasoned, were not the enemy. They were, he insisted, only doing the jobs that they had been hired to do.

Whenever confronted by a police situation, Teddy reacted, and counseled his fellow felons to also react by not confronting those police. This earned him a certain respect from the patrolmen who walked and drove the streets of Hell's Kitchen.

One of them, however, a Patrolman named Edward Flanagan, was not fooled. Knowing full well of McCobb's sometimes violent nature, Flanagan knew that it was only a matter of time, and a rather precise situation before that particular volcano would finally blow.

Ed occasionally subscribed to the old axiom, "Keep your friends close, but keep your enemies closer."

He felt that the rule especially applied to Teddy McCobb. He had even gone so far as to address the young man usually as Don, his given name.

"Why not Donnie?" Teddy had asked him one day in front of Embrey's market.

"I don't know you that well Don." Ed had responded. "You're a man, not a boy, so I think Don is more appropriate than Ted Teddy, or Donnie. But, hey, it's your name. You tell me what you would prefer. I'll go along with whatever you decide. I'd rather not get my ass kicked just yet."

"Uh, I don't know Ed. I would imagine you've kicked a few asses yourself. I still hear rumors of broken noses. I wouldn't want to be on the receiving end of one of those butt-kickings either."

Ed Flanagan knew that Teddy/Donnie's education never went past the tenth grade, but his speech was virtually slang free.

"He must read a lot." Ed correctly surmised.

The time had come, so the Westies leadership had decided, for Teddy McCobb to prove both his mettle and his loyalty.

He was a brawler, for sure, but could he kill? They had no doubt that Teddy could kill in defense, but could he do it in a cold-blooded manner.

There was a numbers runner whom the gang thought might be skimming. It wasn't much, but enough to warrant curiosity. Further examination proved that indeed he was robbing from his employers.

It was felt that an example needed to be made. With this opportunity, young McCobb would be able to prove both his mettle and his loyalty.

The leadership put it to Teddy on how would he handle just such a matter.

Without even blinking, Teddy said "Baseball bat, with gloves, naturally."

"How would you determine whether he was dead or not, and how would the public determine why he had been killed?" The bosses demanded, although not precisely in those words.

They could tell by Teddy's demeanor that he was neither upset by their demands nor even cowed by their power of life and death. That might prove to be a problem in the future, but for now it was a talent to be used whenever necessary.

"You've seen me swing a bat." Teddy replied, "Two or three times in the head would insure death.

"I would place some crumpled money of your determination in his mouth and then whack it shut with the bat. If you decide that it should not be your money, then I would use some of mine, just to prove myself to you.

"I wanna make one thing perfectly clear. I want to be close to you bosses, but I do not want any of your jobs.

"I also have a warning. If you decide to come after me, don't miss. I take exception to people who do not like me anymore. However, if you do not, I will be your most loyal soldier."

After Teddy was dismissed, the various leaders had a discussion about him. There was some very good praise, but there were a few nervous remarks as well.

Three days later the body of Roscoe P. Limony was found in an alley behind a local bar. His head had been crushed by a blunt instrument. His knees, hips, shoulders and elbows had all been shattered, supposedly by that same blunt instrument.

The next day, when the Coroner was finally able to pry the man's mouth open, one hundred dollars in cash was found lodged between the broken teeth. It was not Teddy McCobb's money. It had come from Limony himself with the gang's blessing.

When Teddy presented the balance of what had been in Limony's pockets, just over seven hundred dollars, to the Westies' leadership, he was told to keep it and was presented with an additional three hundred dollars.

As Teddy had foretold, word got around as to why Limony had been killed, but strangely no one had seen anything and the identity of the killer was unknown.

Ed Flanagan was absolutely sure that young Don McCobb had been the culprit. He mulled in his mind how the authorities should best handle the situation.

The very next day after that, a bloody baseball bat was found a block away in a garbage can. The handle had been shattered, and parts of the fat part of the bat were splintered. A number of those splinters were found on several parts of Roscoe Limony's body and head.

The blood, as well, was identified as Roscoe's.

There were no prints, but several slivers of inexpensive leather were found imbedded in the bat's broken handle.

CHAPTER 21

NOT A GOOD IDEA SKIP

Sometimes a series of events string themselves together like a necklace of beads. Occasionally the events are connected, but then not necessarily so. In Skip Layne's case they were entirely connected.

Skip was presently living up in Westchester County, just north of New York City. He felt he was far enough away up in Rye, NY to be out from under NYPD scrutiny, but close enough should opportunity call him.

The present problems which the city was enduring, the Covid virus and Police Defunding while riots attempted to choke the City's very breath seemed to be the opportunity he was looking for. In the past year, he had lost his cousin, Jimmy "Squirrel" O'Malley when some bitch in Queens had killed him during a home invasion attempt. O'Malley had been Skip's cousin on his Mom's side of the family. Skip, whose real name was Steven and Jimmy had been kids together although, Jimmy was several years older. He was Skip's hero.

Luckily, the invasion was a newsworthy event and foolishly, some dorky reporter had released the address.

Then on his father's side of the family, through his Aunt Doreen, his uncle, Doreen's husband had been set up and arrested by a scumbag cop. Al MacGruder, an up and coming member of the famed Westies was Skip's uncle. Skip didn't really care for Uncle Al, but, "Hey," he reasoned, "Family is family." Skip had recently discovered that the bitch in Queens was actually the scumbag cop's daughter. Well, Skip decided, maybe that bitch didn't deserve to live any longer.

On his way into the city Skip grew hungry. He saw the lights of a pizza place just ahead and pulled over.

Just as he pulled into the lot, most of the outer lights were extinguished. A neon sign reading "Closed." blinked on.

The back door was open and he peeked into the kitchen. An older woman was counting cash at a low table while a Hispanic looking man was mopping the floor. Apparently they really were closed.

"Probably some left-over pizza lying around too." Skip told himself, "And, what th' hell, some extra cash wouldn't hurt either."

Skip screwed a silencer onto the pistol tucked in his waistband.

As he stepped through the doorway he shot the man with the mop.

The man gasped as he fell to the floor, unable to even call out as Skip's bullet had found the back of his head

His gasp however and the loud thump as his body hit the floor alerted Rhonda Italo who quickly wheeled about to see what might be wrong. She too gasped when she saw Jose's fallen form, but said nothing else as a bullet entered her chest and threw her back against a counter.

Unconscious, but not dead, she fell to the floor as well.

Grabbing a plastic bag, Skip pushed all the cash into the bag. Some bills fell to the floor, but Skip thought that escaping unseen was far more important than a handful of fives tens and perhaps a twenty or two.

Just as he had thought, a single pie, still in its box lay upon the counter. Scooping that up as well, he left the building as quickly as possible.

Having just used the bathroom upstairs, minutes later Amy Italo walked into the kitchen.

Skip chuckled as he heard Amy's scream. He pulled into the sparse late night traffic.

While working in a restaurant kitchen in Rye, Skip had made an interesting discovery which he thought might be ready to bear him fruit.

While taking out the trash on a clear sky, but sweltering summer evening he saw a truck park at an adjacent building. Two things immediately caught his eye. It was a Con-Edison truck and the driver had left the windows open.

A cursory search revealed a Con-Ed jacket, cap and clipboard.

He had stashed them in his own trunk and held them until opportunity warranted their use.

Apparently, that day had arrived. Unable to duplicate a Con-Ed step van that quickly, he searched the lower Bronx for one to steal. It didn't matter if someone stumbled upon the vehicle he would be leaving behind, as it was also stolen. Ever careful, he always wore driving gloves and therefore, left no fingerprints.

Obviously, however, Con-Ed drivers in the Bronx were a lot more careful than they were in Westchester, since Skip could not find an open or even easily accessible truck.

He did, however find a later model light blue and white pickup truck.

While the owner did not leave his keys, the pickup, by being an older model, was easier to hotwire and steal.

The next day he had already decided to kill the bitch in broad daylight. Who knew how many people might be in the house after dark.

Killing everybody in the house was certainly doable, but also brought on a much greater risk. Getting oneself killed or incarcerated could put a real damper on getting revenge.

"Besides," he told himself, "a grenade in the funeral home might just achieve what I cannot do by myself."

Donning his Con-Ed jacket and cap he drove slowly passed the home in question. Sitting on the front porch was a trio of women. There was an older woman, one a bit younger and another still younger.

"Probably the middle one," he told himself, "but just to be sure, I'll kill all three."

With that in mind he drove around the block.

Theresa, her mother and daughter were all waiting to hear from Davy.

The previous night, having come down to help her mother close up the restaurant Amy had discovered Ronnie and Jose shot upon the floor. She had run to her mother first. Rhonda was still breathing and just barely awake. "Jose…." Rhonda rasped. Trying to point to the fallen dishwasher, but nothing else came out except for more labored breathing.

Running quickly to the foot of the stairs she called loudly, "Gerrie, come quick. Mom's shot."

Gerrie Contadina, who had been convalescing, quickly came running.

In the large kitchen she found Amy kneeling beside her mother and calling Nine-One-One. Pointing at the fallen dishwasher, Amy said, "I don't know about Jose, but Mom is just barely alive."

"You check on Jose." Gerrie ordered, "I have more experience with gunshot wounds."

Amy did as told and sobbed loudly as she realized Jose was dead. Jose had also been training to become Italo's assistant manager.

Rushing back to Gerrie and her mother, she knelt and held her mother's hand.

Italos was a police restaurant. It was owned by the widow of and mother of New York cops. The local precinct responded accordingly.

Nunzio and Davy were both working that night in a different precinct. It was the Four-Eight.

Amy had called Nunzio's cell and given him the bad news. Sergeant Marciano immediately dispatched both of them in their police car to the hospital where Rhonda was being taken.

And now, the next day, Theresa, Marie and Maria were sitting upon their front porch awaiting news from Davy about Rhonda.

Skip Layne had parked his pickup truck one block over and to the rear of the McGinty house.

Before exiting his vehicle he had screwed the silencer upon his pistol and tucked it in the back of his waistband. Picking up the clipboard he made for the house directly behind the McGinty residence. He paused for several minutes and pretended to be reading the electric meter. Nodding once he made a check on his clipboard's page. His jacket hung down and concealed his weapon.

Seeing no one actually watching him he strolled casually over to the set of low bushes surrounding the McGinty property and deftly straddled them to enter the yard.

Realizing that if he crept his way to the house someone might see him and call the cops, he once more strolled languidly to the McGinty's electrical box and paused to take his fake reading.

Noting the large rock with flowers and a bush on the side of the house, he decided that his escape route should be on the outer side of that rock. Casually, for the moment, however, he strolled toward the front of the house and the three women on the porch.

He started whistling so as not to startle them when he appeared. Skip didn't want any of them to get away. He figured he should shoot the oldest one last as she would not be as agile as the other two.

All three of them were still there although an odd feeling told him that something was slightly different.

He placed a broad smile upon his face as he stepped around the corner and said, "Good morning Ladies."

Dropping his clipboard he quickly reached behind for the pistol in his belt. The shock upon his face was quite blatant as the middle aged woman pulled a three fifty seven magnum out from under her apron and leveled it towards his chest.

As he attempted to pull his gun around, the silencer caught upon his wallet and her bullet, accompanied by a very loud bang, entered his chest. Still conscious as he fell to the ground, Skip realized exactly what had been amiss. The youngest woman and the one who had shot him had changed positions.

As death overcame him his trigger finger jerked twice, shooting into the ground beside him.

Kicking his gun away Theresa knelt beside him and felt the pulse at his neck.

"He's dead!" she said to no one in particular and then she began to cry.

The loud retort of a .357 magnum will certainly draw attention in a quiet neighborhood.

Several calls were made reporting the noise to the local precinct, Nick Evanopolis' precinct.

Sergeant Omar Brown immediately realized the address and yelled over to the precinct commander, Captain Evanopolis.

Nick was out the door before Brown even finished.

With Artie Melman as his driver, Nick proceeded directly to the McGinty house. Enroute he called first Mike at One Police Plaza and then Maeve to have her meet him at Theresa's.

When he got to Theresa's house two other vehicles including Omar's had beaten him there. The dead guy was beneath a plastic sheet with his gun and wallet in plastic evidence bags. Theresa's gun was in a separate evidence bag.

She, Marie and Maria were on the porch being interrogated by Detective Sergeant Marty Kassellmann. Theresa sat between her mother and daughter. Marie and Maria each had their arms around her, consoling her as she sobbed intermittently.

"I, I don't know." He heard Theresa say between sobs, "When he drove past, there was just something about him that didn't seem right. I can't put my finger on it. He was just so out of place."

She paused momentarily to organize her thoughts.

"I went into the house to get my gun. If you check your records you'll see that it's registered to me and not Mike."

She was surprising herself, as her narrative continued she found herself being more self-assured and less uncertain.

"When he pulled his gun out, I pulled mine from under my apron. I was hoping he would immediately drop his but he just kept bringing it up.

"This is my daughter and my mother here. Either one of them could have been injured or killed."

"Or both," Nick offered as he approached the porch, "Or probably all three of you Tere.

"I've already called Mike and Maeve Theresa. They're both on their way. Mike said he'd call Davy and Melly.

"Right now, you are my main concern. As soon as the detectives finish here we'll dispose of this piece of trash. For now, if you'd like we can conduct any further interviews in the house."

Before she could react, Theresa's cell phone rang. It was Davy.

He was fiercely concerned for his Mother's well-being, but he also had a bit of good news.

Ronnie Italo was going to recover. The lower lobe of her right lung had to be removed, but despite being weary from overworking, she was in very good shape. Of course, Amy would have to run the restaurant. When and if Ronnie would recover enough to resume her role was anybody's guess. At this short a notice even the doctors could not be sure.

"I'll be there in about an hour Mom." Davy told her.

"No Davy," Theresa told him, "Stay with Amy for now. She's gonna need you more than me.

"Nick just said that both Mike and Maeve are on their way.

"I have to say though; this is not something I could get used to."

CHAPTER 22
BUT, HOW

"Sonuva Bitch!" Mike exclaimed as he shut his phone. His hand was trembling and anger contorted his features into a red mask.

"What?" Theresa asked, unsure if she even wanted to know the answer. The fact that he was mad rather than hurt meant that it probably had nothing to do with either Davy or Melanie.

"What?" she repeated.

"It's about that scumbag that you shot last week. That was Roger Brimley, Chief of Detectives for the City. He had some very weird and quite explanatory news.

The guy's name was Steven Layne. His nickname was Skip. Here's the weird part though. Jimmy "Squirrel" O'Malley, the other guy you shot was his cousin."

Theresa gasped and placed her hand upon her cheek.

"Brimley thinks that this was probably a revenge killing attempt and not really a home invasion. His gun had a silencer on it. That makes this guy somewhat of a professional.

"But, there's more. Remember that story I told you of my rookie days when your Dad not only saved my life, but he caught that crooked cop Jimmy Casertas and that Westie hoodlum Al MacGruder. Well, Layne was MacGruder's nephew, although Brimley tells me there was no love lost between MacGruder and Layne."

Theresa was shaking her head.

"This is all so unbelievable Mike." She said wearily. "Where do these people come from?"

"There's more." Mike said somberly, "They took a ballistics test of Layne's gun. They're absolutely sure that Layne is the one who shot Amy's mother the night before. Cameras from a nearby computer repair store show him leaving the restaurant at just the time that Ronnie and her worker were shot. He was carrying a pizza box and a plastic bag. The camera showed him climbing into a stolen car which was abandoned where he stole the pickup truck which Nick's guys found one block over.

"When they searched the truck they found a plastic bag with almost five hundred dollars in cash.

Mixed in with the cash was a funny white powder that was later described as pizza flour."

"Let me guess," Theresa replied, with a look of wonderment on her face, "Ronnie had pizza flour on her hands when she was counting the night's receipts."

Mike nodded somberly.

Theresa and Ronnie sat together in Ronnie's hospital room. This was the first day Ronnie had been allowed to sit up in a chair. When Nurse Lois Conway found out that Rhonda was a friend of Theresa's, Ronnie became her number one patient.

With all the problems that New York was then experiencing Lois found herself being shifted about the City on a weekly basis.

Earlier Theresa had explained the sequence of events which had led to Ronnie and Jose being shot, and the killer's eventual demise at Theresa's hand.

Theresa was heartbroken. She felt entirely guilty for all that had befallen her son's future Mother-In-Law and Rhonda's employee, Jose. She pressed a check for one thousand dollars into Ronnie's hands. "For Jose's family." Theresa explained, "I am so sorry."

"It's from my mom, my daughters, my sons and my friend Maeve."

"Hey," Ronnie responded, "it isn't your fault, Dearie. These pigs made those decisions to hurt and kill people. They are responsible, and nobody else.

"Theresa, believe me, I know what you go through on a daily basis.

My husband was a cop. My son is a cop, just like yours. In fact those two stupidi idioti, both of our sons, do this every day and usually together.

"But, again, even though it's their decisions to be cops, it's still all on the bad guys."

"I know," Theresa replied wearily, "but you have to admit, it does keep us up at night."

Ronnie nodded sagely.

"A long time ago," Ronnie explained, "I decided to take out extra insurance on all my employees. There's that for Tomasa, Jose's wife. Plus, if she decides to sue the restaurant, I have insurance for that as well.

"Worse comes to worse, I also have a small emergency fund set aside. If she wants, Tomasa can have that too.

"She was here to see me earlier. She's a good woman."

Ronnie appeared to be tiring quickly. Theresa pressed the nurse's summoning button. Lois appeared almost immediately.

With emergency sources stretched throughout the city on every level, Lois had been transferred temporarily from Manhattan to the Bronx.

With an aide, Lois helped Ronnie back into bed. As Ronnie began to drift off to sleep, Theresa gave her a kiss on the cheek and said in Italian, "Sogni piacevoli Caro." Which meant pleasant dreams dear. Theresa had looked it up on line before leaving that morning.

As she was strolling out Theresa was pleasantly surprised to meet her son, Davy and Davy's fiancée, Amy walking in.

"Hey you two!" Theresa greeted, "How about a cup of coffee?"

Turning to Amy, Theresa said, "They just got your Mom to sleep. Apparently she's been up and down all night. She's so worried about Jose's family."

Amy laid her hand lightly upon Theresa's arm. "Thank you so much for stopping by to see her Mom. She really likes you." Theresa smiled her thanks.

"Is it true Mom?" Davy asked, "Was that guy you killed really the one who shot Amy's Mother and Jose?"

"Well," Theresa answered, "apparently there are a whole lot of coincidences involved with this case. Mike had a long talk with Chief of Detectives Brimley.

"It appears as if Skippy Layne was on a mission to kill me and anyone else who was with me."

Both Davy and Amy gasped when she said that.

"You know that first guy I had to kill, O'Malley, well Layne was his cousin."

"What?" Davy asked with a highly incredulous tone to his voice.

"Oh, there's more Sweetie. One of the people that your grandfather put away, back in the beginning of Mike's career was Layne's uncle. At the time Layne's uncle was planning, along with a dirty cop, to kill Mike and Blame it on Daddy, or vice-versa. Apparently their plans were quite fluid depending upon the circumstances. The true horror of this whole story, however, is on his trip down to murder me he stumbled upon Ronnie's place, shot up Ronnie and Jose and robbed them to boot."

"And yet," Amy wondered aloud, "With all this increased crime and mayhem, Lord Muckety Muck in City Hall feels as if defunding one of the best police departments in this country is his GOD given right."

Her brows were knit and her mouth was a tight line.

Davy slipped his arm around the woman he loved.

"It's okay Honey," he crooned softly, "its okay."

"Davy," she answered, just as softly, "I almost lost the two most important women in my life." Her words filled Theresa's heart with warmth.

CHAPTER 23
WHAT THE........

The air was thick with dust and bits of whatever the criminals had blown up. Both Nunzio and Gerrie had been wounded in the explosion. Gerrie, at least was able to help pull Nunzio to safety, so hopefully her wounds were minimal. Davy was concentrating on glints of light in the distance, down the alley and out, possibly in the street.

His gas mask was limiting his vision, but of course, the settling residue of the explosion had a lot to do with that as well.

To his right, Sergeant Marciano admitted to vision problems too.

Suddenly, to Davy's left, he heard a moan of pain immediately after hearing the crack of a rifle, off down the alley, and then out, in the open beyond.

Unknown to Davy, Marciano had seen a brief flash. He aimed for where he had seen it and pulled the trigger on his own automatic rifle.

As he did so he shouted "Duck" and then dropped behind his barricade. Hoping that the six or so men who were still with him had done so too, he was satisfied to hear a scream of pain from the thugs they were facing.

"Stay down." He cautioned, nervously, "These guys are a lot smarter than I first gave them credit for. They're smart enough to pause just long enough for us to stick our heads up again."

Five voices all called back, "Okay, or some other form of agreement. Kelly's voice was strained, obviously in pain as he returned, "No argument from me Sarge. I'm down for the count."

Marciano's intuition was rewarded moments later as the staccato of automatic fire assailed them from the opposite direction.

Just then, they heard even more automatic fire, but it sounded different, like that of a Heckler & Koch MP5 Submachine Gun, which was a 9mm police weapon. It came from a different direction too, near to but off to the side of their adversaries.

To most people there is no difference in the sounds of gunfire. However if one has used those weapons long enough, he or she can tell.

Several screams were heard and then a voice pleading for help. The sounds of weapons clattering to the ground were almost as loud.

Then a voice called out, "Hey, Viduch, you still in command? We got these guys. Come on down, but come carefully. There may be a guy or two in the alley. I'd spray it but I don't want to hit any of you."

Leaving Davy to care for Kelly, Marciano led his small group down the alley. While he was careful, fortunately there was no one there. Out in the street he came across Sergeant Jaime "Jimmy" Ramirez who was presently wrapping things up.

Eight of the thugs were dead and three were wounded. Two were still standing. Well, at present, they were kneeling with their hands cuffed behind them and then also cuffed to their bent legs.

"Hey," one of them whined, "My legs hurt."

"Too bad Jerk-off," Ramirez snapped angrily, I have three cops down, one of them a fatality. Jeez I wish they would bring back the death penalty."

The manacled thug chuckled. Marciano slugged him in the back of his head with the butt of his policeman's rifle.

"There's another reason for you to laugh, Jerk-off." Marciano snarled at the limp figure, "They'll probably bring me up on charges for that. You just helped to end my career as well. I sure hope His Majesty the Mayor can live without me."

"I didn't see anything." Ramirez remarked with a wry smile. "I'm guessing a piece of that rubble over there fell off of a building to clip the poor bastard."

"Hey, watch your language Sarge," Frankie Wheeler said from the side, "Cop-killing poor bastards have feelings too. Ain't that what some of those Northwest Prosecutors are sayin'?"

"More seriously," Marciano asked Ramirez, "whose dead Jim? Is it Italo?"

"No. Ramirez answered gravely, "It looks as if Italo will recover. He'll have another scar on his forehead, but thank GOD the shrapnel missed anything else.

"It was Maddox. He caught one in the throat and bled out before anyone could get to him. He took a couple in the arm and shoulder too, which certainly didn't help, but the throat shot is what did him in.

"I just wish we could bring some of these politicians up on accessory charges, or at the very least, conspiracy charges."

Several of the men around him voiced their approval.

One of the sentences that Ronnie Italo hated most was just spoken by her daughter's boyfriend, "He's okay, but, Nunzio was wounded Mom."

More recently, Davy had begun calling Ronnie Mom.

"He's in Bronx General Hospital, but that's just a formality. I'm bringing him home in a little while. Gerrie got injured too. She has to spend the night in the hospital.

"The doctor recommends that Nunzio should stay at your house so he doesn't have to climb any stairs, other than your front stoop."

"Please tell Amy that I'm okay, but Mom. I wish I had been hit instead of Nunz."

"A-a-hhh, I don' need nobody being hit." Rhonda wailed into the phone. "Amy don' need you getting' shot neither. I see you later. Davy, you be careful too, eh."

A small headache was forming between Theresa's eyes. It wasn't very painful, but it was still an irritation. She had come out onto the porch to wait for Mike's arrival home.

He was stopping at the doctor's to have the bandage on his forehead checked, for possible removal.

She laughed to herself as she regarded her thoughts. It might have been that he was stopping to have his head examined. Thinking about it, she laughed out loud.

She sat upon the deck chair which was nearest the door. At that point in the day it was more sheltered from the sun. Her usual iced tea was in her hand.

The telltale sound of Mike's engine down the street alerted her to the fact that he was almost home.

Coming down the street he was travelling slowly. It was his neighborhood and his neighbors and he wanted to keep them safe.

"He really should get a new vehicle," she told herself, "But as usual, money is tight." This was the SUV he had been driving when they had met and it was several years used back then. It had been a vehicle assigned to him as a Catholic counselor. He had bought it from the Church at a very reasonable price when he had resigned.

As he pulled up she noted that his bandage was still in place. It seemed a bit whiter so more than likely it had been changed.

She also noted the frown upon his face. A dozen different thoughts which all centered upon the same person entered her mind.

"Sonuva bitch!" she muttered to herself.

Once more she was worried for Davy's safety.

"Why," she asked herself, couldn't he become a computer repairman, or a dairy farmer?"

Amusement briefly allayed her worries as she imagined her son milking cows.

"No, of course not," Theresa scolded no one in particular, "He's a frickin' cop like his father and his grandfather."

Mike had parked and was walking up the driveway. Seeing the worried expression on his wife's face, he called out, "Davy's fine Theresa, not even a scratch."

"Then who, what," Theresa called back, "Is it Nick?"

"Nick's fine too." Mike replied as his foot reached the first step, "Nunzio and Gerrie were both injured, as well as a couple of other cops.

"Another cop named Arty Maddox was killed. I don't know him, but Davy seemed pretty upset about it.

"He has to drive Nunzio home, but apparently Gerrie has to stay overnight in the hospital and that has Nunzio all upset as well. Davy said as soon as he gets Nunzio home he'll call you. I only briefly talked to Davy. Sergeant Marciano filled me in on most of it. He's….."

"I Know who Marciano is Mike." Theresa thundered back at him, "I'm not a fucking idiot."

All of the lights were off except for the glow in the hallway. Gerrie Contadina's headache was monumental. She had tiny shrapnel wounds on her neck and cheek. She also had another bump on her head, although opposite to the one she had gotten weeks previously.

Through the window she saw lights in the building across the street. They cast an eerie luminescence upon the shadows in her room.

She did not have a roommate, although the possibility of getting one later in the night was very distinct.

Gerrie closed her eyes and tried to think of happier thoughts, but her mind always kept settling on Nunzio.

His wounds supposedly had been less than hers, but still she worried for him.

Like her, he always seemed to get it in the head.

"Hard headed guineas!" she thought silently and a small laugh escaped her lips.

She was surprised that the slight movement did not elicit any pain. "Apparently the meds have taken effect." She guessed.

A slight noise at the door brought a soft groan from her.

Apparently the threat of a roommate was about to be fulfilled.

Gerrie kept her eyes shut tightly anticipating the room light coming on. She was surprised when it did not. Forcing open her lids just a bit, she saw two figures standing at the foot of her bed. Knowing that a doctor or nurse would have needed the light, and quite sure that it was too late for visitors, Gerrie used her thumb to flick on the overhead light via the remote control in her hand.

She gasped as the faces of her sometimes partner, Davy Keith and Davy's girlfriend, Amy came into view.

"Davy, Amy," she called out weakly, "Hi....i...i!"

Amy was at Gerrie's side instantly. She took Gerrie's hand in her own and surprised Gerrie by kissing the wounded woman on her cheek.

"Don't try to speak Honey." Amy urged, "Nunzio's out like a light, so Davy thought we should be here with you. So did I."

"We were worried about our sister." Davy added. "You will be our sister, sometime in the future Ger, but right now you're more than that. You and I have been through a lot together Gerrie. We have fought like a brother and sister and we have commiserated as well.

"More importantly, we have shared enough life and death situations together. That makes us closer than any two siblings could ever be.

"I can't promise that I won't piss you off from time to time, but I'll still be your little brother as well."

Gerrie squeezed his proffered hand tightly. With their smiles seared into her brain she was finally able to fall asleep.

When morning came, and Gerrie awoke, Amy was still with her.

After explaining that Davy had gone to work, Amy said that she would stay with Gerrie until she was released, and then drive Gerrie home to the Italo family house.

Ronnie Italo had already told her daughter that the restaurant could do without Amy's services for that day.

Ronnie's wound and missing lung's lobe had not bothered her in several days. She wondered however, what kind of damage a long day without Amy might bring.

Two slugs to the middle of the chest and one to the shoulder, even though wearing body armor will certainly knock the wind out of one's sails.

That was the thought trapped in Davy Keith's mind as he sat propped against a brick wall trying to catch his breath. He did not know what had happened to him nor what had actually transpired, since those shots seemingly had come out of nowhere.

Fortunately, the shoulder shot was just a graze, with a minimum of blood.

He did not know where his helmet was but was certainly aware that it no longer sat upon his head.

"Hey Keith," the voice of Joel Ashburn came from beside him, "Whatta ya think your Grandfather woulda said about this?"

Davy strained to turn his head. There was pain, but it seemed to be manageable.

Ashburn was bleeding from a wound to his left bicep. Davy could also see where another slug had flattened out upon Joel's chest armor.

"S-so-nuva bitch musta sucked at the range, huh?" Ashburn quipped and then groaned from the pain it elicited.

Davy was still trying to catch his breath, between minor gasps of air.

"I wonder if this is what Nick felt like." He pondered, but naturally received no answer.

A short while later, Dr. Herb Silverman of Bronx General Hospital said to Sergeant Vito Marciano, as Ashburn and Keith lay beside each other in room twenty seven, "Ya know Sarge, we really don't need the business. The Covid keeps us pretty busy without the shot cops."

Silverman was holding up an x-ray before a fairly bright lamp.

"We can release Keith now if you like. He doesn't have any permanent damage, and he seems to be breathing evenly. I'd suggest light duty, but knowing how pressed you guys are for personnel right now, I know that light duty might just mean a smaller gun.

"Ashburn will have to stay a bit longer. That one bullet creased an artery. Thankfully it didn't do as much damage as it could have, but I'd like to keep an eye on him."

Joel Ashburn twirled his finger in a whoop-de-doo manner and closed his eyes for a nap.

"Crap," Davy rasped softly, "I wonder what my Mom is gonna say about this."

"Well, you're about to find out." Theresa's voice came from the door. "Sergeant Marciano and I have a working relationship. If not the first, I'm usually the second person to find out."

Davy looked to the sound of her voice.

She was smiling, quite lovingly, in fact.

"You're a cop Davy." She said, calmly, "I can only pray for you and hope any damage is minimal. I will always love my oldest son and try to be there for him.

"Mike is on his way Davy, but I did bring along some back-up."

At that she stepped aside to reveal a half smiling, half frowning Amy.

Just behind Amy was a grinning Gerrie Contadina in a wheelchair.

"Hey Keith," she called out, "We gotta stop meeting like this. Marciano's startin' to get a complex."

Marciano chuckled, in spite of himself.

Mike arrived minutes later. He was obviously out of breath and explained between gasps that he had not wanted to wait for the elevator.

"You'd think a hospital would have old-man friendly stairs." He said between gasps.

"Ah, but you aren't old, Sweetie." Theresa assured him while stoking his chin and cheek.

"I am now." He admitted wearily.

Gerrie had been discharged, along with Davy.

Maeve, who had driven Theresa, followed by Mike, formed a two car caravan to drive the not so far distance to the Northern area of the Bronx.

Maeve, Theresa and Gerrie rode in the first SUV while Mike, Amy and Davy rode in the second vehicle.

They had called ahead and even though they went directly to the Italo home, lunch from Italos Restaurant was waiting for them.

After a cursory hello to Mike, Theresa, Maeve, Davy and her daughter, Ronnie gushed over Gerrie and did whatever she could to make the startled young woman comfortable.

Noting Gerrie's puzzled expression, Rhonda touched Gerrie's belly and said, "Who knows how many grandchildren are gonna come outta here Darlin'."

Ronnie carelessly pointed a thumb in her daughter's direction and said, "I can't put all my money on that one. You're my backup Sweetie."

Softly fondling Gerrie's slightly damaged forehead, Ronnie added, "I ain't pushin', but we might wanna rethink the cop idea too."

She turned to Theresa and asked, "How do you do it Theres?"

"I got two, Nunzio an' this girl here. And I share that one with you." At that she indicated Davy with a nod of her head.

"I'm still trying to figure that one out, myself." Theresa assured Ronnie.

After thanking Ronnie for lunch and kissing Davy and Amy goodbye, Theresa and Maeve left. Maeve and Theresa supposedly went straight back to Queens. Mike would be dropping Ronnie off at her restaurant.

"Hopefully Amelia can take care of that crew." She told Mike, "I gotta business to run. The Bronx don't feed itself."

They were quite surprised when they got to Italos and both Maeve and Theresa were waiting there. As they pulled into the parking lot Mike explained that Theresa was addicted to Ronnie's Shrimp Fra Diavalo. "She might not admit it, but she thinks it's the best she's ever eaten." Mike assured the restaurant owner.

He and Ronnie were both totally surprised when they were confronted by the pair of women with an entirely different proposal.

"Maeve and I both waitressed in college to make ends meet." Theresa told Ronnie. "Since you're down a waitress, maybe we can fill in. I'm sure even together we won't be as good as Amy, but maybe we can pick up at least some of the slack."

"Yea," Maeve chimed in, "And we work cheap too. Tere tells me you make the best Shrimp Fra Diavalo in the Universe. I'd work for just one of those."

At that, Mike had nodded knowingly to Ronnie, while winking.

Ronnie smiled slyly. "Ah, we gotta negotiate. You can't expect me to just buckle like that. My counter offer is two Shrimps apiece, one in the dinner hour an' one each to take home."

With a shocked expression, Theresa said, "But that's......"

"Hey, no arguments." Ronnie replied, "Those are my terms. If you don't like it, there's the door."

Since they had not yet entered the restaurant, Ronnie pointed over at her eatery's entrance.

Mike smiled at the surprised expressions on Maeve and Theresa's faces.

Since the women would be at Italos all night he decided to go back to One Police Plaza. He hoped sincerely that no gun wielding thugs would be waiting for him along the way.

CHAPTER 24

THERE'S ALWAYS SOMETHING

"How'd it go?" Ron Beymon asked Mike McGinty as McGinty entered his office.

"Thank GOD for body armor." Mike returned gravely, "Without it he'd probably be dead. Hell, we both know that there would be a lot more dead cops."

Beymon nodded. He had a somber caste to his features.

Mike seemed to be out of breath. It did not go unnoticed by Beymon.

Sitting just a bit heavily in one of Beymon's chairs, Mike unfastened his own body armor and let it hang loosely from his frame.

"Well, it certainly was NOT a heart attack." Doctor Steve Vascaro said bluntly, emphasizing the word, not. "That doesn't rule a heart attack out, however, and not all that far down the line."

Steve Vascaro was the partner of Jim DiPrietro. They were the co-owners of Vascaro and DiPrietro, Heart Surgery.

Vascaro presently sat across from Lieutenant Michael McGinty of the NYPD. McGinty worked for one of Vascaro's other patients Assistant Police Chief Ron Beymon.

"It is not Covid - 19, either. Vascaro assured him, twirling a yellow pencil around his fingers in such a dexterous way that it impressed McGinty.

"I'd like to do a few more tests, but for now I'm inclined to say that it's angina, but not yet severe.

"From all you've told me about Davy and Melly and the rest of your friends and family, I'm reasonably sure that you are probably worrying too much about the people you love. Add to that all the crap that's plaguing our police right now and, well, I guess you can see where this is heading.

Pointing to the bandage on Mike's head, Dr. Vascaro added, "And that doesn't help either. Beymon told me how you got it."

Vascaro shook his head gently.

"Angina at your level is nothing to be exceedingly worried about, but neither can you ignore it.

"I'd suggest discussing this with your wife and Ron Beymon. I'm sure that you are aware that I will be sending Ron a full report.

"I assume you were made aware of the needs of the NYPD over patient confidentiality before you even came here."

"Yes Doctor, painfully aware." Mike answered, "Is this the end of my career then?"

"No, not at all." Vascaro assured him. "You'll have to go through counseling of course, something along psychotherapy lines, naturally. But, just from the discussions that you and I have had, I think you'll do just fine. Unless you prefer your own doctor, I and my partner, Jim DiPrietro, are available as well.

Pressing a button on the console before him, Vascaro said, "Eleanor, could you come in, and bring your book?"

Looking up at Mike, Vascaro said, "It isn't really a book, but it irritates her when I say that." His eyes were bright with laughter.

"So Doctor," Mike replied, with a twinkle in his own eyes, "Are you trying to encourage angina in your employee?"

The light faded from Vascaro's eyes. "Uh, that's a good point Mike." He said, "Maybe I should tone it down a bit."

When his assistant sat down beside Mike, Vascaro introduced them. She was Eleanor DiGuiseppe, a registered nurse practitioner.

"Mike just told me that by pulling that book joke all the time I might be causing you angina, Eleanor."

"Not angina," Eleanor replied, "But it certainly leaves a foul taste in my mouth."

Dinner had been fairly quiet. Theresa had seen that Mike was in a somewhat surly mood and had kept her end of the conversation to a minimum. Both Kenny and Maria chatted amicably and even Marie had added a snippet or two.

Mike however as Theresa had noticed had been somewhat somber. Reasoning that he would tell her when he was up to it, she kept quiet.

Since both Maria and Kenny had school work, Theresa helped her mother clean up after dinner. Mike went out onto the front porch to stay out of their way. He had taken a beer, and was nursing it slowly as he sat upon the chaise lounge.

Theresa appeared at the door. She was carrying two more bottles of beer. Sitting beside him she noted his half full bottle and set one of the new ones next to her chair. Drinking from the other, she warned herself silently, "It's gonna be a long night."

"Angina." Mike said softly but still loud enough that she could hear him.

"W-what?" she stammered, just as softly.

"I have angina. Beymon noticed something about me and he sent me to one of the police medical facilities. It was a heart place that he had been using. They said I don't have a specific heart problem, but my body is in pain because I've been anticipating all the stuff that's been happening to Davy and to an extent, Melly. They said anticipation of your pain regarding what might be happening to Dave or Mel, was a contributing factor as well.

"I'm sorry Tere. I'm supposed to be the strong one, and here I am, letting you down. I am just so sorry."

Standing and moving onto Mike's seat, Theresa lightly banged her hip against his.

"Scoot over." She ordered him, and settled comfortably against him. Placing her beer upon the floor she wrapped both arms around his shoulders and pulled herself tightly against his side.

Kissing his cheek wetly she said softly, "You shut up Michael McGinty. You are not now nor have you ever let me down. You can be infuriating at times, but you have always been there for me, for all of us.

"I can see why you're upset, what with all that's going on lately. But, Mikey Boy, you are the concrete foundation of our life together. With all the bad that we have experienced, Mike you have always been there for me, for all of us.

"GOD bless you Michael, and please, know that I am here for you as well, now and forever."

Kissing his cheek again, she murmured softly, "If it wouldn't set off the angina, Doctor Theresa has a treatment of her own. Do you think you're up for it, My Sweet?"

A day later, Theresa's mind was elsewhere. Mike had been talking about sports and she really wasn't interested. She had been speaking to Mike's daughter Melanie, earlier that day and questions about Melly's real Mom were now filtering back and forth in her mind.

Theresa had known Jennifer. She had met Jennifer several times when Mike and Jennifer had visited Theresa's parents, Ed and Marie.

They had not been best friends, but they had gotten along, and obviously liked each other.

They had sat, side by side on West Street and then again on Barclay Street during the entire 9/11 nightmare, handing out bottles of water and occasionally sandwiches. Together they agonized over that dire situation which was placing both of their husbands and Theresa's father in deadly crosshairs.

The difference back then was that Jennifer at least had some idea of where Mike might be. Theresa was totally in the dark about Dominic.

It was not for several days before they would find parts of his broken mangled body. She had gone to visit her father, Ed Flanagan, who had also been injured on Nine-Eleven in the hospital. Fortunately Ed had been carried to safety by none other than her present husband, Mike McGinty, after a portion of rubble had fallen on Ed.

Ed had been both Mike's inspiration for joining the NYPD and his mentor once Mike had actually become a cop.

On that particular day, while they had been partners, Ed had taken that day off to be with his family for brunch.

Mike had been in the area, not too far north and had witnessed the first plane hitting the first of the Tower targets.

Mike, Ed later told his daughter, had worked tirelessly to dig Ed from that rubble before any more could fall, and then carried Ed to safety.

With only a scraped scalp and a broken leg, Ed had been relatively unscathed compared to so many others, Firemen, Policemen and civilians alike.

The more severe damage to Ed's leg and lower spine had not been discovered until almost a year later.

It was when Theresa had visited her father in that Hospital, Saint Vincent's Catholic Medical Center, a few days later, that he had told her of the authorities finding Dominic's body. Ed had been sobbing as he related what had been told to him.

Even with all the terror and pain she was then feeling, it broke Theresa's heart to see her Dad in such terrible agony.

Dom was the son he had never had, and the thought of his three young grandchildren, now fatherless, caused Ed to suffer so fearfully.

And, even with all that Theresa was then going through, it would not be letting up for her in any way.

Now, Dominic's family had to be notified. One of his brothers, Jimmy had come up to New York to bring Theresa's and Dom's kids. Jimmy had stayed, and was still searching in the rubble for his brother. He had to be notified. Theresa shivered at the thought.

Dominic's brothers were both Philadelphia policemen, and might possibly be somewhat more understanding, but Dom was the youngest and telling his mother would be so very heartbreaking.

As stated, Jimmy Keith had brought Dom and Theresa's kids up and they were presently with Marie, Theresa's Mom. Jimmy, she was certain, was probably still down at the WTC searching for his brother.

A severe pain lanced through Theresa's mind. The kids, how was she going to tell the kids?

Thoughts which had previously passed through Theresa's mind kept re-introducing themselves, captured and re-captured by her incessant confusion.

Someone else would be watching the kids on this day, however. When notified of her husband's injuries, Marie Flanagan had told them she was on her way to the hospital.

Theresa resolved that she and not one of Dom's brothers must be the one to tell Alaina Keith. It might mean that Alaina would possibly resent her daughter-in-law for bringing her such terrible news. Then again, perhaps they might bond over the sad situation. Dom's kids were after all, Alaina's grandchildren.

Fortunately, if indeed any of that horrible situation could be deemed fortunate, Alaina and Theresa did bond. Alaina's love and caring was almost overwhelming.

All of the thoughts and memories of all the events which surrounded the destruction of the World Trade Center came rushing back into Theresa's mind, visibly shutting her down.

In the past year she had lost her father, been shot during an aborted bank robbery, and been forced to kill two home invaders.

The Trade Center, and its memories, seemingly was the one thing which might be pushing her over the edge.

Sensing a stiffening of his wife's already tense body, Mike paused and turned to her.

Immediately he drew her into his arms, and enveloped her protectively. He pressed his cheek against hers, trapping some of her glossy auburn hair between the two of them.

"OH, LORD, Theresa," he lamented, "What is it? What's wrong, My Love? How can I help you?"

Instinctively she folded herself into his embrace. Her tears rolled from her eyes and down both her cheeks and his.

As he pulled her even more tightly to him, his own tears mingled with hers. Although he was still unaware of what was bothering her, her pain was his pain.

She told him of her thoughts. It reminded him of all the people he had to tell when Jenna died from Cancer. He decided not to bring that up, reasoning that Theresa was the most vulnerable now. He decided that she must be made to feel that she was the center of his Universe at that very moment.

"Oh hell," he told himself, "she is my universe, isn't she?"

Apparently his embrace and soothing tone were a big help and she relaxed noticeably.

She seemed to be collecting her thoughts.

"Why" she asked, without actually looking at him, "Did you and Nick like hanging out with my Dad?"

"Well, to tell you the truth, I guess that was all on me. I was dreaming about being a cop, even at that young age. Nick, I suppose was there because of me."

"Didn't Nicky want to be a cop too?" Theresa asked.

"Not at first." Mike answered with a wry chuckle. "Back then, he was torn between becoming a fireman and a cowboy."

"A cowboy?" Theresa questioned, suddenly becoming more animate, "Are you kidding me?"

"Nope. He was a big fan of John Wayne and Randolph Scott, and all of those other TV Cowboys. He was especially a big admirer of Clint Eastwood.

"He took one of his mother's old blankets and made a poncho out of it, just like that one Eastwood character had. His Mom hit the roof when she found it."

Theresa was shaking her head. A broad smile had replaced her frown.

"Does he even remember any of that?" she asked.

"Oh yea. He still watches those old westerns and he still has that blanket. It's kind of worn and threadbare now. I think he air-sealed it in one of those clothing preservation bags. Maeve tried to talk him into getting rid of it just after they married, but he said no."

"She doesn't lose all that many arguments with him, I must admit." Theresa said.

"He sure won that one though." Mike replied with a loud guffaw.

"Why did he become a cop then?" she asked, "Did he follow you?"

"No," Mike admitted, "Actually he got out of the Navy several months before I left the Air Force. He had already graduated from the Police Academy when I got out.

"You've heard him. He still calls me rookie from time to time. Haven't you and Maeve ever discussed this?"

"No, my Darling, I can't say that we have. I'm certainly going to ask her about that blanket though."

"How did you ever meet Jennifer?" Theresa asked, "I know she was from New England someplace. Did you meet in the city?"

"No, I met her in Germany. She was an Air Force brat, as they used to call them. She was my Squadron Commander's daughter, and I have to say, he did not like me dating her.

"I must admit though, he was pretty fair-minded. There were any number of things he could have done to try and discourage me, but he did let us date.

"He lightened up a little when I started going to college in my spare time.

"The fact that I had talked her into going as well got me a few brownie points too.

"I was taking College English and a German History/Culture course. Both classes were taught by the same guy, but the culture course included field trips. And those field trips included gasthaus stops. Uh, those are bars.

"Old John, the professor was a big fan of World War Two. He was always talking about some place or another that he might want to write about. He was British.

"Little did I know that he was already a published author. When I got out, I was browsing through a big bookstore in Manhattan, and Bingo, there he was. There were at least ten or twelve books that he had written."

Mike pointed to a bookshelf on the opposite side of the parlor. "There are a few of them over there." he told her. "John Menlow. He's British. He served in Africa and was also present for D-Day."

"Oh yea, I read a couple of those. They're interesting and well written, but just a bit too dry for me." She replied.

"Now, back to Jennifer." Theresa urged.

"Well, as you already know, I went to Saint John's University here in Queens when I got back. I also signed up to become a cop. One day I got home from school and there she was, sitting on the sofa talking to my Mom. The rest, as they say, is history."

CHAPTER 25
WAS IT FATE OR CHANCE

"How did you of all people, get to partner up with my Dad?" Theresa asked with a wistful look in her eyes.

"Well, actually I was his partner twice. You obviously know about the events of 2001.

"But, when I was a brand new big eyed, smack, outta my diapers rookie, I was his partner as well. I'm sure he arranged that, but he would never admit it. Your 'Old Man' knew how to pull some strings.

"The only problem was, his beat at that time was Hell's Kitchen in Manhattan. Your Dad was an honest cop. Hell he was probably the most honest cop that ever came down the pike. As such, he had a big red target painted on his back.

"The Westies ran 'The Kitchen' back then and the very last thing they wanted in their midst was an honest cop. Little did I know that by my being his partner placed a target on my back too. My target was slightly different though. They wanted to eliminate Ed. Me; they wanted to turn to the dark side, as they said in that movie.

"The lynch pin to their whole scheme was a guy named Jim Casertas. Casertas however had different plans for me. He had decided to eliminate me completely.

This is the stuff that also led to freakin' Skip Layne's attack on you."

Mike paused as a look of alarm crossed his face. He muttered the word "Bastard......." And let his voice trail off.

"Jimmy Casertas was the proverbial bad cop." He continued with less enthusiasm.

"I think he grew up down on the lower east side of Manhattan, not far from where your granddad lived.

"He was already somewhat tainted, the kinda guy who shook down merchants and such.

"Well, old Jimmy got passed over for sergeant a couple of times and so unknown to us at that time, he got his promotion from the Irish Westies in 'The Kitchen'."

Mike rubbed his chin as he pondered his next words.

"I didn't know it at the time, but your Dad had already suspected Jimmy of being in bed with the Westies.

"He thought that Jimmy was getting a little too chummy with one Albert "Allie" MacGruder. They also called him Allie Mack or simply Mack. He, as you know was Layne's uncle.

MacGruder, as I said, was the uncle of Skip Layne.

Layne had been the second home invader that Theresa had been forced to kill. She shuddered as it all came back to her. Mike wrapped his arms around her trembling body. He kissed the top of her head and lifted up her beer to her lips.

She shook her head and pushed it away. Pulling his lips against hers she murmured, "No Sweetie, this is what I need."

When they pulled apart she urged him to continue.

"Well, together, and again, unknown to us, Casertas and MacGruder came up with a scheme to kill your Dad, plant the evidence on me and turn me into one of their pawns. It was just one of their ideas.

"An alternate thought was to kill me and blame it on your dad so he would go to prison for my murder.

"With either idea, though, either your Dad or I were going to die, or possibly even both of us.

"Remember when you guys took that trip to Cape Cod for whale watching?"

"Yea," Theresa answered nodding, "We had to cut the trip short for some police emergency back here in the city.

"Mom was really upset. He was on the phone and she turned to me and told me to never, ever marry a cop.

"Fat lotta good that did me. She should have also warned me about marrying two cops, and having a son for a cop."

"Well, Jimmy Casertas was my partner while your Dad was on vacation." Mike continued "I didn't really care for him. He was always trying to put something over on whomever we were dealing with.

"Unknown to me at that time, Casertas had mentioned to another cop that he wasn't so sure about patrolling with me. He said he was worried that my being so close to your Dad, the Westies might try to hurt me and him in the process.

"What he didn't know is that just like I mentioned earlier, your Dad did not trust him, although Ed never let on.

"Apparently part of Casertas' plan involved him knocking me out, which he did.

"I never expected it from a fellow cop. He then called in that I had disappeared, and that he was searching for me.

"I was tied up in an alley with MacGruder watching over me."

Mike thought for a moment and then started to chuckle.

"What's so damn funny?" Theresa demanded. She was anxious for the end of the story. Obviously her Dad and future husband had gotten out of the situation safely, but she saw no humor in any of this.

Mike could not stop smiling. "I was in an alley with Allie." He revealed, but quickly stopped smiling when his wife continued to frown.

She was sitting up on her chair, quite stiffly. Her arms were folded and wrapped, almost protectively about her shoulders. Her bare, shapely legs were crossed, but the foot which was hanging slightly was shaking, nervously.

The story was quite obviously upsetting her, as she realized all the implications.

He knelt upon the floor beside her. As he wrapped his arms around her she seemed to stiffen even more.

"Honey," he said softly, "its history. The Westies are pretty much gone and everyone in the story but the bad guys turned out okay, at least until those frickin' planes hit the Towers."

"That's just it, Mike. It's never really over. Sure, Dad's gone, but I have to worry about you, Davy and Melly every single day. It's never over."

He stood and went into the kitchen. He returned carrying a glass of ice tea with lemon and ice, and handed it to her. Theresa still sat stiffly, but had lowered her arms. She raised one of them to accept the tea.

"Thanks." She stated flatly. "Now, you were in the alley with Allie, if I remember correctly."

"You want me to continue?" he asked, slightly confused.

"Sure." She answered, casually flipping her hair back, "If I visualize it as two other guys, it isn't quite as bad.

"Well, anyway, I was out cold. MacGruder was guarding me and Casertas thought he was hiding to ambush Ed with my gun.

"Like I said, your Dad suspected Jimmy Casertas from the beginning and had been following him at a distance in an old Navy Pea jacket and a Yankees baseball cap.

"He later old me that he didn't know which was more difficult, seeing me unconscious, or having to wear that damn Yankees cap.

"So, as Casertas waited for Ed to show up, Ed snuck up behind him and hit him with a black jack of all things.

"After Casertas was cuffed and his legs were tied, your Dad woke him with a small vial of smelling salts. "Ed fired a shot in the general direction of me and MacGruder, but into the ground. He yelled, 'I see them Jimmy. Thanks for the tip.'

"Well, Allie Mac took off like a bat outta hell and Your Dad untied me and had me sniff some smelling salts. Together we lugged Jimmy down to the precinct house.

"Knowing that MacGruder suspected that he had been compromised by Jimmy made Jimmy sweat like he saw his own doom written on the wall.

"He rolled on MacGruder, and your Dad, with an entire squad picked Allie Mac up.

"MacGruder knew the score though. He kept his mouth shut. He ended up doing time upstate somewhere. I heard he got shanked over some argument with somebody.

"Jimmy however made a plea deal and was sent out west somewhere. Ed told me he died of a heart attack or something, just a few weeks before he was going to be released.

Theresa was watching him, noting the animation in his face as he told the story. He didn't seem at all fazed by memories of how close he had come to death. The entire story in Mike's mind seemed to be of how Ed Flanagan had saved the day.

He obviously did not see it from her point of view. He didn't see it as how close Theresa had come to losing two of the three most important men in her life. She thought for a moment and then placed Kenny and Davy into that equation as well.

Mike gazed at her longingly. His counselor mode went into full gear.

"I guess men are stupid, aren't they?" he offered, again kneeling beside her.

"All we see is the danger and action. We don't always allow for the pain it causes our loved ones, do we?"

She reached out and caressed his cheek gently.

"Well, Mikey Boy," she murmured softly, "I guess you're a work in progress. Aren't you?"

There had been a case of Covid-19 down at One Police Plaza, a young patrolman who had been involved in some riot prevention.

During an altercation he, John Epidaro, had been jostled from behind and had lost both his hospital mask and plastic face shield. Although he might have caught the disease elsewhere it was assumed that the riot incident had been the deciding factor. As a result, the Headquarters was in a limited lockdown of sorts.

Because of the Corona incident, Mike had returned to the sanitizing process which Kenny had set up months previously.

As he emerged from the basement, showered and sprayed, Theresa was clicking her cell phone off.

"Maeve?" he asked as he finished drying his hair.

Theresa nodded, and added, "Yea, Uncle Joey is acting up again.

"Nick refers to them as his cartoon show nightmare.

"Just this morning Maeve apologized to Nick for Joey and Aunt Carol's antics.

"Know what he said?"

Mike shrugged and Theresa continued, "He said, 'Where else would they be Honey? I may whine from time to time, but I know that this is the place for them. Besides, if you should apologize to anyone, I'd pick

Michelle. We may all have to deal with Joey, but Michelle is the one who bears the burden of both Aunt Carol and Joey as well.

"Maeve told me she fell in love with him all over again."

Theresa glanced at Mike's forehead. He had gotten to the point where he was able to change the bandage himself. He had removed it for the shower but had still not replaced the old one.

It was somewhat puckered. Several stitch marks and scars still covered the reddish area. It would obviously be permanent, but she noted with satisfaction that it did not really detract from his good looks.

His eyes were still deeply engaging, still clear and bright. His nose, while not completely straight, was also still somewhat attractive.

And of course, Mike's smile, when not deferred by one of his frowns, was as engagingly bright as ever.

I'm sorry you're stuck here so much." Mike apologized, shaking his head.

"Oh, it could be worse." Theresa admitted, smiling.

"I have my two Maries and bi-weekly calls to Melly when she isn't home. And of course, I call Maevy every day. You must see the phone bill."

Mike asked, "What do you and Maeve talk about each day?"

"Girl stuff!" Theresa replied.

"Enlighten me." Mike had urged, "In all my days upon this planet, I still don't know what 'Girl stuff', implies."

Theresa touched the side of her cheek with a tapping finger as she contemplated Mike's question. Her eyes flitted all about as a variety of thoughts filtered back and forth through her mind. She mentioned clothes and recipes and Rock bands until one thought in particular lit her eyes brightly and enticed a broad, knowing grin.

"Boys and sex!" she stated emphatically.

Mike grew a little nervous. He chuckled, but his chuckle was not particularly decisive.

"What th' hell does that mean?" he asked tentatively.

"Well," she continued brightly, "Just this morning we were comparing first times."

She noted the uneasiness of his expression.

"We both agreed that it had been nice, but no explosions or earth rumbling roars.

Maeve wouldn't tell me who her first was, but mine was Vinnie Companardo, from High School."

"T-the fireman?" Mike stammered.

"No," she answered, "His brother. You might not know him. He moved to California long ago. I think he's a lawyer or something. The fireman is called "DD".

"Uh, oh yea," Mike stated, more to cover his embarrassment, "I remember now, Derek David"

"How about you Lover Boy. Who was your first? Don't worry, I won't be jealous."

Mike thought for several moments. A fine reddish sheen of embarrassment crept up into his complexion.

"Uh, Jenna." He admitted soberly.

"You didn't have sex until you reached Germany?" Theresa stated as much as asked. Her eyes were wide and unblinking.

"Uh, n-no, ah, actually," Mike stammered just a bit, "Not until we were married."

He fumbled to place his hands in his pockets, missing the left one completely.

"I was kind of a dopey kid, I guess. I took everything the priests and nuns told us literally. I was a virgin until we were married. Jenna kept pushing, but I resisted. We almost broke up at one point because of it, but thankfully, she hung in there."

Theresa was incredulous. "Where the heck did you learn all the stuff you amaze me with all the time, then?"

"Uh, Jenna was a good teacher, and I guess, once we finally got involved, I was a pretty good student."

"She taught you all that oral stuff?" Theresa exclaimed unbelievingly.

"Well, no actually. I came up with that all on my own. She was just as surprised as you."

Theresa grabbed his left hand, the one that couldn't find his pocket.

"Are you hungry?" she demanded, "I mean would you mind if we postponed dinner for a while?"

He grabbed her hands, both of them and led her toward the stairs. Three things happened all at once. Kenny, who had obviously entered the house from the outer basement door, called up, "Hey, can I get some clean clothes?"

And, Marie and Maria who had been folding laundry upstairs began to descend the stairs together. Maria irritated her grandmother by grabbing the older woman's arm to steady her.

"I ain't a cripple yet." Marie protested heartily.

"Yea and it's my job to keep you that way." Maria answered saucily.

Seeing Mike and Theresa together, Marie said, Tere, you wanna start dinner now. I'm done foldin' clothes."

Mike pulled his wallet out and handed the entire thing to his mother-in-law.

"Here Mom," he said nervously, "Order from Alberto's Pizzeria, my treat. We have to go over some bills. We'll be down a little later. You guys go ahead and start without us."

As they walked quickly up the stairs, Marie was grinning.

She winked at their retreating backs.

"I'm not really in the mood for Pizza Grandma," Maria said, "I wonder if they would mind if I ordered a shrimp dinner."

"Go ahead and order whatever you want Sweetie." Marie encouraged, "They won't even know until they get the bill. They might not even know then, either."

The older woman chuckled and remembered similar situations in her own marriage. She sighed deeply, which went unnoticed by her granddaughter.

"Hey," Kenny's voice came from the basement, "Can I get some clean clothes or what

CHAPTER 26
EVEN THE PAIN MAY HELP

Because he had been moping for several days, Mike McGinty now sat before the desk of his immediate boss, NYPD Assistant Police Chief Ronald Beymon.

Mike had tried to keep his moods to himself, but the ever vigilant Beymon had noticed the change in Mike's demeanor from when first it had begun.

The date was September Third. The fact that it was indeed the ninth month of the year was in itself a hard clue.

"Coming up on the 11th." Beymon noted in a somewhat somber voice.

September 11th was a rather special date for all New Yorkers, but especially for cops, firemen and EMTs, not to mention the surviving family members and then the actual building survivors of Nine-Eleven.

Mike simply gazed back at Beymon, with a hollow look in his eyes. He fidgeted noticibly in his chair. Finally, he merely shrugged his massive shoulders.

"I have noticed your moodiness Mike." Beymon revealed with a shrug of his own. He attemted to maintain an even tone in his voice, although within he was unerved to see his friend and employee so worn down.

"My guess is that you're thinking about a lot of other people right now, eh Mike." Beymon continued, "I'm not adverse to you taking a little time off if you think you need it."

Mike shook his head slowly from side to side. His eyes were sad, but a small half-smile creased his face.

"Nah, Chief." He returned softly in a hollow tone.

"Personally, I kinda need work to keep me occupied from my thoughts. However, if you feel that I'm not contributing, then I understand if you don't want to pay me while I'm in these freakin' doldrums."

"No," Beymon answered wearidly, "I'd rather not do that."

Beymon held his chin in one hand. He seemed to be contemplating all that they had said.

"Do you want to go down to the new Trade Center?" he asked, earnestly.

"No!" Mike answered, a bit quickly and rather emphatically.

"I thought, maybe at lunchtime I'd go over to Stuyvesant High School." McGinty added.

"Not Barclay Street?" Beymon asked, his tone laced with puzzlement.

"Sometimes that entire period from the morning of the attacks right up until they finally pulled us off that damn site, all runs together in my mind." Mike revealed.

"Jenna was on Barclay near the end, But so much of her's and Theresa's time was spent on West street in front of the high school. They were doing pretty much that exact same thing, handing out water and occasionally sandwiches to the emergency personnel and other volunteers."

"Stuyvesant High School, eh?" Beymon surmised as well as asked.

Mike nodded. His head felt heavy with the memory.

"On West Street?" Beymon added, and reddened as he realized the sillyness of his statement.

Ignoring his boss's embarassment, Mike nodded once more.

Mike then added, "Well, they were on West Street, but there were others on Chambers Street and in and around the entire area.

"I personally didn't go there at first, but Jenna later told me about it. Theresa, in fact confirmed it just last night.

"Like you Chief, she's pretty good at reading my moods."

"Well, considering what time of the year it is, it's no big deal on my part Mike." Beymon remarked, offhandedly.

Without acknowledging Beymon's comment, Mike continued with, "Theresa told me that both she and Jenna were absolute wrecks. There was still no mention of Dominic and only one firemen was able to confirm that Theresa's Dad and I were still working.

"Jenna told me that same thing some days later after they had actually occured. She admitted to being concerned for any missing time between that report and what might still be going on.

"She said that at times her imagination would run away from her. She imagined that it must have been far worse for Theresa, and of course, it was.

"Unfortunately, Theresa's worst fears did become reality. Dom was dead and Ed was fairly badly injured."

At a loss for words, Beymon nodded sagely. He stood and walked the few steps around his desk. Gently, he laid his hand upon Mike's shoulder.

McGinty sighed, audibly and shook his head sadly.

Looking down, Beymon noted the red and wrinkling scars upon The side of Mike's forhead. That shotgun blast that had shattered the window could probably have done far more damage. Thankfully it had not.

Beymon noticed a tiny divot of missing eyebrow, not far from Mike's eye. It too was red withthin white wrinkles of damaged flesh.

"Thank GOD it did miss his eye." The Chief thought silently. "McGinty, you're a tough old bird."

"Thank Heaven you're one of the good guys." Beymon added quietly in his mind.

"Naturally, both Theresa and Jenna were equally worried about their kids." Mike thought aloud, his voice soft and contemplating.

"Melanie was with my Mom while Theresa's mother was watching her three kids after Dom's brother had brought them up here."

He shook his head once more. A wan smile crossed his lips as he mentioned, "It's hard, sometimes to realize that they're all grown into young men and women. Davy's a cop and Melly's a nurse. The other two'll soon be making their way in life as well.

"Poor Marie was worrying about everyone, Dom, Ed, Theresa and even Jenna and me.

Plus, as I said, Dom's brother Jimmy had brought Theresa's kids up from Philly and Marie was watching them. Jimmy then went off to look for Dom."

Abruptly changing the subject, Mike said, "Theresa mentioned that in the morning when the sun was bright and shining overhead they would move their chairs and water under the Tribeca pedestrian bridge over West Street. You know, Chief, between the High School and the College across the highway.

"Then, later on when the Sun ducked behind Stuyvesant in the afternoon it could become downright chilly. It makes me sad to think of their sacrifice, all the while, worried sick about their men."

"How typical of you McGinty." Beymon thought, again, silently to himself, "With all that you went through to worry so much for others. Ah, but is that not just another reason why I need you on my team?"

Standing totally erect, Chief Beymon pressed his clenched fists into the small of his back. He groaned slightly, but it was a groan of pleasure. His back crackled beneath the stiff pressure.

"How about if I drive you over there?" Beymon suggested as he returned to his seat.

"Ah, no Sir, but thank you." Mike replied. "Actually I have a change of plans.

"I thought I might knock off early, say around three thirty or so. I could walk on over there. It's only six or seven blocks. The walk will give me time to think."

Mike chuckled. "I could certainly use the exercise."

As three thirty approached, less than ten minutes away, Mike knocked on the Chief's door.

"I'm going now Sir." He informed Beymon.

"If you need to take tomorrow off as well, just let me know Mike."

Beymon paused, obviously a specific thought running through his mind. Beneath a wrinkled brow, his mouth was a tight line.

"Mike," he said somberly, "I sincerely hope the rest of your day is much better."

As he ambled over to the elevators, Mike wondered why there had been a gleam in Beymon's eye.

After McGinty's departure, Sergeant Bobby Conway called Beymon on the intercom.

"Chief of Patrol Meyer on line three Sir." Conway informed Beymon. "He says it's important Sir."

"Got some bad news Ron." Meyer said grimley.

VITO BELCASTRO

A chill ran down Beymon's back. He shuddered as he tried to imagine what the grave news might be.

"We lost the Commisioner, just about an hour ago. We think we might have him until the end of the month, but then after that, he's gone. We're not even sure about that. Chief Agrarian is checking it out now. When I know better I'll let you know.

"Deputy Commisioner Mulcahy is in charge for now, but his Honor is bringing in an outsider to replace Commisioner Gibson.

"Apparently the new guy is more in tune with the Mayor's way of thinking on how a police department should be run.

His name is Tom Freedon. He comes from a small city in Pennsylvania and he'll probably be here on Thursday."

"Do you think His Majesty knows the difference between a small city in the hinterland, and one of the largest police forces in the world?" Beymon asked drily. "He's still whining about the crooks he released due to Covid and the way they stabbed him in his back by returning to a life of crime."

"I'm seriously considering retiring Ron." Meyer aswered, "Do you want my job?"

It took Mike a little over three quarters of an hour to reach Stuyvesant High School. Technically, at that moment he was standing across West Street from the school's eastern face. The main entrance was on Chambers Street. He was actually standing on the corner of Chambers and West.

He had walked the six or seven blocks at a less leisurly pace than he had intended. He had planned to count the number of blocks as he walked them but had too much on his mind to really pay attention. Some blocks were longer than others, so he surmised that it really didn't make all that much difference.

The next time he was on a computer he decided he would bring up a map of the area.

He had thought perhaps that he would dwell on things other than Nine-Eleven, but as is often the case, things don't always go as planned.

As a kid he had been told that memories often fade over a period of time.

Certain of Mike's memories of September in the year Two Thousand

176

and one were as vivid as on the actual days they had occurred. Sometimes they ran together in his mind as a bloody, blurry vision, but often they were as graphic as ever.

However, in the last half hour, pushing the Trade Center from his mind led to even darker thoughts. The thoughts of Jenna's last days hammered at him with an intensity that made him cringe.

He found himself back, at her bedside. She was semi-concious as a myriad of drugs kept her pain free.

She was never awake for more than a few minutes at a time. The soothing lull of primarilly morphine kept pulling her back into sleep.

At one particular moment, however, although her complexion was quite pale and she obviously was wearing no make up, her eyes fluttered open with an odd brightness to them. When she saw him smile it lit up her own wan expression.

"Hi!" she rasped softly, "I love you."

"Hi. He returned, momentarilly at a loss for words from this sudden surprise.

Quickly recovering he said, "I love you too, My Sweet, more than you can imagine."

"Oh," she answered, with only the slightest falter, "I can imagine. It's written all over your face."

His brow broke out in a fine, sweaty sheen.

Jenna smiled even more broadly, but then immediately fell back asleep.

Mike had changed into civilian clothing before leaving the office. He did not want to attract any undue attention.

As he stepped out onto the corner of Chambers and West Streets he glanced first right then left, up and down the broad thoroughfare. It looked nothing like it had in the second week of September in Two Thousand and One.

The mobs of people and the tightly packed congregation of emergency vehicles was gone. The coating of dust and grit clinging everywhere to everything was no longer there either.

He stared across at the tall edifice which was Stuyvesant High School. It looked to be around fifteen or so stories high counting the circular rotunda on the top.

It was small, compared to the many skyscrapers which filled the Island of Manhattan, but for a secondary school, it was really quite large.

Mike glanced to his right and up at the somewhat long span of the Tribecca bridge.

It was a footbridge crossing West Street so that students would not have to fight the busy, busy traffic of the street beneath it. Mike had driven many times below it. He had passed under it so many times that he rarely noticed it anymore.

Looking toward the far end of the bridge, Mike sighed. He was sure that the bridge ended at the School's eastern entrance. He would have to fight the vehicular traffic of West Street to get to the other side. Yes, there were traffic lights, but as ever, that was no guarantee that cars and trucks would stop.

A rather cool breeze wafted in from the Hudson River. Even though at that point he could barely see the river, he imagined it's length and breadth. He remembered that magazine cover that separated the country into two distnctly different parts. There was New York City, and then there, across the Hudson, there was the rest of the USA.

Sucking in a lungful of relatively fresh air, he waited for the light to change and then proceeded across.

Even though he was in no mood to proceed quickly, he did just that. In no time he was standing on the opposite curb, breathing just a bit heavilly.

While crossing the street Mike had pulled the hospital type mask to his chin. Reaching the curb, and more people, he quickly pulled it back up over his mouth and nose.

Glancing before him he saw a set of stairs leading down from the bridge.

"Whoa," he said aloud with a slight chuckle in his tone, "way to be observant McGinty. You're getting' too old for your own damn good."

Walking out into the middle of the sidewalk he stood loosely with one hand in his jacket pocket. He caught sight of himself in the school's glass doorway facing West Street.

His reflection stared back at him from the glass. The eyes were judgemental beneath a worn New York Mets baseball cap.

He shook his head sadly and gazed down to the new World Trade

Center. It was a single tower which rose just a bit higher than the original Twin Towers.

His eyes drifted back to the building which loomed over him.

Where stairs from the school reached the sidewalk facing Chambers street sat what appeared to be a young woman. Her posture seemed familiar. She was too nicely dressed to be homeless.

Mike started towards her. As he did he unconciously adjusted his hospital mask. It wasn't police issue, however. It also sported the NY Mets logo. He had bought it in a dollar store, to match his cap. He had bought two, one for Nick Evanopolis.

The woman glanced up at him. She too wore a Mets logo mask, just a bit dangerous here in Yankee territory. Although the lower part of her face was covered her eyes lit up with a smile. She wore a Mets blue ski cap which also sported a Mets logo patch.

"Hi Dad!" she said just as he reached her. Her voice was warm with greeting.

"My Mom, Jennifer sent me to be with you. She thought you might need someone who cares about you to talk to."

"Beymon!" Mike thought silently as his eyes lit up and he reached for Melanie's hand, "Freakin' Beymon."

"Melly," he said aloud as he sat beside her on the step, "You are precisely the one person I needed to see. I love you so much Honey. Thank you for being here."

He enveloped her with both arms and pulled her tightly into his embrace.

Standing, they moved away from the stairs.

"How are you Daddy?" Melanie asked, a touch of concern in her tone.

"Oh, good and bad, Sweetie. I guess you should be used to my September moods by now."

As Mike said the word September, he glanced down at the spire of the new World Trade Center building. It did not go unoticed by his daughter.

"I never really get used to them Dad." Melanie replied, a longing, hollow tone to her voice.

"It hurts to see you in such pain Dad. I realize all that you went through back then, followed up a bit later by Mom's death.

"I kinda think that's what's filling your mind more than anything right now. Isn't it?"

Mike nodded, although he wasn't even aware that he was nodding.

The thought of what she had said caught up to his present thinking process moments later. He turned back to look at her. Her eyes were just a bit less clear than a few minutes previous. The stain of tears darkened the cloth across her cheeks.

"To tell you the truth, Melly it's just a bit more complicated than that. I'm constantly thinking about both of your Moms.

"Sometimes it gets to where I can't think about one of them without bringing the other one into the situation, whatever that may be.

"It may seem silly, but there are times when I feel like I'm cheating on either one with the other."

"And quite honestly, I suppose that's to be expected." came Theresa's voice from behind them.

To Mike's surprised expression, Theresa added, "You didn't think Ronny wasn't going to invite me to this party, now, did you?"

Although a soft pink ski-cap covered her auburn tresses and a matching pink hospital mask covered the lower portion of her face, the large, green and vibrant eyes between them were definitely Theresa's.

Mike's own eyes were smiling beneath curiously raised eyebrows.

"Actually," he replied as he reached for her arm, "I was wondering where you were. I know, ah, Ronny better than you think I do."

Melly had put on a pair of large sunglasses with a tortoiseshell frame. Behind the dark lenses her eyes flitted back and forth between her step-mother and her father. She had known Theresa would be in the neighborhood since Theresa had driven the two of them into the City. Her step-mother had gone just down on Warren Avenue to park in a garage.

Theresa had picked Melanie up in Nassau and made her way over to the Brooklyn Bridge to cross the East River.

"Is everything okay, Mom?" Melly asked.

"No Honey." Theresa answered, "It's a crazy mixed up world, and like you and your Dad, I'm just a tiny piece in the puzzle."

Mike stood, legs apart, hands tucked beneath his arms, listening to them.

Theresa stolled around twenty or so feet to the middle of the broad sidewalk.

Most comuters passing it by thought it to be the front of the High School, but the entrance was actually on Chambers Street, around the corner.

Theresa's hands were thrust deeply into her coat pockets. It was a gray fleece jacket which fell gently to her softly rounded hips. She wore faded blue jeans which clunge tightly to her shapely, muscular legs. They ended above pink woolen socks which were slightly darker than the pink of her cap.

Mike could see that her yard sneakers were covering her feet. She looked warm enough, but still a visible shiver ran the length of her body.

"It was right about here on that first stinkin' day." She thought aloud, as her brows drew down above her deeply reflective eyes.

Stepping back one pace, Theresa glanced from side to side as if to reassure her statement in her mind.

"The school authorities had brought out tables, desks and chairs. That first day we handed out only water. I don't know where the water came from. It was cool enough, but certainly not chilled.

"I was still wearing the clothes I had been wearing at breakfast."

She paused, sorting her thoughts. A sudden, wan smile became a frown.

"Of course, you idiot!" she berated herself, "Where would I have changed, and what inna hell would I have changed into?

"You know what Dopey," she chided, "You don't even remember what you were wearing, do you."

For a moment, Theresa shut herself down. After a deep breath she reopened her tightly shut eyes. They were moist.

Mike reached for her. She let him hug her, but kept her hands in her pockets and did not hug him back. Nor did she snuggle into his embrace. He left his hand loosely on her shoulder.

"My Mom was with me." Theresa continued, an extremely somber tone to her voice.

"She asked everyone who came up for water if they had seen Dom or my Dad. I was content to let her do the talking. I suppose I was still in shock, plus she had been a cop's wife much longer than I had."

Theresa paused. She seemed to be plunging her hands even more deeply into her pockets if that was at all possible.

Her brows were taut as she began again. "At one point, Jack Esposito came trudging up. He looked so much like Dominic. His clothes were gray and dusty and his face had black smudges all over it.

"I called him Dom. I reached out to him."

Her eyes flooded with tears and her voice had climbed an octave. Mike pulled her even more tightly into his embrace. Melanie wrapped her arms around the both of them. Both Mike and his daughter were also crying.

Theresa trembled, violently within Mike's grasp. He kissed the top of her head.

"Oh Mom," Melanie gasped, "I'm so very sorry."

"Oh. Look at me." Theresa sobbed as embarassment colored her face a bright pink, which shone almost as brightly as the pink garments upon her head.

"I'm supposed to be here for the two of you. I'm sorry."

"We are a family, Theresa Marie," Mike admonished gently, "We are here for each other, the three of us."

Withdrawing one hand from her pocket, Theresa caressed first Mike's and then Melly's cheeks. With her sleeve she blotted the tears from her eyes.

"Aren't I the lucky one." she said as a smile lit up those beautiful eyes.

Stepping several paces to her left, Theresa spread both arms and said, "I think this is where Jennifer was sitting. After that first day, we sat together, but initially we were just a bit apart.

"Yea, Jen was alone that first day. She had a chair, but not a desk or table. She kept the water beside her chair and just handed it up to ….whomever.

"We both spent a lot of time searching the faces of those we served.

"I'm guessing a bit at those thoughts regarding Jennifer. I was so preoccupied that I did not pay much attention to anyone else.

"Although, I remember that Mary Espinosa sat just a short way in front of and between us. I remember that specifically because I saw Mary when some Fire Captain came to tell her that her husband Tommy, also a fireman, had been killed.

"Tommy and Mary and their four kids lived around the corner from my parents. Dad had a weekly poker game and Tommy was a regular.

Mary used to make meatballs in sauce for them and send it over with Tommy. Tommy always called it gravy instead of sauce. Heh, imagine that."

Mike remembered those poker games and that sauce.

His memory was quickly brought back to the present as Theresa said, "Poor Mary immediately broke down and that Fire Captain had trouble holding her up.

"Your Mom Jennifer, Melly, quickly rushed to their side to support Mary. She wrapped her arms around that poor woman and spoke so soothingly to her.

"My Mom and I were sobbing too, and holding each other. Just then an EMT guy told us that they were taking Mary away and that they would take good care of her.

"Jennie sat back down. She began to cry too."

Theresa sighed and trembled gently as a flood of memories sifted through her mind.

"On around the third or fourth day," she continued "my mother was watching the kids. Apparently the first signs of Alaina's Alzheimers had become evident.

"Who knows, perhaps the shock of learning that your son is missing in that hell hole of Nine-Eleven brought it on."

Theresa's trembling became a very visible shudder.

"I guess you were with your Grandmother McGinty Melly."

Melanie nodded.

"I was an emotional wreck." Theresa admitted, I was asking everyone, no matter if they had just come from the site, or even if they had been sitting just feet away from me, if they had seen Dom. My guess is most, if not all of them did not even knew what Dom looked like.

"Of course, back then, almost everyone looked like everyone else, coated in all that refuse from the Towers.

"I referred to him in so many ways. I used his name, his description, the fact that he had a Phillies baseball cap, which I'm not even sure he was wearing.

"I don't think I may have mentioned this. If I did, I don't remember, but at one point, Jennifer could see what a wreck I was. She dragged her table, chair and whatever water she had over beside me. By then we also had sandwiches and she brought them too.

"Of course I was aware of how very worried she was about you then Mike, but she was the sweetest, most sympathetic woman on the entire planet. She also began asking people if they had seen Dom."

Theresa covered her eyes with one hand. Memories flooding back simply overcame her.

Mike stepped closer to her and pulled her even more tightly into his embrace. In the back of his mind he felt Jenna's embrace as well. His other arm was around his daughter.

"Sometime, I'm really not sure when, a cop named Jim Holman came to tell me that my Dad had been injured. He didn't mention that you, Mike, had carried him away from that building.

"I knew that you were his partner, but what with all that was going on it did not occur to me that you were the one who carried him to safety."

All of a sudden Mike tensed up quite visibly.

"What a jerk I am!" he uttered emphatically. "What a foolish, self-centered jerk."

Startled, both women stared up at him. Worry flickered in both sets of eyes.

Mike pulled them both in even more tightly. An immense sigh escaped his lips.

"Here I am whining about my problems and the two of you with your own terrible memories are trying to support me.

"What a baby I am."

Mike's expression was set.

Despite his anger with himself, they felt the love of his embrace.

"Yea," he muttered softly, "I lost a lot. Everybody did, but look what I've gained. Look what I have. Look at who loves me.

"Freakin' Beymon. This is why he's the Chief and I work for him.

"Therese, Melly, I love you two more than anything. Thank you both for being in my life.

"Thank you for loving me. Thank you for letting me love you.

"Lets go home." He announced enthusiastically. "We can pick up pizza at Albertos and take it home with us."

Theresa nudged him with her elbow. "Shrimp Francese too?"

It sounded like a question, but Mike knew better.

"Shrimp Francese." He agreed with a chuckle.

Together they strolled down West Street to Warren Street and Theresa's SUV.

"My car is fine over by One Police Plaza." Mike told them, "I'll ride home with you guys.

"Melly why don't you call Jim and see if he can join us?"

Back at One Police Plaza Ron Beymon was replacing his desk phone into it's cradle. He chuckled and warned himself not to feel too full of himself. He had just received a call from his subordinate, Michael McGinty.

McGinty had thanked Beymon and assured his boss that indeed, he, Mike would be in tomorrow morning.

CHAPTER 27
DAMN THOUGHTS AND MEMORIES

The morning was reasonably cool. Mike had gotten up earlier than he needed to.

Theresa had woken, sensing that her husband was missing from beside her. She heard him moving about in the bathroom, with running water and such.

She had known that this particular Friday would be affecting him, as it had for the last eighteen years.

It had affected her father in the exact same way, right up until he had died.

It had, in fact, affected every member of her family in a similar, if not exactly the same way.

It was September eleventh, the nineteenth anniversary of the multiple tragedies at the Pentagon, the World Trade Center, and a rural field out in Shanksville, Pennsylvania. Almost three thousand people had been lost in multiple attacks by the radical wing of the Muslim terrorists who had arrayed themselves against the Democracies of the free world. The casualty number grew in the ensuring years as Cancer stemming from the unsightly debris also took its toll.

There were also a handful of the terrorists who had lost their lives as well, but Ed Flanagan had always insisted that those lives did not then nor would they ever count.

Mike came out of the bathroom all showered and shaved. He was wearing an undershirt and his uniform trousers but had yet to don his outer shirt, socks and shoes.

"You look even more troubled than I thought you might." Theresa told him as she also rose.

"Well," he answered, "this day is bad enough, in and of itself, but I don't want to leave you alone."

"I'll be okay Mike." She answered, calmly, "I have Mom and Marie. I think Melly might be safe, at least physically. While she did not actually lose anyone on 9/11, there is that suspicion that her Mom eventually died from it.

"Even though she now has Jimmy, I'm sure thoughts of Buck will be plaguing her for much of the day, as well.

"I'm most worried about Davy though, Mike. He lost his Dad on this day, as you well know. I only hope it will not interfere with his thinking while working."

"I'm pretty sure that he'll be okay, Therese. He is his grandfather's progeny. As much as 9/11 bothered your Dad, he knew enough to keep it from interfering with his thoughts."

"Yes, Mike, But Daddy was no longer a cop. Davy is a cop and those thoughts might just possibly get in his way."

Mike picked his phone up from his side dresser. He punched in a single number and held the device to his ear.

After a single ring, he heard Davy's voice.

"You can't sleep either, huh? How's Mom?"

"I'll give her the phone in a minute. But, I know how frustrating this day is gonna be. Please don't let it interfere with your head as you go about the job today."

"Well, Dad, I have some relatively good news, depending upon your point of view. If you don't mind, I'd like to tell Mom first."

"Sure Buddy," Mike replied "here she is now."

"Davy…." Theresa said tentatively, "how are you Honey?"

"Well, Mom I have some rather good news. I hope this puts your mind at ease."

"W-what?" Theresa asked expectantly.

"I got a call from Chief Meyer last night. It was Chief Beymon's idea, but Meyer had arranged it.

"I'm going to be at the Trade Center site to help read the names of the various people who were lost at that site on that day. I'll be reading Dad's name as well as a few on either side of his alphabetically."

"Oh my GOD Davy," Theresa exclaimed excitedly, "that's wonderful. Uh, do you think that might be even tougher on you?"

"No Mom. I feel that it brings me even closer to him and Granddad and Mike as well."

"I'm giving the phone to Mike Dave. Tell him what you told me."

Davy explained all that he had told his mother. Mike sighed, and felt a just bit better about the day.

He told Davy that he would be in the vicinity, but several blocks away. Mike had been assigned to traffic control in and around One Police Plaza.

Davy promised to stop by and see him a bit later.

As Mike finally clicked off the phone Theresa was exiting the bathroom.

"Your son will be calling you from the Trade Center just before he's scheduled to appear. I told him that you would know it since it is in alphabetical order. I'm not sure how many Ks there are, but with almost three thousand names it could be quite a few.

Marie, Theresa and Maria sat side by side. They had decided to each watch the program for an hour at a time until the Ks were called. Instead, they, all three, sat raptly watching the entire program.

Occasionally one would go to the bathroom, or fix tea and/or coffee for herself and the others. A platter of un-eaten sandwiches covered in plastic wrap sat to one side.

Basically, however, they sat there for the entire procedure. From time to time tears would appear in their eyes as they listened for and heard the grief in all those voices. Marie, more than her daughter and granddaughter knew many of the first responder names already. When the Ks began however, the tears were more abundant. When they saw Davy, they cried like babies.

Davy was fairly calm, but then he came to his father's name, and his voice caught. A tear definitely formed and slid down his cheek. They all agreed that he looked so handsome in his NYPD uniform.

The dream was back, although, technically it had never really left. It was prevalent now, at this time every year in early September. It was always there on the nights of the Tenth and Eleventh. It did manifest itself from time to time throughout September and even throughout the rest of the year.

The worst part was Mike's inability to breathe.

Being enveloped by that rambling, light stealing cloud was especially bad as well.

As a young man he had met with a fortune telling gypsy at a local carnival, while stationed in Germany.

He did not believe in such things, but he was courting Jenna at the time, and it was her idea.

She was the daughter of his commanding officer, Major Thomas Robert Ryan. Major Ryan did not approve of Airman McGinty.

The gypsy had already given fortunes for several of his friends. They had all been tales of good fortune, of good health and monetary gain. He had been the last, and the gypsy had told him he would be dead by the age twenty five.

He had smiled at the notion, but Jenna had been quite upset.

Outside he had explained to her that since the old woman had spoken so glowingly of all the others' fortunes, she had needed to give at least one bad prophesy to make her seem legitimate.

He had laughed it off, much to Jennifer's chagrin.

In later years he would call her Jenna. Back then however, for those early years she was Jennifer.

Mike had gone back the next day to confront the old lady. He went alone because he did not want to embarrass the gypsy. Mike only wanted to get the truth as he saw it.

She had already forgotten the incident, just one in so many forecasts given in a single day.

She had then given him some good advice though. She had asked if he had ever suffered nightmares.

He admitted to a few, mostly when he was young, but nothing recurring.

"You must confront your fears, face to face." She had told him.

Her German accent was somewhat thick, but he had understood her perfectly.

Little had he known at that time that her advice would need to be heeded and long after his twenty fifth birthday.

As he woke up in a mild sweat from just such a dream, he stared his demons with their red beady eyes back into oblivion. The memories quickly receded and he began to breathe more evenly.

One unnerving thing did bother him after every such session, however.

Jenna had been twenty six, almost twenty seven when he had lost her to the cancer. He felt that it was close enough to age twenty five to mean something. A part of him had died that morning that he had lost her.

Mike stirred in his bed which was now damp with his sweat.

He spied Theresa sitting in the easy chair across the room, watching him keenly.

It had become her habit to watch him from another position in the room whenever one of his episodes encroached.

Once he was awake she would set the shower for him and place clean clothes beside the shower for his use. While he washed, she would change the bed, and prop his pillows.

A kiss and a hug always greeted Mike when he was ready to return to bed. Sometimes a cup of hot chocolate would be waiting too.

Tonight was such a night. He found the chocolate on his bed table.

"The cloud?" she asked him, fully knowing what his answer might be.

He nodded, and sipped the warm beverage. He detected a wee bit of the spirit, as his mother-in-law, Marie was wont to say.

His eyes perked brightly and he offered a salute to his wife with the cup.

"Aaah, I thought you might need it. From the little I observed, your mood appeared to be a bit more intense this time.

"Was Daddy with you?" she asked.

He nodded and took another sip of the spicy cocoa.

"They always seem to be the worst." Theresa observed with her narrowing eyes quite intense.

"This is just a guess, but was Jennifer present?"

He gazed back at her. She always seemed to amaze him with her keen ability to read right through him.

"How do you do that?" He asked worriedly. "Yes she was there. You might be surprised to know that Dominic was there, and Johnny Cello and a multitude of others, both cops and firemen.

Father Mychal Judge was there as well. In life, I only knew him in passing. He usually counseled firemen while later, after his death, I worked with cops. Once or twice our paths crossed when I was a patrol cop. We had met each other, but we were never really buddies. I doubt he even knew my name.

"Oddly, however, it was the same small chamber in which your Dad and I were briefly trapped, but all of those lost souls kept appearing, one after another. They didn't ask for anything, they only smiled and told me mentally to care for Ed.

"Only Jenna had something else to say. She told me to watch over Melly and to love you as I had loved her."

"Smart woman!" Theresa remarked, linking her arm in his and laying her head upon his shoulder.

As they sat she noticed a darkening blackish bruise on his upper thigh. It was red around its perimeter and it looked quite tender.

"What's this Michael?" she asked pointing to it.

Not wanting to hurt him, she refused to actually touch it.

"Ah, I knew that you would spy that sooner or later.

"That's a gift from His Honor, the mighty Police Defunder."

To the confused look upon her face, he explained, "We decided to call any wounds or bruises received from rioters as gifts from Mr. Mayor.

I got hit by a piece of masonry during crowd control down at One Police Plaza yesterday.

"Before the guy could do any more damage however, a patrolman, Joey Lovanno clubbed him with his nightstick. The guy went down like a sack of potatoes.

"Sadly, one of His Majesty's minions from City Hall witnessed it and now there's talk of bringing Joey up on charges.

"Theresa, what inna hell has happened to our city?"

Despite telling Theresa that he was okay, Mike had trouble getting back to sleep. Even though still awake, when he closed his eyes he could still see that terrible, giant rolling cloud as it raced up Manhattan's streets. At that point Mike had been on the northern side of what had formerly been the Trade Center. At least he could see the clear blue skies of Uptown until the cloud finally did envelope him. What of those poor folks east, west and south of the site. They had been enveloped just as quickly and the confluence of the East and Hudson rivers, and Upper New York Harbor, was one helluva restriction.

He wondered if departing ferries were able to sustain themselves as they fought their way toward Staten Island. He had seen photographs of the Towers collapsing from both Brooklyn and New Jersey. But, he had never seen the view from Richmond County, Staten Island.

Briefly, at around seven o'clock he had finally begun to doze off, but the rolling cloud was waiting for him.

It did not jump out of nowhere. It sat, calmly awaiting his departure from the state of his awareness. As he slowly sunk back into the world of Nine-Eleven, The cloud sat waiting, like an old friend with all the patience in the world.

His sleeping persona, which was suddenly surrounded by his wife, Jenna, Eddie Flanagan, Dominic Keith, and Johnny Cello reached out to touch the cloud. The cloud wrapped itself around his bare hand, but he could not feel it.

His dream persona had entered the netherworld dressed simply in the tee shirt, jockey shorts and his old sleeping shorts that Jenna had given him.

Within a short period of immeasurable time, however, he was dressed in the police uniform he had worn on that fateful day.

Once more he was caked in the grime and thick gray dust of the collapsing buildings. He looked around him. All the others, including Jenna were all cloaked in that dusty filth.

He shouted Jenna's name and reached for her. Their fingertips barely touched and suddenly they were each pulled in separate directions.

He was pulled north to Hell's Kitchen. She was pulled east to Wall Street. Ed, Dominic and Johnny just stood there complacent in whatever fate awaited them.

Dominic waved.

He was suddenly awake again. Theresa was bending over him. A warm washcloth was in her hand and she swabbed at his brow, gently. With light dexterity she just barely touched the bandaged portion of his brow. She noticed that the edge of the bandage closest to his nose had a drop of blood.

CHAPTER 28

WEST, THEN BARCLAY STREETS

Barclay Street had been thoroughly littered and dusted with trash and debris from the collapsing buildings.

When Jenna and Theresa had been sitting there little over a week later, however, it had been somewhat, although not completely, a bit more clean.

He suddenly realized, again, that when Jenna and Theresa and several other people had been handing out refreshments initially, it had been up a ways up on West Street, just beside that big high school.

Mike slapped the side of his head with that realization. The shudder from it made his healing head wound sting.

He could not remember the school's name, only that there was a foot bridge over the highway. All of a sudden it hit him. They had actually been at the High School, and of course the school was still there.

"Stuyvesant, Stuyvesant!" he told himself, "Stuyvesant!"

He recalled and then embraced the memory of Him, Theresa and Melly meeting there the previous week.

The school also had been engulfed by that heinous cloud. Most of, if not all of Southern Manhattan had.

Thoughts collided with each other, bringing bits and pieces of confusion.

Further down on West Street, closer by far to the Trade Center had been the Fire Department's emergency headquarters. Mychal Judge had left from there just a bit before he was killed in one of the towers. McGinty seemed to remember it being the North Tower. Most people regarded

Father Myke as being the first ground fatality on Nine-Eleven. Obviously the poor people on that first plane, and those folks at the impact site were the very first.

Even though the North Tower had been struck first, the South Tower collapsed first.

When the North Tower had fallen, the Fire Department's temporary headquarters had gone with it, killing Fire Chief Peter Ganci Jr.

Even knowing that the North Tower was about to fall, Ganci had refused to leave his men.

"Whatta guy!" Mike said to himself silently.

"You saw Jenna again, didn't you?" Theresa stated, as much as asked.

"Yea," he answered, "And your Dad and Dominic and Johnny Cello. We were all covered in that horrendous dust and grime again, but that's how it actually happened to Ed, Johnny and me. I don't really know about Dominic, since I never really encountered him on that day, but Ed, Johnny and I were all caked in that shit. But, in my dream, Jenna was also wrapped in that foul crap. That obviously never happened."

"Yes it did Michael. When those buildings fell, the cloud came roaring up West Street as well. We were all battered by it, me, Jennifer and my Mom too.

Feeling for him, Theresa shook, violently. She grabbed onto him, as much to calm herself as to make him feel better.

"I'm so sorry Mike." She told him with a weary rasp in her voice. "I wish I could relieve you of all this pain you're going through."

Even though he was once more sweaty, she pulled him tightly into her embrace. She pressed her cheek against his and told him that she loved him. She felt him sigh and relax, if only slightly.

His voice, tired, and in a slightly lower register, said, "The pain is not as bad as this cure is amazingly good. Thank you for being there for me Theresa. I love you too."

At the breakfast table Mike was staring blankly at the wall above the refrigerator. His coffee cup, still completely full, was cooling before him. He would blink from time to time, but his eyes remained focused on the wall.

Theresa was unsure if she wanted to interrupt his train of thought.

She was positive that he was still dwelling upon Nine-Eleven.

Somehow, caring for him was alleviating some of her pain. Plus, her kids, the three of them, were always there for her.

Mike seemed slightly pallid, but he wasn't shaking.

She seemed to recall watching him occasionally while he and her father had travelled back and forth between the two collapsed buildings and the small break area up on West Street. At the same time, she did not actually remember seeing either of them.

Most of her thoughts back then were naturally about Dominic. Part of her fervently prayed for his return. Perhaps he might be injured in a hospital, but still alive. Part of her however feared the very worst. Her mind had jumped back and forth between hope and the terrible possibility that he might be gone forever.

With every thought, whether hope or fear, her children always entered the grim equation.

Dom's brother Jimmy had brought the kids up and they had been with her mother, Marie, in Queens.

Jimmy had remained to help search for his brother. There were ranking police officials who thought it a bad idea, but no one had the heart to tell him.

Maria had balked at coming, however, because she and her cousin Kimmy, Jimmy's daughter, were almost like sisters. Kimberly was Jimmy's daughter from a previous marriage. Kimmy's mom, Eve had died in a car accident before September 11th.

Ed and Mike had only been to the High School once on Nine-Eleven, but for whatever reason she thought it happened more.

When they had taken that very brief break Ed had spoken to his daughter and Mike had spoken with his wife. Jimmy took his breaks elsewhere. Even then Jennifer had seemed just a bit unwell.

But, again, Theresa could only remember illusions of Ed and Mike. Too much had been hidden in darker recesses of her mind.

Neither man had hugged the women they were with. Both men were grimy and covered in dusty debris, if indeed they had been there at all.

For whatever reason, Theresa could not remember exactly when her father's injury had taken place. As with Mike, sometimes all the various things ran together in her mind.

Very few bodies were found among the rubble. Many body parts however were found. DNA supplied by family members was the main source of identification.

It took almost an entire month before a part of Dom had been identified.

The DNA had been supplied by his mother and his two brothers. Davy, just a child, insisted that his DNA should be added to the pool. At first Theresa had vehemently resisted. But eventually, she could no longer bring herself to deny the stalwart young boy.

It was right about then that she had begun to rely upon him.

Once ID had been made and several body parts had been identified as his, Dom's funeral was finally planned.

As each body part had been found and correctly identified, the funeral director had incinerated that particular item and later combined all of the ashes into a single receptacle. Because of Dominic's police service and the brave way he had died, the funeral home kept their costs to a very minimum.

It was a somber affair. Any number of Philadelphia relatives, friends and neighbors had assembled to honor him. Many other Philadelphia cops were in attendance. A small contingent from New York was there as well. Theresa's parents naturally came and several of her cousins. Papa Jay and Momma Ellie with both of their sons were also there.

Theresa's best friend Maeve Evans and her husband Nicky had come as well as Mike and Jennifer McGinty.

Jennifer was obviously already in the grip of the cancer that would eventually kill her.

Jennifer, like Mike, Nick and Maeve was a smoker. Being near all that toxic debris while handing out water could not have been good for her, either.

Plus, she worked on Wall Street which was in a close enough proximity to the fallen buildings to be considered a part of the danger zone.

As always the question of why she and Johnny Cello had gotten cancer but Mike and Ed had not reared itself.

At that point in time, it was yet another of dozens of theories, but the fact that Stuyvesant High School had been in the direct path of that terrible cloud of asbestos and so many other contaminants also came into play.

As said, Jenna, Theresa and all the other volunteers had also been consumed by that huge billowing mass. Later on, a Stuyvesant teacher and a prominent alumnus both came down with Cancer, possibly from those 9/11 conditions. Make that probably rather than possibly.

It had all been mentioned in 2019 during the House Judiciary Committee hearings in Washington.

Just after Jennifer's death, Maeve had given cigarettes up. Mike took a little longer, at least another twelve or so years. Nick had been the last to succumb, stopping just a month or so before Mike and Theresa's wedding.

Mike lifted his cup to his lips but did not sip it. Placing it back down, he rose and went out onto the front porch.

Theresa filled a small glass with ice and two shots of Jameson's whiskey.

When she found him seated on the top step she handed him the glass. He raised it in the direction of Manhattan and said, "Slainte!"

A single tear slid down his cheek and he swallowed both shots in one loud gulp,

"More?" Theresa asked.

"I think not," Mike returned, "I don't want to spend any more nights on Woody Kingsley's church steps."

Theresa smiled faintly, but her thoughts were drawn to Woody's and Erica's loss of their daughter Carole to Covid.

It was something which also gnawed upon Melly's heart whenever Melanie thought about poor Carole.

Even though Melanie was presently working for Dr. Feldstrup, she would volunteer in the Emergency room on either Saturday or Sunday, depending upon the workload. Since it was the 9/11 weekend, she had felt she should be closer to her parents.

While Mike and Theresa were sitting on the front porch, a car pulled up in front of the house. It was a taxi type service, and both of them were delighted when Melly emerged from the vehicle.

Mike rose and smiled, leaving his glass on his chair.

Theresa called out, "Melly What, no work today?"

"I thought my parents might need me more." Melly answered, "Besides, 9/11 affected me as well. I guess maybe I needed you."

"He's not doing all that well." Theresa answered Melly's question as they sat drinking iced tea at the kitchen table.

Mike was still on the front porch. He had switched to coffee, but was still staring, longingly in the direction of Manhattan.

"What about you?" Melanie asked, grasping her step-mothers hands, "You've got just as much to be upset at as he has."

"I mourn Dom quite often, Melly. Your father understands and encourages that, for which I am eternally grateful. He's always there when I need him. And, I don't even have to ask. He just seems to know when I'm feeling sad, even if I try to hide it.

"I was there at that horrendous site, but I was not where he was. He saw things that few people will even understand.

"Because of all that he and Daddy had already done, they could have quit at any time. They were policeman though. They chose not to leave.

"Sure there are bad cops. There are bad people in every walk of life, but there are also people, dedicated people, like our two fathers as well."

Theresa covered Melanie's hands with one of her own.

"Obviously, I can't see the future, Honey, but when you find that certain someone I can only hope that he is like your father."

Melly nodded slowly with a big smile on her face. Jim Cantner's face flashed through her mind.

While Melanie cleaned the few dishes that had been used Theresa went out onto the porch to check on her husband.

Mike was seated on the top step of the porch with his legs dangling down two steps to the bottom. He raised his feet to the top step when he heard the door.

His head lay upon his arms, crossed between his two knees.

"He-e-eey," Theresa called out as she stepped into the open air, "that's Maeve's spot."

He looked up at her. His face was flushed and he was breathing just a bit heavy.

"I've seen things Theresa," he began, "That I'll never be able to un-see. I was just now thinking of a poor woman who it seems had leapt from one of those higher floors.

"Your Dad saw it too. Know what he said to me? First off, he took the LORD's name in vain. Then he said that he could only hope that she passed out before she hit the ground.

"Then he made the sign of the Cross and kissed his thumb, but he left his thumb in place for what seemed like hours, even though they were probably only seconds.

The arms and legs we gathered with those poor firemen. We never knew if they were civilian's body parts or cops or firemen or whatever. I don't know about your Dad, but I never found a head, thank GOD."

Mike shuddered. He grasped both of his shoulders with his opposite hands but the shudders continued.

Theresa sat beside him and wrapped her arms about him. The shudders did not stop, but they did ease up slightly.

"This is why I never watch horror movies." He admitted. "How scary can zombies and werewolves be when compared to the inhumanity that man strikes himself with, continuously, throughout history.

"There may well be an Armageddon, but Mankind will inflict it upon itself long before the planet blows up."

His eyes filled with tears and he buried his face in Theresa's shoulder.

Her blouse became soaked as did the ends of the hair on the right side of her head.

She held him even more tightly. It seemed to help.

The sun peeked from behind a cloud. Its warmth splayed all over the two of them.

The shudders ended, but Mike still clung tightly to his wife.

"I love you Honey." He said hoarsely, "Thank you for being in my life."

She stood, holding onto his hand.

"It's getting a little cool out her Mike," she pointed out, "Let's you and I go in. The City will still be there tomorrow if Corona and the rioters don't destroy it."

"And the politicians." Mike added with a wry chuckle.

"Yes, Darling," Theresa echoed, "The politicians, GOD help us."

As they passed through the doorway, Mike looked back at Manhattan.

The corner of his house blocked his view, but still, in his mind he saw two very tall buildings, side by side. The upper floors belched fire and smoke.

Several people plunged from those uppermost floors. Among them, were Ed Flanagan, Johnny Cello, Dominic Keith and Mike's first wife, Jennifer. They were holding hands as they plummeted. They were all smiling and on one end, Jenna was waving.

Mike stifled a sob as he closed the door.

Nine Eleven dreams don't just disappear once the date has passed. They are ever present entities that ebb and flow with what ever might be affecting Mike McGinty at that particular moment.

Sometimes his mind purposefully reaches out for them, afraid to forget the past and the people no longer there that he had cared for.

Dispite the somewhat cathartic release of the afternoon on the corner of West Street and Chambers, Mike was again having trouble sleeping. He had slept a bit uneasily for an hour or so, as a variety of dreams and nightmares floated through his mind.

An amalgam of weeping women with bottles of water swirled in and out of visions of falling masonry and bloody uniformed bodies. Occasionaly the vision of a civilian body dropping from a great height interspersed itself with all the other horrors.

He awoke suddenly, in a sweat and breathing hard.

After a quick trip to the bathroom he was at his bedroom window staring at the calmness of a very early morning.

Not wishing to wake up Theresa, who was lying on her side, he left the bedroom. With faint echoes of her soft snores ringing in his ears he decided to go out onto his front porch. He had slippers on his feet and long pajama bottoms on his legs. He silently proposed to himself to get a leather jacket and his Mets cap from the coat closet and sit out on the front porch.

Mike's plans changed at the foot of the stairway when he saw Theresa's mother, Marie, sitting on the sofa staring at a blank TV screen.

"Works better if you use the remote." He quipped softly, hoping he had not startled her.

Apparently he had not as his silly joke only elicited a wry chuckle.

"I guess you can't sleep either, eh?" Marie murmured just loud enough for him to hear.

"You must have the September Grumbles too." She added.

"Grumbles?" he questioned, sitting down beside her.

"Yea, Grumbles Copper. You got a problem with that?"

Mike laid a gentle hand on his Mother-In-Law's arm.

"No Mom," he answered softly, "But why the Grumbles?"

"Well," she answered "I usually try to hide my September feelings from everyone else. For this family, Melanie included, 9/11 was a very destructive and hurtful time. I know that each one of us goes through painful memories both real and imagined.

"I assigned a silly name to my own experiences to try and keep my moods a bit more light when I'm around the rest of you."

"So you stay up late at night to suffer in silence, eh?"

The way he phrased it it was as much a statement as a question.

He was on her right side and she reached across with her left hand and placed it on his.

"Still the Catholic counselor, eh Mikey?" She acknowledged, "Some habits are hard to get rid of.

"But thank you for saving my Ed."

"Yea, but you must know that your Ed saved my fat butt too, Mom. Thank you for that. You raised him right."

They both chuckled together.

They were startled, however when Theresa's voice called out, "Hey, private party? Shall I make some coffee and tea?"

"I'll have tea." Her daughter Maria said. She was standing behind Theresa.

"Yea, me too." Melly echoed from a step further up.

Jim Cantner had midnight duty and had left earlier for the hospital.

The voice of Kenny, climbing the basement stairs yelled "Coffee for me Mom, thanks."

Mike stood, smiling, and extended his hand to his Mother-In-Law.

"C'mon Mom, let me help you up."

Reaching up to his forehead, Theresa said, "Let me change your bandage Mike. It's half off now."

The wound when exposed was gleaming from his sweat and was a bright, ugly red. It was accentuated by a bevy of thin red scratches which encircled the area not hidden by his hair.

Seating him at the kitchen table she cleaned it and dried it off. After the new bandage was applied he thanked her and went into the other room.

Mike sat, listlessly, watching the TV. He was watching but not really seeing the program.

The Mets were off on that day so he was watching another game.

When they played the National Anthem several players knelt. In disgust he rapidly changed the channel. Other than an angry snort, he made no sound. So far, to the best of his knowledge, only one Met had knelt during the Star Spangled Banner. He could of course be wrong about that, but he was willing to make allowances for his beloved Mets.

"Ah, ya big idiot." He chided himself mentally.

The ensuing silence was broken by Theresa, who asked, "The kneeling?"

"Yea," he answered disgustedly, "The freakin' kneeling."

"So, would you make it against the law then?" she asked further, a bit nervous for what he might say.

Mike thought for several moments.

"Nah!" he answered, with a grunt. "It's a form of free speech, and guaranteed by the Constitution. I swore to uphold those rights in the Air Force, and then again when I became a cop.

"Whether or not I like it, it's still the law of the land.

"Do you remember a guy named Tim Klineman?"

Theresa thought for a moment. Her eyes fluttered and she said, "Oh yes, Melly's friend from High School. Wasn't he a Marine in Afghanistan? He was killed over there as I recall."

"Yea," Mike replied, "That's the guy. "Right at this moment, that's the name that came into my mind, but it's only representative of so many others. I had friends who had died in the last months of Vietnam. There were oh so many in Vietnam, in World War Two, and Korea, not to mention Iraq and so many other places.

"When I see those very well paid Athletes kneeling during My National Anthem, I see all those dead Military guys, who died for everyone else's freedom, including those stupid ballplayers.

"Like that freakin jerk cop in Minnesota, I see them kneeling on the necks of our guys in war."

Just then the phone in Mike's pocket rang. Mike saw that it was Nick. For a moment he almost did not answer it. So many things were plaguing him at the moment. He wasn't sure if he were up for Nick's whining over having to stay at home.

On the third ring, he answered anyway, thinking maybe Nick's problems might take his mind off of his own.

"Nicky, you old so and so. What's up?"

"Guess what happens on Tuesday?" Nick asked in a sing-song voice.

"Well," Mike answered, "It can only be one thing with that silly tone. "You're goin' back to work, but why Tuesday? Why not Monday?"

"Ah, a couple o' doctors appointments, mostly paperwork to cover the Department's ass. It's worth it though.

"While I love being here with Maeve, her relatives are drivin' me nuts, especially freakin' Uncle Joey."

There were several seconds of silence and then Nick said, "I think this'll be more of a relief for Maeve though. One less baby to whine about how bad he has it. I have to admit, I can be a real pain in the butt sometimes.

"I bet there are moments when she regrets crowning that home invader with her best frying pan. They took it for evidence and never returned it."

"I would think," Mike retorted, "That's the last thing she wants back"

"How are you doin'?" Nick asked caringly, "These past few days could not have been very good for you."

"Oh, same old, same old." Mike answered, "There were the usual apparitions and bad memories. I got Theresa though, and she helps me over the more severe humps."

Several more minutes of conversation took place.

As he clicked off his phone, Mike started to laugh.

Knowing his tenuous state of mind, Theresa became worried.

"Honey, are you okay?" she asked, placing her hand upon his arm.

"Not really," he replied, "But I'm better than I was. I just remembered a couple of incidents that tie back into Jenna, things that she and I both laughed over several times. I choose to think of her laughing. She was always at her best then."

He stared down at the floor between his feet.

Theresa waited patiently, knowing he would tell her when he wanted to, if he wanted to.

After a sigh, he began.

Maria and Marie had just entered the room. Marie sat upon the sofa next to Theresa. Maria squatted on the floor next to her grandmother's legs.

Seeing that he had a full audience, after a sigh, he did begin.

"I was in the Air Force, and Sergeant McCormack, uh, Don McCormack was having a special meeting It was early in the morning and we were scheduled to work the four PM to Midnight shift.

"Well, McCormack was checking to see if we needed any equipment replaced. Winter was about to begin and the winters there were very wet and cold. So, ah, he was obviously checking for wet and cold weather gear.

"When he got to me, I didn't have a bunty cap. A bunty cap is like a knitted ski cap except that it has ear covers and a soft bill all of which fold up into the cap when they're not needed.

Naturally, being military issue its color was olive drab.

"So, anyway, McCormack told me to go down to base supply and get a new bunty cap, and to get a haircut while I was there since the barber was in the same building.

"So, when we all showed up for guard mount, McCormack asked to see my new bunty cap. I explained that they were currently out of them, due to arrive at the end of the week. I showed him a paper that they had given me stating just that.

He then asked me where my haircut was. I told him that, since I didn't have a bunty cap I was protecting my neck until the caps finally came in. He slapped the back of my head with his clipboard.

"He hit me pretty hard too."

Mike was smiling as he tried to pull the rest of the story together in his mind.

His audience waited patiently.

"Anyway," he began anew, "Here it is, in summer of the year two thousand.

"Me and Stevie Crenshaw are patrolling Fifth Avenue right at the Empire State. We're waiting at the light where Thirty Third Street comes out to Fifth Avenue and just as the light turns green in our favor this guy shoots out of Thirty Third, against his light.

"Did you see that?" Stevie exclaimed, as he spilled soda onto his pants.

"Yea I shot back as I turned on the light and hit the siren.

"The car stopped within two blocks. The curb was lined with other cars so he just double parked.

"When I got to the driver's window, lo and behold, it's Sergeant McCormack.

"Even before I asked for his license I said, 'Do you know why I stopped you Donald?"

"He thought for a minute and then said, "Well, I assumed because of the light back th......., Hey, how do you know my name?"

"I showed him my nametag and he immediately recognized me. Then, I imagine he remembered the pile cap incident, and started to frown. I think all sorts of things were running through his head. He started to hold up his license, I would guess imagining a very big ticket.

I said, "I don't need that Sergeant McCormack. I think I can let an old Air Force Buddy slide.

"Then I asked if he remembered Major Ryan, our squadron commander.

"When he said he did I told him that Ryan was now a full-bird colonel.

"How do you know that?" he asked.

"I married his daughter." I said and his jaw dropped."

Mike could barely finish his story. He had tears in his eyes and he was laughing hoarsely.

"Geez," his mother-in-law quipped, wryly "You tell stories like Ed did."

The night was lengthening. Darkness had set in and Midnight was not that far off. The air was clear, unlike those days after the Towers had fallen. McGinty sat once more upon the steps. He was wondering where his life might have led if things had been different.

"Shoulda, woulda coulda!" he told himself with just a touch of sadness.

He remembered a fireman named James Thomas "Cappy" Jorgensen from the old neighborhood. Jimmy Jorgensen had gotten the name Cappy when he had been named a Captain in the New York Fire Department, with a fire house in Brooklyn. His had been one of the first firehouses responding on Nine-Eleven, and Cappy had been one of the first responders to enter the South Tower.

Cappy's wife Genevieve nicknamed Genny was an employee of a company on the sixty fifth floor.

As Cappy was racing up the stairway to find his wife amid the rampant chaos, he met her coming from the other direction. She was guiding several of her co-workers. Having warned them not to use the elevators, Genny was herding them like a sheep dog to their safety. After a brief kiss, Genny continued to escort her friends to safety. Cappy continued on up into the doomed building. They saw each other once more when Cappy brought more of the building's tenants out into safety. Genny was moving the newly saved people out and away from the building. She was sending them to what she hoped was safety up on Broadway.

After one more, quick kiss, Cappy returned to the building. He was never heard from again. After about a week or so, body parts were found which later were determined to be Cappy's after DNA samples had been offered with his hair brush and toothbrush back in the firehouse.

Genny continued to raise their son and daughter. Kevin was a fireman like his dad. Mandy, Amanda, was a nurse, in Melly's hospital.

At first Mandy steered away from Melanie for two reasons. Having lost her dad in the same way that Dominic had gone, Mandy was just a bit jealous of Melly, whose father had survived.

The second reason was that Melly had lost her mother and Mandy feared that Melanie might be equally jealous of Mandy, whose mom had survived.

Whenever two people are in such close proximity, however, and if those two people do share like experiences, often they will come together.

Add to that the fact that both of them had been close friends of Carole Rutherford. In commiserating with each other over their loss of Carole, they had discovered a warm and lasting friendship.

CHAPTER 29

BAD NEWS AND GOOD NEWS

"Ah, thanks Chief." Mike called from Beymon's door the following day. That had taken place one week past.

"I'm certainly not perfect, but I do feel a bit better. Thanks for sending my two girls to cheer me up the other day."

"Come on in Mike." Beymon called out, "I have some news to share."

As Mike began to enter the office, a familiar voice behind him said, "Yea Tubby, quit blocking the door."

Quickly stepping to one side a very startled Mike McGinty moved to allow Police Commisioner Bob Gibson to enter.

"Uh, sorry Sir." Mike stammered, "I, ah didn't see you there."

Gibson patted Mike's shoulder and said, "Don't let it bother you Mike. I'm going around to certain people to say goodbye, and I followed you in."

To Mike's very shocked expression Gibson said, "Oh, I guess Ron hasn't had time to tell you yet. I submitted my resignation to Mayor D'Alorio.

"I'm tired of watching him dismantle this department. The Govenor's placing me in charge of an oversight committee to keep an eye on NYC's city government. It should be fun.

"When I told Mayor D'Alorio's this morning he was eating a muffin. I thought I was gonna have to perform the Heimlich Maneuver.

"Do you know how hard it is to apply the Heimlich while you're grinning from ear to ear?"

With a twinkle in his eye, Gibson wondered how the Mayor was going to react when the Governor announced that Gibson's new title would be Assistant Attorney General.

"At any rate, my coming here was two-fold. I came to say goodbye to the two of you, although I will stay in touch. My duties should bring me into the City fairly often.

"But, there is something else."

At that, Gibson reached into his pocket and pulled out several sets of Captain's bars.

Beymon immediately rose to his feet. His smile was beaming.

Mike stood there, mouth agape, unsure of what to do.

"This isn't my last official act, Mike," Gibson related, "But it's certainly one of my most favorite.

"And I don't want an argument Buddy. If anybody deserves them, you do."

"Thank you Sir." Mike replied, "I'm overwhelmed."

"And, the reason why a promotion to Captain is so much better than a promotion to sergeant is you don't have to cut off any insignia nor do you have to sew any new stripes on.

"Pretty cool, huh."

"If you don't mind Sir," Beymon interjected, "May I pin them on for him?"

"Sure Ron, not a problem. I would have liked to have made you full Chief Ron, but The Mayor has to approve that, and right now he isn't too fond of me or any of my favored subordinates. Plus, a full chief would definitely be moved somewhere else. I think that for now, the department needs you right here.

"Although, there's a good chance you might lose the Captain here. If that happens I apologize."

"Ah, we'll cross that bridge when we get to it." Beymon replied as he placed the second set of bars on Mike's collar.

Mike left them to their discussion and called Theresa to tell her both the good and bad news. She was, of course, thrilled at Mike's promotion, but sorry to see the Commisioner leave.

Garret Holmes stared through the windshield, watching the various vehicles ahead of them, cruising just a bit faster than the thirty mile an hour speed limit.

The Covid Pandemic had taken a sharp toll on policemen who would have enforced the speed laws. Defunding did not help either.

His driver, Captain Michael McGinty was driving his own, late model SUV. Although it had replaced the one that they had been shot at in, it was still a used vehicle.

Mike was humming along to the radio. A glance at McGinty told Garret that despite the humming, Mike's attention was firmly on the road ahead as well as the surroundings which they were riding through.

It was a nice part of town, Third Avenue on the Upper East Side of Manhattan. They were approaching 88th Street, whose eastern terminus was Carl Schurz Park. The park was the location of Gracie Mansion, the home of His Honor, the Mayor whom everyone at One Police Plaza referred to as The Great Defunder.

Back in the 1950s, there had been a wonderful song by a group called The Platters. It was called, The Great Pretender. As one may expect, in 1PP it was often heard, with the name Defunder substituted for Pretender. Any changing of the lyrics was in no way appreciative.

Garret breathed an inward sigh of relief when Captain McGinty steered straight through the intersection and continued to drive north.

Technically, Garret Holmes was an appointee of His Honor the Mayor, but there was no love lost between the two men. If there was any way in which the Mayor could have relieved himself of Holmes he would have. Garret however was the unicorn of modern politics, an honest man. Any excuse would have been held up to close scrutiny by the public, and torn apart by a clever and seemingly omnipotent press.

They were on their way to the second trial of Brian Eugene O'Dell, a member of the white supremacy group named Caucasian Infinity. Because of his refusal to initially reveal his identity he had then been referred to as John Doe. O'Dell had been planted within a BLM protest up in the Bronx where a policeman had been killed, allegedly by a missile thrown by O'Dell.

Ironically, the officer killed by Brian O'Dell was a black policeman, named Sergeant Kwame O'Dell.

Brian O'Dell having finally been revealed as a member of Caucasian Infinity, had released his attorney, Edward Winston Preston, a liberal political activist, and was now being represented by a lawyer hired by Caucasian Infinity.

They finally arrived at the Mario Merola Building, the name given to the Bronx County Courthouse in honor of Mario Merola, a former Councilman and Bronx District Attorney. The name had been changed in 1987 by then Mayor Ed Koch.

The building also served as Bronx Borough Hall. Because of so many official vehicles Mike was forced to park in a parking lot over one block away, closer to Yankee Stadium.

Holmes always referred to it as the NEW Yankee Stadium.

While he had to admit that Stadium amenities were more plentiful, and quite a bit nicer, "Nothing," he always told himself "would ever replace 'The House That Ruth Built'."

Nodding towards the Stadium, Garret said, "Uh, sorry Buddy. I know how this must hurt an old Mets fan like you."

"Actually," Mike replied, leaning closer and speaking in a whisper, "After the Mets, I like the Yankees too. They're my favorite American League team."

With a confused expression on his face, Holmes asked "Why the whispering?"

"Oh, I don't know where old Ed Flanagan might show up. It'd be just like him to haunt Yankee Stadium. My money's on Citi Field, though."

As they walked toward the Courthouse Garret Holmes laughed into the hospital mask he had adjusted before dismounting the SUV.

Just then, Mike was startled as his step-son, David Keith walked up beside them.

"Hi!" Davy called out, seemingly appearing out of nowhere.

He was clutching two cups of what appeared to be coffee. Offering them, he said, "I already had mine. My fellow patrolmen, er, people, are already in the building. Trial begins in another fifteen minutes."

Twenty minutes later they were standing side by side as the new Judge was being announced.

Judge Lennox had in fact, recused himself. He was an African-American Judge. While he knew that he would be totally fair he did not want to give the defense any ammunition for an appeal motion based on the possibility that he might have been unfair because of his own skin color.

The new Judge had been borrowed from Manhattan. He was neither black, nor Jewish. He was in fact, a 'Good Ole Boy' from Chattanooga Tennessee.

He was Judge Charles Robert "Charlie" Patton.

Willis James "Will" Culbertson, Patton's bailiff called the Court to order. Culbertson was also white, something the former Justice, Lennox, had included in his plan as well.

In a soft Tennessee accent, Patton spoke directly to the younger defendant, and included O'Dell's attorney at the same time. "Mister O'Dell, are you and your attorney ready to begin?"

The Judge seemed to be very accommodating, but Roger Aimsley, O'Dell's lawyer knew better. While not overtly pro-minority, Patton, like Lennox was a strict, by the book Jurist.

Unfortunately for Mr. O'Dell, Judge Patton was not a prejudiced man.

"We are, Your Honor." Aimsley answered, "Mr. O'Dell pleads not guilty."

The trial proceeded quickly. Everything seemed to be going in favor of the Prosecution. Along with forensic evidence, several witnesses had come forward for the Prosecution. It was clear to Lead Prosecutor Erica Lomonico that their previous resistance had been because they had thought O'Dell was one of them. Knowing him now to be a supremacist had loosened their tongues.

"What the hell," Erica reasoned, "you take what you can get. Eh?"

After a brief consultation with his client Aimsley asked to approach the Bench. Aimsley and O'Dell accepted a plea, which was yet to be determined, and that portion of the trial ended.

Garret Holmes informed Mike that he would be riding back with Judge Patton's contingent, in order to discuss mutually important business.

Mike offered a ride to Davy and his crew, which was heartily accepted.

Theresa was at work at Queen's Mercy Hospital, not too far from her home. She had gotten into the habit of walking to and from work, except when Mike, Maeve or one of the kids would pick her up or drop her off.

With the extra exercise, her legs and lungs had gotten stronger. Always a rather hale and hearty woman anyway, she delighted in the new and exciting strength coursing throughout her.

Her present assignment required some of that new-found strength and flexibility. With the sudden absence of some of the aides because of the Covid, as low girl in seniority Theresa found herself assigned to many of the aides' tasks.

She did not complain, however. Knowing that she was last on the famed totem pole, and feeling lucky to have a job at all, she was content.

She was especially aware that hearing nurses complain was not a prescribed mode for a patient's healing.

Mrs. Guthrie, one of Theresa's more vocal patients, was presently complaining about the way Theresa was treating her.

"Now, now Betty, we're almost done. Are you still in pain?" Theresa asked, almost fearful for Mrs. Guthrie's answer.

"Well, the weary woman answered, somewhat tentatively, "Not really as much as before. I do feel better Theresa. I suppose I should be thanking you. Sorry for my complaining."

"Hey," Theresa replied with a smile, "you complain all you want. Listening to you is part of my job."

Pulling the covers up to Betty's neck, Theresa had to stop herself from kissing the ailing woman on her forehead. She snickered inwardly as she told herself, "Not one of your kids Terri Darlin'."

As Theresa reached the Nurses' station, Missy DuBois showed up unexpectedly.

Despite her face being covered, she wore a nametag which read, MISSY DUBOIS.

"Hey Sweetie," Missy said with a smile, "Cara says it's time for your break. Want some coffee?"

CHAPTER 30

MORE CHANGES

The very bright sunlight of a new spring day was filling the office of Acting Police Commissioner James Michael "Jimbo" Mulcahy. Dust motes danced all about the office. He had been a Deputy Commissioner under his predecessor, Bob Gibson, who was now attached to the Governor's office in Albany.

The irony was however, that Gibson was not in Albany. He had been assigned as a watchdog to monitor Police matters in New York City by the Governor.

Mayor Ron D'Alorio's newly appointed commissioner; Burton Thomas Freedon had yet to take office. Apparently he was tying up some loose ends in the town he was leaving, Squiresville, Pennsylvania. It was a small town in western Pennsylvania. Considering the size of Squiresville, Pennsylvania almost everyone in the City wondered what exactly qualified Tom Freedon to run a police department the size of New York's.

Most, if not all of New York's precincts were each, in and of themselves larger than Squiresville.

Apparently, as Jimbo Mulcahy had been told, the new commissioner preferred Tom rather than Burt or Burton.

"Speaking of names, "Mulcahy told himself silently, "I should probably use James or Jim rather than Jimbo."

Former Commissioner Bob Gibson didn't mind it, but who knew how the new guy might react.

Sandra Louise "Sandi" Halstadt was Mulcahy's Assistant. She rang him startling him from his thoughts.

"Yes Sandi?" he asked, depressing the button on his desk. He was still in his regular office, as he knew he would be moving back anyway when Freedon took over.

"Sir," Sandi answered, "Chief Beymon and Captain McGinty are here for their appointment."

"Okay Sandi," Mulcahy answered, "Send them in. Oh, and you need not come in. This is somewhat unofficial."

When Beymon and McGinty heard that they looked at each other a bit uneasily.

They entered Mulcahy's office somewhat tentatively.

"Uh, you wanted to see us Commissioner?" Beymon asked.

"Ah, yes Chief." Mulcahy answered, "Please, sit down.

"Technically Ron, I only need to see Captain McGinty, but I felt that your presence would be a big plus.

"As you both know, I am only temporarily in this position. His Honor, the Mayor has appointed a new commissioner from out of state.

You might know, what with all the scuttlebutt that his name is Burton Freedon. For whatever reason, he prefers Tom to Burton. Of course, the three of us will call him Commissioner or Sir.

"At any rate, I'm a bit worried that he might not approve McGintys promotion to Captain.

"I spoke yesterday to Tim Rogers over at the Detective's Endowment Association. He said he would like to agree with me but he has to check it out first.

"The crux of the situation is, if we can get you into that Union, they might be able to protect your promotion.

"In view of the work you guys did on that case involving that actress robbing those older people, you would probably qualify as a detective. You already have the gold shield. Whatta you say?"

Staring back at Commisioner Mulcahy Beymon tapped his gold shield with a slender forefinger. Mulcahy was looking at his notes.

"Well, Sir," Mike began, "First and foremost, thanks for your concern. I'm really quite flattered.

"But, not to seem ungrateful, and while I really appreciate the extra pay, I don't think I'm quite ready to butt heads with a new Commissioner."

Mulcahy nodded, knowingly. In the back of his mind he realized the sagacity of McGinty's words.

"I'm sure you already know, Sir about my wife returning the Key to the City. The mayor is not one of my biggest fans as it is. I'd rather not give him any more fuel just yet."

"Not to bring up Nine-Eleven," Mulcahy replied, "But you do have that ace in the hole."

"Ah, yes Sir, but that's not an ace I'd like to pull out at any given time. I did what I did because that is what I knew I should do. Should I use it to get something; I feel that what I did might then be minimized.

"Whether I'm right or wrong, Sir, it's just how I feel.

Mulcahy smiled a gentle smile. He was shaking his head yes.

"I do know what you mean, Mike, and I guess I do understand your reasoning."

In the back of his mind Mulcahy had to admit, he had just been thoroughly chastised. He also admitted to himself that he probably deserved it.

"Well Gentlemen," the Commissioner said as he rose, "I guess that about covers everything. Thanks for coming.

"Sometime in the near future you will be meeting our new boss.

"Also, sometime in the near future I imagine Assistant Attorney General Bob Gibson will be talking to us."

"Assistant Attorney Gen........." Chief Beymon began, but was cut off.

"Uh, yea," Commissioner Mulcahy interrupted, "but you didn't hear that from me."

The day had seemed longer than it really was. Theresa was working twelve hour shifts. She had just been starting the eleventh hour when Doctor Mieliastro, the Emergency Room attending had noticed just how tired she seemed to be. She was presently in the cafeteria drinking coffee and resting her head upon her fist.

Having nodded asleep, Theresa awoke suddenly to see Dr. Mieliastro standing over her. The combination of sleeping, however briefly, and seeing her supervisor startled her.

"Mrs. McGinty," Mieliastro said somberly, "Please, come with me."

"Oh, I'm so sorry Doctor." She apologized, "I didn't mean to take advantage. Please forgive me."

"Uh, oh no, Mrs. McGinty, that's not it. Uh, please….uh, your son was just admitted. Please come with me." His voice had become softer, more caring.

Theresa's face drained of color. She was almost as pale as a fresh snowfall. Standing abruptly she became slightly dizzy. Then, forgetting to reapply her surgical mask she lurched forward banging her knee on an adjacent chair.

"D-D-Davy?" she stammered softly, but still with a trace of panic in her voice.

"Uh, no," Dr. Mieliastro replied, "They said his name was Kenneth. I didn't even know he was your son until another nurse told me. What with the last name difference. Then, it hit me like a lightning bolt. My cousin Kathy was your sister-in-law when you were married to Dominic."

Mieliastro slapped his head to illustrate his foolish feeling.

"But, I assure you, Dr. Ramos told me that uh, Kenneth is going to be alright."

"What, ah, did he fall?" Theresa asked as she shuffled toward the exit.

"Ah, no, Mrs. McGinty, it was a, ah, gunshot wound, but Dr. Ramos assured me he will be okay. I assume it was only a flesh wound."

Theresa gasped, but kept going. She was now moving a bit quicker, and Mieliastro, though several years younger, struggled to keep up with her.

Kenny was alert, if somewhat fuzzy from the pain medicine they had administered. His eyes flickered, defensively when he saw his mother.

"Now, Mom, I can explain." He tried to justify.

Her eyes went immediately to the large bandage on his right calf. It had a trace of blood escaping from the edge of the bandage.

"Kenny!" she rasped, touching the thin trail of blood gingerly. Unconsciously she wiped her hand upon her scrubs.

Captain Nick Evanopolis appeared suddenly at the doorway. His trained eyes took in the entire situation immediately. Mentally, he thanked Providence that he was not in Kenny's shoes.

"Theresa, Kenny, I heard everything down at the precinct. How is he?"

"Well, Uncle Nick," Kenny replied, gaining just a bit more daring as he spoke, "It's not as bad as it looks. Whatever they gave me took the pain away.

"I guess I was stupid though. This guy tried to rob the store. He was at my cash register with Bud, the manager. I tried to wrestle his gun from him, and it went off.

"As he pulled away from me, Bud smashed a can of peas over the guy's head. He went down like nobody's business.

"Then, I guess, they called your guys."

Theresa's hand was over her eyes. She was shaking her head gently from side to side.

"Eddie Freakin' Flanagan," she asked herself, silently, "just what kind of stinking chromosomes have you placed in all of our bodies?"

"Well, Kenneth, my son," she muttered looking back at him, "I can only hope you've gotten this foolishness out of your system. This image alone is implanted in my mind forever."

Nick placed his arm around Theresa's shoulders. She thought to shake it off, but did not have the strength to.

Kenny had been kept overnight to make sure that the Covid Virus did not exasperate the situation.

Theresa wondered at the sagacity of keeping him in a building where there were indeed Covid patients.

Nick dropped Theresa off at her home. She refused his offer to walk her to the door. Previously she had also refused his idea to stop at his house in order that Maeve might help to comfort her.

Just as she reached the house, and Nick had driven off, Mike's SUV came speeding, quite unlawfully, down the block. His vehicle had barely stopped in the driveway then he was out, up the pathway to his wife and was hugging her tightly.

"Well Michael," she related softly, "The good news is that Nick bore most of my ire. You can get all the hugging and kisses. I should warn you though, don't go overboard. I'm really not in the mood."

Mike just held her a little more tightly. She smelled of antiseptics and other hospital aromas, but he didn't care.

As she stepped into the kitchen to get a decent cup of coffee, Theresa's Mother handed her the landline phone.

"Am I still in the doghouse?" Kenny asked earnestly.

"No," Theresa returned in a softening tone, "But I can't make any promises for when you come home tomorrow."

"Maybe I should just go straight to work at the Market." Kenny told himself silently, but instead said "I love you Mom."

"I love you too Kenny." Theresa answered, "You should know that by now. This is why seeing you hurt is so damn hard."

When he saw his mother's face the next morning, Kenny wondered just what he had gotten himself into. While her expression wasn't angry, it was in no way pleasant. She appeared to be more disappointed than anything.

He could not know, at least at that point, that her disappointment was for another reason.

It was however still attached to Kenny's circumstances.

Another nurse had succumbed to Covid. Thankfully it had not been fatal, but still, the Hospital could not do without Theresa on that particular day. Maria and her boyfriend, John would be driving Kenny home. At first the thought of an ambulance had been brought up, but Dr. Ramos determined that the car would be just fine.

Dr. Ramos had also apologized to Theresa since she had been forced to work.

In the back of her mind, however, Theresa was thanking GOD that her own mother would be there to tend to Kenny until Theresa came home. Of course, the shift would be at least twelve hours long but hopefully no longer.

At lunch time, Theresa was given a full half hour.

Under the circumstances, Doctor Mieliastro felt that they should not push her too much.

As Theresa walked to the cafeteria, she was surprised to see a policeman's blue uniform in the corner of her eye.

She was even more surprised to hear her husband's voice call out "Hi Honey."

When she paused, Mike stepped up to her side. He was carrying a white Styrofoam box in his left hand.

"I'm sorry, it isn't Italos, but at least it's from Alberto's." He said with a wan smile.

She smiled just a bit more warmly. "Oh, Michael," she said, grabbing on to his right arm, "I was so looking forward to a hospital cafeteria sandwich. I don't suppose you brought any coffee from home, did you?"

His smile disappeared.

She squeezed his arm even more tightly. "Oh, Mike, I'm kidding. Thanks for that, whatever it is."

"Oh," he returned, smiling again, "I'm sure you know exactly what it is, Sweetie."

As they neared the cafeteria she asked if he could stay with her to protect her from hungry co-workers.

"For a little while," he assured her, "But then I have to get back into the City."

As she already knew, he had been to Nicky's precinct that morning on specific business for Chief of Patrol Meyer.

"I, ah, checked on His Majesty before coming here, ah, Kenny, that is. He seems to be doing fine. Your Mom has him set up on the living room sofa so he doesn't have to climb stairs. She's fussing over him like a mother hen. He was watching soap operas when I left."

"You, ah didn't.....? Theresa began, nervously.

"No, I did not say anything." Mike assured her, I have more sense than that. Heck, he's wounded."

Fifteen minutes later after Mike had left; Theresa gave her unfinished Shrimp Alfredo to two other nurses, downed her hospital coffee and went back to work.

Just as she thought might happen, yet another nurse called out sick. Thankfully, it had nothing to do with Covid. As a result, Theresa was there for an additional two hours.

She was understandably grumpy when Mike picked her up, but tried not to show it. Mike, of course picked right up on her mood. He knew, however that the very best thing he could do was to get her home to her wounded cub as quickly as possible. Once more, he exceeded the speed limit.

Knowing why, Theresa wisely kept quiet.

CHAPTER 31
OH, OH, WHAT NEXT

As John and Maria had driven off, with Kenny sprawled across the backseat of Theresa's SUV, Maria's mind had been drifting back to her family's first meeting with John. Nick had stopped by but then they had heard an unfamiliar voice call out. She was finally able to piece it together after getting everyone else's version.

The Sun had been exceedingly bright. John wore large aviator sunglasses to shield his eyes. A Mets ski cap with ear flaps covered his head and an almost matching Mets logo mask had covered the bottom part of his face.

Tuesday's snow still covered the ground a bit, but thankfully the roads were clear.

It was cold, but not extremely so.

John's bicycle wobbled slightly since it was a winter street and had a few ruts and gouges from plowing.

He was John Petros, twenty four years old, and he lived in the Sunnyside neighborhood in Queens Borough of New York City. Fortunately for him, his jobsite was within walking and bicycling distance of his apartment. His method of travel depended entirely on the weather of the day. On Tuesday, with that snowfall, he had walked to work, and left an hour earlier.

He worked at the One-One-Oh Police Precinct, there in Queens. His Captain as it turned out, was a man named Nick Evanopolis.

Like John's Great Grandfather, Captain Evanopolis' forebear had come though Ellis Island, in New York Harbor. Also like John's Great Grandfather, the Captain's ancestor had had his name simplified and changed by a bureaucrat who was probably too uneducated to get it correct. While Evanopolis had gotten it changed back, however, John's Dad, and John, himself, were content to keep their name as Petros.

The only problem though, was that because of the spelling, people often mistook him for Italian. Add to that the fact that he was dark haired and tanned reasonably well.

In truth, John was Polish. The family name had been Petrovska. John's Dad, Robert reasoned that there were probably too many consonants at the end of the name and the confused Government guy had decided to correct it.

John was almost to that house. It was a cop house, identified by the American Flag with the thin blue line emblazoned on it. Obviously someone connected with that family had been a policeman who may have died in action.

He had seen Captain Evanopolis sitting on their porch with other police officers and a few women. One woman in particular had caught his eye. She was young, perhaps a year or so to either side of twenty. She was quite pretty, although he had to admit, all of the women on that porch, young or older, were all pretty.

Most often she was reading, either from a Kindle, or sometimes, an actual book.

As he neared the house, he could see that indeed she was there with her Kindle in her hand. She was dressed warmly, and even had mittens on her hands. Since it was her house, and she appeared to be alone, she wasn't wearing a mask.

Apparently something funny had appeared upon her device's screen because a broad smile suddenly brightened her already beautiful face.

Going against his normally shy nature, he stopped. He held himself up with his feet planted firmly on either side of his bike.

Tugging his mask beneath his chin, he called out nervously, "Hi! My name's Johnny Petros."

She glanced up at him. She wasn't frowning, but neither was she smiling. He was aware of the home invasion problems they had had in the past.

Pointing at the Blue Line Flag, he said, "I know this is a Policeman's house. I'm a cop too. I work for Captain Evanopolis at the One-One-Oh.

He saw movement in her face when he said One-One-Oh instead of One-Ten.

Just then, Evanopolis, another captain and two women walked out onto the porch.

"Evanopolis called out, "Did someone mention my name?" then, "Hey, Petros, what's up? Did you need me?"

"Uh, no sir, Captain. I didn't even know you were here. I was saying hello to the lady."

He saw the younger of the two older women grimace when he revealed his intentions.

"Well, move on Petros." Evanopolis yelled back, "There's a gaddam pandemic out there. Move on son."

With a lump in his throat, John half saluted the Captain and prepared to leave. He noted that the woman who had frowned relaxed her expression. He also noted a gleam in the young woman's eyes as she waved goodbye to him.

The wave did not go unnoticed by Maria's mother, Theresa.

Kenny had told them that he was back on the cash register. One of the check–out women had called out sick. "Sinuses," Naomi had told Bud, the manager, "Not the Covid."

So far, the day had been uneventful. Kenny was quite content, since he had no desire to vault the protective screen again.

Five people had already passed through his line since his afternoon break. He had glanced up and saw a young policeman with a small amount of groceries upon the line.

Noticing the cop's nametag he had chuckled and said, "She likes you John."

The policeman seemed slightly confused. His eyes grew large above his light blue hospital type mask.

"Ah, what?" he had asked, then, "Are you talkin' to me?"

"My sister, Maria. You stopped by the house on your bike yesterday. Uncle Nick scared you off."

"Oh," John murmured, "Are you ah,…."

"Kenny Keith," Kenny had replied with an unseen smirk beneath his own hospital mask, "I'm Maria's brother. She said you weren't flirting, but that you were definitely interested. I guess girls know when that happens, eh."

After the customary shower and change of clothes Kenny had taken a couple of soft drinks from the refrigerator and strolled out onto the porch. His Mother was sitting on the sofa next to his Grandmother watching the news on TV. He kissed them both before exiting the front door.

"Hey!" he had said to his sister sitting at the very end in the lounge chair with her feet up.

"Hey, yourself!" Maria had responded while keeping her eyes on the Kindle screen on her lap.

"Johnny says Hi too." Kenny said, watching her closely for whatever reaction he could see.

Her head never moved as she asked, "Did you tell him what we had discussed last night?"

"Yea," Kenny replied, "I even mentioned Mom, Mike, and their worries and concerns about you dating a cop."

That got her attention. She looked up at him with knit brows and said, "Really? What did he say?"

As she sat upon her front porch Theresa felt all of her muscles aching from the rigid day she had just experienced at Queen's Mercy Hospital. All of her training and experience as a nurse had gotten her hired there. It was right there, in Queens, not far from their house. She presently worked the ambulatory wing, caring for patients with broken limbs, either legs or arms, or occasionally, both.

Because of the pandemic, she was required to be an aide as well. Cleaning bodies and administering for bodily functions were part of her job.

"Oh, well," she reasoned, "I raised three kids, so I'm already experienced."

Theresa's Mother, Marie was often alone. Her granddaughter, Maria was usually nearby, but college occupied young Maria and she was too often involved with that. They did dine together, and Maria seemed to like it when her Grandmother sat with her on the porch, weather allowing.

With Mike, Theresa, Davy and Kenny all working, she spent a lot of her time alone.

Occasionally that young cop, John Petros would stop by to see young Maria. On those occasions Marie would try to give them a little privacy.

Theresa was aware of Officer Petros' visits. It obviously bothered her, but so far Theresa hadn't mentioned it. Of course, who knew what she said to Mike behind closed doors.

On a day when Maria was on her main computer, studying for a test, it was a warm forty six degrees out. At least it seemed warm after the blast of Arctic air which had been punishing them for over a week.

Marie bundled up with a warm hat, mittens and a very warm goose down coat she had received for Christmas, and sat on the porch with a hot cup of coffee.

Across the way, Mr. O'Malley was sitting on his porch, dressed in a similar manner with a cup of something in his hands too.

O'Malley's first name was Conor, but he preferred just plain O'Malley. He was around six or seven years older than Marie and was a retiree from the New York Fire Department.

Spotting her, he raised his mug in greeting, but said nothing.

Laying her mug on the table beside her, she waved back.

He took another sip. Unknown to her, naturally, his cup also contained coffee, but it also had two shots of Bushmills Irish Whiskey instead of milk or cream.

"O'Malley," she called out, "How are you on this fine warm Thursday?"

"Ach," he called back after another sip, "This damn bloody heat is killin' me. How about yerself?"

She laughed, in spite of herself.

"Me too." She hollered back, "I think I need a pair of thinner mittens."

He surprised her when he rose and strolled across the street to the end of the McGinty driveway. Standing there he finished the liquid in his mug and nodded.

"I know poor Ed hasn't been gone all that long, Mrs. Flanagan, but I hope ye won't be mindin' me sayin' yer still quite the fine lookin' woman, if ever I saw one."

She had watched him cross the street, noting that although elderly he still cut a dashing figure for one so old. He was almost completely erect, and he moved with a grace not usually seen in a man his age.

Lines filtered downward on either side of his nose and mouth, but they weren't deep nor very prominent. A myriad of tiny wrinkles appeared as crinkling around his eyes when he smiled. While not thin, other than a very small paunch he was reasonably well built.

And she knew from the warmer months that an unruly thatch of white hair covered his head beneath his hat. Not even a thinning at the back could be seen.

"Ach," he murmured just loud enough for her to hear, "I've got to go back. Me cup is dry."

Smiling, she said perhaps a bit loudly, "Well, I have coffee if that's what you're drinking."

"Ah, coffee it is, but instead of Dairy, I be drinkin' it with a wee bit o' the demon."

With a coy smile she asked him, "Bushmills, Jameson or Tullamore Dew?" I have all three O'Malley."

If he was indeed slumping slightly, he stood a bit taller as a bright light entered his slightly rheumy eyes.

"Sonuva.......ye don't say?" he muttered, also a bit loudly.

"Ah, but I do say O'Malley. I have to warn you though, there are several pictures of Ed about the room and I will not turn them to face the wall for anyone."

"Well, don't I wish that poor Ed was here with us that he might have a wee dram of the demon himself." O'Malley answered with an extremely bright grin.

She wondered if his slight brogue was real or made up for effect.

Pulling a threadbare hospital mask from his pocket he asked her, "Will I be needin' this, then, Darlin'?"

"I don't think so O'Malley." She answered with a smile, "The way you crossed that street, I doubt seriously that you have the Covid.

"Perhaps, however, you should be worried about me." She added.

"Ach, sure now aren't you too pretty for such a nasty disease. I'll take me chances, and it's Bushmills, if ye don't mind. I know it's Protestant, but sure don't they just have the proper knack for brewin'?"

After pouring two more mugs, and joining him with the Bushmills, they talked for a bit.

O'Malley had been in New York since just before his fifth birthday. He had been born in the Galway town of Loughrea, not too far to the east of Galway City.

His father before him, a mechanic in Ireland, had also become a New York fireman.

As Marie already knew, he was presently living with his daughter, Lydia Pretalamo, and her husband Tony, who was also a fireman. And as Marie also already knew, they both called him O'Malley as well.

CHAPTER 32

LIVE YOUR LIFE

John Petros had finished his shift, the eighth shift in a row. Because of his close proximity to the station house, he had gone home for a short while after each of those twelve hour shifts. His present work period had lasted only eight hours. His Captain, Nick Evanopolis had decreed that he take at least twenty four hours off to regenerate.

"I don't need anybody succumbing to exhaustion." Nick had stated emphatically.

As Petros prepared to leave, Evanopolis motioned for John to enter his office.

When John stepped through the doorway, The Captain handed him a cell phone and said, "Try not to ruffle her feathers Petros."

Placing the phone to his ear, John said "Hello." somewhat tentatively.

A voice, which sounded familiar, but which he did not immediately recognize, said, "You tell his highness there what he can do with that feathers remark."

John, slightly confused, could only stammer, "Uh, Ma'am, I can't do that. Uh, s-sorry."

"I guess I know that John." She said, "I'm sorry I asked you to.

"This is Theresa, Maria's Mom. I have a rare day off and I was able to cook a nice dinner with my Mother. How would you like to stop by?

"I'd like to get to know the fella who's courtin' my daughter a little better.

"My husband, Mike will be here. As you know, he's a captain, but no other ranking cops will be gracing our table.

"So, what do you think? I am a good cook, and my Mom is superb."

"Uh, sure Mrs. McGinty," John answered, softly, "What time?"

"Well John, that depends. Do you have your bike or are you walking today?"

"Ah, I ah, have my bike." He replied, wondering just what was he getting himself into.

"How about fifteen minutes then?" Theresa said, "That'll be right about the time that Mike will be home.

"It'll just be you and the family, except for my son Dave. I'm sure Maria has told you that Dave is a cop up in the Bronx.

Mom's new beau, O'Malley from across the street will be there too. You up for that?"

"Ah, yes Ma'am." He answered and handed the phone back to Evanopolis.

"Go easy there Petros." Nick said but not in an unfriendly way. "I'm sure Maria has filled you in on all the fears that her Mother has, but maybe you could tread lightly just the same.

"She's not an unreasonable woman, and the needs of her kids are one of her major priorities."

John and Maria were standing on the front porch just after dinner. It had gone fairly well, and Mike had gone out of his way to downplay the difference in their ranks. He had purposely changed into civilian clothing. It was a lesson he had learned well when courting his first wife, Jennifer. He remembered everything his future Father-in-law, the Major had done to intimidate Mike, and did the exact reverse with John.

Maria excused herself to go to the bathroom. She used the one on the first floor, near the front door.

She groaned softly when she heard her mother say, "Hi John, may I have a private word with you?"

Finishing up, Maria rushed out of the bathroom without washing her hands, hoping desperately that she would not be too late.

Theresa was returning into the parlor with a somewhat confused John Petros just behind her.

"You should know, Sweetie," she said to her daughter, "I would never go behind your back.

"Come, let's all sit on the sofa and talk. The words 'Shut up Mother,' will be allowed when and if, you think them necessary."

Tentatively, Maria and John sat down. Theresa had placed the young man between the two of them.

Maria noticed that everyone else was somewhere else, and obviously not in the living room. She briefly wondered where her Grandmother and O'Malley were.

Theresa explained her fears and her trepidations of another police officer in the family to John, but Maria marveled at how quickly she had done so. John sat nodding, and it was obvious that he was doing so studiously.

"You seem to be a good listener John." Theresa stated with a knowing smile.

"I like you, and Nick Evanopolis assures me that you're a good man.

"Don't break my daughter's heart John, but then, don't let her break yours, either."

At that, Theresa rose, and kissed both young people on their cheeks.

Entering the kitchen she said, "I need coffee with something stronger than cream. O'Malley you'll have to share that stuff!"

Later, when John had left, despite it bring pretty cold out, Maria was on the porch thinking. Her thoughts were disturbed when her mother came out on to the porch to stand beside her daughter.

"Let me just finish what I have to say Sweetie, and then I'll leave you to your peace." Theresa began.

"Ten years ago I wouldn't even imagine having this conversation with you. Even though you have been quite mature for such a long time now, you are still my little girl.

"Although, that certainly isn't a little girl's body you have. I'm afraid you've inherited quite a few assets from both the O'Toole and Flanagan families. No wonder John was initially so attracted to you."

O'Toole was Marie Flanagan's maiden name.

"By the way, I really do like him. He's a very nice young man."

Theresa paused, weighing her words carefully before she shared them with her daughter.

"Now, I'm not telling you what or what not to do." Theresa opened with. "I'm just letting you know what Mike, your Grandmother and I think. And I assure you, we are all on the same page about this.

"It's a mean world out there Honey. This Covid thing is far from over. We don't know where it's gonna take us, no matter what these silly politicians say, or hell, don't say. Add to that this stupid, utterly stupid, police defunding which places our policemen and policewomen in more danger than they have ever been.

"What I'm trying to say Maria, is that you have to grab onto life while you can.

"Maybe you and John aren't meant for each other. But then, maybe you are. The only way you're going to determine that is to explore it yourselves.

"As I said, I'm not telling you what to do or what not to do, but Kenny is gone during the day. Whatever you may or may not do in that basement, clean up after yourselves.

"Also, here's a suggestion, and I assure you, I do not have an ulterior motive. Take a load of laundry down with you. It gives you an excuse to be there and perhaps the background noise will cover-up any other sounds."

Maria's expression had changed several times during her Mother's discourse. While she had been faintly smiling for the last five or so minutes, at the mention of laundry, her smile became a silly grin.

"I don't know Mom," she said, giggling, "sounds like an ulterior motive to me."

Theresa's own grin became even brighter. She kissed her daughter on the cheek and without another word, went into the house.

To Mike and her own Mother, side by side on the sofa, she said, "I need a glass of wine."

It was Theresa's turn to shower and scrub. Mike had gotten home almost one hour prior. Thinking that she might be just around the corner he had waited in his car in the driveway. With his radio playing he had sat patiently, drumming on the steering wheel with his fingertips.

Mike had nodded to O'Malley when the old man had crossed over from his house to the McGinty-Keith-Flanagan home a few minutes later.

O'Malley had raised the half full bottle of Bushmills Whiskey in his hand as an offering, but Mike had shook his head no, with a bright smile.

"Maybe later," he told himself with a chuckle, "if there's any left!"

Finally, one half hour after arriving, his bladder and kidneys got the best of him.

Phoning Theresa, he got her voicemail. Prancing with his need to pee, he left the message, "Nature is calling loudly Honey. I waited for one half hour to give you dibs on the shower, but I can't wait any longer."

At that, he snapped his phone shut and started down the back stairs to the outside cellar door. As he looked up, Mike saw his Mother-in-law, Marie glancing out the window. She was grinning and knowingly gave him a thumb up.

Theresa arrived moments later and checked her phone messages. From the porch, Marie waved and indicated the basement with her hand. Theresa slapped herself lightly on the side of her forehead and made for the backyard.

From the Boiler, washer-dryer side of the basement she could hear Mike singing in the shower. She too was dancing from foot to foot as the cascading sound of the shower was inducing her need to urinate.

"Come on ya big lug," she called out loudly, "you must be clean by now. Give a girl a break."

His smile was classic as he reentered the living space side of the basement.

Not stopping to dry off, he had simply pulled on a fluffy terrycloth robe and strode wet and dripping into the living area.

"Your shower awaits, My Lady." He announced with a wave of his hand towards the steaming room.

"The hell with the shower," she muttered as she sped past him, "I gotta pee."

When done with her emergency Theresa did indeed make use of that shower. Upon exiting it she dried off and wrapped a fluffy white towel about her. Waiting in the outer room was a very satisfied looking Mike, fully dressed except for shoes and an outer shirt.

His feet were upon the coffee table, but he wasn't sipping coffee. A large mug of beer rested on his stomach, supported by his left hand. In his right hand was a large wine glass with ice and what appeared to be White Zinfandel wine.

Stacked next to his feet was a pile of what appeared to be Theresa's casual clothing.

Accepting the wine, she sat beside him and fingered the clothing. It definitely was hers.

It was warm and smelled of fabric softener.

"Where'd you get this?" she asked softly.

"From the dryer." He answered with a smack of his lips. He had just sipped his beer.

She sipped her wine. It was cold, and exactly the right thing for her to be drinking at that moment.

"Oh, Mikey, Mikey, Mikey, "She murmured softly, "if I wasn't worried about Mom and O'Malley popping in, I would jump your bones, right here, right now."

"Yea, Old Folks," Mike agreed, "gotta make sure you don't do anything to upset those old tickers. I'm sure your Mom could handle it, but I am not too sure about O'Malley. No matter what he may have seen in the past, he has never seen anything like my Theresa.

"Can I get a rain check for later tonight?"

As if on cue Kenny called out from the outer cellar door, "Comin' down. I need the bathroom Tres vite!"

Shrugging, Mike asked, "What the hell is that? What is it with you Keiths and French?"

"It means very fast." Theresa explained drily, "And I'm no longer a Keith, Sweetie. In case you've forgotten, I switched to McGinty when we got married.

"You remember that don't you? There was a priest and a lot of people, oh, and a lot of rain too."

"Shaking his head and grinning profusely, Mike called out, "Come on in Ken. We'll go upstairs and leave you to your privacy."

The stairs from the basement opened upstairs into the dining room.

They heard snoring and as they entered the parlor they caught sight of O'Malley, asleep on the sofa. His bottle was embraced firmly within both hands which were crossed upon his chest.

The up and down movement of that bottle on that chest assured them that he was breathing. Retrieving a blanket from the coat closet, Theresa covered him gently. She was a bit surprised when she was easily able to pry the bottle from his hands and set it on the coffee table.

"Maybe I should place this in the kitchen." She remarked to no one in particular.

"Really?" Mike asked, "Did we not just have a conversation about old people's hearts?"

Nodding sagely, Theresa left the bottle there and strolled into the kitchen to help her Mother with dinner.

Mike shook his head slowly. He turned on the TV for the news but muted it so as not to disturb O'Malley.

O'Malley continued to snore and occasionally smack his lips.

CHAPTER 33

WHO IS IN CHARGE

David Edward Keith, NYC patrolman, currently assigned to the Bronx Borough was presently hunkered down behind a large rusty green trash dumpster. He had wisely dropped several cinder blocks beside the wheels to block any stray bullets. In his mind he remembered slivers of concrete that ricocheting bullets had once driven into the flesh of his legs.

After an initial spray of bullets from his adversary there had been no more firing. Since Davy had yet to shoot back, either the guy was waiting for Davy to expose himself, or quite possibly had already taken off.

Davy had kept his voice as low as possible when he had called in his situation. Since the guy already knew where he was, he didn't want him to hear any possible planning.

He heard Marciano's voice, also quite soft. Marciano informed him that help was already there, on the opposite end of the alley where Davy was hidden. But, so far, a shooter had not been seen.

When he notified whomever it might be that he was surrounded and to throw down his weapon, Davy was rewarded with another spray of bullets. He pressed himself against the wall to avoid any ricochets.

There was a slight gap at the back of the dumpster. As he heard police firing from the opposite direction he did indeed feel the sting of a stray round as it rebounder off the wall into his exposed shoulder. Fortunately it only creased the outer flesh of his deltoid. A minimum of blood stained his shirt.

"Still," he told himself, "Mom's gonna have a fit."

In the back of his mind, however, his Grandfather's voice told him, "Get that crap outta your head Boy! There are more important things to tend to. Concentrate on your situation."

Vinnie Calabrese's voice came loud and clear from the opposite direction.

"Hey, Jerk-off," Vinnie called out, "You're sealed in between cops. Now this can go either way. We can sit here until you starve to death or we can spray the freakin' alley with bullets."

There was a pause as Vinnie let his words sink in.

"Of course, Jerk-off, it ain't your decision, now is it?

"Keith," he shouted just a bit louder, "Stay hidden. If this guy don't answer in the next five minutes, bullets will be coming his way."

"Alright, alright," a gruff voice called back, "here's my gun. I'm throwin' it your way."

The sound of a larger weapon clattering upon the ground echoed in the alley.

Calabrese began to rise from his position behind an entirely different dumpster. Patrolwoman Gerrie Contadina was just behind him.

Davy Keith peeked from behind his own dumpster. Immediately he took in the two cops and the perp standing loosely with his hands at his side.

As more of Vinnie Calabrese's body became exposed the perp reached for another gun, an automatic pistol tucked into his the back of his waistband.

With no time to call out an effective warning, Davy brought up his own weapon. Shouting "Gun!" at the same time he shot the hoodlum, dropping him immediately.

Moaning in pain, the tough squirmed with tremendous strain upon the ground. His gun had fallen and scattered several feet away from him.

The bullet had hit his lower back, missing both lungs and his heart, but who knew what organs may have been hit.

Gerrie immediately called for an ambulance and apprised Marciano of what had taken place.

Unheard by any of them, Marciano also groaned. With the climate stemming from City Hall, a back-shot was bound to bring an investigation.

Marciano envisioned the last time he had confronted a councilman named Mort Lieberman. While nothing really serious had really come of it, still, the confrontation had not gone well.

Two emergency technicians showed up within minutes, followed by an ambulance from Bronx General Hospital which was just three blocks away.

The hoodlum, whose name was Theodore Robert "TR" Kleinman was given immediate first aid and taken to the hospital with a police escort.

One EMT remained behind to tend to Davy's wound.

As it turned out, Kleinman's own wound was too severe and he died on the way to Bronx General

Marciano was simultaneously correct and incorrect in his assessment of the back shooting incident. He, his commander, Captain Diego Rodriguez and the three patrol persons involved were waiting in the anteroom of the new Police Commissioner, Burton Thomas Freedon. The three patrol people were Vincent Calabrese, Geraldine Contadina and David Keith. Keith had fired the shot which had sent the perp to his death.

Marciano wondered at the intelligence of summoning five police people from the same precinct in the middle of an epidemic and a very foolish police defunding folly.

He reminded himself to only speak when being addressed and not to say anything stupid.

Commissioner Freedon's secretary, one of two, whose name was Alice Agrippo told them all to go into the Commissioner's office. Alice did not care that Freedon preferred the title secretary to assistant. His other secretary, Enid Bloch felt lucky just to be gainfully employed.

Commissioner Freedon was reading a series of documents when they entered. They all stood at a loose parade rest awaiting his attention. Marciano wanted to clear his throat to announce their presence, but once more berated himself not to be foolish.

"Well," Freedon finally said, in a somewhat authoritative voice, "Firing a pistol on a crowded street which resulted in the death of a New York citizen. Do I have those facts correct Captain?"

"Not exactly Sir." Captain Rodriguez answered.

Freedon looked up. Surprise briefly flitted in his eyes. He noted Rodriguez's captains bars. He quickly took in Marciano's nametag and sergeant's stripes.

The implication, quite obviously was that he did not expect a man of Hispanic extraction to be in a position of authority.

"Ah, Captain," he said looking directly at Rodriguez, "Were you on site during this incident?"

"No Sir....." Rodriguez began, but was immediately cut off by the Commissioner.

"Then, let someone who was actually there address this incident. Sergeant, what can you tell me?"

"Ah, Sir, I was not on site either. These three patrol people were there."

Freedon's expression changed. It went from bland to irritated within seconds.

"They were unsupervised?"

Although meant to be a question, it was clearly a statement.

"Yes Sir," Rodriguez intervened, "Considering the size of this City....."

"I was talking to the Sergeant" Freedon snapped, standing up.

"Uh, yes sir." Rodriguez replied and was then silent.

In the outer office, three men, Freedon's next appointments, heard everything. Both Alice and Enid kept their heads down and pretended not to hear.

The three men were Police Chief Walter Agrarian, Chief of Patrol Dennis Meyer and Civilian Garret Holmes, the Mayor's appointed police watchdog.

The three men glanced at each other and shook their heads.

Quickly changing back, Commissioner Freedon looked to David Keith and said, "Keith, was it really necessary to kill that man. Couldn't you have shot him in the leg or arm?"

"No Sir," Keith responded, "It was a do or die situation. Had I missed at that distance there's a good chance, Vinnie, ah that is Patrolman Calabrese might be dead, ah, Sir."

With a disgusted look, Freedon glanced back down at the papers on his desk.

"It says that you had been wounded Keith. Isn't possible that you shot that man in retribution for his having shot you?"

Again, Freedon's implication was very clear.

"No Sir!" Davy answered with a trace of irritation entering his own voice, "That's not the kind of cop I am. I was trained by the best and I strive every day to merit that training."

"I'd shut up if I were you Keith." The Commissioner warned. His tone was just a bit ominous.

Just then, the door to the outer office opened. In marched Holmes, Agrarian and Meyer. None of them looked particularly happy.

Freedon knew Agrarian and Meyer from their pictures. He assumed that the black man must be Holmes since that was his other appointment.

Wisely he decided not to ruffle any of their feathers, just yet.

"Gentlemen," he said, "This is a private meeting. If you'll just wait out in the anteroom, I will get to you soon enough."

"I'm sorry Commissioner," Chief of Patrol Meyer spoke up, "But if you are going to threaten some of our finest cops, without knowing or understanding the true story, then I am making it my business."

Both Agrarian and Holmes were nodding.

Freedon stood back up. He held onto his desk to steady himself as he felt his anger coursing through his body.

"Meyer," he snapped nastily, "Your job is no safer than anyone else in this room. Do yourself a favor and shut the fuck up."

Meyer smiled. His face was flush.

Freedon eyed him warily, wondering just what was going to come next.

Stepping up to the Commissioner's desk, Chief Meyer snapped the shield from his chest and tossed it on the desk. He laid his service pistol in its holster, beside it.

While Commissioner Freedon wondered just what Meyer might do next, Walt Agrarian did the exact same thing. As if on cue, the other five uniformed police personnel in the room did the exact same thing.

Freedon stood there with his mouth open and his eyes wide. As he struggled to form words in his mind, Agrarian said to him, "Ah, Burt is it; you might want to get someone to escort all of us out of the building.

"Uh," Holmes said aloud, "I'll go inform the Mayor so that he can start making new plans."

"Just stand right there Holmes." Freedon snapped harshly, "I haven't dismissed you yet."

"Uh, sorry Burton," Holmes replied with an evil grin, "I don't work for you. I work directly for the Mayor and he most certainly needs to be apprised of this situation. "Ah, come on Walt and Dennis. I'll escort you from the building."

"STOP!" Freedon shouted loudly. "No one is fired and I would appreciate it if no one quits. All of you please go back to work and please, clean all this hardware from my desk."

As they all turned to leave, the Commissioner said, "Keith and Captain Rodriguez please stay and relate exactly what happened so that I might place everything in its proper prospective."

Freedon sighed heavily and then told Holmes that he, Freedon would fill the Mayor in on just what took place.

"Yes Sir," Holmes replied, "Will do. However, please inform the two Chiefs and me as to what your report might say, and I assure you we will concur. I'll make sure that nobody else will add or detract anything from whatever you say."

A day later, Burton Freedon was seated at his desk. A lazy arc of sunlight shone through a spot in his venetian blinds where several slats had separated. Burton had punched those blinds just that morning.

He sat, elbows on his desk, head in his hands, wondering just what had he gotten himself into.

His Subordinates back in Squiresville were far less combatative than the police hierarchy here in New York.

Since they had arrived unannounced, Freedon was unaware of his new guests until they burst through his office door. Additionally, Mayor Ron D'Alorio had instructed Alice and Enid not to announce him.

The two ladies were currently wondering where their next job might be.

"Tom," D'Alorio called out as he entered the office with several suited individuals in tow. "How're your first few days on the job? Certainly not Pennsylvania, now is it?"

Bringing up the rear was Garret Holmes.

Commissioner Freedon groaned inwardly when he saw Holmes.

"Garret tells me you're adapting well to our City." D'Alorio said as he took a chair opposite his new Police Commissioner.

The Mayor was taller than everyone else in the room.

Fanning his hand outward he introduced the two men whom Freedon did not yet know.

"This is Deputy Mayor Jim Collins." D'Alorio said, indicating an average height Caucasian man with grayish brown hair and squinty eyes which appeared to be brown. The second man was African-American, dark with grayish black hair and rather dark piercing eyes.

D'Alorio introduced him as Steven Brent, also a Deputy Mayor.

"And of course, you already know Garret." The Mayor added.

"Garret tells me that you handled that problem from The Bronx rather easily and he gives you kudos for your efforts.

"As I'm sure you already know, we're in a bit of a situation here. The Media is ready to pick-up on anything we might do wrong, and smear it all over the public's rather unwitting conciousness.

"Naturally, whatever we do correctly is overlooked. Ah, but such is politics in the Big City, eh."

The Mayor and his entourage left as suddenly as they had arrived, after a "Good Job!" from D'Alorio.

Only Holmes remained behind.

Once the door had been shut Holmes winked at the Commissioner.

"As I mentioned the last time, Commissioner, things are a bit different here. A career can end at a moment's notice. The Mayor may have defunded his Police Department, but since then he's come to realize all the problems he's facing because of it.

"He does not take credit for any problems which arise. He looks for scapegoats and usually either finds or creates them.

"His Honor has been doing a lot of back pedaling lately. His key phrase has become 'Damage Control' and he adheres to it as much as possible."

Tom Freedon shook his head and wondered just what had he gotten himself into. A higher salary meant little if it could disappear at any moment.

He thought about what Holmes had just said, damage control and scapegoats. Several plans began to form in his mind.

He reminded himself; however, "Big City cops don't just roll over and fold at any kind of confrontation. That, in and of itself bears watching."

Vito Marciano could not believe what he was reading. He recalled the scorn and accusations that they had been subjected to in the new Commissioner's office. Even two Chiefs and Marciano's own Captain had been laced into by that, ah, lunatic.

And now, Marciano held a document lauding the three patrol people, Keith, Contadina and Calabrese for the fine job they had done in protecting the public from such a dangerous killer.

In addition Marciano and Captain Rodriguez were praised for the excellent leadership and training which they had provided.

The document further called for citations for all five individuals. It had been counter-signed by Chief of Patrol Dennis Meyer.

With his disbelief blatant in his expression, Sergeant Marciano took the document in to show Rodriguez.

Rodriguez possessed his own copy. He had been just as amazed as his sergeant had been.

His reaction had been a tremendous gulp. Glancing up at the ceiling he remarked, "I wonder when the other shoe is going to fall."

The Captain's phone rang and he just stared at it. Rodriguez noticed Marciano staring at the ringing phone and indicated the device with a simple nod of his head.

Picking the receiver up, Marciano offered a very tentative "Uh, hello."

"Ah," Chief of Patrol Dennis Meyer's voice came over the line, with a chuckle, "It sounds as if you've already read the document. Has Captain Rodriguez read it yet?"

"Uh, ah, yes Sir." Marciano replied, "He's staring up at the ceiling and wondering when the other shoe is going to drop."

"Yea," Meyer replied, "That was my first reaction too. I haven't seen the Commissioner since his little temper outburst.

"His girl Alice brought it in and instructed me to countersign it. She told me to then send it to Diego, uh, Captain Rodriguez.

"I showed it to Walt Agrarian. He just laughed and urged me to do as Freedon wanted. So, now you have it.

"We'll probably have the medal ceremony down here, but I'll check with his Lordship to see how he wants to handle it.

"My guess, however, is if there is another shoe to fall, you'll be calling Ron Beymon the new Chief of Patrol.

"Remember Sergeant, nothing is permanent in this man's police department, nothing, at all."

Both Mike and Davey had been inoculated against the Covid virus by the Police Department. Theresa, Melanie and Maria, all health professionals, had received the injection through their hospitals.

Kenny had been able to get his through the Pharmacy section at his store.

Only Marie, Theresa's Mother was left.

Theresa was taking a much needed break in the hospital cafeteria. Having eaten half of a sandwich, the other half was wrapped and in her pocket.

Her empty coffee cup was crumpled and in the next few moments she was going to drop it in the trash on her way back to the Emergency Room.

A smile creased her lips as she wondered why they called it a room when it was a suite of many chambers, including various testing rooms.

Just then, Dr. Mieliastro sat down at her table with two fresh coffees. He set one in front of Theresa.

"Mrs. McGinty," he began, "When I found out your son's name was Keith, and then found out that he had grown up in the Philadelphia area, I did a little checking.

"I grew up in Bensalem. As you already know, my cousin, Kathy O'Toole married Tim Keith.

"I actually knew Dominic. I guess you and I are kind of related."

Mieliastro's smile was broad and engaging.

Theresa's eyes were quite large and her own smile of surprise was just as bright.

"Well," she replied, "And, as I imagine you already know, three of my four kids are Dominic's kids as well."

What came next was more Angelo Mieliastro's idea, but Theresa readily agreed to it.

Mieliastro had suggested coming to Theresa's home and inoculating whoever needed it with the Covid vaccine. As it turned out, only her mother needed it.

Even old Conor O'Malley had already gotten his.

Theresa immediately thought of Nick and Maeve's extended family. Nick and Maeve were already vaccinated, but Uncle Joey, Carol and Michelle probably were not.

"Consider it done." Mieliastro assured her. Plus, I think I should now get to know this family that I am somewhat a member of a bit better."

Mike, Marie and the kids had immediately liked the Doctor.

O'Malley wasn't as sure when Mieliastro remarked that too much alcohol wasn't good for a man of O'Malley's age.

"Well, I'll be eighty soon enough and I'm already lookin' forward to breakin' that hundred mark as well." O'Malley snorted back to him, followed by a straight swig of Bushmills Irish whiskey.

With a furtive glance to each other, Mike and Theresa both smiled wanly and shook their heads gently.

"An' don' be shakin' your head at me now McGinty." O'Malley snapped, "I'll be prayin over yer grave sooner or later, now won't I."

CHAPTER 34

WHAT'S A BROTHER FOR

Tim McGreevy woke up in his usual panic mode. He had been dreaming again and as always his dreams were quite far from pleasant. He did not dream as often as he had in the past, but his dreams were just as intense as they had been ever since Nine-Eleven.

Once more, in his dream he had lain there in the immense shadow of Building Number One as it at first had begun to crumble and then fall down around him with an angry blast of hot air. Once the building had fallen and dust was swirling everywhere, he saw that it had missed him completely.

Tower-One had lain, strewn all about him in ugly, crusty, one ton or more chunks. Scattered among the rubble were pieces of human bodies including open-eyed faces, one of which belonged to his brother Trevor.

Trevor had been born with the name Thomas, but at the age of eleven he had felt a change was needed. All of his legal documents still bore the name Thomas, but everyone had since called him Trevor.

In his dream, Tim was missing all four of his limbs. But oddly enough, every one of his extremities had been itching terribly in that dream, both hands and both feet.

While a portion of the building had indeed fallen on him he had been nowhere near the devastation that his nightmares usually elicited. And, he had not been the one who had found Trevor's body parts.

Upon awakening, Tim sat up. His pillowcase, blanket and sheets were all damp with his sweat.

He swung his one leg over the side of the bed and lit himself a cigarette.

Tim actually still had both arms and that one leg. He had, however lost his right leg on that horrible day in September of two thousand and one.

More terribly, however, he had also lost four of his five brothers.

Tim and four of his brothers were firemen. His youngest brother Ian had been a Port-Authority policeman.

The brothers were Laurence, or Larry, the oldest, Dominic, Trevor, Roger and Ian.

Trevor and Ian had both died on that terrible day. Roger had died one week later from injuries sustained while helping people out of Tower number Two. Dominic had died within the year, from cancer. His death was not sudden, nor was it painless. It was horribly unpleasant.

In addition, Tim had lost friends. They had been co-workers, who were almost like brothers to him as well.

Laurence and Tim had both been injured, Larry superficially and Tim much more severely. His career had ended with his missing leg, severed above the knee. Tim had died twice upon the operating table. Fortunately, as an A-Positive blood type there had been plenty of blood to be had.

The smoke from his cigarette drifted lazily upward. He no longer enjoyed cigarettes, but for whatever reason found it virtually impossible to give them up.

Peggy, his former wife had also been a smoker, but had foregone the habit soon after Tim had lost his leg. She had cited his refusal to stop smoking as one of the reasons for the divorce.

Not smoking, however, was just an excuse. The true reason, also cited, was his inability to get along with her, or anyone for that matter except for Larry.

There were moments, however when he drove Larry absolutely crazy.

Deeply underlying was his inability to give her even an inch in any disagreements between them. Generally, Tim's disposition was the prime reason for any arguments.

Early on she had always tried to back off. Just before the divorce, however Peggy found herself standing up to him more and more.

While she would not admit it, even to herself, caring for a somewhat thankless cripple was not what she had signed on for. Had Tim shown at least a trace of love or simply just a bit of gratitude, things might have been different.

His loss of Peggy, however, had been a wakeup call. It was a resounding crash of emotional cymbals to either side of Tim's head. Perhaps a few bits of love still remained within that angry mind.

There had been Fire Department councilors, and the advice of the only person he would ever really listen to, his brother, Larry.

Larry, he reasoned, knew exactly where Tim was coming from. Larry had been there. Larry had seen and felt everything that Tim had. Perhaps he hadn't lost his leg, but like Tim, 9/11 waited each and every day to pounce upon Larry's heart and soul. As with Tim, 9/11 was an ever present entity drawing energy from either fireman's hearts, souls and minds.

Larry however was constantly making the effort to escape his mental bonds.

A knock on the apartment door brought Tim's attention back to the present.

He considered donning his artificial leg, but decided it might take too long.

Grabbing his crutch, he half hopped, half hobbled over to the door. Without checking the security peephole he pulled the door open.

Tim was pleasantly surprised to find his former wife, Peggy standing there, an anxious look upon her face.

Peggy normally was an attractive woman. Although she was over fifty years of age, she actually looked several years younger. Despite a few streaks of gray in her normally light brown hair, and a series of facial wrinkles, her nervous smile gave her a much younger appearance.

Braced for whatever tirade he might fling at her she was mildly surprised when he also smiled.

"Peggy," he said cordially, "come on in. I just woke up, but I can have coffee ready in a few minutes."

She noted his disheveled appearance and the dark stains of perspiration at his armpits.

"Nine-Eleven still haunting you Tim?" she asked.

He noted a tone of concern in her voice.

246

"Yea, you know how it is." He told her, "You already put up with enough of my crap to realize that."

After setting his machine for the first cup, he placed a container of milk and two spoons beside the sugar bowl on the table.

"I just want to clean up a little." he informed her in a not unpleasant tone. "Just fix your coffee however you want. I'll be back in fifteen or so minutes."

Although neither of them timed it, Tim was back in twelve minutes. His face was freshly washed. He had scrubbed just a bit roughly, attested to by the reddish glow to his skin. He had changed into a clean though worn tee shirt with a FDNY logo on its breast.

He was surprised to see that she had also made him a cup of coffee. A sip told him that it was exactly as he normally took it.

"Now, Peggy," he said pleasantly, "to what do I owe this visit? Are there more papers to sign?"

Peggy stared into her cup. He could see the mechanics of her mind at work by the expression on her face. She opened her mouth to speak, but nothing came out.

"Let me put your mind at ease Peg." He said with a kindly tone to his voice, "I've reconciled myself to the divorce. I have to live with my grouchy old self on a daily basis. So I do have an idea of what you had been putting up with.

"Just tell me what it is, and I'm sure we can work our way through it.

"I must warn you though," he added with a chuckle, "If you've found another guy, I'll give you my blessing, but I won't walk you down the aisle. Get your brother for that."

An uneasy smile crept into Peggy's eyes. She knew he was kidding, but wasn't sure just how much he was.

"Well the question is moot." She told herself, "Since I'm not even looking for another guy."

Remembering just how much in love she had been with Tim, and having seen how badly that had broken down, Peggy was much too nervous to even consider another man.

Tim's voice startled her as he asked, "How is Brian, anyway?"

He was referring to her brother.

"Tell ya the truth; Peggy, I miss him almost as much as I miss you."

"Y-you m-miss me?" Peggy stammered, unsure of which direction the conversation had suddenly taken.

"Sure I miss you!" Tim replied. "We were married for twenty one years. I'd like to think I wasn't an asshole for the entire time."

"N-no, of course not." She answered and then was once more silent.

"Well, I'm sure old memories are not what have brought you here. Let's have it. What can I do for you?"

She noted keenly the kinder tone to his voice.

Suddenly she did not want to ask him. To show him that she did still care for him, she took his empty cup and started to make him another cup of coffee.

As she stood before the coffee maker Peg chastised herself for even thinking that her gesture in any way compared to what she was about to ask him for.

After setting the cup before him, she indicated a print hanging above the sofa. It was a Picasso, and even though only a print, it had been signed by the artist. It had been appraised back when her parents had given it as a wedding gift, at over five thousand dollars.

Naturally, they hadn't paid that much.

She had recently checked on line and at auction it could bring twelve thousand dollars or more.

"It's worth around twelve or more at auction." She informed him "I guess obviously, half of that would be six. I can't pay you all of that at once, but I have three hundred for a down payment and a couple of hundred a week until it's paid off."

"How about it?" she asked nervously.

Tim stood. With his crutch he hobbled over to the print and removed it from the wall.

Hobbling back he offered it to her.

"This was a gift from your parents, GOD rest their souls." He said softly.

"Timothy Dennis McGreevy will not be takin' advantage of a woman he once loved."

Gazing steadily into her unflinching dark eyes, he continued, "And by GOD Darling, I still do."

Peggy had left. It was obvious that she was quite a bit confused when she stood to leave. Nervously she had placed the print, protected by a pillowcase, under her arm.

Tim stared at the door after she had left. The soft aroma of her bodywash still hung in the air. He pondered over how uneasy she had appeared, since it had not been his intention to upset her.

He, himself was also somewhat confused. While he hadn't had any kind of a vision, still his way of thinking had changed just a bit. Perhaps the catalyst had been their divorce. Though he felt himself changing in so many ways, he could still not form any kind of a solid plan in order to figure out where he was going next.

He wondered if his brother Larry might have any thoughts on the matter.

Larry answered his cell phone on the first ring. There was a chuckle in his voice as he answered.

"Hey he said, I was just going to dial your number. What are you getting psychic in your old age?"

"Actually," Tim answered, "And as a matter of fact, I kind of feel like I'm just a bit younger than I was yesterday."

"Oh and what might the reason for that be?" Larry asked, marveling at the change in Tim.

Truthfully, Larry spent almost every day worrying about his brother.

They had so much more in common than just their genetics and career choice.

"How about I pick something up and come on over?" Larry suggested.

To tell you the truth, Laurence me boy, I think I'd like to go out to eat. It's been so freakin' long. What say you?"

Unable to keep the surprise from his voice, Larry said, "Well, uh, Scruffy's has a big tent set up in their parking lot. They have several portable heaters. It's not real warm, but at least we won't freeze our cajones off.

"Remember though, ya gotta wear a hospital mask before they seat you and whenever the waitress approaches."

Taking care, since it wasn't something he did often, Tim prepared his stump and attached his artificial leg. He was a little clumsy with it since he did not wear it very often. Deciding to take a walking stick just in case, he selected a tall stout piece of carved wood. Even though it was just a walking stick, he laughingly called it his shillelagh.

As he approached Scruffy's, his brother hailed him with a waving arm. Larry was dressed for winter with a slightly faded dark blue, hooded and fur lined parka. He also had on a ski hat and bright green mittens. He wore sturdy work boots and faded blue jeans.

Tim felt slightly underdressed with his Brooklyn Dodgers cap and team jacket. Since his artificial leg was clad in a black and white sneaker, its mate was upon his good foot. Tim wore loose-fitting jeans as well, and his one nod towards the weather was a bright, though faded blue and white Brooklyn Dodgers scarf and brown leather gloves.

Tim chuckled at the slight ache in his non-existent leg. "Well," he told himself, "at least the ache is not as persistent as the freakin' itch."

Scruffy's wasn't all that warm so they kept their coats and hats on. Gloves and mittens were placed in jacket pockets.

Once more Larry marveled at how alike they were as they both ordered rare burgers with raw onions and ketchup. Both ordered doubly fried steak fries and each had a Smithwicks beer. As any fireman in Brooklyn would know, they had each called it Smiddicks.

So," Larry began, "what seems to be startin' your engine lately? Did the dreams go away?"

"No," Tim replied, as he sipped his beer, "in fact I had one just this morning. It was slightly different though."

"How so?" Larry asked.

"Well, for the most part, it was pretty much the same. Only, this time, when I was surrounded by the building and all those body parts, it was just a tad different."

Tim paused and Larry could see that his brother was examining his thoughts. Larry waited patiently for Tim to continue.

"Trevor's Head was still there, as usual, but this time, just before I woke up, he winked at me and smiled. Then, Bingo, the morning light was shining in my eyes.

"Then I was sweating, and sitting on the edge of my bed with a smoke. Somebody knocked at the door, and when I got there it was Peggy."

"Peggy?" Larry echoed, "Is this still part of the dream?"

"No Lar, I was awake and she had actually stopped by. I made her coffee. Well, actually, I just turned the damn machine on. She made coffee for both of us while I cleaned up."

At the end of his sentence, Tim had looked up and was staring at the top of the tent.

"I was out to see the folks in the cemetery just last week." Larry revealed.

"As you know, Mom and Dad were there, side by side. Dom Ragh and Ian were side by side, but there was room next to Ragh and Ian for their wives.

"Trevor was in the next row and they also had a space saved for Inga.

"Did you know that she put Trevor on his grave stone? She put Thomas as a middle name."

Laurence laughed out loud but Tim only smiled.

Forty minutes or so later they were strolling down Eleventh Street in Park Slope. Well, Larry was strolling while Tim limped along. It was a quiet night in Brooklyn. It had gotten colder as the late afternoon had approached earlier.

Firehouse Engine 220 with Ladder 122 loomed, just down and across the street. One side was a brick and stucco building which fit in nicely with the neat, also brick, buildings around it.

The other side was made up of yellowish stone blocks which contrasted nicely with its brick neighbors.

Larry was trying to think of some way to avoid the building. While Tim fully understood why he was no longer a fireman, occasionally he resented it. It had never been mentioned when Larry had still been on the job. Larry wondered how this might set back the good mood which had encompassed Tim on this day.

"Hey," Tim called out, "The old house. Whoa, doesn't she look pretty. Hey, Larry, let's stop by; see if anybody we know is still on the job."

A large number of Firefighters had perished both during and soon after the Nine-Eleven attacks, several from this very firehouse.

Early on both Tim and Larry had attended one of those televised ceremonies on one of the Nine-Eleven Anniversaries. Tim had read Trevor's name as Inga was still heavily grieving and unable to do so, herself. Larry had read Dominic's name.

Not knowing why, Tim had purposely placed the name Thomas before Trevor. He regretted it as soon as he had said it, but by then it was too late.

Larry's voice had caught near the end of his dissertation and tears had flowed freely. He was wearing his Fireman's uniform.

Tim, dressed in a starkly black suit, white shirt and black tie, had stood stiffly. Leaning heavily upon his two crutches, he stated what he had memorized instead of reading it. He stared steely eyed directly at the camera.

In the background he heard people whispering. Almost everyone there had lost someone in the Towers' collapse, but somehow Tim had imagined that they were all only talking about him. Perhaps some of them had been, but Tim had never gone back again. Larry worried how the Firehouse might now influence Tim.

When they entered the building, there were only a few firemen standing around. Their conversation had stopped abruptly as they turned to view the strangers. Tim's leg and walking stick were immediately noted. Larry guessed that they might have been discussing sports, but he had no way of knowing.

"Uh, hi!" Larry said tentatively, "I'm Larry and this is Tim McGreevy. We used to work outta this barn."

"Oh," one of the firemen acknowledged, "He's in the kitchen. It's his turn to cook."

"Uh who's in the kitchen?" Larry asked, an uncertain and wan smile gracing his face.

Tim just stood, motionless except for a little swaying. His eyes travelled all over the garage bays, taking in the rigs, other equipment and the men's uniforms. A great many thoughts and memories collided in his mind. He wasn't aware that he was smiling.

"Ah, who's in the kitchen?" Larry repeated.

"McGreevy!" came the answer, "Ain't that who you're here for?"

Just then from the rear and to the left, a voice called out, "Yo, Dinner's ready. Come now or I'm throwin' it out to the alley cats."

Everyone, including Tim and Larry turned towards the voice.

"Sal," Larry called out, "Hey Sal!"

"Sal," Tim questioned in his mind, "Did he say Sal?"

Salvatore Ian "Sal" McGreevy was the son of an Italian American mother, Sophie, and Tim's brother Ian. Tim had not known that Sal was a fireman. There were a lot of things that Tim chose to no longer be aware of. Accordingly, Larry never brought them up.

Sal came forward, wearing an apron which read "Head Barbecue Artist". He was holding a long spatula and there was a touch of reddish sauce on his cheek as well as on the apron. He unconsciously wiped the sauce on his face with his sleeve.

Tim was amazed. Sal looked just like his father, Ian, but he had his mother's dark eyes and shiny black hair.

Larry was not quite as amazed as Tim since he had attended Sal's graduation from the Fire Academy. Larry had thought of the possibility of Sal being there on that night. It was yet another of his worries for Tim's peace of mind.

"Sal," Tim called out hoarsely, but with warmth in his voice, "is that you?"

Immediately, Tim chastised himself. "What a stupid thing to say." He berated himself, mentally.

"Whoa," Tim added, "isn't that the wrong uniform?" Tim immediately regretted that statement as well. His brother, Sal's father, had been a Port-Authority policeman.

Sal's expression briefly changed, but a broad grin leapt to his face as he approached his two uncles.

"Uncle Tim, Uncle Larry," he called out, "it's so good to see you guys."

Since he saw Larry on a semi-regular basis, he immediately went to Tim.

Extending his free hand, Sal was surprised when Tim wrapped both arms around his startled nephew. The spatula was caught between them and Tim's walking stick fell to the floor.

Caught unaware, Sal almost staggered beneath Tim's weight, but immediately recovered with Larry's help.

"Whoa," Uncle Tim," Sal said, "that's some grip you got there."

"Sorry Buddy." Tim responded, expelling a lungful of air simultaneously, "I was just so surprised to see you. When did you become a fire chaser?"

"A few years ago." Sal answered.

Sal debated mentioning Larry's influence throughout much of Sal's life. He decided that then was not the time to say so.

"I know what you're thinking though. Dad was a Port-Authority Cop, why not me." Sal shook his head sadly.

"No Buddy," Tim returned, "Not at all. I understand completely. Let's don't forget, I been on my own downward spiral for the last twenty years. Nobody, but nobody has been feeling more sorry for himself than yours truly.

"I'm sure you've always had the desire to be on the front lines. Hey, maybe even because of the way we lost your Dad. How you decide to fulfill that need ain't anybody's business but your own. And anybody, me included, that can't see that, is an asshole. And, believe me; I know exactly how an asshole thinks."

"Well said!" came a booming and familiar voice from behind them.

They all turned to see a tall imposing, salt and pepper brown haired man with a thin gray mustache and captain's bars on his collar.

Sal immediately said, "Cap, you're just in time. Dinner's ready, if you're up for it."

Tim said, "Sonuva bitch! Lew freakin' Mason, and with jewelry on his collar. Sonuva bitch!"

"Jeez, Timmy," Mason replied, "you're startin' to repeat yourself. Aren't you a sight for these tired old eyes?"

Once more Tim threw his arms around another person who wasn't quite prepared for the extra weight. Both Larry and Sal were prepared, however. Together they kept Captain Mason and Tim from collapsing to the floor.

Mason shook Larry's hand, once they had disentangled.

"How about it?" Mason asked, "Your nephew has cooked dinner. Don't tell him I said this, but young Sal here is becoming quite the chef. He's a pretty good fireman too. Of course I'm a bit prejudiced on that part."

A question flashed through Tim's mind, but he remained silent for the moment.

Larry and Tim tasted a bit of Sal's fare to be polite. They were, however a bit full from the earlier lunch at Scruffy's. They did agree that it was delicious.

The coffee however was fantastic.

"I gotta say," Tim related, "I don't remember Firehouse coffee ever bein' this good."

Later, as the other firemen had gone back to other things, and Larry was helping Sal load the dishwasher, Tim and Lew sat talking.

"This might sound funny Lew, all things considered," Tim said in low very soft tone, "but I need your help Buddy.

I'm just startin' to come outta my funk and I need to talk to someone."

"Sure," Lew said, "Ask away."

"Uh, don' take this the wrong way Lew, but it ain't you. It's one of your friends. You know that Catholic priest, McGinty? I'd like to talk to him."

Tim laughed out loud. "Even if he's a Police Counselor, but, he was there. He'll know exactly where I'm comin' from."

"Uh, well, uh, yea." Lew answered drily, "I can arrange that, easily enough, but he isn't a priest or a counselor anymore. He gave up the priesthood. In fact, I attended his wedding."

Tim's eyes were as large as saucers, as the saying goes.

"Really," he said, as a multitude of thoughts swirled about in his slightly dazed mind, "don't that beat all?"

"What, did he retire?" Tim asked while trying to sort through all the thoughts and questions in his mind.

"Uh, yes and no." Lew answered drily, "You must watch television Tim. Have you seen the various allegations of the Catholic Church trying to cover up signs of sexual abuse among the clergy?"

"Well, ah, yea." Tim answered.

"The thing is, the Church has lost a lot of parishioners in the last twenty or so years." Lew related.

"As have a lot of religions." Lew pointed out.

"Yea, that's true." Tim admitted, "But I guess the Vatican has just been tryin ta stem the flow, so to speak."

"Be that as it may," Lew answered, "It turned Mike off completely."

"Plus soon after he quit the priesthood, he ran into the daughter of his old partner, Eddie Flanagan. You remember Flanagan Tim. He was pretty active down at the Trade Center too. Turns out his daughter lost her first husband there as well. Funny thing was that he was a Philadelphia cop.

"It also turns out that Eddie's daughter, whose name is Theresa, had a hand in raisin' Mike's own daughter after her mother died from Cancer, and Mike became a priest."

"Wow, "Tim intoned solemnly, "Lotta stuff circling around and stickin' to one another there."

"Yea, I guess that's one way of puttin' it." Lew agreed.

"Larry could have hooked you up though. He knows Mike almost as well as I do." Lew added.

They sat sipping their coffee as each mulled the previous conversation.

Tim finally spoke. "Hey," he said, what was that remark about you bein' prejudiced over my nephew Sal?"

"Oh," Lew answered with a quizzical expression on his face, "I guess Larry didn't tell you."

"Tell me what?"

"Uh, Betsy died a few years ago. She had a heart attack. I been grievin' over her, but a couple of months ago I started dating Sophie, Sal's Mom. Sal was already assigned to this house, so I hope there wasn't any impropriety."

Tim punched Lew lightly on the shoulder. "Well, I'll be......" he let his voice trail off. "I never thought we'd be related, but Lew, I'm really sorry about Betsy. GOD rest her soul."

Lew nodded sadly and placed his hand over Tim's.

CHAPTER 35

SEEMS LIKE A PLAN

The waitress appeared beside them with fresh coffee. Though the lower part of her face was covered, there was a glint in her eyes.

"I haven't seen you ladies in a while." Agnes, the server said, "More coffee?"

"Peggy McGreevy said, "Sure, fill 'er up."

Sophie McGreevy merely nodded and pushed her cup forward.

Once the waitress had left, Peggy tugged her mask below her chin. She was grinning.

"So, what d'ya think about my Tim news Soph.?" she asked as the grin lit up her entire face.

"Well, Honey, I'm afraid I have even more news on that Tim subject." Sophie answered, "Guess who was at the firehouse last night with Larry, Lewis and my son Sal?"

"You're kidding!" Peg exclaimed, unable to hide the shocked expression on her face.

"Not only that, Peggy my dear, but guess who's staring in the window at us?"

Peggy's head snapped around. Her surprised expression did not change.

Tim, smiling, and with his mask hanging from one ear, waved to her, and then to Sophia.

Readjusting his mask over his face, Tim entered the café. He sat at the table with his ex-wife and sister-in-law.

"I saw Sal and Lew last night." He informed them.

"Yea, Lewis called me this morning." Sophie said. Her eyes sparkled with humor. "I just told Peggy."

"I got something to say, and I would like to say it with Sophie present, so I got a witness." Tim further informed them. He then sat quietly awaiting their reactions.

Sophie merely shrugged, but Peg leaned forward expectantly.

After a minute or more of silence, Peggy said, "I kinda have an idea of where this might be goin' Tim, but I ain't in the mood for guessing games. What's on your mind, if it wouldn't be too much trouble?"

"Geez," Tim exclaimed, "How I miss that mouth!"

He paused while he centered his thoughts. His eyes were somewhat knit and his mouth was open ever so slightly.

"Well," he said softly, "while I realize that me wantin' it don't mean it's gonna happen, but, I would like to court you Peggy Elizabeth McConnell McGreevy."

"So you wanna get back together?" Peg stated as much as asked.

"I didn't say that." Tim returned with a crinkling smile.

"Far too much has happened between us for me to expect that to happen right outta nowhere. I've let you down far too many times Peg. I would however, like a chance to make up for all I have failed to do in the past."

He was quiet once more. He was thinking and when the waitress approached he readjusted his mask and asked for a coffee plus two more for the ladies.

As the waitress left to fill the order, he cleared his throat and said, "Just one date Peggy, and then we can see where that takes us."

"Give me a little time to sort through this, huh?" Peggy asked.

'Why don't you step outside for a cigarette and let me discuss this with Sophie."

"I'll give you your space right now, but I gave up the smokes last night after I got home."

Both women looked at him with widely open eyes and gaping mouths. Peggy shook her head from side to side.

"Uh, Captain, There's a guy out here named McGreevy to see you.

He says he has an appointment." Sergeant Robert Conway informed Mike McGinty.

As Tim and Larry McGreevy appeared at the door of Chief Beymon's office, Mike motioned them in.

"This is my brother Larry, Captain," Tim said nervously, "Can he wait out there while just you and I talk, uh, Sir?"

"Sure, no problem." Mike answered, winking at Larry.

Mike hit the intercom switch and said, "Bob, one of these guys is gonna sit out there with you. Play nice"

Tim turned briefly to see Larry's expression. Larry nodded and stepped back with a faint smile.

When Tim turned back towards McGinty, he saw him removing his captain's bars and placing them in his pocket.

"Ain't no rank in here Buddy. We're just two guys talking."

"Lew told me a little of your background and I took it upon myself to research it a bit more. You've had some really serious setbacks Tim. Uh, may I call you Tim?"

"Sure Captain," Tim replied, "Tim's fine."

"Yea, but like I said Tim, there isn't any rank in here. We're just a couple o' old warhorses tryin' to muddle through some thoughts.

"Call me Mike. For one thing, you ain't even a cop. You were a fireman, and after everything I saw down on the site, you guys have my total respect."

Mike paused. He shuffled a few of the papers on the desk to regain his composure.

Finally he said, "I learned that paper shuffling thing from my boss, Chief Beymon. This is his office. I normally sit out there with Bob, uh the sergeant, but Beymon let me use his office to give you a little privacy.

"The Chief was down there too. He respects you guys as much as I do.

"I knew Myke Judge. We weren't buddies, or anything like that, but my Father-In Law, who back then was my partner, introduced us. When I heard that we had lost him, it hit me pretty hard.

"I, uh, I also know your brother Larry."

"Oh yea, Lew told me that." Tim replied, unsurely, "Things get a little muddled in my head though. This reaching out is totally new to me."

"I guess you know about the priest thing." Mike added, "I'm sure Lew must have told you if you didn't already know. There were a lot of reasons for that, some I'm not particularly proud of. One of the better inspirations however was Father Myke.

"Where do you want to start Tim? I can guide you, but it's your show. You're the one who's pushing your way through this dense forest. How may I help you?"

Mike paused momentarily, as much to allow Tim to think things through as to gather his own thoughts together.

"If it's any help, I have to deal with my own nightmares and visions." Mike continued, "Fortunately for me I have a built in support team. Each of them has their own 9/11 experience and none of those are particularly good, either."

"Well, for the longest time I thought I was the only one with any problems." Tim responded, "My brother Larry lost almost as much as I did. I always reasoned though, somewhere in the depths of my mind, that at least Larry still had both legs. At least Larry was still a fireman. I guess I felt like a total failure."

"That's all a part of the whole picture Tim. What was it, you lost four brothers?"

"Yea," Tim replied, "Three were firemen and one was a Port Authority policeman."

Mike was shaking his head. "Sounds kinda like that World War Two thing with the five Sullivans. They were all on the same ship when it was attacked."

"Yea, I saw that movie when I was a kid." Tim reflected, "Never thought it could happen to me, but here I am.

"Just what do I need Capt...., uh Mike."

"I'm sure you've heard this from other counselors, family and friends. But, you have to believe in yourself. You have to know that avoiding these thoughts for the last twenty years in no way makes you a failure.

"A failure would have given up completely years ago."

While he knew he would never say it out loud, the thought of certain cops committing suicide flashed through Mike's mind like a bolt of lightning. Some called it eating their gun. Mike had known at least two guys who had done that. He also knew Johnny Cello who had fought with grit through all the pain and discomfort that plagued him just so that he could be there for Phyllis, his wife.

"You sound like my brother Larry." Tim returned.

"Well, there ya go. You have your own built in counselor. And, Tim, just because he's your brother don't disavow his advice. Like you said, he lost almost as much as you did.

"I lost my wife to cancer a year later. I tried to escape by becoming a priest. While I was able to do some good as a police counselor, clearly I was trying to escape something similar to what you were hiding from.

"My present wife had lost her husband, a Philadelphia policeman who happened to be there that day. He went back into one of those buildings, and it took his life."

Tim could see thoughts circulating in Mike's eyes. He briefly looked away, unsure as to what might come next. He had to admit that the policeman impressed him. Or, maybe Tim was just ready to move on.

"Strike that, it wasn't the building that took his life." Mike added, "It was those stinkin' rottin' fuckin' scumbags who flew that plane into that building. Almost three thousand people died on that day. Then, how many died from the cancer that followed. "How many kids lost parents or grandparents? How many people lost lovers?"

Tim was sitting on the edge of his chair. He was trembling and his face was a bright red. A smooth sheen of perspiration coated his brow and his breath was shallow as it escaped and then reentered his lips.

"I need to be useful again Mike." He rasped through tightly clenched teeth. I can't sleep my life away any more."

They talked for another fifteen or so minutes.

Finally done for the moment, they entered the outer office.

Beymon was sitting in Mike's chair chatting with Larry McGreevy. While they had not known each other, they did have a couple of mutual friends.

After introductions were made and Beymon retired to his own office, Mike walked Tim and Larry out into the hallway. As they approached the elevators, Mike asked if the two of them were free for dinner on Saturday. Mike invited them to his house. Tim asked if he could bring a date. He explained that he was attempting to rekindle his marriage.

Mike agreed and after they had departed, called Theresa.

Saturday came, right on time. It came just after Friday and right before Sunday. Both Tim and Larry were nervous as they approached the McGinty house.

Peggy was with them. She had insisted that she sit in the back seat. Her reason was that Tim might need the extra room.

Tim knew better, but knowing of all the hell that he had already put her through, he agreed readily.

Her thought was that she wanted to move slowly and see just where they might be going in their relationship. Having lived with Tim as he had sunk deeper into the abyss of his mind, she was still a bit skeptical.

Mike and Theresa were waiting at the door for them. Mike had sprinkled extra salt upon the driveway and sidewalk, in lieu of Tim's artificial leg.

The salt had been enough and they were at the open front door in several minutes.

It was discovered that Peggy, a nurse knew exactly who Theresa was, including the return of the key to the City.

As planned by Mike, a wide ranging discussion centered, more or less on the events of 9/11 and their aftermath.

All of them, the Firemen, Mike and their dependents, each became even more aware of the suffering of the others.

Mike admitted freely that his hope was for some cathartic healing for everyone at the table including his own wife, mother-in-law and himself.

It had been pointed out that Ed Flanagan had been forced to retire as well. Ed still had both of his legs, but problems with his back had taken away his ability to walk freely.

While not specifically speaking of it, Tim had acknowledged it with a nod.

During dessert and coffee Maria, Davy and Amy showed up. Kenny was still at the market, working.

The presence of Maria and Davy brought two new facets to the discussion. Theresa had already touched upon their needs and problems from Nine-Eleven, but their presence brought even more depth to the exchange.

Watching as Tim would occasionally fidget in his chair, Maria coupled it with thoughts of one thing that was absolutely necessary to the subject of their discourse, Nurses.

Adding to the fact that both Melanie and her mother were nurses stoked the fire blazing through her young mind. Peggy also being a nurse added more fuel to her thoughts.

Seeing and knowing just how cleansing the experience had been for his family, Mike hoped sincerely that That Tim, Peg and Larry had all found a way to feel better as well.

He stated as much when the McGreevys stood up to leave.

Once the McGreevys had left everyone else returned to the kitchen. Dave and Amy had not been by for a while. Even though they all kept in touch with their phones, face to face time simply could not be replaced by devices.

After a couple of hours of conversation, interrupted only by Kenny's return, everyone started to drift away from the table.

Kenny went down to the basement to study, Marie although in good shape for a sixty year old woman, had gone to bed. Mike and Theresa were washing the dishes and Amy, having worked all day at Italos had also retired.

Davy and his sister sat side by side on the sofa, trying to relax.

"So, a cop, eh?" Davy finally said.

"Yea," Maria answered, "Mom wasn't too happy about it at first, but John seems to b growing on her. He works for Uncle Nicky, so that's a point in his favor. Even though he's Polish, his name sounds Greek, so Uncle Nick is pleased with that, as well.

"He have any battle scars?" Davy asked.

"A couple, but we haven't told Mom yet. Maybe Mike, uh, Dad may know something, but he hasn't let on yet, at least not to me."

"So, do you think it's serious?" Davy asked.

"I'm not sure Dave." Maria answered, "I mean, I really like him and I can see it going further. For now, however, it's just boyfriend-girlfriend."

Maria seemed to be thinking about something. Finally she said, "Hey Davy, what d'ya think about me becoming a nurse?"

Davy's grin was broad and beaming. At first Maria thought he was laughing at her.

Then he reassured her of his understanding with, "I knew it, Sweetie.

It was only a matter of time before the family legacy took hold of you too. I bet it was always there, just waitin' to pounce.

"Hey Maria, first Mom, then Melly, and now you.

"I think you would be a great nurse Honey. I'm all for it."

"So am I!" came Theresa's voice from the kitchen.

"It's bad enough that you're dating a policeman, but if it will keep you from becoming a cop then all the better.

"Don't get me wrong now Sweetie, I like John well enough. But I'd rather my own kids weren't cops.

"Uh, take that any way you want to Davy. I still love you."

As it turned out, Saints Bridget and Patrick hospital in Nassau County had its own accredited Nursing School. With the intervention of one Nurse Melanie McGinty, and with the help of Doctors Seamus O'Malley and Sylvia Feldstrup, Maria was admitted to their program.

Also in her favor was the fact that the Hospital Administrator, Hal Ablemeyer, felt that Dr. Feldstrup could walk on water. If Sylvia Feldstrup had decided that she wanted the actual planet Jupiter on her desk as an ornament, then Hal Ablemeyer would have entertained the notion in his head.

On one of those rare moments when Maria Keith had a few minutes with the so-so coffee in the cafeteria, she was able to converse with fellow nurse McGinty.

"This is really hard work Mel." She said between sips and grimaces at the pungent taste.

"But I gotta admit, nothing has ever given me such satisfaction. I really feel like I'm contributing here."

"Let me guess, Maria, there's half a sandwich in your pocket right now, isn't there?"

Maria smiled.

As Maria rose to return to work, Melanie added, "And of course, a few years back you wouldn't have been training amidst a worldwide pandemic."

Maria nodded knowingly and tugged all of her facial protection into place. With a glint in her eyes she gave Melly a sharp thumbs up and left.

Melly was thinking about the rest of her family when the sound of a male clearing his voice brought her back to the bright overhead glow of the cafeteria lights.

"Hi Sweetie." She chortled as she glanced up to see Jim Cantner approaching her table with three cups of coffee secured between his two hands.

"Who are those for?" she asked coyly as she batted her eyes.

"Well, one each for me and you," Jim replied as he batted his own eyes in a burlesque manner, "and the other's for O'Malley."

Melanie glance over at the cash register just in time to see a figure who appeared to be Doctor O'Malley's body type receive his change. He was carrying a couple of sandwiches in plastic wrap.

Through conversations with the doctor she had already determined that he was not related to their neighbor.

"McGinty," he called out as he approached the table, "I hope my sister is treating you well."

"Could not be better, Doctor." She stated definitively s she tugged her mask down to sip the coffee, "And thanks for the coffee."

"Yea," O'Malley replied, but I gather your sister doesn't care for our coffee. Does she?"

"Uh, how's she working out Doctor?" Melanie asked, "Any problems?"

"O'Malley chuckled. "You know I'm not supposed to discuss training nurses with other personnel, McGinty. Even if she's just as good as her sister, I'm not allowed to say so.

"A little decorum McGinty, oh, and ah, thanks for recommending her."

Staring into his coffee cup, Jim Cantner only smiled.

CHAPTER 36
LONG AGO AND SO VERY FAR AWAY

On a rare day off Salvatore McGreevy had gotten up early and stopped for coffee and a bagel at Fineman's Delicatessen, one of his favorite establishments in Williamsburg, Brooklyn.

There were any number of Hasidic people on and around the streets outside, but within Fineman's the other customers were all Goyem like Sal. While Sid Fineman enjoyed the color and attraction of the Hasidic Community, he, himself was of a more lenient branch of Judaism.

Breakfast over; Sal drove north to the Long Island Expressway.

His destination was his Mother's house in Queens and then the cemetery out in Nassau County where his Dad, Uncles and Grandparents were buried.

When his Mother, Sophia, entered the car there was a Fineman's bagel wrapped and on the dashboard for her. She munched it slowly while they conversed. It seemed as if most of the traffic was headed for Manhattan. The Covid pandemic still had the City, if not the entire Nation in its grip.

Within twenty minutes they were at the cemetery. After parking they walked slowly toward Ian's grave. Of course, Ian was buried near his brothers and parents.

Two figures stood at Ian's grave. They were easy to recognize. One was taller, a bit rangy and slumped. The other had a pair of crutches.

Sal smiled twice, once when he recognized them and again when he heard his mother gasp.

Larry and Tim turned simultaneously when they heard Sophia. Larry watched his brother nervously, afraid that Tim had turned too quickly. Tim only smiled.

Sophia seemed just a bit nervous. She kissed Larry's cheek as he leaned over. With a quick turn she stepped lightly over beside Tim and pecked his cheek as well.

"How's Peggy?" she asked softly. Sophia knew it was a touchy subject. She wasn't sure how touchy though.

"Could be better," Tim answered with a shrug, "but I guess I placed myself in this position. I might add, it could be a lot worse."

Sophia nodded nervously.

"Well," she said, "You understanding that seems like a big step in my book."

"A very big step!" Tim echoed with a silly grin.

"How's it going with the cigarettes?" she asked anxiously.

"Uh, not as well Soph. I still haven't lit up, but it's driving me nuts. You might say, though, it takes my mind off all of my other problems.

"How's the new fireman doing?" he asked, indicating Sal with a raised crutch.

"Oh, don't get me started." Sophia replied as her faint smile became a frown.

"Between him and Lew I have a mild heart attack every time I hear an engine's siren. I never felt this way with your brother."

At that she glanced wistfully at Ian's grave.

"I mean, I know he was a first line of defense, but until 9/11, who knew how truly dangerous that was."

At that, tears appeared in her eyes. Placing both crutches in one hand, Tim drew her into an embrace.

Sal stepped over to his Mom and uncle and threw his arms around both of them. Feeling just a little left out, Larry joined them as well.

After several minutes they all separated. Larry and Tim walked back and forth staring at each grave, including their parents. They were silent, but obviously an amalgam of thoughts slipped in and out of each man's head.

Sal and Sophia stood, just as silently, at Ian's grave.

Hearing the words announcing Ian's death still rang in Sophia's mind. She hugged her son even more tightly.

"I love you Sal." She said softly.

"I know Mom. I love you too."

"Hey, is this a private party, or can I get some of those hugs and kisses too?" Peggy called out as she approached the small group.

Tim began to smile broadly.

"Okay, you win McGreevy." She announced, "Let's try this one more time."

Within seven or so steps she reached his side. When he tried to kiss her cheek she grabbed his jaw within both hands and pulled his lips to hers.

"Don't worry if you forgot how," she told him in between kisses, "I remember enough for both of us."

CHAPTER 37

HOW VERY STUPID

It had begun as a lark. Too often, situations which suddenly get out of hand have begun innocently enough.

They had been friends since before High School.

Having had already graduated, they were all gainfully employed. Tommy and Lara were the only ones going to college. Tommy was a student at a County school in New Jersey and Lara was attending a two year business school. They both worked part-time, Tommy in a service station and Lara in a pharmacy.

Jerry, Tom C. and Carla all worked full time. Jerry and Carla worked at a major building supply store and Tom C. worked as a gopher in his father's insurance business. All of them lived in the same town they had grown up in, Paramus, New Jersey.

It was Tom C.'s birthday and the others had taken him into Manhattan to celebrate.

Tommy and Lara were the only couple. He was Thomas DiLibretto and she was Laraine "Lara" Coverton.

The others were Gerald "Jerry" Cohen, Thomas "Tom C" Carstairs and Carla Mendez.

How the party had gotten out of hand, nobody really knew. Surely an excessive amount of drinking was at least one of the causes.

They were in the Bronx having taken the wrong road out of Manhattan and the wrong ramp off the Triborough Bridge.

Of course, a sign which read Welcome to Yonkers, NY was a sure indication that they were nowhere near New Jersey.

Jerry, the driver, did a u-turn right in the middle of whichever road they were on.

After having travelled thirty or so blocks back into New York City, he pulled over, weary, and certainly too drunk to continue driving. While they argued and discussed what their further plans might be, Carla noticed a small house nearby that had lights on in its lower level.

Jerry, Lara and Tommy got out to investigate. Without really knowing why, Jerry took his father's thirty eight caliber revolver from the glove box and tucked it into his waistband.

"Just in case." He answered Carla's quizzical expression, to which she simply shrugged.

They knocked upon the house's front door, which foolishly, had no peephole.

The door opened minutes later and a pale, thirtyish woman wearing a robe over pajamas and with disheveled brown hair peaked out through the slightly opened door. Her eyes were tired looking above a faded blue hospital mask.

She had thought her husband had forgotten his house key.

Almost all at once she noticed their drunken condition, that there were three of them and the gun tucked into the taller one's pants.

It seemed even more threatening that black surgical masks covered their lower faces.

With a gasp, she tried to close the door, but there were three of them and they pushed even harder. Again, without knowing why, Jerry pulled the gun out and pointed it in the woman's general direction.

"P-please," she begged, tearfully, "Take whatever you want. Please, just leave us alone."

While the word coffee blared in Jerry's mind, he said nothing and pushed past the frantic woman.

Lara, in a panic mode herself, tried to get Jerry and Tommy to leave. They ignored her.

Jerry wanted coffee at any cost and Tommy desperately needed a bathroom.

Instead of the kitchen, Jerry found a small room converted into a bedroom with an old, perhaps seventy or so year old man in a hospital bed. Leaning over the man, Jerry rasped, "Hey Old Man, where do you keep your coffee?"

With a quickness and dexterity that shocked Jerry, the old man, though riddled with painful cancer, grabbed the younger man's hand, drew the pistol into his own mouth and pushed sharply against the trigger.

The echoing gunshot was extremely loud within that small enclosed space. Jerry pulled his hand back, without the weapon and with an extremely shocked look upon his very pale face.

All over the neighborhood lights came on and hands reached for telephones.

"What was that?" Lara exclaimed out in the corridor. Both Tom C. and Carla, out in the car, said the same thing.

Lara, still in the hallway, and too afraid to investigate the noise, did not see the fifteen year old boy descending the stairway, with his father's forty five caliber automatic pistol in his hand.

When he asked her who she was she screamed and raised both hands to her face. The sudden gesture frightened the boy and he fired his father's pistol in her direction. The bullet entered the wall, missing her entirely. She took advantage of his horror at what he had done and slipped out through the front door.

Tommy, responding first to one shot, and then to a second one, entered the hallway to search for Lara. Tommy, a larger target and definitely appearing more threatening, was the recipient of the boy's second bullet.

Having missed the first time, the boy aimed more surely, at the larger center mass target of the man's body.

Tommy was dead before he rebounded off the wall and onto the floor.

His blood stained that wall and the soft blue carpet beneath his body. A small amount of splatter hit the front door.

Responding to the incident were Patrolmen Italo, Calabrese and Keith along with Sergeant Vito Marciano.

They had been notified by the initial calls of neighbors, several of them.

The knowledge that two shots had been fired brought them rather speedily. Keith and Italo arrived in the first car followed quickly by Marciano and Calabrese;

When Italo and Keith had first arrived they found Gerald Cohen and Joey Brenner Jr. the fifteen year old boy, sitting side by side on the front steps. There was a car parked nearby with two girls and a young man.

A woman sat beside the boy with her arms around him. She was the only one wearing a surgical mask. Her eyes were worn and showed evidence of crying. As the two policemen approached, both Cohen and the boy, Joey Brenner held up hand weapons balanced on forefingers, holding them by their trigger guards.

Keith grabbed both guns as Italo stood with his own weapon drawn and held before him.

Davy placed both weapons in separate plastic evidence bags and labeled each with whom he had received them from.

After quickly determining who had been the home invader, Marciano handcuffed Cohen and made sure that the Brenner boy would not hurt himself. Both Cohen and Brenner however were extremely distraught.

Detectives arrived fairly quickly as well. They were Bob Eldred and Detective Sergeant Charles "Chico" Kloss

After determining that tests must first be conducted, the detectives reasoned that the initial shooting was probably a suicide and that the second was a form of self defense.

The one glaring factor, as Marciano mentioned, was that no one would have been shot if the young people who obviously were drunk, had not forced their way into the home in the first place.

"Especially," Marciano pointed out "If that jackass, Cohen had not been armed."

"Hey, Viduch," Sergeant Kloss commented, his tone quite weary, "You've always been a decent detective. How'd you like to sort this one out?"

Marciano just shook his head, no. Minutes later a police van pulled up and all the New Jersey kids were herded into it. Jerry Cohen's hands were cuffed behind his back. The others were allowed to be cuffed in front. None of them complained. Cohen appeared to be in shock and Lara Coverton had been crying since finding out that her fiancé, Tommy DiLibretto was dead. She blamed herself, reasoning that if she hadn't made any sudden moves, the young boy might not have been spooked. Each of them felt, individually that if they had shown some restraint, none of this would have happened.

They were certainly correct.

The ambulance and a blue late model SUV appeared at the same time. With Jerry Cohen's car blocking the curb, the ambulance swung out into the street and backed up to the sidewalk. They had not been told that both men were dead.

An SUV was left idling back a few yards from the ambulance. A tall husky man with tired features jumped from the vehicle and ran into the house. His clothes were worn and soiled. His eyes were drawn tightly together and he wore no mask.

By then, the woman, Elise Brenner and her son, Joey Jr. were side by side on the living room sofa. Her arms were wrapped around him. The dead man in the small bedroom was her father, Joey's grandfather, Edgar G. Lomax.

The new arrival was Elise's husband, Joe Brenner Sr. He asked how his wife and son were doing. The boy remained motionless, staring at the floor. Elise shrugged. Joe Senior saw the tracks of her tears, on her hospital masked cheeks and where they had stained her robe.

As the ambulance drivers were in the back with old Edgar, the hallway was empty but for Officer Vinnie Calabrese, Joe Senior and Tommy DiLibretto's inert body.

Suddenly and savagely, Joe Senior kicked the corpse in its ribs. Bones were heard cracking. Joe was wearing steel toed boots.

Jumping quickly to stop the angry man, Vinnie pushed him closer to the front door.

"Hey now," Calabrese said, in a voice that seemed to be somewhat understanding, "He can't feel that. Don't get yourself all upset like that. Your family needs you Buddy. Go on, go in to them."

At that Joe Senior began to cry. He pushed past the policeman and went into his family. Kneeling upon the carpet before them he wrapped his arms tightly around the two of them.

"I'm so sorry guys." He sobbed softly, "I should have been here for you. I'm so sorry."

As they drove back to their precinct house, Davy said, "I'm sure glad our involvement with that case was minimal. There's a whole lot of heartache attached to that one."

Nunzio nodded but remained silent.

CHAPTER 38
WELL, SEEMS LIKE A GOOD START

The day had been long and rather hard. Time wise, it had been no longer than twelve hours, not counting the commute, but they had been extremely difficult hours.

Theresa stood, practically slumped against the wall in the basement shower of the house she shared with her family.

She was weary beyond expression and the warm cascading water seemed to be making her even sleepier.

The door opened and Mike stood there with a big, fluffy towel a set of pajamas, slippers and a robe. The robe, also fluffy white cotton, was slung loosely over his arm.

"Let's get you up to bed Sweetie." He said, offering the towel. Another towel was spread upon the floor to collect dripping water.

Within minutes, she was dry and rubbing her damp hair with yet another towel. Minutes after that, dressed in her pajamas she was seated on the basement sofa as Mike knelt and placed her slippers upon her dainty feet.

"Okay, My Love," Mike began, here's how it works. "We'll get you up to bed and I'll bring your supper up to you. If you don't feel like eating, that's okay.

"If you wake up in the middle of the night and I don't, just nudge me. I will get you whatever you need.

"If, however you simply need the bathroom, I'll help you to go in there, but the rest of that scenario is on you.

"Oh yea, and maybe this bears repeating, I love you Theresa. As previously stated, you are the queen of my heart."

Leaning forward she wrapped her arms around him.

Thankfully he was able to support her as they ascended two flights of stairs.

As predicted, in no time she was asleep with an uneaten meal on the bed table, beside her.

Ron Beymon was tired. His wife, Monique had been up most of the night. Since she had gotten both Covid shots, and her breathing problems were minimal, they finally determined it to be her yearly spring allergies.

Despite his desire to stay at home with her, she finally convinced him that she would be alright.

Since nobody really knew much about the new Commissioner, Monique cautioned Ron to tread lightly around the man.

"Especially since Tom Freedon was such an as yet unknown." Monique told him.

As he stepped off of the elevator, Beymon spotted his subordinate, Captain Mike McGinty exiting the men's room. Mike was disposing of the paper towel he had used to handle the door knob.

When he saw his boss, McGinty half saluted him with two fingers.

"Good morning' Mike." Beymon rasped and then coughed lightly.

"Uh, morning Chief." Mike answered, "Are you alright Sir."

Concern was evident in McGinty's voice.

"Do I look that bad?" Beymon asked with a half smile.

"Uh, yea Chief, you do."

As they passed the ladies room, another subordinate, Sergeant Natalie Eberstein joined them.

"Jeez Chief," she muttered, with a slight gasp, "you get hit by a bus?"

Beymon shook his head and his smile became slightly more evident. "No he answered, "Just a rough, sleepless night with Monique's allergies."

"Yea," McGinty concurred, "Seems to be a lot of pollen this year. Theresa's a little under the weather today too. I tried to get her to stay home, but the hospital is shorthanded between Covid and other cases of allergies."

"Women," Beymon remarked with a snort, "they're a lot tougher than we are."

Although she remained silent, Natalie's smile became a grin.

As they entered Beymon's outer office Sergeant Bob Conway stood abruptly. He seemed a bit upset as he began to gesture toward Beymon's office door. Before he could say anything, the door opened and Chief of Patrol Dennis Meyer emerged, followed by a man in a suit who seemed slightly ill at ease.

"Gentlemen," Meyer began, "And Natalie, uh, Sergeant Eberstein, allow me to present our new boss, Commissioner Freedon."

Beymon congratulated himself on guessing correctly. He also applauded Monique for urging him to come to work.

Mike simply stood there, waiting for the two Chiefs and their new boss to decide what he should be doing.

Natalie wondered why Meyer hadn't mentioned the Commissioner's first name. "Maybe," she thought bemusedly, he only uses one name, like Madonna or Cher."

The Commissioner pushed past Meyer into the outer office.

He walked up to Beymon first and extended his hand.

"Hello Chief, I'm Burton Freedon. I prefer Tom, however in less formal situations. You don't really need to know why."

He then made his way around the room, greeting each person, including Bob Conway whom he had already met.

Meyer turned to Freedon and said, "Well Sir, if you don't need me anymore, I do have other duties."

Freedon dismissed him with a cursory wave of his hand.

Leaving the two Sergeants in the outer office, Freedon herded Beymon and McGinty into Beymon's own office.

"Gentlemen," he began as he took a seat opposite to Beymon's, "Please, sit down if you will. This won't take long."

Mike and Beymon did as directed. They both assumed it to be an order from their boss.

"Well," Freedon said, as he sat back, "I came into this building the other day with my ass on fire. My intention was to disassemble this building and rebuild it in my own image.

"To put it mildly, I had that ass handed to me in a paper bag. I don't intend to give you any details, but let's just admit that it happened.

"I was a bit unsure of myself at that moment and so I contacted Bob Gibson, your former Commissioner as you obviously already know.

"Bob helped me to connect the dots. I now realize that I am in a rather tenuous situation and my butt is as much on the line as every other cop in this city, uh, the guys actually doing the job."

Freedon paused to collect his thoughts.

"Well," he began anew, "I started with Agrarian and Meyer, both of whom had helped to set me straight in the first place, and I'm working my way down the ladder.

"This might place me in a bad light with His Honor, the Mayor, but we'll just have to see how it all plays out."

There was a knock at the door.

Natalie announced over the intercom, "Sirs, Mr. Holmes is here to see you."

Freedon nodded and Beymon told her to send him in.

As Holmes entered the room, Freedon stood and said, "And this gentlemen is one of my instructors."

After a brief discussion Freedon asked Beymon if he might use Beymon's office to talk with Captain McGinty.

After readily agreeing, Beymon picked up two coffee cups. Handing one to Holmes, he indicated the door and they both left.

"Mike," Freedon began, "may I call you Mike?"

"Sir, you're the Commissioner. You can call me anything you like."

"Well," Freedon replied, "to set your mind at ease, I do not want your Captains' bars. I've spoken to Garret and he has already set me straight on that matter.

"I want to talk about something else, and hopefully Garret has pushed me in the right direction on this subject as well."

As he paused, he glanced at McGinty's forehead. The scar was reddish, slightly jagged down near his temple, and pushing just a bit into the fluff of McGinty's eyebrow.

Pointing to it the Commissioner asked, did that hurt much?"

"Hurt like hell." Mike answered, wondering where this conversation might be leading.

"Look, I know this is a painful subject, and I won't press it if you say no." Freedon related slowly with a worried expression on his face. "But Garret tells me to really understand this department and all the other emergency agencies in this City; I have to step back in time, back to Nine-Eleven.

"He tells me that you can tell me some of what I need to know. However, if you cannot, for whatever reason, he says there are many others that I can go to."

He could see the wheels rolling behind Mike's eyes.

"Not just now, however." Commissioner Freedon continued, "If it happens it will have to be when you feel ready. For now, just think about it. Can you do that much for me.?"

Mike nodded. "Give me a day or so, Sir. I realize that the bigger picture is much more important than my needs. Let me mull it over."

Reaching out, Freedon slapped Mike gently upon his shoulder.

"You got it." He replied and got up to leave.

Mike was still sitting in place when he heard Freedon say, "Chief, if you need to take the day off it's okay by me. I can see that you have a good staff here. I, ah, do have your cell number if I need you, but I don't think that'll be necessary."

Mike then heard, "Garret, can you come with me. I need to discuss some things."

Moments later, Beymon reentered his own office.

"I guess you heard, eh?" he said to Mike.

When Mike nodded, Beymon reached for his jacket and hat and said, "You're in charge now, Captain. Keep me in the loop if it's necessary. Like the Commissioner said, you have my cell number."

As Beymon began to exit he glanced back at Mike who had yet to move.

"Oh yea," he barked with a smile, "Don't drink all my coffee." And then he was gone.

It had been a long day, longer; it seemed than the actual nine hours plus those fifty five minutes of commuting time.

Mike had emerged from his shower in the basement to find clean clothes stacked upon the coffee table. Donning the underwear, slacks and

T-shirt, he tucked the sneakers under his arm and trudged up into the Dining Room.

Enticing aromas filled his nostrils. He groaned softly, but in a pleasant manner.

"Is that you Mike?" Theresa called out. "Dinner will be ready in around ten minutes or so."

Her eyes brightened when he appeared in the kitchen doorway.

"Oh wow," she murmured, "You look beat. Rough day?"

She noted with satisfaction that there were no new bandages, lumps or gouges.

"Yea," he answered, "Beymon had to go home because Monique is sick. Ah, she has allergies, not the Covid.

"Also, I met the new Commissioner today. He isn't as bad as they make him out to be. Oh, and I'm still a Captain."

Theresa noticed a certain melancholy in his tone.

"Well then, what's bothering you Honey?" She asked as she dumped a large pot of pasta into a colander in the kitchen sink.

"He wants a better understanding of 9/11." Mike related, "Holmes told him that I could be his best source."

As the rising steam from the draining macaroni drifted upward, Theresa seemed to be pondering Mike's statement. Her perplexed expression relaxed into one of better understanding.

"How about dinner here?" she suggested, "And then I, my Mom and the kids can add to the conversation. We could be your backup team. We can try to arrange it for all of the kids to participate, Melly too."

Mike's eyes lit up.

"I swear," he murmured as a small smile tugged the corners of his mouth higher, "I think I married a genius."

"No Sweetie," she replied, "You just married Eddie Flanagan's daughter."

Coming in from the front porch with O'Malley in tow, Marie Flanagan called out, "Hey, I helped."

"How about the McGreevys?" Mike suggested, "Add a fireman's point of view."

Taking a seat upon the sofa, O'Malley said, "I was there McGinty." His voice trailed off as he repeated, "I was there......"

At first, Commissioner Tom Freedon wondered at the sagacity of a meal at McGinty's. Between the New York Press and his now tentative connection with his boss, the Mayor, it could be a possible mistake.

Overriding his own fears, he had simply enlisted the help of his Security detachment's leader, Sergeant Robert O'Connor. Per O'Connor's advice, the vehicle of choice was a black, unmarked police SUV with unofficial license plates.

Sergeant O'Connor, in plain clothes, drove.

As they pulled into the McGinty driveway, Arianna Freedon mentioned what a beautiful house it was.

Tom Freedon wondered briefly on how a police captain could afford such a house.

Had he inquired he would have found that the house had sat upon the market for over a year while the owner, an independently wealthy man had wanted to get on with his life and secure his new home in Florida.

Add to that the fact that the home had been paid off twenty seven years prior by the man's father, from whom he had inherited the house.

Add also that the man's blind son had been halfway down the stairs between his thirty third floor office in WTC-1 and the street when WTC -2 collapsed on September eleventh in 2001.

A police sergeant named Michael McGinty had met and made certain that the young man had reached safety.

Mike had conversed with the young man as they had descended to keep him calm. Mike's name had been mentioned several times in answer to the frightened fellow's questions.

Mike had paid an extremely inexpensive price for the house to a very grateful seller.

Of course, none of that affected the rather high Queens Boro taxes paid to New York City.

When Marie Flanagan, however, had moved in with her daughter and son-in-law, she had insisted on receiving no charity.

She helped to pay for the current taxes.

When Sergeant O'Connor returned to the vehicle Theresa suggested that he join them. Mike explained the nature of his position as a security professional, much to Freedon's satisfaction after the sergeant had declined.

Theresa nodded in understanding and acceptance.

Because of a pre-scheduled appointment, Tim McGreevy could not attend. His brother Larry and nephew Sal did attend.

Maria and Kenny served the food, but as delicious as it looked and smelled, the subject of the night was dwelling deeply upon each person's mind. Only O'Malley ate with any gusto.

O'Malley's mug was filled with coffee and Bushmills' whiskey. In deference, however to the current subject, he sipped at it sparingly. He was listening though. He had suffered his own 9/11 problems. He usually alleviated his own nightmares with that self-same Bushmills.

As host, Mike felt that he was expected to lead off and did so.

He was reluctant at first, stammering and frequently pausing. He realized however just how sympathetic his audience was. Everyone there had suffered from 9/11. He wasn't sure about the Commissioner and his wife, but then again, who knew.

He spoke first of his reoccurring dreams. Theresa, her mother and all the firemen nodded knowingly. Even young Sal who had lost his Port Authority Policeman Father had his own experiences.

Everyone became especially attentive when Mike spoke of the encroaching ominous cloud. Both of the senior firemen had grave expressions on their faces. O'Malley took an especially large sip from his mug.

Once more, when he spoke of pulling live people from the burning buildings, and then searching for body parts, the firemen grew very rapt in their attentiveness.

Marie Flanagan disappeared momentarily and returned with another large mug. She set it in front of O'Malley who grunted a warm thank you.

She placed a second mug before Larry McGreevy.

"If you don't mind," Commissioner Freedon asked, "Might I have one of those too?"

When Marie glanced at his wife, Arianna simultaneously shook her head and her hand no. Touching her own coffee cup, she said, "No thank you. I'm fine."

When Marie returned with the Commissioner's mug she had brought one for herself.

Mike felt a minor headache building just above and between his eyes. He continued anyway.

He spoke of lost friends, finding body parts and of Jenna's painful life taking cancer.

Several tears ran down his cheeks as he described Jenna's last days and how he felt that the debris and smoke from 9/11 had obviously contributed to her suffering.

Beside him, Theresa grasped his hand tightly. Marie offered him a sip from her cup, which he accepted gratefully.

Next Larry McGreevy stepped up to the plate. While he had suffered greatly in the loss of his four brothers, he related the terrible suffering of his brother, Tim. Tim had also lost those same four brothers. He had lost his job, and his right leg. Eventually, Tim's attitude had also cost him his marriage, although he was then actively attempting to reconcile with his former wife.

Larry mentioned his brother Ian, a Port Authority Cop who was one of his four lost brothers. Nodding toward Sal, Ian's son, he spoke glowingly of Sal's efforts to go on without his loving father. He mentioned so many fireman friends from all over the City who had lost their lives, both then and in the devastating Cancerous loss of life in the following years.

"Last I heard," Larry told them, "somewhere around one hundred and twenty firefighters alone have, or still are suffering from some kind or another of breathing problems. Add to that cops, hospital people and sanitation people."

"Sanitation people?" Freedon interrupted with a questioning tone.

"Yea, somewhere up around 400 or so day laborers and sanitation guys and building maintenance workers tested positive for that crap

"Even at that, however, these guys found themselves battling City Hall so to speak. Not the Mayors, necessarily, but those rat-bastard other politicians.

"And, every now and then you hear about some other poor soul who finds him or herself sick. Even though they can usually trace it back to the Trade Center, usually with a team of physicians confirming, they gotta fight tooth and nail to get any results. How often, I wonder, do they die and their relatives are left holdin' the bag in the midst of their sorrow."

Larry paused. He seemed to be thinking. He was tapping his right cheek with his right forefinger. He blinked several times quickly before he continued.

"They did push for respirator use in the days that followed. I think OSHA was behind that, along with the brass of all the different first responders."

Theresa glanced at Mike from the corner of her eye. He was watching Larry and did not notice.

She worried deeply that Mike might yet succumb to a disease related to Nine-Eleven. That is if he didn't get his damn head blown off on the damn job.

She held her tongue. Now was neither the time nor the place to discuss the topic. She made a check on a list in her mind that was always current. She would suggest another check-up for the man that she loved.

She noted that his forehead damage had gotten just a tiny bit smaller, but was currently somewhat red.

"That was a lot of damn asbestos, ya gotta admit." O'Malley chimed in.

Mike worried that the old fireman might say something out of hand.

He, Theresa and Marie listened keenly, wondering what O'Malley might say next.

"I remember hearing fire chiefs say that the EPA back then said it wasn't so bad. Then I heard it on several radio news shows. I never even saw a TV in the next few months." O'Malley added.

"I remember that Rudy was furious."

"Rudy?" the Commissioner asked.

"Giuliani." O'Malley answered, "I know he has himself in a world of trouble now, but back then he was one hell of a Mayor.

Shrugging his shoulders, O'Malley said, "Better than what we got now."

Theresa noticed that his brogue was not as prominent when he was sober, well as sober as she had ever seen him.

"You have to realize," McGreevy continued, "It wasn't just asbestos. There was fiberglass, lead, silica, mercury and who knows what else."

"Plus all that dust." Sal added, "I know I wasn't there, but I read about the dust clouds all the time. I wonder just what my Dad went through."

Sal's voice caught in his throat as he said, "GOD I miss him. I was just a toddler, but I can still see his smile and hear his laugh."

Larry laid a hand upon his nephew's shoulder and lightly hugged him.

Resolutely, Sal McGreevy held back his tears.

Theresa thought about the clouds in Mike's dreams. They had also intruded upon her dreams from time to time. She remembered that they had swept on up West Street with an unrelenting fury, in life as well as in her nightmares.

Larry did not mention it, but of dead first responders, Firemen suffered the most greatly. That figure included Fire Chief Peter J. Ganci Jr. who had refused to leave his men. It also included Fire Chaplain Father Mychal Judge, a Catholic priest. Both men had died when the North Tower collapsed.

Commissioner Freedon looked over to Theresa.

"Pardon me Mrs. McGinty," he said, "But Garret Holmes told me that you lost your first husband at Nine-Eleven. He said that you were left to raise three small children on your own."

Theresa pointed at each of her three kids.

"I had help." She told him. "Both of my parents, my in-laws and this guy in particular were of tremendous aid."

At that, she pointed her thumb at Davy.

"He's a patrolman up in The Bronx now. He's had his fair share of scrapes too, I'm sorry to say."

Freedon took note of the passion in Theresa's voice as she spoke of her children.

"I might add Commissioner," Mike chipped in, "That there were moments, perhaps far too many moments, when I was not there for my daughter, Melanie. At a point, Theresa stepped in and helped to raise her as well. I am so thankful that she did, too."

Freedon glanced over at Davy, noting mentally that the young man did not wilt beneath his gaze.

"So you're a cop too eh." Freedon said and then asked, "How many cops are in this family, anyway?"

"My Grandfather, my Father, my Son, and my Husband were or still are policemen." Theresa answered. "My first husband, Dominic was a Philadelphia cop as are his two surviving brothers."

Freedon shook his head.

Looking over to Larry McGreevy he said, "And you had four fireman brothers plus a Port Authority policeman? You people amaze me."

It was at that moment that Kenny said, "What about Uncle Nick?"

Looking back at Theresa, Tom Freedon raised his eyebrows expectantly.

"Well," Theresa returned, "Nick is the commander of the precinct we're in. He's not a blood relative, but he's Mike's brother from another mother.

"As boys, they were regaled by tales of police work my Father told. I guess Dad was the primary reason that Nick and Mike became cops.

"And, while we're at it, Davy's partner is a patrolman, but his Uncle and late father were both police captains." Mike interjected.

Freedon gasped and took a sip of water.

"It gets better Commissioner," Mike added, Nunzio, that's Dave's partner, has given his sister Amy to be David's bride if ever we get over this damn Covid."

At that, both Davy and Theresa smiled.

Maria raised her hand shyly, a faint smile upon her lips.

"Oh, yes, lest we forget," Theresa added, "My daughter there is dating a patrolman from this precinct. Nick is his Commander."

"It must get pretty dicey when any one of them is in danger then." Freedon observed drily, although that particular tone had not been his intent.

"You have no idea Commissioner." Theresa replied, shaking her head gently from side to side.

"Sometimes I wonder," Davy spoke up, "Which is worse, the wound or the lecture afterwards."

Keeping silent, Theresa shot her son a rather sharp look.

It did not go unnoticed by the Police Commissioner.

Everyone spoke and by evening's end, Tom Freedon had a very clear picture of what 9/11 had meant to everyone there.

More importantly, he had an extremely clear idea of how the New York Police Department should be run. It did not jive, at all with what the Mayor or City Council wanted.

In the back of his mind, Tom Freedon wondered what could have enticed him to leave Western Pennsylvania.

After Freedon and his wife had left, Larry McGreevy stepped over to O'Malley.

"You're Tony Pretalamo's Father-in-law, aren't you?" he said with a smile.

"You might not remember me, but I dated your daughter, Lydia briefly.

Worst thing I ever did was let her go. Your wife was upset that I was a fireman. She said that one asshole in the family was enough."

"Ah, she did now didn't she. Ye might not think it, but I sometimes ponder for my Liddy callin' me that. Me daughter was named after her darlin' mother." O'Malley returned with a chuckle. "Sure didn't she inherit her mother's Irish temper, now!"

Larry nodded without admitting that he already knew that.

Lydia O'Malley had taken a very large piece of his heart when she had broken off with him. When she had married Tony Pretalamo she had taken the rest.

But that was then and this was now.

"I see Tony occasionally, but I don't ask him about Lydia. How's she doing?"

CHAPTER 39
IT'S A POLITICAL THING

Robert Gibson, former Police Commissioner for New York City, sat quietly. He was in the anteroom of the current Commissioner, Tom Freedon.

Freedon's assistant Alice, had already offered him coffee, which he had declined. Gibson glanced about the office. He noted that the only thing that had changed was the number of assistants. He had employed one, while Freedon had two, Alice Agrippo and......... He strained to read the woman's name plaque. Ah, the name Enid Bloch finally came into focus.

"Oh, crap!" Gibson thought silently, "Time for glasses. Geez, getting old sucks"

His own assistant, Denise Aguilara had followed him to Albany and again to his new assignment in the City. He had been a widower when she was assigned and she was a widow. Sparks had flown, and now they were a couple.

He was thinking, at that moment, a thought which occurred to him often. He had yet to act upon it, and knew if he did not act soon; the situation just might bite him in the ass.

Moments later, after reaching his decision, he called the Governor on his private cell phone.

"Ed," he said bluntly, "I just wanted to let you know that what I mentioned the other night is a fact. With your permission, I'll mention it to the press this afternoon."

Edward Townsend "Ed" Caliva, the present Governor of New York chuckled loudly. He was talking to, or actually, presently listening to his boyhood friend of too many years to calculate, Robert Oliver "Bob" Gibson.

"Not a problem Bobby," Ed replied with still another chuckle. "But, I should warn you. The press is going to be all over you. I just found out that Steve accidentally revealed your new position. Rather than dance around, I just confirmed it to the local Press. I'm sure the City papers and TV media will be all over it within the half hour or even less.

"Oh, and Bob," Governor Caliva continued, "I'm starting to hear good things about that new Police Commissioner, but let's not take any chances. Fill him in on all we just discussed.

"Talk to you later Bud!" Governor Caliva said as he clicked off his own phone.

"He'll see you now Commissioner." Alice informed him, "Just go right in."

Tom Freedon actually met Gibson at the door.

Gibson glanced around the room, noting that nothing had changed.

Freedon noticed him looking and said, "No, I haven't stamped it with my own presence yet Commissioner.

Gibson's expression grew serious.

Gibson was lean in an almost muscular kind of way. While he did work out from time to time he wasn't really a fanatic. Denise made certain that he ate healthy. At best he was allowed an occasional glass of wine and his major weakness, popcorn. However, since Denise had entered his life, butter-free popcorn was the norm.

"Two things Tom, if I may call you Tom. Firstly, please call me Bob. I'd prefer it to any title, between us. We will be consulting rather often, which brings me to the second item.

"As just released by the Governor's office, my new title is Assistant Attorney General. I wanted to tell you myself, rather than have the New York Press ambush you with it. I'll be confirming it to the press this afternoon.

Gibson's eyes suddenly lit up.

"Hey," he revealed, "I just had an idea.

"Now, the decision is entirely yours. You're certainly going to have to take the Mayor into your consideration and whatever you decide is okay with me. But, how about if you come to my press conference with me. That way it won't seem as if you were blindsided."

"May I make a suggestion then?" Freedon asked. Apparently Freedon was a lot quicker than Gibson had originally given him credit for.

Gibson nodded.

"Well, unfortunately for me, I'm beginning to learn the ins and outs of big city politics more and more. It's a bit similar to Squiresville, but comparing the two is like the difference between a mosquito bite and being smashed in the face with a sledge hammer."

Gibson laughed out loud. "You want me to notify the Mayor ahead of time, as well, don't you?" He confirmed.

Freedon nodded nervously. "Uh, yes," the new Commissioner answered, "if you wouldn't mind."

Assistant Attorney General Gibson pulled out his phone once more and punched one number.

On the other end, Mayor D'Alorio looked at the number and answered "Can this wait Gibson? I'm on my way to a press conference."

"No Sir," Gibson responded, "They might have some information that you don't have and I don't want you to get ambushed."

There was a moment of silence on the other end.

Taking it as a sign to continue, Gibson said, "This information was not supposed to be released until next week, but someone in the Governor's office accidentally let it slip a short while ago."

"Well, what is it," D'Alorio snapped, "Or are we playing guessing games?"

"Well Sir," Gibson answered, respectfully despite the Mayors surliness, "My new title is Assistant Attorney General and I have been assigned to your city."

As silly a statement as this might be, the silence on Mayor D'Alorio's end was rather deafening. Gibson waited dutifully as the Mayor regained his composure.

D'Alorio cleared his throat, twice.

"Uh, thank you Mister Attorney General." The Mayor answered, "I really do appreciate the heads up. That could have been embarrassing."

"To be perfectly honest, Your Honor, while I see now what a good idea it was, I cannot take credit for it.

"I'm standing here with Tom Freedon and it was his idea."

"Ah, please tell Tom that I said thank you and that I'll speak to him later. Right now I have to go disappoint a bunch of rowdy media people. I can hardly wait. This'll be my opening statement."

When your leg is fused at the knee, some days seem longer than others, particularly the rainy ones. Sergeant Bob Conway's knee was especially painful on that rainy April morning,

It was barely ten thirty and he felt as if he had been there at work for two or three days. He had taken all the painkillers that he was allowed, but the leg still throbbed sorely.

His desk had been modified. The drawers on the right side as he sat had been removed. In their place, the space was quite open.

He was able to slide down in his chair and place his foot on a small ottoman which Beymon had ordered specifically for Bob's use.

Noting the tiny lines of anguish around Bob's eyes, Natalie Eberstein, Bob's trainer, stood.

"How about a cup of coffee Bob?" she asked, nodding toward the single cup maker, "I'm buying."

Conway smiled and offered her his cup. "Well," he answered, "as long as you're buying."

Across the room, Mike McGinty stirred. He rose, and brought his mug over as well. Looking at Conway, he smiled and tapped his own mug against his leg.

"Rough day, huh Bob?" Mike observed, "Well, sooner or later this weather's gotta let up. I know they're no match for yours, but I have a few aches myself."

"Old guys," Natalie chanted, "Ya can't live with 'em and........"

"Hold it right there Nat," Mike interrupted, "That about sums it up."

"In a nutshell." Conway completed Mike's sentence, with a wry chuckle.

He and McGinty laughed together. As she placed Conway's coffee on his desk, Natalie shook her head and grinned.

Before Mike could step up to the coffee maker, Natalie took his mug from his hand.

"Hey," she reminded him, "I said I'm buying. Go sit down Captain. I'll bring it to you."

She looked at Conway and winked. "Ya just gotta know how to kiss butt." She told him with another wink.

McGinty smiled and he too shook his head.

From the open door to the hallway, came the voice of former police commissioner Bob Gibson.

"Speaking of brownnosing," he said with a chuckle, "Even though I don't work here anymore, can I get a cup too."

"For you Commissioner, anything." Natalie retorted.

"Well, not anything," Gibson replied, "Jim O'Leary is a lot tougher than I am. Just the coffee, please."

While all that had been going on, Bob Conway had depressed the button on his desk intercom to alert their boss of their distinguished visitor.

Chief Ron Beymon had heard almost all of that short conversation. He appeared at the door between the offices.

"Ah, Commissioner Gibson," he called out, "Other than coffee, how may we be of service?"

"Well Ron, I have some information for you. I just told the new Commissioner and his Honor the Mayor. I'm on my way down now to spill it to the press, although Albany accidentally leaked it to them earlier this morning."

"Oh, sounds important." Beymon conceded. "But how does it concern us?"

"Well, Ron, technically it does concern you and the rest of NYPD.

"Governor Caliva has appointed me as an Assistant Attorney General with the City here as my bailiwick.

"Other than Denny, ah Denise that is, nobody really reports to me, but I can live with that.

"Oh, and I'm also going to tell the Press that Denny and I are an item."

"Hey," Beymon returned, shrugging, "You're both adults and both widowed, so I see nothing wrong there."

"Ah, but you're not the Press, looking to hang a politician out to dry, now are you?" Gibson replied as his smile faded just a bit.

From out in the corridor they heard the approaching voice of Commissioner Freedon, "I'm ready when you are, Mr. Attorney General. Let's tackle this together."

As they left, Natalie shrugged and said. "Hmph, I think everybody in this building outranks me."

"Hey," Bob Conway brought up, "We're both sergeants."

"Yea," Natalie answered, "But, you have more time in grade than I do."

Conway shrugged as well, and smiled.

CHAPTER 40

YOU AND ME AND.........

Amy Italo was beginning to understand Theresa McGinty's frustration just a bit more. Between Davy's, Nunzio's and Gerrie's injuries she was worn to a frazzle. Add to that her Mom's wound and Jose's death and some days she just wanted to scream.

She had Meg Thebes' shield number 5274 embroidered on all of her work blouses. She had especially liked Meg.

"Why," she asked herself, "is it always the really nice ones?"

Rhonda Italo was out in the restaurant taking a break. Before being shot, Ronnie rarely took a break. Now they came a little more often than Ronnie appreciated. They had been forced to hire three more employees to take up the slack. The two waitresses, Ginny Melino and Betty Ralston had caught on quickly. Two men had not been able to fulfill Jose's duties to Ronnie's satisfaction. Each had left within a week of being hired. Amy however had come up with the perfect solution. She had recruited a woman to replace Jose. The woman's name was Tomasa "Tomy" Nunez. She was Jose's widow and she was as good a worker as he had ever been.

Most of the time Tomy's sister Ynez watched Tomy's kids, Jose Jr. and Maria.

When it became necessary, Ronnie Italo was happy to have them in the restaurant.

Both Davy and Nunzio had been wounded recently. Gerrie had not, but still had a nagging headache from her head wound suffered from thrown debris.

Amy knew about Gerrie's headaches but had promised to keep the policewoman's secret.

Amy thought perhaps Davy had suspicions of Gerrie's discomfort too, but for whatever reasons he might have, he had also remained silent.

On that particular Thursday, Amelia Italo had far too much on her mind.

Not only was she acting as everyone else's confidant, but she was co-managing the restaurant, waitressing, filling in as cook whenever needed, and losing sleep each night as she worried about everyone else in her life.

Recently she had been experiencing stomach pains and had virtually lost her appetite. She explained her discomfort to herself as her worry for all the others.

At a point, when she had paused to catch her breath and was leaning up against a table in the kitchen, Tomy Nunez asked her, "So, when are you due Honey?"

"Wh-what?" Amy stammered as the stunning realization flashed into her mind.

"The baby," Tomy added, "you're pregnant, right?"

"Who's pregnant?" Ronnie asked as she entered through the swinging doors.

She stopped abruptly when she saw her very pale daughter almost lose her grip on the table she was leaning on.

Hoping to reassure Amy as quickly as possible and keep her from actually falling, Ronnie rushed to her side.

"Hey, Amelia," Ronnie called out excitedly, "You gonna make me a Grandma?"

Reaching Amy's side, Ronnie simultaneously held Amy up and leaned over to listen to Amy's abdomen.

Amy groaned softly.

"Seriously?" Davy grunted into the phone. Unconsciously he moved the phone just a bit further from his ear.

"I'll be off in another hour, Honey." He told Amy, who had called him. "I know you're doin' all the heavy work Babe, but this is great news. But, let's go tell my Mom together. Okay?"

As he turned his phone off, Nunzio said, "What's with the dopey smile Dave? Who was that?"

"Nunzio, my man," Davy answered, almost gushing, "you are about to become an uncle."

"Wh-what?" Gerrie stammered, "What did you just say?"

"And you, Miss Contadina," Davy directed to her, "you, if you marry this crazy Eye-talian, will be the baby's aunt.

"Hell, you're already my sister from another mother. You'll be his aunt no matter what you decide."

With Davy's hand at Amy's back, they entered the McGinty- Keith home.

On the sofa, side by side, Theresa and her Mother Marie were smiling.

"When?" Marie called out, "You have baby written all over your faces."

"You already know?" Davy asked, his voice laced with astonishment.

"Oh, Mom," Amy muttered, placing her hand over her eyes, "You just had to be the one, didn't you?"

"Oh, don't blame her Sweetie." Theresa gently admonished, "You should have heard the abject joy in her voice when she called. You know that she loves you Amy."

Amy lowered her hand. Unconsciously she placed it on her belly.

"Yea, I know." Amy admitted with a shy smile. "She's been looking forward to grandchildren from the moment she found out she was pregnant with me."

Amy chuckled out loud and once more murmured, "Mom!"

Theresa and Marie were immediately on their feet and wrapping their arms around both Amy and Davy.

"Hey, that's my first great-grandchild too." Marie crooned sweetly.

Naturally problems presented themselves almost immediately.

The wedding, planned for the following Saturday was in danger of being postponed indefinitely. Ronnie's Bronx parish was unable to hold it there because of prior scheduling to which current Covid problems might be added.

There was one Catholic Chaplain from the Police program available, but he let it be known that he was not a fan of Michael McGinty. In the end, however The New York Police Chaplain Corps did save the day.

Rabbi Mark Feinstein agreed to officiate and even to give his best rendition of a City Hall type of service. His only condition was that it be changed to the next day, Sunday, for obvious reasons.

As it turned out, when the big day arrived, Mark Feinstein had been able to reach out to a boyhood friend, Father Edwardo Gomez, a Catholic Priest.

Both Davy and Amy however insisted that Rabbi Mark also be a part of the ceremony.

A Yarmulke was not worn by the groom, and neither was a glass broken at the end of the ceremony.

Still, the spirit of two religions honoring the one GOD was kept.

The fact that Patrolmen aren't particularly rich and that Amy placed a lot of her salary back into her Mother's business influenced the young couples living arrangements.

Amy still had her room over the restaurant, so that is where they lived.

Melanie and Jim had their own place. Maria had her own room and Kenny still preferred the basement apartment.

That left at least one empty bedroom in the McGinty household. They considered offering it to O'Malley, but he wasn't interested. As it turned out, he owned the house across the street. Of course his daughter would be inheriting it, but for now, it was still his.

"Besides," O'Malley reasoned, "that's me daily sabbatical now, is it not?" "Where else would I be getting' me exercise?"

Marie Flanagan only shook her head.

Mike thought out loud, "Maybe I should buy some Bushmill's stock, especially if you're gonna outlive me."

"You and all of your great-grandchildren." O'Malley replied with a snort and a chuckle.

Most of the time nevertheless, O'Malley had other things pressing upon his mind.

Back when that Police Commissioner had visited, after all had left but family and O'Malley, the old man had been lost in his thoughts.

They were things which would have been pertinent to that dinner conversation with that Commissioner, but they were things that O'Malley had no desire to share.

In his mind's eye O'Malley saw the two giant buildings tumbling down to the Manhattan bedrock, the North Tower splaying down upon and around the already fallen South Tower.

In his dreams, even the ones on McGinty's sofa, the two towers were transformed nightly and daily sometimes, into two huge, sparkling whiskey bottles. There were never any labels on the whiskey bottles, so they could have been American, Scottish, or perhaps Irish. When awake, however, the spirit from O'Malley's homeland was preferable.

O'Malley had spent sixteen days of the month of September in that hospital up there along the East River. They had said he would never walk again, but he fooled them.

Not only was he able to walk again, but he had returned to work as well. Nine years later, he had been crushed beneath a collapsing building down in Greenwich Village in Manhattan.

Once more the doctors had said he might be crippled for life. Once more, against all odds, O'Malley had fought back. It had required fusing three of his vertebrae together, and had forced him into retirement. Still, he had walked again.

Occasionally he would laugh to himself, "Well I guess my marathon days are behind me, are they not."

Curiously, it wasn't the pain that had led him to drinking. Truth be told, he had been a drinker all of his life, although never to excess. It had been the boredom, especially after his beloved Liddy had passed on.

"Am I a lesser man because of it?" O'Malley often asked himself.

"Ahh," he would answer with a wink and a headshake, "who gives a shit, anyway?"

He was aware, however that both his daughter and her husband Tony rather disapproved of his life style. Naturally they felt that he was a bad influence on his grandchildren.

O'Malley's son, CJ also a fireman, lived up in Westchester County, in the town of Elmsford. He did not approve of his father's drinking, either.

Days later cold gray graves surrounded O'Malley and an even colder breeze enveloped his thin elderly legs. Normally jeans were more than enough to keep him protected against the elements. Today, however a chill from within him reached out to unite with the icy day.

He hadn't been to the cemetery since the Covid scare. Liddy was in a decorative urn on the bookshelf. But, three of his best friends, two of whom had been with him when he had met Liddy, were buried nearby. Joey Cameron, Jesse Ortiz and Bobby Kelly had all been lost to him on that same World Trade Center site which had almost taken his spindly legs.

Joey and Jesse had been firemen and Bobby had been employed three floors above the impact site in Tower number Two.

Bobby's remains had never been found, but Lois, Bobby's wife, had buried her heart in the same cemetery as Joey and Jesse.

A few days previous Mike had noticed O'Malley at the McGinty front door staring across at his own house. The old fireman seemed deep in his thoughts.

A half empty bottle of Bushmills hung at his side, but Mike noticed that he hadn't drunk from it the whole time he had been standing there.

"I recognize that slump." Mike told himself, "Perhaps not as ramrod straight as that old fellow, but that could be me."

At that moment, thoughts of O'Malley's wife, Liddy had been streaming through the old man's mind.

"Ach, Lydia Foyle, ye darlin' daughter of the auld sod, do ye miss me as much as I miss you?" O'Malley had asked the soft breeze wafting through the screen door. It blew the scent of flowers into his face.

"I've taken up with the lovely Marie Flanagan, but I guess up there in the Heaven you already know that don't ye? Tell me Darlin', are ye tellin' The LORD how ta run HIS Universe yet? Is HE listening?"

O'Malley had sighed and leaned heavily against the door frame. Without realizing it he set the whiskey upon a nearby table.

Tears threatened to erupt, but willfully he held them back.

Mike was immediately at the old man's side. He placed a steadying hand upon O'Malley's back.

"Ah, Michael me boy, would ye be doin' an old man a favor now?" O'Malley asked without actually looking at McGinty.

"Me wife is buried, not all that far from here. On a day of yer choosin' might ye take me to see her?

"I'd ask me daughter, but she doesn't care for cemeteries or hospitals. She's a bit of a soft heart, that one. Not at all like her Mother."

"More so," he told himself, "I doubt she'd want ta be seen with the likes of her old drunken father."

"If ye like, Marie and Theresa could come along too."

"I'd like that." They heard Marie's voice from just behind them. A soft smile adorned her face.

"O'Malley," she said, "You have had to endure Ed's pictures all over this room. I would love to see your wife."

"Well, actually, Darlin' Liddy is across the street, at least most of her is. I sprinkled just a bit of her ashes in me boyhood pal Bobby's grave." O'Malley replied softly. "I didna want poor Bobby's spirit ta be lonely, even though our two friends are buried beside him.,

"Bobby ain't there either. He was working just above the impact site back on 9/11. Ach, Nine-Eleven, LORD, I hate those stinkin' numbers.

"They never recovered any bit of him. Sometimes I tell myself that maybe he escaped and is wanderin' around someplace, wonderin' just who the hell he might be. Perhaps he's in California with the amnesia. He always wanted to go there. We were supposed ta go one year, but just the week before, I had met my darlin' Liddy.

"I called him the next day to tell him I couldn't go. I met a girl, I told him, and I think she's the one.

"LORD, LORD, LORD, a truer word was never spoken."

O'Malley sighed loudly. They could see the emotion of it written within his expression.

O'Malley decided that perhaps home was the place to be at that very moment. He cradled the bottle in his arms and then tucked it beneath his left elbow.

With any kind of luck, Tony, Lydia and the wee ones would be so absorbed with that infernal television that he might slip up to his room without them noticing.

Without a word of goodbye, he was gone. Mike watched as the old man strode strongly, specifically and ramrod straight, across the street.

"What?" Theresa said with a trace of concern in her voice as she stepped down from the stairway.

Turning back to her, Mike echoed her query, "What? Did you say something Tere?"

"You have worried written all over your face McGinty." She answered, "What in this evening has brought you down that much?"

Mike opened his mouth to speak but then closed it as he wandered among his own thoughts.

"Ah, I was just listening to O'Malley, Honey.

"Am I too self-centered? I ah, mean, naturally I care about your feelings, and uh those of our entire family. But, look how many people died on that day. Look how many were severely injured. And what of those who have passed on in the subsequent years? What about all those poor people who have lost so many of those other people in their lives?

"They all have stories Theresa. They all have anguish. Mine is but one story in the oh so many."

"Ours, Darling," she corrected him as she placed her arms around his waist, "We don't share the entire story, my Love, but we do share much of it.

"I love you McGinty, ya big lug. Don't ever, ever forget that."

She felt, as well as heard his deep sigh.

"Let me remind you Sweetie," she continued, holding him even more tightly, "Before you and I re-connected, there were an awful lot of counseling sessions, were there not?"

"How many painful stories did you hear? The man I know became a part of each one of them. This I do know!"

Theresa looked about anxiously. Her expression was partially serious, with a wry, half smile parting her lips.

With a gentle tug she led him out onto the porch.

His expression was puzzled as he asked her, "What was that all about?"

"Well, I have something to tell you that was told to me in confidence. I was admonished never to tell anyone, especially you."

"Well then maybe………" he started to say, but was stopped by her forefinger across his lips.

"Shush!" she told him as she waggled her other forefinger. "I need to say this before he gets suspicious.

"Before who…….? Mike started to say, but she pressed her finger even more tightly.

"Daddy" she stated affirmatively as a gleam filled both of her eyes. "He's in several different pictures all about that room.

"I don't necessarily believe in ghosts, but one can't take chances, now, can one?

"He told me not to tell you this."

Mike wanted to tell her that perhaps she should keep her father's secret. But she seemed so excited he could only stare back at her as his own smile creased his face. He raised his eyebrows expectantly.

"This goes no farther Michael," she cautioned him, "I mean that!"

He nodded, reluctantly, but he nodded.

"Daddy told me that although you began slowly, you were the very best partner that he ever had."

She glanced about, furtively, but seeing nothing or no one, returned her attention to her husband.

She was rewarded with a warm, glowing smile. Pulling her into his arms he hugged her fervently and kissed the top of her head. Her hair was fragrant in its cleanliness.

"I love you Theresa Marie, even if you are crazy."

Sunday morning had come, on schedule as usual. Earlier minor rainstorms had given way to a few soft rays of sunshine, heralding a warmer afternoon.

Theresa was at the bathroom mirror applying her makeup. Mike was getting up to answer his cell phone ringing on the bureau.

They, along with Theresa's Mother were going to Church that morning. Although they had all been raised Catholic, that morning they would be attending the Episcopal Church, several blocks away.

Reverend Elwood "Woody" Kingsley was the Pastor there. He and his wife Erica, or "Riki" were both good friends of the McGintys.

When Theresa came out of the bathroom, she was surprised to see Mike sitting, his phone upon his lap, with a somewhat shocked and melancholy expression on his face.

"What, Mike, what is it? Is Davy okay?" she demanded worriedly.

"Uh, Davy's fine Tere. It's Maeve's Uncle Joey. He went to Sainte Xavier of Navarre Hospital last night with breathing problems. He died this morning. They think he had the Covid. Nick and the whole family are quarantined.

"That was Nick, warning us not to stop by today.

"The Police Department is arranging for them to be tested.

"I-I'm sorry Theresa. I liked Uncle Joey. He was a real character."

Losing Uncle Joey had been bad enough, but being locked in their own home was almost as devastating.

Nick, of course had police work. He was able to maintain his connection with his precinct. "Thank Heaven for phones and computers." he told himself.

Carol LeBlanc was so obviously distraught over the loss of her brother, which made Michelle's tasks even harder.

Maeve blamed herself. She had lately been a little freer with her exposure to the rest of the world. She wondered if she hadn't brought the disease back to her Uncle.

In fact, Joey himself had been the bearer of the Covid. He had taken to wandering about the neighborhood and had made a friend of Jimmy Riullo, a homeless man who frequented several different neighborhoods in Queens. Although normally a somewhat hearty man, Jimmy indeed was also infested with the Corona virus.

Unknown to any of them, Jimmy had himself died one day previous in Theresa's hospital, Queen's Mercy. Obviously, no connection had been made.

Fortunately, everyone in the Evanopolis household had already been vaccinated, everyone but Joey. Joey felt that the vaccination was unnecessary. He thought that the virus was just a government hoax geared to keep the common man in his place.

Joey was cremated.

Two weeks later, the quarantine was lifted when no one in the household had tested positive for Corona. Joey's room which had been quarantined separately was sanitized by a crew of professional cleaners who dealt solely with communicable diseases. Even at that, all family members were forbidden access to the room which remained locked.

At the memorial for Joey, three weeks later, Theresa sat beside a grieving Maeve, holding her hand.

Mike helped Nick greet people, as few as there were. When the word pandemic was mentioned most people sent condolences either by mail, Twitter or by Facebook.

Carol LeBlanc sat silently contemplating her brother's sometimes erratic lifestyle. She wondered how soon people would be sitting in a similar room with similar thoughts as her body or ashes lay before them.

Squeezing Michelle's hand tightly, she leaned over and whispered to her daughter, "Honey, I don't tell you this often enough, but I appreciate everything you do for me. I love you Michelle. Thank you for being my daughter."

A half smile crinkled Michelle's lips. "Eh bien, chère Mère, vous étiez plus responsable de cela que moi." she whispered back, which translated to "Well, Dear Mother, you were more in charge of that than I was."

Carol squeezed her hand more firmly. Maeve, who had heard the exchange smiled warmly.

Theresa, who had also heard Carol, squeezed Maeve's hand a bit more firmly.

Unknown to everyone present, Joey's last few moments had been a mixture of being partially awake, hovering within his consciousness and that final lapse into becoming comatose. Somewhere in Joey's mind he must have been aware of his situation. Although he wasn't able to raise his arm more than a couple of inches, in his mind it was fully extended. At that moment Joey realized he had lived a good life since JESUS stood before him, smiling, with both hands outstretched.

Did he imagine it? Perhaps he did, or perhaps not.

Nick explained to Maeve that had she been responsible for Joey's illness, at least one other member of the family would also be sick. They had all been cleared. He also reminded her that Joey had taken to wandering. Who knew who or what he might have come into contact with?

Father Rupert Blousoise of the local Catholic Church had performed the ceremony. In deference to Carol and Michelle's French-Canadian nationality he ended with a French prayer.

The three women from Nick's household were crying. Nick placed his arms around Maeve and Michelle as Michelle pushed her mother's wheelchair.

A dinner commemorating Joseph Robert Sullivan's life was held at McHale's Steakhouse, Joey's favorite restaurant.

CHAPTER 41

NICE TO BE APPRECIATED

Theresa McGinty was pushing wearily through her very long day.

Things were quite different, however in The Bronx.

The one thing that David Edward Keith had in common with his Mother on that day was the long hours.

Sergeant Vito Marciano was concerned that his men were working too much and were being rather overtaxed.

He had been brought into Captain Rodriguez's office to receive a lecture on his behavior during another City Hall hearing of their patrolmen, Nunzio Italo just about a week previous.

Rodriguez assured Marciano that he did not have a problem with Marciano's behavior, and to assure him additionally that Chief of Patrol Dennis Meyer did not either. In fact, Meyer said if he had more men like Marciano he could clean the City up in no time.

Meyer had also said that when things hopefully would become normal again, and when funds were once again available, Marciano was on Meyer's list for better things. Meyer did not elaborate, but Marciano still felt good to be noticed.

Marciano was presently up on the roof. Although coffee runner was not one of his duties, he had no one else and felt that his rooftop guardians needed the hot liquid.

He emerged into their midst with a cardboard box loaded with paper cups, creamers, sugar and sweeteners. A large thermos of coffee was tucked beneath one arm.

"Geez, thanks Sarge." Nunzio stated, reaching to take the box from Marciano's hands.

Keith and Contadina remained at their posts at the front of the building. The back was being covered by Tom Coviescu and Bernie Rosatto.

Keith, Contadina and Italo all had the number 5274 embroidered on the pocket flap beneath their shields. The number was significant as it was the shield number of their friend, Margaret Elaine Thebes. Meg Thebes had been gunned down during a traffic stop in the northernmost part of the Bronx. They had all been hit hard by their loss of her. Most affected though was Gerrie Contadina who had been Meg's best friend.

Marciano noticed the shield number and knew whose it was. He said nothing and returned to his post inside.

"Viduch!" Captain Rodriguez greeted when he got back. Viduch was Marciano's nickname.

"Sir," Marciano answered curtly, "How may I help you?"

Marciano had been a cop for a long time. One would think that a man with that much experience might know the sagacity of rank respect. Marciano, however had far too much experience engrained within him, however, to be cowed by anyone.

If however, that respect had already been earned, Viduch was always ready to return it. Captain Rodriguez was just such a respected man. While the job itself was highly important to the Captain, the welfare of the men in his command was just as significant.

Marciano noticed a large box sitting on one of the desks. Immediately the smell of vinegar reached his nostrils.

"Yea," Rodriguez confirmed, nodding at the carton, "Lunch.

"I figured they're due some kind of respite, so, lunch is on me.

"I had Jeremy open the soda machine too. I'll take care of that as well."

Marciano started to speak, but Rodriguez interrupted him.

"No, Buddy, you keep your wallet in your pocket. I got this. LORD knows, you guys are always making me look good."

After eating and drinking their meal a group of patrol people were sent up to relieve the people on the roof.

Keith, Contadina, Italo, Tom Coviescu and Bernie Rosatto came through the door in single file. Keith brought up the rear. They all settled around a table to eat their own lunch. Since there were only four chairs,

Italo stood next to Contadina. Marciano brought the extra chair from his tiny office and indicated for Italo to sit.

Finishing Lunch the five patrol people were ordered out on patrol to give others a chance for the free lunch.

As they walked in another file out through the door, Marciano thought wryly, "I guess lunch isn't so free if one of them gets hurt out there."

Just a bit later it seemed as if the Sergeant's thoughts were becoming a reality. Warm blood stained David Keith's pants. It wasn't his blood. It belonged to the man who had just attempted to remove Keith's head with a baseball bat. Hearing movement behind him, Davy had ducked just in time as the bat whisked but inches away from the young patrolman's head.

Davy fell heavily to the floor.

As the man swung the bat again, a bullet from Patrolwoman Geraldine Contadina's pistol raked across the assailants back.

Turning sideways and screaming, the young hoodlum fell upon Keith's legs.

Davy quickly pushed the man away and scrambled to his feet. Noting that they were only flesh wounds he cuffed the punk's hands together and looked up and around.

Maybe this guy was the only one, or maybe there were more.

Davy heard the growl of Ed Flanagan's voice muttering in his mind, "Keep yer wits about you boy. Watch out for your partner too."

Looking to his left he saw Gerrie Contadina give him a thumb up. He tapped the visor of his just replaced hat with two fingers. She smiled back.

Just then another shot echoed from a different direction. Both Gerrie and Davy ducked, waiting in case the shooter had them in his or her sight.

They heard movement at the other end of the alley. A heavy grunt tipped off the other thug's position.

Davy stood again, sheltered behind a large dumpster.

Gerrie dropped to the ground flattened out beside a row of garbage cans.

"Give it up," Davy shouted, hugging the wall, "Police."

Another shot pinged off of Davy's dumpster.

Gerrie, having seen his movement, shot their assailant. She had aimed for the largest area, his torso, and placed her bullet almost in the middle of his chest.

Fortunately for him, the shot cleared the man's heart by inches, but unfortunately, it had pierced his right lung.

He lay upon his back, gasping for air.

Unable to control his hands, he allowed the weapon to slip from his grasp. Both Gerrie and Davy had crept forward and Davy kicked the man's gun away from his hand. When the thug's first shot had been fired Davy had alerted their precinct. Gerrie now informed them of the two bullet wounds to both assailants. She requested a medical team, and certainly an ambulance.

Seconds later a police car pulled up with Sergeant Vito Marciano and patrolman Vinnie Calabrese.

While Marciano tended to the severely wounded man, the other three kept watch.

A team of Emergency Technicians arrived soon after, followed, minutes later by an ambulance.

Marciano spotted the blood on Keith's legs and inquired. Keith explained the situation and put the Sergeant's mind at ease.

"What about that blood on your sleeve Contadina?" Vinnie Calabrese asked, motioning toward her left arm.

They all gazed over at her. She looked down.

"Sonuva bitch!" she muttered angrily.

Apparently the bullet which had ricocheted off of the dumpster had clipped her right tricep. It was only a flesh wound, easily treated by the EMTs, but in his mind, Marciano groaned, "Could have, might have."

"Check in at the Emergency Room and then, after reports Gerrie," he informed Contadina, "take the rest of the day off."

As he started to walk toward his cruiser, he stopped, turned back and said, "And for Pete's sake, somebody tell Italo before it gets into the rumor mill....please."

Davy handed his cell phone to Gerrie who immediately phoned Nunzio.

"Listen Babe," she added at the end of the conversation, "could we not mention this to your Mother? She drives me crazy sometimes with the way she hovers over me."

"No problem." Nunzio assured her as he clicked off his own phone.

She did not hear him chuckle and laugh.

CHAPTER 42
O'MALLEY, O'MALLEY

Despite it being spring, it was a reasonably cool day. The ride had not been that long. Even though the Covid Pandemic had opened up slightly because of vaccinations, the roads had been fairly wide open.

A large number of people throughout the country had openly challenged the mask wearing and personal distancing, yet still on this particular Saturday, the challenge was not as strong.

O'Malley knew exactly where he was going. Obviously the others had let him take the lead since he was the only one who actually did know where he was going. The others were Marie Flanagan, Theresa and Mike McGinty, the driver. Theresa's daughter, Maria Keith had come along too. She had grown quite used to the old man's presence in their house and felt that perhaps her support was called for as well.

O'Malley appreciated the support of the other three, but there seemed to be something special about the younger woman's concern.

He had brought his whiskey bottle with a promise to himself that only three swigs would take place, one for each of his comrades buried there.

Well, of course, Bobby Kelly wasn't there, but some of O'Malley's dear wife Liddy's ashes were in Bobby's grave. Bobby had been working just above the impact site in Tower number Two. Nothing, O'Malley had been told, had ever been recovered of his friend.

Bobby had been O'Malley's best friend from childhood. When first the O'Malley family had arrived in New York from Ireland, it was Bobby

Kelly and his gang of young toughs who had beaten up a young Conor O'Malley because he talked funny.

And sure wasn't it that same Bobby Kelly who himself had been thrashed by Conor O'Malley when he had made the mistake of walking alone before the tenement in which an angry young O'Malley had resided.

To O'Malley's surprise, Kelly had extended a hand to young Conor O'Malley, from his prone position on the sidewalk. "Well Boyo," he asked, "how's about helpin' your new best friend to his feet? I could use a bit of ice for my jaw, too if you don't mind."

At that, Bobby Kelly spit out a tooth which O'Malley's fist had dislodged. The friendship had grown strong after that; and soon came to include the two fellows buried beside Bobby Kelly's empty, except for Liddy's few ashes, grave.

They were, as mentioned, Joey Cameron and Jesse Ortiz, both of whom had become firemen like O'Malley.

It was Ortiz who had shortened Conor's name to simply O'Malley.

While they were Manhattan Firemen themselves, Joey and Jesse were attached to two different firehouses than O'Malley's. Both had perished on that same day which had taken Bobby and had almost taken O'Malley.

A breeze was felt, wafting in from the north, undoubtedly from the Long Island Sound. The breeze ruffled the flowering bushes of the cemetery and the fragrance was sweet and enticing.

Despite his fused spine, or maybe because of it, O'Malley felt sore and a bit tired. He had tossed and turned for much of the night, both dreading and anticipating this very moment.

With a knowing nod, Marie Flanagan stepped up beside him and encircled his waist with her right arm.

She guided him forward to Bobby Kelly's grave and said, "Good Day to you Liddy. I have heard so many wonderful things about you from this delightful lug here. He misses you dearly Liddy, as I do miss my darlin' Ed. I hope you don't mind the two of us commiserating together as we mourn our losses."

This here is Bobby Kelly's grave." O'Malley informed her, "Although he ain't even there. LORD knows where his body ended up."

Marie already knew who was buried where, but she did not interrupt him. This was his day and she let him direct it as he wished.

He introduced them to his other two friends. His voice caught slightly as he mentioned their names.

In the back of his mind O'Malley still clung to the possibility of Bobby Kelly wandering about California, wondering just who th' hell he might be.

As planned, O'Malley uncapped his spirits bottle and gave a hoarse salute to each of his three friends, followed by a swallow.

For Bobby he silently wished his friend a warm day on a Pacific Ocean beach with a cold glass of beer to roll across the area of his missing tooth.

A sniper should be intelligent and clear minded. Even when not clear minded he can, but not necessarily will still be a very good shot. His weapon is not a rifle. It is a rifle system.

Snipers are generally more partial to a bolt action weapon, preferably a single shot. The rifle should have a laser attachment to coordinate with the telescopic sight in order to single out that sniper's particular target.

Ralph Caberoso preferred the Barrett M82 for his rifle of choice. It seemed to handle just a bit better than any of the others, at least for him. In Afghanistan it had never let him down.

Moe Petersen however had let Ralph down. Moe's swinging the telescope uncovered had lead to the Afghani sniper shooting the two of them. In that bright a Sun, any glass surface can be reflective. The enemy sniper had taken out Moe first which allowed Ralph to duck quickly, although not quickly enough. The Afghani's bullet had creased Ralph's head right at the hairline. It may not have killed Ralph, but two years later he still had some rather touchy headaches.

Nonetheless, Ralph had returned. A man in Virginia had sold Ralph the system which he presently owned and was using. He had singled out and killed three of the enemy there in that place called The Bronx. They were easy to spot, too. They had disguised themselves as New York policemen, and the third thought he could fool Ralph with that fireman's uniform.

Ralph could see through their charade however. He had singled one each of the enemy every three days and had killed the man. It might have been a slow process, but patience was a sniper's ally.

Sergeant Vito Marciano was about to lose his patience. He and Sergeant

Jimmy Ramirez had scoped out what they thought were the two tallest buildings in their area of the Bronx. Ironically, they were within a block's distance of one another.

Viduch had passed that information along to the Intelligence Officer in his precinct. He had assumed that the officer, Lieutenant Jim Corey had shared said information with his superiors. Marciano certainly hoped that Corey had done so.

Marciano's team consisted of patrolman Nunzio Italo and Patrolwoman Gerrie Contadina.

Ramirez had picked Gerald Duffy and Raheem Davis. They were simultaneously searching and staking out the two buildings in hope of stopping whoever was killing first responders from afar.

The two cops had been killed in two other Bronx precincts. The fireman had been killed in the Four-Four precinct, not far from the Harlem River. Admittedly, that shot could have come from Manhattan.

Ramirez had just checked in, allowing to failure thus far. Marciano was shaking his head. The odds were good that the sniper, whoever he was might not even be in the Four-Eight.

"Hell, he might not even be in the Bronx."

As always, the words "Shoulda, Coulda, Woulda," rolled around in Marciano's head and he knew that such assumptions just did not cut it.

As the sergeant approached a metal air conditioning shed atop the building he noted slotted aluminum grates on the two sides that were visible to him.

Just then, as he noticed a dark cylinder extending out of one of the grates he heard the sharp snap which reminded him of a silencer, a sound suppressing device for firearms.

Suppressors do not completely silence firearms, but they do effectively mute to a specific degree, the normally very sharp report of that particular weapon.

Twenty three stories below and in an alley across the street a sniper's anomaly had taken place.

As Patrolman David Keith stalked through that alley his grandfather's voice could be heard in Davy's mind giving advice in that singular Ed Flanagan way.

"Don't stand up so straight Dummy!" Ed's voice advised Davy, "Stoop, Davy, Stoop. Make yourself a smaller target."

With a light chuckle, Davy did just that. As he did so, Ralph Caberoso's bullet raked across the young policeman's back.

"Agh!" Davy muttered sharply as he dropped fully to the ground. He pulled himself behind a rusty green dumpster, hoping that his assailant did not fire again. He had banged his head lightly in the process.

He noticed traces of blood on the corner edge of the dumpster. A quick examination told him his forehead was bleeding. The bullet had hit his vest and at an angle. It had not hurt him.

Up on the Tall building Sergeant Marciano barged through the aluminum shed's door.

A startled Ralph Caberoso immediately brought his rifle up to bear on the intruding cop. He had just efficiently removed the suppressor, scope and laser, and his reflexes were guiding the weapon back into position.

Caberoso screamed and dropped to his knees as Gerrie Contadina's own bullet hit his back between his shoulders. As he reached for his dropped rifle another bullet struck the area just below his neck. The retort was deafening in that small metal enclosure.

Kicking the rifle away, Marciano saw the shining police weapon barrel of a Sig Sauer P226 automatic pistol extending through the slats of the grate. Its nine millimeter bullets had forced the sniper to the floor of the shed.

Marciano knelt to see how badly damaged the man was. As he did so he asked who his patrol person was that had just fired.

"It's me Sarge, Contadina." Gerrie called out. "Nunzio's coming around the side.

"Is that guy dead?"

Apparently not," Marciano answered. "This guy has body armor that seems to be just a bit better than ours. It looks like he hit his head on some pipes though. I'm cuffing him. Call it in Gerrie. He might still have some severe damage."

"Big deal," Nunzio snorted as he entered the enclosure, "He still killed two cops and a fireman. I hope his back is broken."

Gerrie called it in, mentioning that the perp had been neutralized and was cuffed. She assured them that no cops had been hurt.

The wounded patrolman down below snorted at the transmission.

"Sez you!" Davy Keith mumbled, feeling a harsh soreness across his shoulders and blood sliding down his cheek.

"Ah, shit!" he muttered, envisioning facing Amy and their two mothers, Theresa and Rhonda.

Since Marciano had decided to shield his team from the press, Alicia Malosky had decided to interview the one person who had been wounded in the melee. She caught up to Patrolman David Keith as he sat upon the rear of a Fireman's EMT van, having his wounds tended to.

The camera had zeroed in upon the thin stream of blood upon the side of his face. Davy's frown had absolutely nothing to do with any pain he might then be feeling. He saw the faces of three women reflected in that camera's lens. He wanted to groan out loud but he knew what the reaction of those three women would be.

Davy Keith's worries had just become a reality. Firstly, Ronnie Italo on a much needed break had just switched channels on her TV set to a young cop being interviewed on the back of a paramedics' vehicle.

"Sonuva bitch!" she snapped, spilling her coffee. "Amy!" she screamed, facing the open kitchen door.

"Aw, you gotta be kidding me." Theresa McGinty rasped hoarsely as she slapped her forehead above her right eye.

Replacing the phone after just being notified by Chief of Patrol Dennis Meyer, Theresa's husband Mike, in Manhattan could only stare blankly at the floor.

His boss, Ron Beymon did not know just what Meyer's news had been, but from Mike's expression, he thought Mike might just be taking the rest of the day off.

"Oh Daddy," Theresa moaned softly as she glanced at her father's picture, "What more can happen to this family?"

From the kitchen doorway, Eddie's wife Marie whispered, "What more indeed?"

Printed in the United States
by Baker & Taylor Publisher Services